PENGUIN BOOKS

SHARPE'S ENEMY

Bernard Cornwell was born in London in 1944, raised in South Essex, and educated at London University. He worked for several years as a producer and writer for BBC Television, taking charge of its current affairs department in Northern Ireland, and in 1978 he became editor of Thames Television's *Thames at Six* program. His interest in the Napoleonic Wars, pursued since his schooldays, was ignited by C. S. Forester's Hornblower novels, and in his spare time he began his research for the Richard Sharpe novels. Mr. Cornwell is now a full-time writer.

SHARPE'S ENEMY

RICHARD SHARPE AND
THE DEFENSE OF
PORTUGAL,
CHRISTMAS 1812

Bernard Cornwell

PENGUIN BOOKS

For my daughter, with love

PENGUIN BOOKS
Viking Penguin Inc., 40 West 23rd Street,
New York, New York 10010, U.S.A.
Penguin Books Ltd, 27 Wrights Lane, London W8 5TZ
(Publishing & Editorial) and Harmondsworth,
Middlesex, England (Distribution & Warehouse)
Penguin Books Australia Ltd, Ringwood,
Victoria, Australia
Penguin Books Canada Limited, 2801 John Street,
Markham, Ontario, Canada L3R 1B4
Penguin Books (N.Z.) Ltd, 182–190 Wairau Road,
Auckland 10, New Zealand

First published in the United States of America by
The Viking Press 1984
Published in Penguin Books 1987

LIBRARY OF CONGRESS CATALOGING IN PUBLICATION DATA
Cornwell, Bernard.
Sharpe's enemy.
Reprint. Originally published: New York:
Viking Press, 1984.
1. Peninsular War, 1807–1814—Fiction.
2. Great Britain—History, Military—19th century—
Fiction. I. Title.
[PR6053.075S52 1987] 823'.914 87-7576
ISBN 0 14 01.0430 5

Printed in the United States of America by
Offset Paperback Mfrs., Inc., Dallas, Pennsylvania
Set in Baskerville

'. . . this system is yet in its infancy
. . . much has been accomplished in a short time and there
is every reason to believe that the accuracy of the
Rocket may be actually brought upon a par with that of
other artillery ammunition for all the important pur-
poses of field service.'

COLONEL SIR WILLIAM CONGREVE. 1814.

THE GATEWAY OF GOD

road

THE
PASS

Convent

Castillo
de la Virgen

600

500

550

600

650

N

all contours in feet

| 0 | 100 | 200 | 300 |

yards

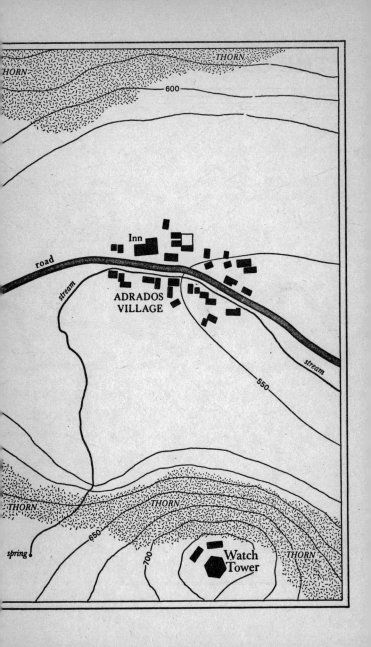

PROLOGUE

On December 8th, 1812, the English soldiers first came to Adrados.

The village had escaped the war. It lay in that part of Spain east of the northern Portuguese border and, though it was close to the frontier, few soldiers had passed through its single street.

The French had come once, three years before, but they had been running from the English Lord Wellington and running so fast that they scarcely had time to stop and loot.

Then in May of 1812 the Spanish soldiers had come, the Garrison of Adrados, but the villagers had not minded. There were only fifty soldiers, with four cannon, and once the guns had been placed in the old Castle and Watchtower outside the village the soldiers seemed to think their war was done. They drank in the village inn, flirted with the women at the stream where the flat stones made laundry easy, and two village girls married gunners in the summer. By some confusion in the Spanish Army the 'garrison' had been sent a powder convoy intended for Ciudad Rodrigo and the soldiers boasted that they had more powder, and fewer guns, than any other Artillery troop in Europe. They made crude fireworks for the weddings and the villagers admired the explosions that flashed and echoed in their remote valley. In the autumn some of the Spanish soldiers deserted, bored with guarding the valley where no soldiers came, eager to go back to their own villages and their own women.

Then the English soldiers came. And on that day of all days!

9

Adrados was not a place of great importance. It grew, the priest said, sheep and thorns, and the priest told the villagers that made the village a holy place because Christ's life began with the shepherds' visit and ended with a crown of thorns. Yet the villagers did not need the priest to tell them that Adrados was sacred because only one thing brought visitors to Adrados, and that was on the Feast on December 8th.

Years before, no one knew how many, not even the priest, but in those far-off days when the Christians fought the Muslims in Spain, the Holy Mother had come to Adrados. Everyone knew the story. Christian Knights were falling back through the valley, hard pressed, and their leader had stopped to pray beside a granite boulder that was poised on the edge of the pass which fell off to the west, towards Portugal, and then it had happened. She had appeared! She stood on the granite boulder, Her face pale as ice, Her eyes like mountain pools, and She told the Knight that the pursuing Muslims would soon stop to pray themselves, to face east towards their heathen home, and that if he turned his tired troop about, if they drew their battered swords, then they would bring glory to the cross.

Two thousand Muslim heads dropped that day. More! No one knew how many and each year the figure grew with the story's telling. Carved Muslim heads decorated the archway of the Convent that was built around the place where She had appeared. In the Convent chapel, at the top of the altar steps, was a small patch of polished granite; the place of the Holy Footfall.

And each year on December 8th, the Day of the Miracle, women came to Adrados. It was a woman's day, not a man's, and the men would go to the village inn once they had carried the statue of the Virgin, its jewels swaying beneath the gilded canopy, round the village bounds and back to the Convent.

The Nuns had left the Convent two hundred years before, attracted to plumper houses in the plains, unable to compete with the towns where the Holy Mother had been more generous in her appearance, yet the buildings were still good. The chapel became the village church, the upper cloister was a store-place, and one day a year the Convent was still a place for miracles.

The women entered the chapel on their knees. They shuffled awkwardly across the flagstones, their hands busy with beads, their voices muttering urgent prayers, and their knees would take them to the top of the steps. The priest intoned his Latin. The women bent and kissed the smooth dark granite. There was a hole in the stone and legend said that if you kissed in that place and the tip of your tongue could reach the very bottom of the hole, then the baby would be a boy.

The women cried as they kissed the stone; not with sorrow, but with a kind of ecstasy. Some had to be helped away.

Some prayed for deliverance from illness. They brought their tumours, their disfigurements, their crippled children. Some came to pray for a child and a year later they would return and give thanks to the Holy Mother for now they shared Her secret. They prayed to the Virgin who had given birth and they knew, as no man could know, that a woman brought forth her children in sorrow, yet still they prayed to be mothers and their tongues stretched down the hole. They prayed in the candled glory of the Convent Chapel of Adrados and the priest piled their gifts behind the altar; the harvest of each year.

December 8th, 1812. The English came.

They were not the first visitors. Women had been arriving in the village since dawn, women who had walked twenty miles or more. Some came from Portugal, most from the villages that were hidden in the same hills as Adrados. Then two English officers came, mounted on big horses, and with them was a girl. The officers had loud braying voices. They helped the girl from her horse outside the Convent then rode to the village where they paid their respects to the Spanish Commandant over cups of the region's harsh red wine that

11

was served in the inn. The men in the inn were good humoured. They knew that many of the women were praying for a child and they would be called on to help the Holy Mother in the prayer's fulfilment.

The other British soldiers came from the east which was strange because there should have been no British soldiers to the east, but no one remarked on the fact. There was no alarm. The British had not been to Adrados, but the villagers had heard that these heathen soldiers were respectful. Their General had ordered them to stand to attention when the Host was carried through the streets to a deathbed, and to remove their hats, and that was good. Yet these English soldiers were not like the Spanish garrison. These red-coated men were foul looking, villainous, unkempt, their faces full of crudity and hatred.

A hundred of them waited at the eastern end of the village, sitting by the washing place next to the road and smoking short clay pipes. A hundred other men filed through the village led by a big man on horseback whose red coat was lavishly looped with gold. A Spanish soldier, coming from the castle to the inn, saluted the Colonel and was surprised when the English officer smiled at him, bowed ironically, and his mouth was almost toothless.

The Spaniard must have said something in the inn for the two British officers, jackets unbuttoned, came into the road-way and watched the last of the soldiers file by towards the Convent. One of the officers frowned. 'Who the devil are you?'

The soldier he had spoken to grinned. 'Smithers, sir.'

The Captain's eyes flicked up the line of soldiers. 'What Battalion?'

'Third, sir.'

'What bloody Regiment, you fool?'

'The Colonel'll tell you, sir.' Smithers stepped into the centre of the street, put a hand to his mouth. 'Colonel!'

The big man turned his horse, paused, then spurred

towards the inn. The two Captains pulled themselves up-right and saluted.

The Colonel reined in. He seemed once to have had the jaundice, perhaps to have served in the Fever Islands, for his skin was yellow like old parchment. The face beneath the tasselled bicorne hat twitched in involuntary spasm. The blue eyes, startlingly blue, were unfriendly. 'Button your bloody jackets.'

The Captains put down their wine cups, buttoned their jackets and pulled their belts into place. One, a plump young man, frowned because the Colonel had shouted at them in front of the grinning privates.

The Colonel let his horse walk two steps closer to the pair of Captains. 'What are you doing here?'

'Here, sir?' The taller, thinner Captain smiled. 'Just visit-ing, sir.'

'Just visiting, eh?' The face twitched again. The Colonel had a strangely long neck hidden by a cravat that he pinned high on his throat. 'Just the two of you?'

'Yes, sir.'

'And Lady Farthingdale, sir,' added the plump one.

'And Lady Farthingdale, eh?' The Colonel mimicked the Captain's plummy voice, then he screamed at them in sudden vehemence. 'You're a bloody disgrace, that's what you are! I hate you! Christ's belly, I hate you!'

The street was suddenly silent in the winter sunshine. The soldiers that had gathered either side of the Colonel's horse grinned at the two Captains.

The taller Captain wiped the spittle flung from the Co-lonel's mouth off his red jacket. 'I must protest, sir.'

'Protest! You puking horror! Smithers!'

'Colonel?'

'Shoot him!'

The plump Captain grinned, as if a joke had been made, but the other flung an arm up, flinched, and as Smithers, grinning, levelled and fired his musket so did the Colonel bring out an ornate chased pistol and shoot the plump Captain in the head. The shots echoed in the street, the smoke drifted in two distinct clouds above the fallen bodies, and the Colonel laughed before standing in his stirrups. 'Now, lads, now!'

They cleared the inn first, stepping over the corpses whose blood was spattered on the lintel of the door, and the muskets crashed in the building, bayonets hunted the men into corners and killed them, and the Colonel waved the hundred men who had been waiting at the eastern end of the village into the street. He had not wanted to start this quickly, he had wanted to get half his men up to the Convent first, but these bloody Captains had forced his hand and the Colonel screamed at them, urged them on, and led half his force towards the big, square, blank-walled Convent.

The women in the Convent had not heard the shots fired five hundred yards to the east. The women were crowded in the upper cloister, waiting their turn to shuffle into the chapel on their knees, and the first they knew that the war had at last come in its horror to Adrados was when the red-coated men appeared in the gateway, bayonets levelled, and the screaming began.

Other men were clearing the village houses, one by one, while yet more streamed across the valley towards the castle. The Spanish garrison had been drinking in the village, only a handful were at their posts, and they assumed that British uniforms belonged to their allies and further assumed that these British soldiers could explain the uproar in the village. The Spaniards watched the redcoats come across the rubble of the castle's fallen east wall, shouted questions at them, and then the muskets fired, the bayonets came, and the garrison died in the mediaeval ramparts. One Lieutenant killed two of the redcoats. He fought with skill and fury, drove more of the invaders back, and he escaped over the fallen wall and ran through the thorn bushes to the watchtower on its hill to the east. He hoped he would find a handful of his men there, but he died in the thorns, shot by a hidden marksman, and the Spanish Lieutenant never knew that the men who had captured the watchtower were dressed not in British red, but in French blue. His body rolled under a thorn bush, crushing the old brittle bones of a raven left by a fox.

There were screams in the street. Men died who tried to protect their homes, children screamed as their fathers died, as their homes were forced open. The musket shots dotted the breeze with small white clouds.

More men came from the east, men in uniforms as varied as the Battalions that had fought for Portugal and Spain in the four years of war in the Peninsula. With the men came women and it was the women who killed children in the village, shooting them, knifing them, keeping only those who could work. The women squabbled over the cottages, arguing who would have what, sometimes crossing themselves as they passed a crucifix nailed on the low stone walls. It did not take long to destroy Adrados.

In the Convent the screams had become constant as the English soldiers hunted through the two cloisters, the hall, the empty rooms, and the crammed chapel. The priest had run to the door, pushing his way through the women, and now he was held, quivering, as the redcoats sorted out their prize. Some women were pushed out of the building, the lucky ones, women too diseased or too old, and some were killed with the long bayonets. Inside the chapel the soldiers took the ornaments from the altar, picked through the gifts that were piled in the narrow space behind it, and then smashed open the cupboard that held the Mass vessels. One soldier was pulling on the white and gold finery the priest kept for Easter. He walked round the church blessing his comrades who pulled women onto the floor. The chapel sounded with sobs, screams, mens' laughter, and the tearing of cloth.

The Colonel had ridden his horse into the upper cloister and waited, a grin on his face, and watched his men. He had sent two men he could trust into the chapel and they appeared now, holding a woman between them, and the Colonel looked at her, licked his lips, and his face twitched in its spasms.

Everything about her was rich, from her clothes to her hair, a richness that spoke of money enhancing beauty. Her hair was black and full, falling in waves either side of a face that was generous and provocative. She had dark eyes that looked at him fearlessly, a mouth that seemed as if it smiled a lot, and her clothes were covered with a dark cloak trimmed in lavish silver fur. The Colonel smiled. 'Is that her?'

Smithers grinned. 'That's 'er, sir.'

'Well, well, well. Isn't Lord Farthingdale a lucky bastard, then. Get her bloody cloak off, let's have a look at her.'

Smithers reached for the fur-edged hood at the back of the cloak, but she pushed the men away, undid the clasp at her neck and slowly took the cloak from her shoulders. She had a full body, in the prime of her youth, and there was something tantalizing to the Colonel in her absence of fear. The cloister stank of fresh blood, echoed with screaming women and children, yet this rich, beautiful woman stood there with a calm face. The Colonel smiled again with his toothless mouth. 'So you're married to Lord Farthingdale, whoever he is?'

'Sir Augustus Farthingdale.' She was not English.

'Oh, dear me. I begs your Ladyship's pardon.' The Colonel gave his cackling laugh. 'Sir Augustus. General, is he?'

'Colonel.'

'Like me!' The yellow face twitched as he laughed. 'Rich, is he?'

'Very.' She stated it as a fact.

The Colonel dismounted clumsily. He was tall, with a huge belly, and an ugliness that was truly remarkable. His face twitched as he approached her. 'You're no bloody English lady, are you now?'

She still seemed utterly unafraid. She covered her dark

16

riding habit with her fur-edged cloak and even gave a tiny smile. 'Portuguese.'

The blue eyes watched her closely. 'How do I know you're telling the bleeding truth, then? What's a Portuguesey doing married to Sir Augustus Farthingdale, eh?'

She shrugged, took from her left hand a ring, and tossed it to the Colonel. 'Trust that.'

The ring was of gold. On its bevelled face was a coat of arms, quartered, and the Colonel smiled as he looked at it. 'How long have you been married, Milady?'

This time she did smile, and the soldiers watching grinned with desire. This was the Colonel's prize, but the Colonel could be generous when he wished it. She pushed black hair away from her olive skin. 'Six months, Colonel.'

'Six months. Still got the shine on it, has it?' He cackled. 'How much will Sir Augustus pay to have you back as a bedwarmer?'

'A lot.' She dropped her voice as she said it, enriching the two words with promise.

The Colonel laughed. Beautiful women did not like the Colonel and so he did not like them. This rich bitch had spirit, but he could break her, and he looked at his men who watched her, and he grinned. He tossed the gold ring in the air, caught it. 'What were you doing here, Milady?'

'I was praying for my mother.'

The grin went instantly from his face. His eyes were suddenly cunning, his voice guarded. 'You were what?'

'Praying for my mother. She's ill.'

'You love your mother?' His question was intense.

She nodded, puzzled. 'Yes.'

The Colonel jerked on his heel, swung to his men, and his finger jabbed at them like a blade. 'No one!' His voice was at a scream again. 'No one is to touch her! You hear me! No one.' The head twitched and he waited for the spasm to pass. 'I'll kill any bastard who touches her! Kill them!' He turned back to her and gave her a clumsy bow. 'Lady Farthingdale.

You have to put up with us.' His eyes searched the cloister and saw the priest, tied to a pillar. 'We'll send the vicar with a letter and the ring. Your husband can pay for you, Milady, but no one, I promises you, no one will touch you.' He looked at his men again, screamed, and the spittle flayed out in the sunlight. 'No one touches her!' His mood changed back just as suddenly. He looked about the cloister, at the women who lay, bloody and beaten, on the coloured tiles, at the other women who waited, fearful and terrified, within the hedge of bayonets and he grinned. 'Plenty for everyone, yes? Plenty!' He cackled and turned, his slim sword scabbard scraping on the ground. He saw a young girl, skinny, scarce out of childhood, and the finger jabbed again. 'That's mine! Bring her here!' He laughed, hands on hips, dominating the cloister, and he grinned at the men in the Convent. 'Welcome to your new home, lads.'

The Day of the Miracle had come to Adrados again and the dogs of the village sniffed at the blood that stiffened in the single street.

CHAPTER 1

Richard Sharpe, Captain of the Light Company of the South
Essex Regiment's one and only Battalion, stood at the
window and stared at the procession in the street below. It
was cold outside, he knew that too well. He had just marched
his shrunken company north from Castelo Branco, ordered
to Army Headquarters by a mysterious summons for which
he had still not been given an explanation. Not that Headquarters often explained itself to mere Captains, but it
annoyed Sharpe that he had now been in Frenada two days
and was still none the wiser about the urgent orders. The
General, Viscount Wellington of Talavera, no by God, that
was wrong! He was now the Marquess of Wellington, Gran-
dee of Spain, Duque de Ciudad Rodrigo, Generalissimo of all
the Spanish Armies, 'Nosey' to his men, 'the Peer' to his
officers, and the man, Sharpe assumed, who had wanted him
in Frenada, but the General was not here. He was in Cadiz,
or Lisbon, or God only knew where, and the British army
was huddling in its winter quarters while only Sharpe and
his Company were out on the cold December roads. Major
Michael Hogan, Sharpe's friend, and the man who ran
Wellington's Intelligence department, had gone south with
the General and Sharpe missed him. Hogan would not have
kept him waiting.

At least Sharpe was warm. He had given his name yet
again to the clerk on the ground floor and then growled that
he would wait upstairs in the Headquarters mess where
there was a fire. He was not supposed to use the room, but
few people wanted to argue with the tall, dark haired Rifle-

man with the scar that gave his face a slightly mocking look in repose.

He stared down at the roadway. A priest sprinkled Holy Water. Acolytes rang bells and swung censers of burning incense. Banners followed the litter-borne statue of the Virgin Mary. Women knelt by the buildings and held clasped hands towards the statue. A weak sunlight lit the streets, winter sunlight, and Sharpe's eyes automatically searched the sky for clouds. There were none.

The mess was empty. With Wellington away most of the officers seemed to spend their mornings in bed, or else sitting in the inn next door where the landlord had been educated in the making of a proper breakfast. Pork chops, fried eggs, fried kidneys, bacon, toast, claret, more toast, butter, and tea so strong that it could scour a fouled howitzer barrel. Some officers had already gone to Lisbon for Christmas. If the French attacked now, Sharpe thought, they could stroll through Portugal to the sea.

The door banged open and a middle-aged man wearing a voluminous dressing-gown over his uniform trousers walked in. He scowled at the Rifleman. 'Sharpe?'

'Yes, sir.' The 'sir' seemed judicious. The man had an air of authority despite a streaming cold.

'Major General Nairn.' The Major General dropped papers on a low table, next to the back numbers of the *Times* and the *Courier* from London, then crossed to the other tall window. He scowled at the street. 'Damned Papists.'

'Yes, sir.' Another judicious reply.

'Damned Papists! The Nairns, Sharpe, are all Scottish Presbyterians! We may be boring, but by God we are Godly!' He grinned, then sneezed violently before vigorously wiping his nose with a huge grey handkerchief. He gestured with the handkerchief at the procession. Another god-damned feast-day, Sharpe, can't think why they're all so bloody thin.' He laughed, then looked with shrewd eyes at the Rifleman. 'So you're Sharpe?'

'Yes, sir.'

'Well don't come near me, I've got a bloody cold.' He walked towards the fire. 'Heard about you, Sharpe. Bloody impressive! Scottish, are you?'

'No, sir.' Sharpe grinned.

'Not your fault, Sharpe, not your fault. Can't help our damned parents which is why we have to thrash our damned children.' He glanced quickly at Sharpe, making sure he was being appreciated. 'Came up from the ranks, didn't you?'

'Yes, sir.'

'You've done bloody well, Sharpe, bloody well.'

'Thank you, sir.' It was amazing how few words were usually needed to get by with senior officers.

Major General Nairn bent down and damaged the fire by bashing its logs with a poker. 'I suppose you're wondering why you're here. That right?'

'Yes, sir.'

'You're here because this is the warmest damned room in Frenada and you're obviously no fool.' Nairn laughed, dropped the poker, and worried his nose with his handkerchief. 'Bloody awful place, Frenada.'

'Yes, sir.'

Nairn looked accusingly at Sharpe. 'Do you know why the Peer chose Frenada as his winter Headquarters?'

'No, sir.'

'Some people will tell you,' and here the Major General broke off to collapse with a satisfied sigh into a vast horsehair armchair, 'that it was chosen because it is near the Spanish border.' He wagged a finger at Sharpe. 'That bears some truth, but not the whole truth. Some people will tell you that the Peer chose this benighted town because it is bloody miles from Lisbon and no snivelling place-seekers and bum-lickers will bother to make the journey up here to annoy him. Now that, too, might contain a grain of the eternal truth, except that the Peer's down there half the time which makes life bloody easy for the sycophantic bastards. No, Sharpe, we must look for the real reason elsewhere.'

'Yes, sir.'

Nairn groaned as he stretched himself out. 'The real reason, Sharpe, the immaculately conceived reason, is that this God-damned excuse for a bloody miserable little hovel of a crippled town being chosen is that it is right in the centre of the best God-damned fox-hunting in Portugal.'

Sharpe grinned. 'Yes, sir.'

'And the Peer, Sharpe, likes to chase foxes. Thus are the rest of us consigned to the eternal torments of this bloody place. Sit down, man!'

'Yes, sir.'

'And stop saying "yes, sir", "no, sir" like a bloody bum licker.'

'Yes, sir.' Sharpe sat in the chair opposite Major General Nairn. The Scotsman had huge grey eyebrows that seemed to be trying to grow upwards to meet his shock of grey hair. The face was good and strong, shrewd-eyed and humorous, spoilt only by his cold-reddened nose. Nairn returned the gaze, looking Sharpe up and down from the French cavalry boots to the Rifleman's black hair, then he twisted round in the armchair.

'Chatsworth! You scum! You varlet! Chatsworth! Heel! You hear me? Heel!'

An orderly appeared who grinned happily at Nairn. 'Sir?'

'Tea, Chatsworth, tea! Bring me strong tea! Something that will rekindle my military ardour. And kindly try to bring it before the New Year.'

'I've already wet it, sir. Something to eat, sir?'

'Eat? I've got a cold, Chatsworth. I'm nigh unto death and you blather at me about eating! What have you got?'

'I've some ham, sir, that you liked. Mustard. Bread and fresh butter?' Chatsworth was solicitous, obviously liking Nairn.

'Ah, ham! Bring us ham, Chatsworth, ham and mustard,

with your bread and butter. Did you steal the toasting fork from this mess, Chatsworth?'

'No, sir.'

'Then find which of your thieving comrades did take it, have them flogged, then bring the fork to me!'

'Yes, sir.' Chatsworth grinned as he left the room.

Nairn smiled at Sharpe. 'I'm a harmless old man, Sharpe, left in charge of this bloody madhouse while the Peer gallivants round half of the bloody Peninsula. I am supposed, God help me, to be running this Headquarters. Me! If I had time, Sharpe, I suppose I could lead the troops on a winter campaign! I could inscribe my name in glory, but I don't have bloody time! Look at this!' He picked a paper from the pile beside him. 'A letter, Sharpe, from the Chaplain General. The Chaplain General, no less! Do you know that he is in receipt of a salary of five hundred and sixty-five pounds a year, Sharpe, and in addition is named advisor on the establishment of semaphore stations for which nonsensical bloody job he receives a further six hundred pounds! Can you believe that? And what does God's vicar to His Majesty's Army do with his well-paid time? He writes to me thus!' Nairn held the letter in front of his face. '"I require of you to report on the containment of Methodism within the Army." Good God Almighty, Sharpe! What's a man to do with such a letter?'

Sharpe smiled. 'I wouldn't know, sir.'

'I do, Sharpe, I do. That's why I'm a Major General.' Nairn leaned forward and threw the letter onto the fire. 'That's what you do with letters like that.' Nairn chuckled happily as the paper caught fire and flared brightly. 'You want to know why you're here, don't you?'

'Yes, sir.'

'You are here, Sharpe, because the Prince of Wales has gone mad. Just like his Father, poor man, stark staring raving mad.' Nairn leaned back and nodded triumphantly at Sharpe. The letter shrivelled to a black wisp on the logs as

Nairn waited for a reaction. 'Good God, Sharpe! You're supposed to say something! God bless the Prince of Wales would do at a pinch, but you sit there as though the news means nothing. Comes of being a hero, I suppose, always keeping a straight face. Stern business is it? Being a hero?'

'Yes, sir.' Sharpe was grinning broadly.

The door opened and Chatsworth edged in with a heavy wooden tray that he put on the floor in front of the fire. 'Bread and ham, sir, mustard in the small pot. Tea's well brewed, sir, and I beg to report that the toasting fork was in your room, sir. Here it is, sir.'

'You're a rogue and a scoundrel, Chatsworth. You'll be accusing me of burning correspondence from the Chaplain General next.'

'Yes, sir.' Chatsworth grinned contentedly.

'Are you a Methodist, Chatsworth?'

'No, sir. Don't rightly know what a Methodist is, sir.'

'You are fortunate indeed.' Nairn was fixing a slice of bread to the toasting fork. A Lieutenant appeared at the open door behind him, knocked hesitantly to attract attention. 'General Nairn, sir?'

'Major General Nairn is in Madrid! Negotiating a surrender to the French!' Nairn pushed the bread close to the logs, wrapping his hand in his handkerchief to keep the scorching heat away.

The Lieutenant did not smile. He hovered at the door. 'Colonel Greave's compliments, sir, and what's he to do with the iron brackets for the pontoons?'

Nairn rolled his eyes to the yellowed ceiling. 'Who is in charge of the pontoons, Lieutenant?'

'The Engineers, sir.'

'And who, pray, is in charge of our gallant Engineers?'

'Colonel Fletcher, sir.'

'So what do you tell our good Colonel Greave?'

'I see, sir. Yes, sir.' The Lieutenant paused. 'To ask Colonel Fletcher, sir?'

24

'You are a General in the making, Lieutenant. Go and do that thing, and should the Washerwoman General want to see me, tell her I am a married man and cannot accede to her importunings.'

The Lieutenant left and Nairn glared at the orderly. 'Take that grin off your face, Private Chatsworth! The Prince of Wales has gone mad and all you can do is grin!'

'Yes, sir. Is that all, sir?'

'It is, Chatsworth, and I thank you. Go now, and close the door silently.'

Nairn waited till the door was shut. He turned the bread on the fork. 'You're not a fool are you, Sharpe?'

'No, sir.'

'Thank God for that. It's possible that the Prince of Wales does have a touch of his Father's madness. He's interfering in the army, and the Peer's damned annoyed.' Nairn paused, holding the bread dangerously close to the flames. Sharpe said nothing, but he knew that the Peer's annoyance and the Prince of Wales' interference had something to do with the sudden summons north. Nairn glanced at Sharpe from beneath the bushy eyebrows. 'Have you heard of Congreve?'

'The rocket man?'

'That's the one. Sir William Congreve who has the patronage of Prinny and is the begetter of a system of rocket artillery.' Smoke came from the bread and Nairn snatched it towards him. 'At a time, Sharpe, when we need cavalry, artillery, and infantry, what are we sent? Rockets! A troop of Rocket Cavalry! And all because Prinny, with a touch of his father's madness, thinks they'll win the war. Here.' He held the toasting fork to Sharpe then proceeded to lavish butter on his blackened slice. 'Tea?'

'I'm sorry, sir.' Sharpe should have poured. He filled two cups while Nairn dressed his toast with a massive chunk of ham liberally smeared with mustard. Nairn sipped the tea and sighed.

'Chatsworth makes a cup of tea fit for heaven. He'll make

25

some woman a lovely wife one day.' He watched Sharpe toast a slice of bread. 'Rockets, Sharpe. We have in town one troop of Rocket Cavalry and we are ordered by the Horse Guards to give this rocket troop a fair and searching test.' He grinned. 'Don't you like it blacker than that?'

'No, sir.' Sharpe liked his toast pale. He turned the bread.

'I like it smoking like the bloody pit.' Nairn paused while he ate a huge mouthful of ham. 'What we have to do, Sharpe, is test these bloody rockets and when we find they don't work we send them back to England and keep all their horses which we can put to good use. Understand?'

'Yes, sir.'

'Good! Because you've got the job. You will take command of Captain Gilliland and his infernal machines and you will practice him as if he were in battle. That's what your orders say. What I say, and what the Peer would say if he were here, is that you've got to test him so bloody hard that he slinks back to England with a grain of sense in his head.'

'You want the rockets to fail, sir?' Sharpe buttered his bread.

'I don't want them to fail, Sharpe. I'd be delighted if they worked, but they won't. We had a few a couple of years back and they're as flighty as a bitch in heat, but Prinny thinks he knows best. You are to test them, and you are also to practice Captain Gilliland in the manoeuvres of war. In plain words, Sharpe, you've to teach him how to co-operate with infantry on the grounds that infantry, if he were ever to go into battle, would have to protect him from the troops of the Proud Tyrant.' Nairn wolfed another bite of ham. 'Personally speaking,' his voice was muffled, 'I'd be delighted if Boney got him and his bloody rockets, but we've got to show willing.'

'Yes, sir.' Sharpe sipped his tea. There was something odd here, something still unsaid. Sharpe had heard of Congreve's rocket system, indeed the army had been having rumours of the new secret artillery for five or six years, but why was

26

Sharpe selected to test them? He was a Captain, and Nairn had spoken of him taking command of another Captain? It did not make sense.

Nairn had another piece of bread by the fire. 'You're wondering why you were chosen, is that right? Out of all the brave officers and gentlemen, we chose you, yes?'

'I was wondering, sir. Yes.'

'Because you're a nuisance, Sharpe. Because you do not fit into the Peer's well ordered scheme of things.' Sharpe ate his toast and ham, saving himself the need to answer. Nairn seemed to have forgotten the toasting fork, that lay on the hearth, and instead had plucked another piece of paper from the table. 'I told you, Sharpe, that Prinny has gone mad. Not only has he foisted the dreadful Gilliland on us with his dreadful Congreve rockets, but he has foisted this on us as well.' 'This' was the piece of paper that Nairn dangled between finger and thumb as if contagious. 'Appalling! I suppose you'd better read it, though God only knows why I don't just put it on the fire with that bloody man's letter. Here.' He held the paper to Sharpe, then returned to his toast.

The paper was thick and creamy. A seal was big and red on its wide left margin. Sharpe twisted it towards the windows so he could read the words. The top two lines were printed in decorative copperplate script.

'George the Third by the Grace of God of the United Kingdom of Great Britain and Ireland, King, Defender of the Faith &c. To Our'. The next words were hand written on ruled lines. *'Trusty and Well-beloved Richard Sharpe, Esq.'* The printing resumed. 'Greeting: We do by these Presents, Constitute and Appoint you to be'. Sharpe looked up at Nairn.

The Major General was grumbling as he scooped butter from the dish. 'Waste of time, Sharpe! Throw it on the fire! Man's mad!'

Sharpe grinned. He tried to control the elation that was

growing in him, elation and sheer disbelief, he almost dared not read the next words.

'*Major in Our Army now in Portugal and Spain*'.

Dear God! Dear, sweet God! A Major! The paper shook in his hands. He leaned back for an instant, letting his head touch the chair behind him, a Major! Nineteen years he had been in this army. He had joined days before his sixteenth birthday and he had marched across India in the ranks, musket and bayonet in his hands, and now he was a Major! Dear God! He had fought so hard for his Captaincy, thinking it would never come, and now, suddenly, out of the blue, from nowhere, this! Major Richard Sharpe!

Nairn smiled at him. 'It's only army rank, Sharpe.'

A Brevet Major, then, but still a Major. Regimental rank was a man's real rank, and if the commission had said 'a Major in our South Essex Regiment', then it would have been Regimental rank. Army rank meant that he was a Major as long as he served outside of his own Regiment, paid as a Major, though if he were to retire now his pay would be computed by his Regimental rank and not his new Majority. But who cared? He was a Major!

Nairn looked at the tanned, hard face. He knew he was seeing someone remarkable, someone who had risen this far, this quickly, and Nairn wondered what drove a man like Sharpe. Sitting by the fire, the Commission in his hand, he seemed a quiet, contained man, yet Nairn knew of this soldier. Few people in the army did not know of Sharpe. The Peer called him the best leader of a Light Company in the army and perhaps, Nairn wondered, that was why Wellington had been angered by the Prince of Wales' interference. Sharpe was a good Captain, but would he be a good Major? Nairn shrugged to himself. This Sharpe, this man who still insisted on wearing the green uniform of the 95th Rifles, had not let the army down yet, and making him into a Major was hardly likely to still the ferocity of his fighting power.

Sharpe read through the Commission to the bottom. He

would well discipline both inferior officers and soldiers, he would observe and follow such orders as were given him. Dear God! A Major!

'Given at Our Court at *Carlton House* the *Fourteenth* day *of November 1812* in the *Fifty-Third* Year of Our Reign.' The words 'By His Majesty's Command' had been crossed out. In their place the Commission read; '*By the Command of His Royal Highness the Prince Regent, in the Name and on the Behalf of His Majesty*'.

Nairn smiled at him. 'Prinny heard about Badajoz, then about Garcia Hernandez, and he insisted. It's against the rules, of course, absolutely against the rules. The damned man has no business promoting you. Throw it on the fire!'

'Would you take it hard if I disobeyed that order, sir?'

'Congratulations, Sharpe! You're beginning as you mean to go on.' The last words were hurried as a sneeze gathered in his nose and Nairn grabbed his handkerchief and trumpeted into it. He shook his head, bullied and blew his nose, and smiled again. 'My real congratulations.'

'Thank you, sir.'

'Don't thank me, Major. Thank all of us by making sure that little Gilliland's rockets go fizz-plop. D'you know the beggar's got over a hundred and fifty horses for his toys? A hundred and fifty! We need those horses, Sharpe, but we can't bloody touch them as long as Prinny thinks we're going to knock Boney bum over tip with them. Prove him wrong, Sharpe! He'll listen to you.'

Sharpe smiled. 'So that's why I was chosen?'

'Good! You're not a fool. Of course that's why you were chosen, and as a punishment, of course.'

'Punishment?'

'For being promoted before your time. If you'd have had the grace to wait for one of your own Majors to die in the South Essex you'd have landed Regimental rank. It'll come, Sharpe, it'll come. If 1813 is anything like this year we'll all be Field Marshals by next Christmas.' He pulled the

29

dressing gown tight round his chest. 'If we live to see next Christmas, which I doubt.' Nairn stood up. 'Off you go, Sharpe! You'll find Gilliland playing fireworks on the Guarda road. Here's your orders. He knows you're coming, poor lamb. Pack him back to Prinny, Sharpe, but keep the bloody horses!'

'Yes, sir.' Sharpe stood up, took the proffered orders, and felt the elation again. A Major!

Bells suddenly clanged from the church, jangling the still air, frightening birds into hurried flight. Nairn flinched at the sound and crossed to the window. 'Get rid of Gilliland, then we can all have a quiet Christmas!' Nairn rubbed his hands together. 'Except for those bloody bells, Major, there's nothing, thank the Good Lord, that is disturbing His Majesty's Army in Portugal and Spain.'

'Yes, sir. Thank you, sir.' God! The 'Major' sounded good in his ears.

The bells rang on, marking the feastday, while, fifty miles north and east, the first English soldiers, red coats untidy, filed into the quiet village of Adrados.

CHAPTER 2

The rumour reached Frenada soon enough, yet in its passing through the Portuguese countryside the story twisted and curled in the same manner that Congreve's rockets tangled their smoke trails above the shallow valley where Sharpe tested them.

Sergeant Patrick Harper was the first man of Sharpe's Company to hear the story. He heard it from his woman, Isabella, who had heard it from the pulpit of Frenada's Church. Indignation in the town flared, an indignation that Harper shared. English troops, not just English, but Protestants to boot, had gone to a remote village which they had looted, killed, raped, and defiled on a holy day.

Patrick Harper told Sharpe. They were sitting with Lieutenant Price and the Company's two other Sergeants in the winter sunlight of the valley. Sharpe heard his Sergeant out, then shook his head. 'I don't believe it.'

'Swear to God, sir. The priest talked of it, so he did, right there in the church!'

'You heard it?'

'Isabella heard it!' Harper's eyes, beneath the sandy-brown eyebrows, were belligerent. His indignation had thickened the Ulster accent. 'Your man is hardly going to lie in his own pulpit! What's the point of that?'

Sharpe shook his head. He had fought with Harper on a dozen battlefields, he would count the Sergeant as a friend, yet he was not used to this bitterness. Harper had the calm confidence of a strong man. He had an unconquerable humour that saw him through battlefields, bivouacs, and the malevolent fate that had forced him, an Irishman, into England's army. Yet Donegal was never far from Harper's mind and there was something in this rumour that had touched the patriotic nerve that smarted whenever Harper thought of how England had treated Ireland. Protestants raping and killing Catholics, a holy place defiled, the ingredients were seething in Harper's head. Sharpe grinned. 'Do you really believe, Sergeant, that some of our lads went to a village and killed a Spanish garrison and raped all the women? Truly! Does that sound right to you?'

Harper shrugged, thought reluctantly. 'I give you it's the first time, I give you that. But it happened!'

'For God's sake why would they do it?'

'Because they're Protestant, sir! Go a hundred miles just to kill a Catholic, so they will. It's in the blood!'

Sergeant Huckfield, a Protestant from the English shires, spat a blade of grass from his lips. 'Harps! And what about your bloody lot? The Inquisition? You never heard of the Inquisition in your country? Christ! You talk about killing! We learned it all from bloody Rome!'

'Enough!' Sharpe had endured this argument too often and certainly did not want it aired when Harper was filled with anger. He saw the huge Irishman about to utter again and he stopped it before tempers flared. 'I said enough!' He twisted round to see if Gilliland's troop had finished their seemingly interminable preparations and vented his anger on their slowness.

Lieutenant Price was lying full length, his shako tipped over his eyes, and he smiled as he listened to Sharpe's swearing. When it was done he pushed his shako back. 'It's because we're working on a Sunday. Breaking the Lord's Day. Nothing good ever came out of working on the Sabbath, that's what my Father says.'

'It's also the 13th.' Sergeant McGovern's voice was gloomy.

'We are working on Sunday,' Sharpe said with forced

patience, 'because that way we will get this job done by Christmas and you can rejoin Battalion. Then you can eat the geese that Major Forrest has kindly purchased and get drunk on Major Leroy's rum. If you'd prefer not to, then we'll go back to Frenada now. Any questions?'

Price made his voice into that of a small lisping boy. 'What are you buying me for Christmas, Major?'

The Sergeants laughed and Sharpe saw that Gilliland, at last, was ready. He stood up, brushing earth and grass from the French cavalry overalls he wore beneath his Rifleman's jacket. 'Time to go. Come on.'

For four days now he had practised and rehearsed with Gilliland's rockets. He knew, or thought he knew, what he would have to say about them. They did not work. They were entertaining, even spectacular, but hopelessly inaccurate.

They were not new in war. Gilliland, who had a passion for the weapon, had told Sharpe they were first used in China hundreds of years before, and Sharpe himself had seen rockets used by Indian armies. He had hoped that these British rockets, the product of science and engineering, might prove to be better than those which had decorated the sky at Seringapatam.

Congreve's rockets looked just like the fireworks that celebrated Royal days in London, except these were much bigger. Gilliland's smallest rocket was fully eleven feet long, two feet of which was the cylinder containing the powder propulsion and tipped with a roundshot or shell, the rest made up of the rocket's stout stick. The largest rocket, according to Gilliland, was twenty-eight feet long, its head taller than a man, and its load more than fifty pounds of explosive. If such a rocket could be persuaded to go even vaguely near its target it would be a fearful weapon.

For two hours again, beneath a cloudless sky in which the December sun was surprisingly warm, Sharpe exercised Gilliland's men. It was probably, he thought, a waste of all their time for Sharpe doubted if Gilliland would ever need to liaise with infantry in battle, yet there was something about this new weapon that fascinated Sharpe.

Perhaps, he thought as he cleared his thin skirmish line for the fourth time from the front of the battery, it was the mathematics of the rockets. A battery of artillery had six guns, yet it needed a hundred and seventy-two men and a hundred and sixty-four horses to move it and serve it. In battle the battery could deliver twelve shots a minute.

Gilliland had the same number of men and horses, yet at full fire he could deliver ninety missiles in the same minute. He could sustain that rate of fire for a quarter of an hour, firing his full complement of one thousand and four hundred rockets, and no artillery battery could hope to rival that power.

There was another difference, an uncomfortable fact. Ten of the twelve cannon-fired shots would hit their target at five hundred yards. Even at three hundred yards Gilliland was lucky if one rocket in fifty was even close.

For the last time that day Sharpe cleared his skirmish line. Price waved from the far side of the valley. 'Clear, sir!'

Sharpe looked at Gilliland and shouted. 'Fire!'

Sharpe's men grinned in anticipation. This time only twelve small rockets would be fired. Each lay in an open-ended trough so that it would skim the ground when it was ignited. The artillerymen touched the fire to the fuses, smoke curled into the quiet air, and then, almost together, the twelve missiles exploded into movement. Great trails of smoke and sparks slammed backwards, the grass behind the troughs was scorched by fire, and the rockets were moving, faster and faster, rising slightly above the winter-pale field, filling the valley with their tangled roar, screaming above the pasture as Sharpe's men whooped with joy.

One struck the ground, cartwheeled, its stick broke and the loose head smashed down into the earth spraying flame and dark smoke into the valley. Another veered right, collided with a second, and both dived into the grass. Two seemed to be going perfectly, searing above the field, while the rest wandered and made intricate patterns in smoke above the grass.

All except one. One rocket thrust itself in a perfect curve, higher and higher, pushing up so that it was hidden by the smoke that was pumped out and seemed to stack itself beneath its fiery tail. Sharpe watched it, squinting into the brightness of the sky, and he thought he saw the stick flicker in the smoke, turning, then he saw flame again. The rocket had flipped over and was plunging earthward, accelerating before the rush of fire, screaming down at the men who had fired it.

'Run!' Sharpe yelled at the artillerymen.

Harper, his indignation at the massacre temporarily forgotten, was laughing.

'Run, you idiots!'

Horses bolted, men panicked, and the sound grew louder, a thunderbolt from the December sky, and Gilliland's shrill voice was shrieking confusion at his men. The artillerymen dived to the earth, hands over their heads, and the noise grew and suddenly crashed into nothing as the solid six-pound shot of the twelve pound rocket buried itself in the soil. The stick quivered above it. For a second the rocket propellant still flamed hungrily at the cylinder's base, then it died and there were only flickering blue flames licking at the stick.

Harper wiped his eyes. 'God save Ireland!'

'The others?' Sharpe was looking upfield.

Sergeant Huckfield shook his head. 'All over the place, sir. Nearest to the target area was probably thirty yards.' He licked the pencil and made a note in the book he was carrying, then shrugged. 'About average, sir.'

Which was, sadly for Gilliland, true. The rockets seemed to have a mind of their own once they were in motion. As Lieutenant Harry Price had said, they were superb for frightening horses so long as no one cared which horses were frightened, French or British.

Sharpe walked Captain Gilliland up the valley among the smoking remains of his missiles. The air was bitter with powder smoke. The notebook said it all, the rockets were a failure.

Gilliland, a small, young man, his face thin but lit with a fanatical passion for his weapon, pleaded with Sharpe. Sharpe had heard all the arguments before. He half listened, the other part of his mind sympathetic to Gilliland's desperate eagerness to be part of the 1813 campaign. This year was ending sourly. After the great victories of Ciudad Rodrigo, Badajoz and Salamanca the campaign had ground to a halt before the French fortress of Burgos. The autumn had seen a British retreat back to Portugal, back to the foodstocks that would keep an army alive through the winter, and the retreat had been hard. Some fool had sent the army's supplies by a different road so that the troops slogged westward, through pouring rain, hungry and angry. Discipline had broken down. Men had been hung by the roadside for looting. Sharpe had stripped two drunks stark naked and left them to the mercies of the pursuing French. No man in the South Essex became drunk after that and it was one of the few Battalions that had marched back into Portugal in good order. Next year they would avenge that retreat and for the first time the armies of the Peninsula would march under one General. Wellington was head now of the British, the Portuguese and the Spanish armies, and Gilliland, pleading with Sharpe, wanted to be part of the victories that unity seemed to promise. Sharpe cut the speech short. 'But they don't hit anything, Captain. You can't make them accurate.'

Gilliland nodded, shrugged, shook his head, flapped his hands in impotence, then turned again to Sharpe. 'Sir? You once said a frightened enemy is already half beaten, yes?'

'Yes.'

'Think of what these will do to an enemy! They're terrifying!'

'As your men just found out.'

Gilliland shook his head in exasperation. 'There's always a rogue rocket or two, sir. But think of it! An enemy that's never seen them? Suddenly the flames, the noise! Think, sir!'

Sharpe thought. He was required to test these rockets, test them thoroughly, and he had done that in four hard days work. They had started the rockets at their full range of two thousand yards and quickly brought the range down, down to just three hundred yards and still the missiles were hopelessly inaccurate. And yet! Sharpe smiled to himself. What was the effect on a man who had never been exposed to them? He looked at the sky. Midday. He had hoped for an easy afternoon before going to see the performance of *Hamlet* that the officers of the Light Division were staging in a barn outside the town, but perhaps there was just one test that he had forgotten. It need not take long.

An hour later, alone with Sergeant Harper, he watched Gilliland make his preparations six hundred yards away. Harper looked at Sharpe and shook his head. 'We're mad.'

'You don't have to stay.'

Harper sounded glum. 'I promised your wife I'd look after you, sir. Here I am, keeping the promise.'

Teresa. Sharpe had met her two summers ago when his Company had fought alongside her band of Partisans. Teresa fought the French in her own way, with ambush and knife, with surprise and terror. They had been married eight months and in that time Sharpe doubted if he had spent more than ten weeks with her. Their daughter, Antonia, was nineteen months old now, a daughter he loved because she was his only blood relative, but a daughter he did not know and who would grow to speak a different language, but still his daughter. He grinned at Harper. 'We'll be all right. You know they always miss.'

'Nearly always, sir.'

Maybe they were mad to try this test, yet Sharpe wanted to deal fairly with Gilliland's enthusiasm. The rockets were inaccurate, so much so that they had become a joke to Sharpe's men who loved to watch the veering, crashing and burning of Gilliland's toys. Yet most of the rockets did travel towards the enemy, however curious their path, and perhaps Gilliland was right. Perhaps they would terrify and there was only one way to find out. To become the target himself.

Harper scratched his head. 'If my Mother knew, sir, that I was standing against a wall with thirty bloody rockets aimed at me . . .' He sighed, touched the crucifix around his neck.

Sharpe knew the artillerymen were jointing the sticks. Each twelve pounder needed two lengths of stick. The first length was slotted into a metal tube on the side of the rocket head and then fixed in place by crimping the metal with pliers. A similar metal tube, similarly crimped, joined the two sticks into a ten-foot shaft that balanced the rocket head. The shaft had another use, a use that intrigued and impressed Sharpe. Each trooper in the Rocket Cavalry kept a lance-head in a special holster on his saddle. The lance-head could be hammered onto the jointed sticks and then carried into battle on horseback. Gilliland's men were not trained to fight with the lance, any more than they were trained in the use of the sabres they all carried, but there was an ingenuity about the detached lance-head that pleased Sharpe. He had appalled Gilliland by insisting that the Rocket Troop rehearse cavalry charges.

'Portfires alight!' Harper seemed determined to keep up a commentary on his own death. Sharpe could see his own Company sitting by Gilliland's rocket 'cars', his specially fitted supply wagons. 'Oh, God!' Harper crossed himself.

Sharpe knew the portfires were going down to touch the rocket fuses. 'You said yourself they couldn't hit a house at fifty yards.'

'I'm a big target.' Harper was six feet and four inches tall.

There was a wisp of smoke far down the field. That one

rocket would already be moving, burning the grass, leaping like quickfire above the soil, hammering in front of its fire and smoke. The others burst into life.

'Oh, God,' Harper groaned.

Sharpe grinned. 'If they're close, just jump over the wall.'

'Anything you say, sir.'

For a second or two the rockets were curious twisting dots, haloed by fire, centred on their pulsing smoke trails. The trails weaved as the missiles climbed and wandered and then, so fast that Sharpe would have had no time to throw himself behind the low stone wall, the rockets seemed to leap towards the two men. The sound filled the valley, the fire blazed behind the spread of missiles, and then they were past, screaming above the wall and Sharpe found he had ducked even though the closest rocket had been thirty yards away.

Harper swore, looked at Sharpe.

'Not so funny here, eh?' Sharpe found himself feeling relieved that the rockets had gone. Even at thirty yards the noise and fire was alarming.

Harper grinned. 'Wouldn't you say our duty was done, sir?'

'Just the big ones, then it's done.'

'For what we are about to receive.'

The next volley was not to be ground fired, but to be aimed upwards in firing tubes supported by a tripod. Gilliland, Sharpe knew, would be working at the mathematics of the trajectory. Sharpe had always supposed mathematics to be the most exact of all the sciences and he did not clearly see how it could be applied to the inexact nature of rocketry, but Gilliland would be busy with angles and equations. The wind had to be ascertained, for if a breeze was blowing across the rockets' path then they had a perverse habit of turning into the wind. That, Gilliland had explained, was because the wind put more pressure on the long stick than on the cylinder head, and so the tubes had to be aimed down-wind for an upwind target. Another calculation was the stick length, a longer stick giving more height and a longer flight, and at six hundred yards Sharpe knew the artillerymen would be sawing off a length of each rocket's tail. A third imponderable was the angle of launch. A rocket travelled relatively slowly as it left the firing tube and so the head fell towards the ground in the first few feet of flight and the angle of launch had to be increased to compensate. Modern science at war.

'Hold your hat, sir.'

The smoke and flames were easily visible beneath the firing tubes, even at six hundred yards, and then, with appalling suddenness, the missiles leaped into the air. These were eighteen-pounder rockets, a dozen of them, and they sliced the air above the lingering smoke trails of the first volley, climbing, climbing, and Sharpe saw one slam off to the left, hopelessly off course, while the others seemed to have coalesced into a living flame-shot cloud that grew silently over the valley.

'Oh, God.' Harper was holding the crucifix.

The rockets, strangely, seemed not to be moving. The cloud grew, the flame surrounded dots were still and hovering, and Sharpe knew it was an illusion caused by the trajectory bringing the missiles in a curve pointing straight at the two of them. Then a single dot dropped from the cloud, fire at its edges, smoke dark against the clear sky behind. The noise burst on them; a screaming roar, flame-born, and the dot grew larger. 'Down!'

'Christ!' Harper dived right, Sharpe left, and Sharpe clung to the soil by the wall and the noise hammered at him, growing, seeming to make the stones of the wall shake, and the air was throbbing with the noise that came closer and closer and filled their whole world with terror as the rocket slammed into the wall.

'Jesus.' Sharpe rolled over and sat up. The rocket, the most accurate of the week, had demolished the stone wall where he and Harper had been standing. The broken stick toppled slowly off the wreckage. The cylinder smoked innocently in the next field. Smoke drifted over the burned grass.

They started laughing, beating the dirt off their uniforms, and suddenly it seemed hilarious to Sharpe so that he rolled onto his side, helpless with laughter. 'Holy Jesus!'

'You'd better thank Him. If that had been a shell instead of roundshot.' Harper left the thought unfinished. He was standing and staring at the ruins of the wall.

Sharpe sat up again. 'Is that frightening?'

Harper grinned. 'You'd regret having a full belly, that's for sure, sir.' He bent down and picked up his shako.

'So maybe there is something to the mad Colonel's invention.'

'Aye, sir.'

'And think if you could fire a whole volley at fifty paces.'

Harper nodded. 'True, but there's a lot of maybes and ifs there, sir.' He grinned. 'You're fond of them, aren't you? You fancy trying them out, yes?' He laughed. 'Toys for Christmas.'

A figure in blue uniform, leading a second horse, was riding towards them from the firing point. Harper pulled his battered shako low over his eyes and nodded towards the galloping man. 'I think he's worried he's murdered us, sir.'

Clods of earth flew up behind the galloping horses. Sharpe shook his head. 'That's not Gilliland.' He could see a cavalryman's pelisse across the blue uniform shoulders.

The cavalryman skirted a burning rocket wreck, urged his horse on, waved as he came close. His shout was urgent. 'Major Sharpe?'

'Yes.'

'Lieutenant Rogers, sir. Headquarters. Major General Nairn's compliments, sir, and would you report at once.'

Sharpe took the reins of the spare horse from Rogers, looped them over the horse's head. 'What's it about?'

'About, sir? Haven't you heard?' Rogers was impatient,

41

his horse fretful. Sharpe put his left foot in the stirrup, reached for the saddle, and Harper helped by heaving him upwards. Rogers waited as the Sergeant retrieved Sharpe's shako. 'There's been a massacre, sir, at some place called Adrados.'

'Massacre?'

'God knows, sir. All hell's loose. Ready?'

'Lead on.'

Sergeant Patrick Harper watched Sharpe lurch as his horse took off after the Lieutenant. So the rumour was true and Harper smiled in satisfaction. Not a satisfaction because he had been proved right, but because Sharpe had been summoned and where Sharpe went, Harper followed. So what if Sharpe was a Major now, supposedly detached from the South Essex? He would still take Harper, as he always took Harper, and the giant Irishman wanted to help take revenge on the men who had offended his decency and his religion. He began walking back towards the Company, whistling as he went, the prospect of a fight pleasant in his soul.

CHAPTER 3

'Damn, damn, damn, damn, damn, damn, damn.' Major General Nairn, still in a dressing gown, still with a cold, stared out of the window. He turned as Lieutenant Rogers, having announced Sharpe, left the room. The eyes, under the straggling eyebrows, looked at Sharpe. 'Damn.'

'Sir.'

'Cold as a parson's bloody heart.'

'Sir?'

'This room, Sharpe.' It was an office, one table smothered in maps which, in turn, were littered with empty cups and plates, snuff boxes, two half eaten pieces of cold toast, a single spur and a marble bust of Napoleon on which someone, presumably Nairn, had inked embellishments which made the Emperor of the French look like a simpering weakling. The Major General crossed to the table and lowered himself into a leather chair. 'So what have you heard about this bloody massacre, Major? Cheer an old man up and tell me you've heard nothing.'

'I'm afraid I have, sir.'

'Well what, man?'

Sharpe told him what had been preached in the church that morning and Nairn listened with fingers steepled in front of his closed eyes. When Sharpe finished Nairn groaned. 'God in his heaven, Major, it couldn't be bloody worse, could it?' Nairn swivelled in the chair and stared across the roofs of the town. 'We're unpopular enough as it is with the Spanish. They don't forget the seventeenth century, blast their eyes, and the fact that we're fighting for their bloody country doesn't make us any better. Now the priests are preaching that the heathen British are raping anything that's Catholic with a skirt on. God! If the Portuguese are believing it, what the hell are they believing over the border? They'll be petitioning the Pope to declare war on us next.' He turned back to the desk, leaned back and closed his eyes. 'We need the co-operation of the Spanish people and we are hardly likely to get it if they believe this story. Come!' This last word was to a clerk who had knocked timidly on the door. He handed Nairn a sheet of paper which the Scotsman looked through, grunting approval. 'I need a dozen, Simmons.'

'Yes, sir.'

When the clerk had gone Nairn smiled slyly at Sharpe. 'Be sure your sins will find you out, eh? I burn a letter from that great and good man, the bloody Chaplain General, and today I have to write to every Bishop and Archbishop inside spitting distance.' He mimicked a cringing voice. 'The story is not true, your Grace, the men were not from our army, your Holiness, but nevertheless we will apprehend the bastards and turn them inside out. Slowly.'

'Not true, sir?'

Nairn flashed a look of annoyance at Sharpe. 'Of course it's not bloody true!' He leaned forward and picked up the bust of Napoleon, staring it between its cold eyes. 'You'd like to believe it, wouldn't you? Splash it all over your bloody *Moniteur*. How the savage English treat Spanish women. That would take your mind of all those good men you left in Russia.' He slammed the bust onto the table. 'Damn.' He blew his nose noisily.

Sharpe waited. He was alone with Nairn, but he had seen much coming and going as he entered the Headquarters. The rumour, whatever its truth, had stirred Frenada into activity. Sharpe was part of it, or else Nairn would not have sent for him, but the Rifleman was content to wait until he was told. The moment had evidently come, for Nairn waved

Sharpe into a chair by the small fireplace and took the chair opposite. 'I have a problem, Major Sharpe. In brief it is this. I have a nasty mess on my doorstep, a mess I must clear up, but I don't have the troops to do it.' He held up a hand to stop an interruption. 'Oh yes, I know. I have a whole bloody army, but that's under Beresford's control.' Beresford was in nominal command of the Army while Wellington politicked in the south. 'Beresford's up north, with his Portuguese, and I don't have time to write a "please, sir" note to him. If I ask for help from one of the Divisions then every General inside ten miles is going to want a finger in this pie. I'm in charge of this Headquarters. My job is to pass the papers and make sure the cooks don't piss in the soup. However, I do have you, and I do have the so-called garrison battalion of Frenada, and if you're willing then we might put the lid on this peculiarly nasty pot of snakes.'

'Willing, sir?'

'You will be a volunteer, Sharpe. That's an order.' He grinned. 'Tell me what you know of Pot-au-Feu. Marshal Pot-au-Feu.'

Sharpe shook his head. 'Nothing.'

'An army of deserters?'

That did ring faint bells. Sharpe remembered a night on the retreat from Burgos, a night when the wind flung rain at the roofless barn where four hundred wet, miserable and hungry soldiers had sheltered. There had been talk there of a haven for soldiers, an army of deserters who were defying the French and the English, but Sharpe had dismissed the stories. They were like other rumours that went through the army. He frowned. 'Is that true?'

Nairn nodded. 'Yes.' He told the story that he had gleaned that morning from Hogan's papers, from the priest of Adrados, and from a Partisan who had brought the priest to Frenada. It was a story so incredible that Sharpe, at times, stopped Nairn simply to ask for confirmation. Some of the wildest rumours, it seemed, turned out to be fact.

For a year now, perhaps a few months longer, there had been an organized band of deserters, calling themselves an army, living in the mountains of southern Galicia. Their leader was a Frenchman whose real name was unknown, an ex-Sergeant who now styled himself as Marshal Pot-au-Feu. Nairn grinned. 'Stockpot, I suppose that translates. There's a story that he was once a cook.' Under Pot-au-Feu the "army" had prospered. They lived in territory that was unimportant to the French Marshals or to Wellington, they subsisted by terrorizing the countryside, taking what they wanted, and their numbers grew as deserters from every army in the Peninsula heard of their existence. French, British, Portuguese and Spanish, all were in Pot-au-Feu's ranks.

'How many, sir?'

Nairn shrugged. 'We don't know. Numbers vary between four hundred and two thousand. I'd guess six or seven hundred.'

Sharpe raised his eyebrows. That could be a formidable force. 'Why have they come south, sir?'

'That's a question.' Nairn blew his nose into the huge wrinkled handkerchief. 'It seems that the Frogs are being pretty lively in Galicia. I don't know, bloody rumour again, but there's a whisper that they might try a winter attack on Braganza then on to Oporto. I don't believe it for a second, but there's a school of thought which maintains that Napoleon is in need of some victory, any victory, after the Russian catastrophe. If they capture the north of Portugal then they can trumpet that as some kind of achievement.' Nairn shrugged. 'I can't think why, but we're told to take the possibility seriously and certainly there's a lot of Frog cavalry lumbering about in Galicia and our belief is that they drove our friend Pot-au-Feu towards us. And he promptly sends his British deserters to attack a village called Adrados where they murder a small Spanish garrison and go on to make themselves free with all the ladies. Now half of bloody

Spain thinks that the Protestant English are reverting to the Wars of Religion. That, Sharpe, is the story in its rancid little nutshell.'

'So we go up there and turn the bastards inside out?'

Nairn smiled. 'Not yet, Sharpe, not yet. We have a problem.' He got to his feet, crossed to the table, rummaged through the mess of papers and litter, and returned with a small, black leather-bound book. He tossed the book to Sharpe. 'Did you see a tall, thin man when you arrived here? Silver hair? Elegant?'

Sharpe nodded. He had noticed the man because of the flawless uniform, the look of bored distinction, and the obvious wealth of the man's spurs, sword and other ornaments. 'I did.'

'That's him.' Nairn pointed at the book.

Sharpe opened it. It was new, the covers stiff, and on the title page he read 'Practical Instructions to the Young Officer in the Art of Warfare with Special Reference to the Engagements now Proceeding in Spain'. The author was named as Colonel Sir Augustus Farthingdale. The book cost five shillings, published by Richard Phillips, and was printed by Joyce Gold of Shoe Lane in London. The pages were mostly uncut, but Sharpe's eye was caught by a sentence that ran over a page and so he took out his pen-knife and slit the next two pages apart. He finished the sentence and smiled. Nairn saw the smile. 'Read it to me.'

' "The men, during the march, should keep their files, and no indecent language or noise be allowed".'

'God! I missed that one.' Nairn grinned. 'You will note that the book has an introduction by my friend the Chaplain General. He recommends frequent divine service to keep the men quiet and ordered.'

Sharpe closed the book. 'So why is he a problem?'

'Because Colonel Sir Augustus Farthingdale has taken himself a wife. A Portuguese wife. Some filly of a good family, it seems, but a Papist. God knows what the Chaplain

General would say to that! Anyway, this spring flower of Sir Augustus' autumn wants to go to Adrados to pray at some bloody shrine where miracles are two a penny and guess who meets her there. Pot-au-Feu. Lady Farthingdale is now a hostage. If any troops go within five miles of Adrados they'll turn her over to the rapists and murderers who make up their ranks. On the other hand, Sir Augustus can have her back on payment of five hundred guineas.'

Sharpe whistled, Nairn grinned. 'Aye, it's a pretty price for a pair of legs to wrap round you in bed. Anyway, Sir Augustus swears the price is fair, that he will do anything, anything to bring his bride safe home. God, Sharpe, there's nothing so disgusting as the sight of an old man in love with a woman forty years younger.' Sharpe wondered if there was some jealousy in Nairn's words.

'Why would they want to ransom her, sir, if she's their insurance against attack?'

'You're not a fool, are you. God knows the answer to that. They have deemed to send us a letter and the letter informs us that we may send the money on a certain date, at a certain time, and so on and on. I want you to go.'

'Alone?'

'You can take one other man, that's all.'

'The money?'

'Sir Augustus will provide it. He claims his lady wife is a pearl beyond price so he's busy writing notes of hand to get her back.'

'And if they won't release her?'

Nairn smiled. He was huddled back in his dressing gown. 'I don't believe they will. They just want the money, that's all. Sir Augustus made a half-hearted offer to deliver it, but I turned him down much to his relief. I suppose two hostages are better than one and a Knight of the Realm makes a useful bargaining piece. Anyway, I need a soldier to go up there.'

Sharpe raised the book. 'He's a soldier.'

'He's a bloody author, Sharpe, all words and wind. No,

you go, man. Take a look at their defences. Even if you don't bring the filly back you'll know how to go and get her.'

Sharpe smiled. 'A rescue?'

Nairn nodded. 'A rescue. Sir Augustus Farthingdale, Major, is our government's military representative to the Portuguese government which means, between you and me, damn all except that he gets to eat a lot of dinners and meet pretty young ladies. How he stays so thin, God only knows. He is, however, popular in Lisbon. The government likes him. His wife, moreover, is supposed to be from some high-up family and we're not going to get letters of thanks if we casually allow her to be raped by a gang of scum in the mountains. We have got to get her out. Once that's done our hands are free and we can cook Pot-au-Feu in a very hot cauldron. You're happy to go?'

Sharpe looked through the window. A score of smoke trails rose vertically from the chimneys of Frenada, smoke fading into a flawless cold sky. Of course he would go. Nairn had not let Sir Augustus go because the Colonel might become a hostage himself, but Nairn had not expressed any such fear about Sharpe. He smiled at the Major General. 'I assume I'm expendable, sir.'

'You're a soldier, aren't you? Of course you're expendable!'

Sharpe was still smiling. He was a soldier, and a lady needed rescuing, and was that not what soldiers throughout history had done? The smile became wider. 'Of course I'll go, sir. With pleasure.'

In the churches of Spain they were praying for revenge on the perpetrators of Adrados's misery. The prayers were being answered.

CHAPTER 4

La Entrada de Dios.

The Gateway of God.

It looked it, too, from two hundred feet below on a bright winter morning as Sharpe and Harper walked their patient horses up the track which wound between rocks whose shadows still harboured the night's frost. Adrados lay just beyond the saddle of the pass, but the pass was the Gateway of God.

To left and right were rocky peaks, a nightmare landscape, savage and sharp. In front of them was the smooth grass of the road through the Sierra. Guarding that road was the Gateway.

To the right of the pass was the castle. The Castillo de la Virgen. El Cid himself had known that castle, had stood on its ramparts before riding out against the curved scimitars of Islam. Legend said that three Muslim Kings had died in the dungeons beneath the Castle of the Virgin, died refusing to profess Christianity, and their ghosts were said to wander wraith-like in the Gateway of God. The castle had stood years beyond number, built before the Wars of God were won, but when the Muslims had been thrown back across the sea, the castle had begun to decay. The Spanish had moved from the high places of refuge, back down the passes into the softer plains. Yet the castle still stood, a refuge for foxes and ravens, its keep and gatehouse still holding the southern edge of the Gateway of God.

And on the northern side, two hundred yards from the castle, was the Convent. It was a huge building, low and square, and its windowless walls seemed to spring from the granite of the Sierra's rocks. Here was the place where the Virgin had stood, here was where they had built a shrine about her Footfall and a castle to protect it, and the Convent had no windows because the nuns who had once lived in its rich cloisters were supposed not to look upon the world, only at the mystery of the smooth patch of granite in their gold painted chapel.

The nuns had gone, taken in leather-curtained carts to the mother house at Leon, and the soldiers whose surcoats had decorated the walls of the castle had gone too. The road still led through the hills, a road that wound up from the deep-ravined rivers of the Portuguese border, but there were newer and better roads to the south. The Gateway of God guarded only Adrados now, a valley of sheep, thorns, and Pot-au-Feu's desperate band of deserters.

'They'll have seen us by now, sir.'

'Yes.'

Sharpe pulled out the watch that Sir Augustus Farthing-dale had lent him. They were early so he stopped the three horses. The third horse carried the gold and, it was hoped, would provide a mount for Lady Farthingdale if Pot-au-Feu kept his word and released her on payment of the ransom. Harper climbed off his horse, stretched his huge muscles, and stared at the buildings on the skyline. 'They'd be bastards to attack, sir.'

'True.'

An attack on the Gateway from the west would be an uphill assault, steeply uphill, with no chance of approaching the pass unseen. Sharpe turned. It had taken him and Harper three hours to climb from the river, and for much of that time they would have been visible to a man with a glass on the castle ramparts. The rocks to left and right of the pass were jumbled and steep, impassable to artillery, barely climbable by infantry. Whoever held the Gateway of God barred the one road through the Sierra, and it was fortunate

51

for the British that the French had never needed these hills and so no battle had ever been fought up this impossible slope. The hills had no value because the roads to the south by-passed the Sierra, making a defence of Spain impossible in these hills, but to Pot-au-Feu the old buildings were a perfect refuge.

High above them were birds, circling slowly, and Sharpe saw Patrick Harper staring lovingly at them. Harper loved birds. They were his private retreat from the army.

'What are they?'

'Red kite, sir. They'll be up from the valley looking for carrion.'

Sharpe grunted. He feared that they might provide lunch for the birds. The closer they rode to the high valley the more he believed it was a trap. He did not believe that Farthingdale's bride would be released. He believed the money would be taken and he wondered whether he or Harper would leave alive. He had told the Sergeant that he need not come, but the big Irishman had jeered at such pusillanimity. If Sharpe was going, he would go.

'Come on. Let's go on.'

Sharpe had not liked Sir Augustus Farthingdale. The Colonel had been condescending to the Rifleman, amused when he discovered that Sharpe did not possess a watch and could not, therefore, time his arrival at the Convent to the exact moment stipulated by Pot-au-Feu's letter. Ten minutes past eleven, exactly. Yet beneath the Colonel's bored voice Sharpe had detected a panic about his wife. The Colonel was in love. At sixty he had found his bride, and now she was being snatched from him, and though the Colonel tried to hide every emotion beneath a mask of elegant politeness, he could not hide the passion which his bride engendered. Sharpe had not liked him, but Sharpe had felt sorry for him, and he would try to restore the lost bride.

The red kites slid their spread wings and forked tails over the castle ramparts and Sharpe could now see men on the walls. They were on the ramparts of the keep, on the turret of a great gatetower that faced into the pass, and behind the castellations of the wall around the courtyard. Their muskets were tiny lines against the pale blue of the December sky.

The road was zig-zagging now as the pass narrowed. It crossed the saddle of the pass close to the Castle wall, too close, and Sharpe pulled his horse off the road and set it at the steep grass bank of the pass's last few yards. The Convent was to their left now and Sharpe could see how it had been built on the very edge of the pass so that its eastern wall, facing the village, was just a single storey high while the western wall, looking towards Portugal, was two floors high. In the southern wall, facing across the pass, a big hole had been crudely smashed into the lower floor. The hole was covered by a blanket. Sharpe nodded at it. 'You'd think they'd put a gun in there.'

'Good place for one.' Harper said. The gun would fire straight across the neck of the pass.

They breasted the last few feet, their horses scrambling up the steep turf, and there was the high valley of Adrados. A quarter mile ahead of them was the village itself, a huddle of small, low houses built around one larger house that Sharpe supposed to be the village Inn. The road turned right once it was through the village, sharp right, turning to the south, and Sharpe almost groaned aloud. There was a hill that made the pivot of the turning valley, a hill that was steep, thorn covered, and crowned by an old watchtower. The Castillo de la Virgen guarded the pass, but the watchtower was the sentry post for the whole Sierra. The tower looked old, its summit crowned by castellations like the Castle walls, but at its foot he could see the scars of earthworks and he guessed the Spanish garrison had made new defences there. Whoever controlled the watchtower controlled the whole valley. Guns put at the summit of the watchtower hill could fire down into the courtyard of the Castle.

'Let's keep going.' They were five minutes early and

Sharpe did not turn towards the Convent, instead he led Harper on the track which ran, past a spring, towards the village. He wanted to see the eastern face of the Castle, the face that looked onto the village, but as he rode there was a sudden shout from the gatehouse and then a rattle of musket shots.

'Friendly.' Harper grinned. The shots had gone hopelessly wide, intended only as a warning. Sharpe reined in and stared at the Castle. The gatehouse faced him, massively turreted, topped with men who jeered towards the Riflemen. The archway, its gates long gone, was barricaded with two peasant carts, presumably stolen from the village, while the gatehouse turrets above seemed solid and untouched by the passage of time. The keep had not been so fortunate. Sharpe could see daylight through some of the holes in its upper floors, yet the stairways must still wind to the very top for men stood on the ramparts staring at the two horsemen in the valley.

They had ridden far enough to see along the length of the eastern wall, and their excursion had been worthwhile. Most of the wall was gone, nothing now but a heap of rubble marking the line of the old wall. The rubble line would be simple to cross, a ready made breach into Pot-au-Feu's fastness.

They turned toward the Convent. No one stared from its apparently flat roof, no smoke drifted from its cloisters. It seemed to be abandoned. One doorway faced east, a doorway that was flanked by two small barred windows that Sharpe guessed had been the only normal channels of communication with the outside world. The door itself was huge, decorated with strange heads carved into the stone archway, and Sharpe dismounted beneath their eroded gaze and tied the horses' reins to the rusting bars of the left hand window. Harper heaved the saddlebags off the third horse, the gold heavy, and Sharpe pushed at one of the doors.

It creaked open.

The watch said ten past eleven, the scroll-worked minute hand precisely pointing to the Roman II.

The door, hinges rusted, swung fully open.

It showed a cloister beyond the entrance tunnel. A century of neglect had made the cloister ragged, but it kept its beauty. The stone pillars that supported the cloister arches were carved, their heads a riot of stone leaves and small birds, while the cloister floor was paved in coloured tiles, green and yellow, now edged with weeds and dead grass. In the centre was a raised pool, empty of water but filled with weeds, and in one corner of the courtyard a young hornbeam had pushed its way through the tiles, cracking them around its bole. The cloister seemed empty. The roof line of the southern and eastern walls was etched in shadow on the tiles.

Sharpe took the rifle from his shoulder. He was a Major now, the ranks long in his past, yet he still carried the rifle. He had always carried a long-arm into battle; a musket when he was a private, a rifle now he was an officer. He saw no reason not to carry a gun. A soldier's job was to kill. A rifle killed.

He cocked it, the click suddenly loud in the dark entrance-way, and he walked on soft feet into the sunlight of the cloister. His eyes searched the shadows of the arches. Nothing moved.

He gestured to Harper.

The huge Sergeant carried the saddlebag into the court-yard. The coins chinked dully inside the leather. His eyes, like Sharpe's, searched the roofline, the shadows, and saw nothing, nobody.

Beneath the arches doors opened from the cloister and Sharpe pushed them open one by one. They seemed to be storerooms. One was full of sacks and he drew his huge, clumsy sword and slit at the rough cloth. Grain spilled onto the floor. He sheathed the sword.

Harper dropped the saddlebag beside the raised pool and took from his shoulder the seven-barrelled gun and pulled back the flint. The gun was a gift from Sharpe and it fired seven half-inch bullets from its seven barrels. Only a hugely strong man could wield the gun, and they were few in number, so much so that the Royal Navy, for whom the guns had been made, had abandoned the weapon when they found its recoil wounding more of their own men than its bullets wounded of the enemy. Harper adored the gun. At close range it was a fearful weapon and he had become used to the massive kick. He lifted the frizzen and checked with his finger that there was powder in its pan.

On the left of the courtyard there was just the one door beneath a window dark with stained glass. It was a large door, ornate with decoration, larger than the door on the western side which Sharpe had tried, pushed, and found firmly barred from the far side. He tried the lever handle of the decorated door and it moved. Harper shook his head, gestured at the seven-barrelled gun, and took Sharpe's place. He looked questioningly at his officer.

Sharpe nodded.

Harper shouted as he jumped through the door, a fearful screaming challenge designed to terrify anyone within the building, and he threw himself to one side, crouched, and swept the seven-barrelled gun around the gloom. His voice died away. He was in the chapel and it was empty. 'Sir?'

Sharpe went inside. He could see little. The stoup that had held holy water was empty and dry, its bowl lined with dust and tiny fragments of stone. The light fell on the tiles of the chapel floor by the doorway and Sharpe could see an untidy brown stain that flaked at the edges of the tiles. Blood.

'Look, sir.'

Harper was standing at a great iron grille that made the area they were standing in into a kind of ante-chamber to the chapel proper. There was a door pierced in the grille, but the door was padlocked shut. Harper fingered the lock. 'New, sir.'

Sharpe craned his head back. The grille went to the ceiling where gold paint shone dully on the beams. 'Why's it here?'

'To stop outsiders getting into the chapel, sir. This is as far as anyone could go. Only the nuns were allowed in there, sir. When it was a convent, that is.'

Sharpe pressed his face against the cold bars. The chapel ran left and right, altar to the left, and as his eyes became accustomed to the gloom he saw that the chapel had been defaced. Blood was splashed on the painted walls, statues had been torn from their niches, the light of the Eternal Presence ripped from its hanging chains. It seemed a pointless kind of destruction, but then Pot-au-Feu's band was desperate, men who had run and had nowhere else to flee to, and such men would wreak their vengeance on anything that was beautiful, valued, and good. Sharpe wondered if Lady Farthingdale was even alive.

Horses' hooves came faintly from outside the Convent. The two Riflemen froze, listened.

The hooves were coming closer. Sharpe could hear voices. 'This way!'

They moved quickly, quietly, out into the cloister. The hooves were closer. Sharpe pointed across the courtyard and Harper, astonishingly silent for a huge man, disappeared into the dark shadow beneath the arches. Sharpe stepped backwards, into the chapel, and pulled the door close so that he and his rifle looked through a slit onto the entrance tunnel.

Silence in the courtyard. Not even a wind to stir the dead leaves of the hornbeam on the green and yellow tiles. The hooves stopped outside, the creak of a saddle as a man dismounted, the crunch of boots on the roadway, and then silence.

Two sparrows flew down into the raised pool and pecked among the dead weeds.

Sharpe moved slightly to his right, searching for Harper, but the Irishman was invisible in the shadows. Sharpe crouched so that his shape, if seen through the crack, would be confusing to whoever came out of the dark tunnel.

The gate creaked. Silence again. The sparrows flew upwards, their wings loud in the cloister, and then Sharpe almost jumped in alarm because the silence was shattered by a bellowed shout, a challenge, and a man leaped into the cloister, moving fast, his musket jerking round to cover the dark shadows where assailants might wait, and then the man crouched at the foot of a pillar by the entrance and called softly behind him.

He was a huge man, as big as Harper, and he was dressed in French blue with a single gold ring on his sleeve. The uniform of a French Sergeant. He called again.

A second man appeared, as wary as the first, and this man dragged saddlebags behind him. He was in the uniform of a French officer, a senior officer, his red-collared blue jacket bright with gold insignia. Was this Pot-au-Feu? He carried a cavalry carbine, despite his infantry uniform, and at his side, slung on silver chains, was a cavalry sabre.

The two Frenchmen stared round the cloister. Nothing moved, nobody.

'*Allons*.' The Sergeant took the saddlebag and froze, pointing. He had seen Harper's bag beside the pool.

'Stop!' Sharpe yelled, kicking the door open with his right foot as he stood up. 'Stop!' the rifle pointed at them. They turned.

'Don't move!' He could see their eyes judging the distance of the rifle shot fired from the hip. 'Sergeant!'

Harper appeared to their flank, a vast man moving like a cat, grinning, the huge gun gaping its bunched barrels at them.

'Keep them there, Sergeant.'

'Sir!'

Sharpe moved past them, skirting them, and went into the tunnel. Five horses were tied outside the convent beside the three he and Harper had brought and, having noticed them, he pushed the Convent door shut, then went back to look at the two prisoners. The Sergeant was huge, built like an oak tree, with a tanned skin behind his vast black moustache. He stared hatred at Sharpe. His hands looked large enough to strangle an ox.

The man in officer's uniform had a thin face, sharp eyed and sharp featured, with intelligent eyes. He looked at Sharpe with disdain and condescension.

Sharpe kept the rifle pointing between them. 'Take their guns, Sergeant.'

Harper came behind them, plucked the carbine from the officer then pulled the musket from the Sergeant. Sharpe sensed the massive resistance of the huge Sergeant, twitched his rifle towards the brute of a man, and the Sergeant reluctantly let the musket go. Sharpe looked back to the officer. 'Who are you?'

The reply was in good English. 'My name is not for deserters.'

Sharpe said nothing. Five horses, but just two riders. Saddlebags just as he and Harper had carried. He stepped forward, his eyes on the officer, and kicked the saddlebags. Coins sounded inside. The French officer's thin face sneered at him. 'You will find it all there.'

Sharpe stepped back three paces and lowered his rifle. He sensed Harper's surprise. 'My name is Major Richard Sharpe, 95th Regiment, an officer of his Britannic Majesty. Sergeant!'

'Sir?'

'Put the gun down.'

'Sir?'

'Do as I say.'

The French officer watched the seven barrels sink down, then looked at Sharpe. 'Your honour, M'sieu?'

'My honour.'

The Frenchman's heels clicked together. 'I am Chef du Battalion Dubreton, Michel Dubreton. I have the honour

59

to command a Battalion of the Emperor's 54th of the Line.'

Chef du Battalion, two heavy gold epaulettes, a full Colonel no less. Sharpe saluted and it felt strange. 'My apologies, sir.'

'Not at all. You were rather impressive.' Dubreton smiled at Harper. 'Not to mention your Sergeant.'

'Sergeant Harper.'

Harper nodded familiarly at the French officer. 'Sir!'

Dubreton smiled. 'I think mine's taller.' He looked from his own Sergeant to Harper and shrugged. 'Maybe not. You will find his name appropriate. Sergeant Bigeard.'

Bigeard, reassured by his officer's tone of voice, stiffened to attention and nodded fiercely at Sharpe. The Rifleman gestured to Harper. 'Their guns, Sergeant.'

'Thank you, Major.' Dubreton smiled courteously. 'I assume that gesture means we are enjoying a truce, yes?'

'Of course, sir.'

'How wise.' Dubreton slung the carbine on his shoulder. He might be a Colonel, but he looked as if he could use the weapon with skill and familiarity. He looked at Harper. 'Do you speak French, Sergeant?'

'Me, sir? No, sir. Gaelic, English and Spanish, sir.' Harper seemed to find nothing odd in meeting two enemy in the Convent.

'Good! Bigeard speaks some Spanish. Can I suggest the two of you stand guard while we talk?'

'Sir!' Harper seemed to find nothing odd in taking orders from the enemy.

The French Colonel turned his charm onto Sharpe. 'Major?' He gestured towards the centre of the cloister, bent down and dragged his saddlebags until they rested beside the one Sharpe had brought. Dubreton nodded at it. 'Yours?'

'Yes, sir.'

'Gold?'

'Five hundred guineas.'

Dubreton raised his eyebrows. 'I presume you have hostages here, yes?'

'Just one, sir.'

'An expensive one. We have three.' His eyes were looking at the roofline, searching down into the shadows, while his hands brought out a ragged cheroot that he lit from his tinder box. It took a few seconds for the charred linen to catch fire. He offered a cheroot to Sharpe. 'Major?'

'No thank you, sir.'

'Three hostages. Including my wife.'

'I'm sorry, sir.'

'So'm I.' The voice was mild, light even, but the face was hard as flint. 'Deron will pay.'

'Deron?'

'Sergeant Deron, who now styles himself Marshal Pot-au-Feu. He was a cook, Major, and rather a good one. He's quite untrustworthy.' The eyes came down from the roofline to look at Sharpe. 'Do you expect him to keep his word?'

'No, sir.'

'Nor I, but it seemed worth the risk.'

Neither spoke for a moment. There was still silence beyond the Convent, and silence within the walls. Sharpe pulled the watch out of his pocket. Twenty-five minutes to twelve. 'Were you ordered here at a specific time, sir?'

'Indeed, Major.' Dubreton blew a stream of smoke into the air. 'Twenty-five minutes past eleven.' He smiled. 'Perhaps our Sergeant Deron has a sense of humour. I suspect he thought we might fight each other. We very nearly did.'

Harper and Bigeard, either side of the cloister, watched the roofs and doors. They made a frightening pair and encouraged Sharpe to believe that they all might leave alive. Two such men as the Sergeants would take a deal of killing. He looked again at the French Colonel. 'Can I ask how your wife was captured, sir?'

'Ambushed, Major, in a convoy going from Leon to

61

Salamanca. They stopped it by using French uniforms, no one suspected anything, and the bastards went off with a month's supplies. And three officers' wives who were coming to join us for Christmas.' He walked over to the door in the western wall that Sharpe had already tried to open, tugged at it, then came back to Sharpe. He smiled. 'Would you be Sharpe of Talavera? Of Badajoz?'

'Probably, sir.'

Dubreton looked at the Rifle, at the huge Cavalry sword that Sharpe chose to carry high in its slings, and then at the scarred face. 'I think I could do the Empire a great service by killing you, Major Sharpe.' He said the words without offence.

'I'm sure I could do Britain an equal service by killing you, sir.'

Dubreton laughed. 'Yes, you could.' He laughed again, pleased at his immodesty, but despite the laughter he was still tense, still watchful, the eyes rarely leaving the doors and roof.

'Sir!' Harper growled from behind them, pointing his gun at the chapel door. Bigeard had swung round to face it. There was a small noise from inside, a grating noise, and Dubreton threw his cheroot away. 'Sergeant! To our right!'

Harper moved fast as Dubreton waved Bigeard to stand behind the officers and to their left. The Colonel looked at Sharpe. 'You were in there. What's there?'

'A chapel. There's a bloody great grille behind the door. I think it's being unlocked.'

The chapel doors were pulled open and facing them, curtseying, were two girls. They giggled, turned, and fetched a table from behind them which they carried out the door, beneath the cloister, and placed in the sunlight. One looked at Bigeard, then at Harper, and made a face of mock surprise at their height. They giggled again.

A third girl appeared with a chair which she placed beside

the table. She too curtseyed towards the officers then blew them a kiss.

Dubreton sighed. 'I fear we must endure whatever they have planned for us.'

'Yes, sir.'

Boots clattered in the chapel and soldiers filed out, left and right, into the cloisters. They wore uniforms of Britain, France, Portugal and Spain, and their muskets were tipped with bayonets. Their faces were mocking as they filed to line three of the four walls. Only the wall behind Dubreton and Sharpe was unguarded. The three girls stood by the table. They wore low cut blouses, very low, and Sharpe guessed they must be cold.

'*Mes amis! Mes amis!*' The voice boomed from within the chapel. It was a deep voice, gravelly, a great bass voice. '*Mes amis!*'

A ludicrous figure came out of the shadow, through the cloister's arch, to stand by the table. He was short and immensely fat. He spread his arms, smiled. '*Mes amis!*'

His legs were cased in tall black leather boots, cut away behind the knees, and then in white breeches that were dangerously tight about his huge fat thighs. His belly wobbled as he laughed silently, ripples of fat running up his body beneath the flowered waistcoat he wore beneath a blue uniform jacket that was lavishly adorned with gold leaves and looping strands. The jacket could not button over his immense front, instead it was held in place by a golden waist sash, while a red sash was draped across his right shoulder. At his neck, below the multitude of chins, an enamelled gold cross hung. The tassels of his gold epaulettes rested on his fat arms.

Sergeant Deron, now calling himself Marshal Pot-au-Feu, took off his hat, wondrously plumed in white, and revealed a face that was almost cherubic. An aging cherub with a halo of white curls, a face that beamed with goodwill and delight. '*Mes amis!*' He looked at Sharpe. '*Parlez-vous Francais?*'

'No.'

He wagged a finger at Sharpe. 'You should learn the French. A beautiful language! Eh, Colonel?' He smiled at Dubreton who said nothing. Pot-au-Feu shrugged, laughed, and looked again to Sharpe. 'My English is very bad. You the Colonel meet, yes?' He twisted his head as far as the rolls of fat on his neck would allow. '*Mon Colonel! Mon brave! Ici!*'

'Coming, sir, coming! Coming! And here I am!' The man with the yellow face, the toothless grin, the blue, child-like eyes, and the horrid ungovernable spasms, leaped grotesquely through the door. He was dressed in the uniform of a British Colonel, but the finery did nothing to hide the lumpen gross body or the brute strength that was in his arms and legs.

The capering figure stopped, half crouching, and stared at Sharpe. The face twitched, the voice cackled, and then the mouth twisted into a smile. 'Sharpy! Hello Sharpy!' A string of spittle danced from his lips as the face jerked.

Sharpe turned calmly towards Harper. 'Don't shoot, Sergeant.'

'No, sir.' Harper's voice was full of loathing. 'Not yet, sir.'

'Sir! Sir! Sir!' The yellow face laughed at them as the man who called himself Colonel straightened up. 'No "sirs" here, no. No bloody airs and bloody graces here.' The cackle again, obscene and piercing.

Sharpe had half expected this, and he suspected that Harper had expected it too, yet neither had voiced the fear. Sharpe had hoped that this man was dead, yet this man boasted he could not be killed. Here, in the sunlight of the cloister, spittle dangling from his mouth, stood ex-Sergeant Obadiah Hakeswill. Hakeswill.

CHAPTER 5

Obadiah Hakeswill, the Sergeant who had recruited Sharpe into the army, the man who had caused Sharpe to be flogged in a dusty Indian square. Hakeswill.

The man who had Harper flogged earlier this same year, who had tried to rape Teresa, Sharpe's wife, who had held a saw-backed bayonet at the throat of Sharpe's baby daughter, Antonia. Obadiah Hakeswill.

The head twitched on its long neck. The spittle dropped in a glittering cartwheel from his mouth. He hawked, spat, and shuffled sideways. This was the man who could not be killed.

He had been hanged when he was twelve. It was a trumped-up charge of stealing sheep, trumped-up because the vicar whose daughter young Hakeswill had tried to molest did not want to drag his child's reputation in the mud. The magistrates had been happy to oblige.

He was the youngest of all the prisoners being hanged that day. The executioner, wanting to please the massed spectators, had not given any of his victims a neck-breaking drop. He had suspended them slowly, letting them hang and throttle themselves to death, letting the crowd enjoy each choking sound, each futile kick, and the executioner had tantalized the crowd by offering to tug on the ankles and responding to their shouts of yes or no. No one cared about the small boy at the end of the gibbet. Hakeswill had hung, feigning death, cunning even as he slipped into nightmare-ridden darkness, and then, before the end, the heavens had opened.

The street outside the gaol was hammered and sluiced by

the cloudburst, lightning slammed and bent the weathercock on the high church steeple, and the wide market street cleared as men, women and children ran for shelter. No one cared as Hakeswill's uncle cut the small body down. They thought the boy was dead, that the body was being sold to a doctor eager for a fresh corpse to explore, but the uncle took Obadiah into an alleyway, slapped him into consciousness, and told the child to go away, never to return. Hakeswill had obeyed.

He had started twitching that day and the twitching had not stopped in thirty years. He had found the army, a refuge for men like himself, and in its ranks he had discovered a simple code for survival. To those who were superior, the officers, Hakeswill was the perfect soldier. He was punctilious in his duty, in his respect, and he was made into a Sergeant. No officer with Hakeswill as his Sergeant needed worry about discipline. Sergeant Hakeswill terrorized his Companies into obedience and the price of freedom from that tyranny was paid to the ugly Sergeant in money, liquor or women. It never ceased to amaze Hakeswill what a married woman would do to keep her soldier husband from a flogging. His life was dedicated to revenge upon a fate that had made him ugly, unloved, a creature loathed by its fellows, useful only to its superiors.

Yet fate could give blessings too. It had cheated death for Obadiah Hakeswill. He was not the only man or woman to escape a hanging. So many survived that some hospitals charged the cost of caring for the living-hanged on the ghouls who fought to snatch fresh corpses from the gallows to sell to doctors, yet Hakeswill saw himself as unique. He was the man who had survived death, and now no man could kill him. He feared no man. He could be hurt, but he could not be killed, and he had proven that on battlefields and in back alleys. He was the favoured child of death.

And he was here, in the Gateway of God, Pot-au-Feu's Lieutenant. He had deserted from Sharpe's Company in

April, his careful rules for survival in the army shattered by his lust for Teresa, his court-martial and execution guaranteed by his murder of Sharpe's friend, Captain Robert Knowles, and so he had slipped into the black-red darkness of the horror that was Badajoz at the siege's end. Now he was in Adrados where he had found other desperate men who would play to his evil, pander to his madness, follow him into the murk of his lusts.

'A pleasure, yes?' Hakeswill laughed at Sharpe. 'Got to call me "sir" now! I'm a Colonel!' Pot-au-Feu watched Hakeswill fondly, smiling at the performance. The face jerked. 'Going to salute me, are you? Eh?' He took off the bicorne hat so that his hair, grey now, hung lank over the yellow skin. The eyes were china-blue in the ravaged face. He looked past Sharpe. 'Got the bloody Irishman with you. Born in a pig-sty. Bloody Irish muck!'

Harper should have kept quiet, but there was a pride in the Irishman and in his voice was a sneer. 'How's your poxed mother, Hakeswill?'

Hakeswill's mother was the only person in the world he loved. Not that he knew her, not that he had seen her since he was twelve, but he loved her. He had forgotten the beatings, his whimpering as a small child beneath her anger, he remembered only that she had sent her brother to take him from the scaffold, and in his world that was the one act of love. Mothers were sacred. Harper laughed and Hakeswill bellowed in uncontrollable rage, lurched into a run, and his hand fumbled for the unfamiliar sword at his side.

The cloister was stunned by the size of this hatred, the force of it, the noise that echoed through the arches as the huge man charged at Harper.

The Sergeant stood calm. He let the flint down onto the steel of his gun, reversed it, and then thrust the heavy brass-bound butt into Hakeswill's belly, stepped to one side and kicked him in the side.

The muskets of Pot-au-Feu's men twitched into their

shoulders, flints back, and Sharpe dropped to one knee, rifle steady, and the barrel was aimed straight between Pot-au-Feu's eyes.

'*Non! Non!*' Pot-au-Feu screamed at his men, flapping a hand towards Sharpe. '*Non!*'

Hakeswill was on his feet again, eyes streaming in pain and anger, and the sword was in his hand and he whipped it at Harper's face, the steel hissing and blurring in the sunlight, and Harper parried it with the butt of his gun, grinned, and no one moved to help Hakeswill for they feared the huge Rifleman. Dubreton looked at Bigeard, nodded.

It had to be ended. If Hakeswill died then Sharpe knew they were all doomed. If Harper died then Pot-au-Feu would die and his men would avenge him. Bigeard strode calmly behind the officers and Hakeswill screamed at him, shouted for help, but still no one moved. He lunged with the sword at Harper, missed, and swung helplessly towards the vast French Sergeant who seemed to laugh, moved with sudden speed, and Hakeswill was pinioned by the great arms. The Englishman fought with all his strength, wrenched at the hands which held him, but he was like a kitten in the Frenchman's grip. Harper stepped forward, took the sword from Hakeswill's hand, stepped back with it.

'Sergeant!' Dubreton's tone was a warning. Sharpe still had his eyes on Pot-au-Feu.

Harper shook his head. He had no intention of killing this man yet. He held the sword handle in his right hand, the blade in his left, grinned at Hakeswill and then slammed the sword onto his knee. It broke in two and Harper threw the fragments onto the tiles. Bigeard grinned.

A scream cut through the Convent, an awful scream, agony slicing the air.

No one moved. The scream had come from within the Convent. A woman's scream.

Pot-au-Feu looked at Sharpe's rifle, then at Dubreton. He spoke in a reasonable tone, his deep voice placatory, and

Dubreton looked at Sharpe. 'He suggests we forget this small contretemps. If you lower your gun, he will call his man back.'

'Tell him to call the man first.' It was as if the scream had never happened.

'Obadiah! Obadiah!' Pot-au-Feu's voice was wheedling. 'Come 'ere, Obadiah! Come!'

Dubreton spoke to Bigeard and the French Sergeant slowly released his grip. For a second Sharpe thought Hakeswill would throw himself at Harper again, but Pot-au-Feu's voice drew the shambling, yellow faced figure back towards him. Hakeswill stooped, picked up the fragment of sword with its handle, and thrust it pathetically into his scabbard so that at least it looked correct. Pot-au-Feu spoke softly to him, patted his arm, and beckoned to one of the three girls. She huddled next to Obadiah, stroking him, and Sharpe lowered his rifle as he stood up.

Pot-au-Feu spoke to Dubreton. The Colonel translated for Sharpe. 'He says Obadiah is his loyal servant. Obadiah kills for him. He rewards Obadiah with drink, power and women.'

Pot-au-Feu laughed when Dubreton had finished. Sharpe could see the strain on the Colonel's face and he knew the Frenchman was remembering the scream. His wife was held here. Yet neither officer had asked about the scream, for both knew that to do so was to play into Pot-au-Feu's hands. He wanted them to ask.

It came again, wavering to a shrill intensity, sobbing in gasps to silence. Pot-au-Feu acted as if it had never sounded. His deep voice was talking to Dubreton again.

'He says he will count the money, then the women will be brought.'

Sharpe had presumed that the table was for counting the money, but three men dragged the coins to a clear patch of tiles and began the laborious task of piling them and counting. The table had another purpose. Pot-au-Feu clapped his podgy hands and a fourth girl appeared who carried a tray. She put it on the table and the fat Frenchman fondled her, took the lid from the earthenware pot on the tray, and then spoke lengthily to Dubreton. The rumbling voice seemed full of pleasure; it lingered lasciviously on certain words as Pot-au-Feu spooned food into a bowl.

Dubreton sighed, turned to Sharpe, but his eyes looked into the sky. Smoke was rising where there had been none twenty minutes before. 'Do you want to know what he said?'

'Should I, sir?'

'It's a recipe for hare stew, Major.' Dubreton gave a thin smile. 'I suspect rather a good one.'

Pot-au-Feu was eating greedily, the thick sauce dripping onto his fat, white-breeched thighs.

Sharpe smiled. 'I just cut them up, boil them in water and salt.'

'I can truly believe that, Major. I had to teach my own wife to cook.'

Sharpe raised an eyebrow. There was an inflection in Dubreton's words that was intriguing.

The Frenchman smiled. 'My wife is English. We met and married during the Peace of Amiens, the last time I was in London. She has lived the ten years since in France and is now even a creditable cook. Not as good as the servants, of course, but it takes a lifetime to learn how simple cooking is.'

'Simple?'

'Of course.' The Colonel glanced at Pot-au-Feu who was delicately picking up a lump of meat that had fallen onto his lap. 'He takes his hares, cuts the flesh off the bones, and then soaks them for a full day in olive oil, vinegar and wine. You add garlic, Major, a little salt, some pepper, and a handful of juniper berries if you have them. You save the blood and you mix it with the livers which you have ground into a paste.' There was an enthusiasm in Dubreton's voice. 'Now. After a day you take the flesh and you cook it in butter and bacon fat.

70

Just brown it. Put some flour in the pan then put it all back into the sauce. Add more wine. Add the blood and the liver, and heat it up. Boil it. You will find it superb, especially if you add a spoonful of olive oil as you serve it.'

Pot-au-Feu chuckled. He had understood a good deal of what Dubreton had said, and as Sharpe looked the fat Frenchman smiled and lifted a small jug. 'Oil!' He patted his huge belly and broke wind.

The scream came once more, the third time, and there was a helplessness in the agony. A woman was being hurt, horribly hurt, and Pot-au-Feu's men looked at the four strangers and grinned. These men knew what was happening and wanted to see the effect on the visitors. Dubreton's voice was low. 'Our time will come, Major.'

'Yes, sir.'

Hakeswill and his woman had crossed to the piles of money and he turned with a grin on his face. 'All here, Marshal!'

'Bon!' Pot-au-Feu held out a hand and Hakeswill tossed him one of the golden guineas. The Frenchman held it up, turned it.

Hakeswill waited until the twitching of his face had subsided. 'Want your woman now, Sharpy?'

'That was the agreement.'

'Oh! The agreement!' Hakeswill laughed. He plucked at the girl beside him. 'How about this one, Sharpy? Want this one, do you?' The girl looked at Sharpe and laughed. Hakeswill was enjoying himself. 'This one's Spanish, Sharpy, just like your wife. Still got her, have you? Teresa? Or has she died of the pox yet?'

Sharpe said nothing. He heard Harper move restlessly behind him.

Hakeswill came closer, the girl with him. 'Now why don't you take this one, Sharpy. You'd like her. Look!' He brought his left hand round and plucked at the strings of her bodice. It fell open. Hakeswill cackled. 'You can look, Sharpy. Go

71

on! Look! Oh, of course. Bleeding officer, aren't we? Too high and bloody mighty to look at a whore's tits!'

The men on the edges of the cloister laughed. The girl smiled as Hakeswill fondled her. He cackled. 'You can have her, Sharpy. She's a soldier so the money you've brought means she's yours for life!' She was a soldier because, like the men in the ranks, she would serve for a shilling a day. The girl pursed her painted lips at Sharpe.

Pot-au-Feu laughed, then spoke in French to Dubreton. Dubreton's replies were brief.

Hakeswill had not finished with his game of taunting Sharpe. He pushed the girl towards him, pushed her hard so that she stumbled against the Rifleman, and Hakeswill pointed and laughed. 'She wants him!'

Sharpe slung his rifle. The girl's eyes were hard as flint, her hair dirty. He looked at her and there was something in his eyes that made her ashamed and she dropped her gaze. He pushed her gently away, took the strings of her bodice and pulled it up, tying the knot. 'Go.'

'Major?' Dubreton's voice was low. He gestured beyond Sharpe to where the locked door in the western wall had been opened. Beyond it was another door, a grille, and beyond that Sharpe could see the sunlight of another cloister. 'He wants us to go through there. Just the two of us. I think we should go.' Dubreton shrugged.

Sharpe walked past the raised pool, the Frenchman beside him, and the soldiers at the western side of the cloister parted as the two officers stepped under the arch and into the doorway. The grille swung open to the touch, they were in a short, cold passageway, and then they were on the upper balcony of the inner cloister. Hakeswill followed them, and with him were half a dozen soldiers who stood either side of the officers. Their muskets were cocked, their bayonets pointing at Sharpe and Dubreton.

'Jesus God.' Sharpe's voice was bitter.

This inner cloister had once been beautiful. Water had

been channelled through its court to form a maze of small, decorated canals. The shallow channels were brilliant with painted tiles, yet the water had long ceased to flow, the canals were broken, and the stones of the court were cracked.

All that Sharpe saw in a few seconds, as he saw the thorn bushes that grew like weeds in one corner, the vines that straggled winter-dead up the fine, pale stonework, as he saw the soldiers on the courtyard below. They looked up and grinned at their audience. A brazier burned in the cloister's centre, burned so that the air shimmered above it, and in the bright burning bayonets rested.

A woman was tied on her back in the courtyard's centre. Her wrists and ankles had been tied to iron pegs that had been driven between the cracked stones. She was naked to the waist. Her chest was bloody, black marks beneath the blood that trickled down her ribcage. Sharpe looked at Dubreton, fearful that this was his English wife, but the Frenchman gave the smallest shake of his head.

'Watch, Sharpy.' Hakeswill cackled behind them.

One of the soldiers went to the brazier and, protecting his hand with a hank of rag, he took a bayonet from the flames. He checked that the head was glowing hot, turned with it, and the woman began to jerk, to gasp in panic, and the soldier put his boot on her stomach, half-hiding his work, and the woman screamed. The red hot blade went down, the scream filled the cloister, and then the woman must have fainted. The soldier stepped away.

'She tried to run away, Sharpy.' Hakeswill's breath was foul over Sharpe's shoulder. 'Didn't like it with us, did she? Can you see what it says, Captain?'

The smell of burned flesh came to the upper storey. Sharpe wanted to haul the great sword free of its scabbard, to give the edge its freedom on the bastards in this convent, but he knew he was powerless. His moment would come, but it was not now.

Hakeswill laughed. '*Puta.* That's what it says. She's Span-

ish, you see, Captain. Lucky she's not English, isn't it? Got
another letter in English. Whore.'

The woman was scarred for life, branded by evil. Sharpe
supposed her to be one of the women from this village, or
perhaps a visitor from another village who had tried to run
down the long twisting road that led westward from the
Gateway of God. It would be as hard to escape from Adrados
as it would be to approach the Castle ramparts unseen.

The soldiers pulled the pegs out of the ground, cut the
bonds, and two of them dragged the woman across the stones
and out of sight beneath the arches of the lower storey.

Hakeswill had walked round the corner of the upper
cloister so that he faced the two officers across the angle. He
rested his hands on the stone balustrade and sneered at
them. 'We wanted you to see that so you know what will
happen to your bitches if you try and come up here.' The face
twitched, the right hand pointed to the bloodstains by the
brazier. 'That!' Two bayonets still rested in the fire. 'You
see, gentlemen, we have changed our mind. We like having
the ladies here, so we're bleeding keeping them. We don't
want you to have all the trouble of taking the money back, so
we're keeping that too.' He laughed, watching their faces.
'You can take a message back instead. You understanding
this, Froggie?'

Dubreton's voice was scornful. 'I understand. Are they
alive?'

The blue eyes opened wide, feigning innocence. 'Alive,
Froggie? Of course they're bloody alive. They stay alive as
long as you keep away from here. I'll show you one of them in
a minute, but you bloody listen first, and listen good.'

He twitched again, the face jerking on its long neck and the
pinned cravat slipped, showing the scar on the left side of his
neck and he pulled at the cravat till the scar was hidden. He
grinned, showing the blackened stumps of his teeth. 'They
ain't been hurt. Not yet, but they will be. I'll burn them first,
mark them, and then the lads can have them, and then

74

they'll die! You understand?' He screamed the question at them. 'Sharpy! You understand?'

'Yes.'

'Froggie?'

'Yes.'

'Clever aren't you!' He laughed, eyes blinking, tooth-stumps grinding in his mouth. The face twitched suddenly, once, then stopped. 'Now you've brought the money so I'll tell you what you've done. You've bought their virtue!' He laughed again. 'You've kept them safe for a little while. Course we might want more money if we decide their virtue's expensive, follow me? But we got women now, all we want, so we won't use your bitches if you pay up.'

Sharpe dreamed some nights of killing this man. Hakeswill had been his enemy for nigh on twenty years and Sharpe wanted to be the man who proved that Hakeswill could be killed. The rage he felt at this moment was impotent.

Hakeswill laughed, shuffled sideways down the balustrade. 'Now, I'll show you one bitch and you can talk to her. But!' His finger pointed again at the brazier. 'Remember the spikes. I'll carve a bloody letter on her if you ask her where we keep her. Understand? You don't know which bloody building they're locked in, do you? And you'd like to know, wouldn't you? So don't bloody ask or else I'll mark one of the pretties. You understand?'

Both officers nodded. Hakeswill turned and waved at a man who stood in the courtyard close to where the first woman had been dragged away. The man turned, called to someone behind him.

Sharpe sensed Dubreton stiffen as a woman was brought into the courtyard. She was dressed in a long black cloak and she stepped delicately over the broken canals. Two men guarded her, both with bayonets. Her hair, golden and wispy, was piled loosely on her head.

Hakeswill was watching the two officers. 'Chose this one special for you. Chatters away in French and English. Would you believe she's English and married to a Froggie?' He laughed.

The woman was stopped in the centre of the courtyard and one of the soldiers nudged her, pointed upwards, and she looked at the balcony. She gave no sign of recognizing her husband, nor he of her, and Sharpe knew that both were proud people who would not give her captors the satisfaction of knowing anything about her.

Hakeswill sidled back towards the officers. 'Go on, then! Talk!'

'Madame.' Dubreton's voice was gentle.

'Monsieur.' She was probably, Sharpe thought, a beautiful woman, but her face was in shadow, was marked by tiredness, and the strain of captivity had deepened the lines either side of her mouth. She was thin, like her husband, and her voice, as they spoke, was dignified and controlled. One of the soldiers guarding her was French and he listened to the conversation.

Hakeswill was bored. 'In English! English!'

Dubreton looked at Sharpe, back to this wife. 'I have the honour to introduce Major Richard Sharpe, Madame. He is of the English army.'

Sharpe bowed, saw her incline her head in acknowledgement, but her words were drowned by a great cackle from Hakeswill. 'Major! They made you a bleeding Major, Sharpy? Christ on the cross! They must be bloody desperate! Major!' Sharpe had not put a Major's stars on his shoulders; Hakeswill had not known till this minute.

Madame Dubreton looked at Sharpe. 'Lady Farthingdale will be pleased to know you were here, Major.'

'Please pass on her husband's solicitations, Ma'am. I trust she, and all of you, are well.' Hakeswill was listening, grinning. Sharpe desperately searched in his head for some form of words, any form of words, that might hint to this woman that she must give some indication of where the hostages were kept. He was determined that he would avenge this day's insults, that he would rescue this woman and the other women, but Hakeswill had been right. If he did not know in which building they were kept, then he was helpless. Yet he could not think of anything that he could say which would not sound suspicious, which would not provoke Hakeswill into ordering the branding of Dubreton's wife.

She nodded slowly. 'We are well, Major, and we have not been hurt.'

'I'm pleased to hear that, Ma'am.'

Hakeswill leaned over the balustrade. 'You're happy here, aren't you, dearie?' He laughed. 'Happy! Say you're happy!'

She looked at him. 'I am withering in my bloom, Colonel. Lost in solitary gloom.'

'Ah!' He grinned. 'Doesn't she speak nice!' He turned to the officers. 'Satisfied?'

'No.' Dubreton's face was harsh.

'Well I am.' He waved at the soldiers. 'Take her away!'

They turned her and, for the first time, her poise went. She pulled at her captors, twisted, and her voice was pleading and desperate. 'I'm withering in my bloom!'

'Take her away!'

Sharpe looked at Dubreton, but still his face was a mask showing no reaction to his wife's distress. The Frenchman watched her until she was gone and then turned, wordlessly, towards the upper cloister.

Harper and Bigeard were standing together and their faces showed relief as their officers came back into the cloister. The door was shut behind them, the soldiers once more were arrayed against the western wall, and Pot-au-Feu, still in his chair, spoke in French to Dubreton. When he had finished he spooned more of the stew from the great earthenware pot.

Dubreton looked at Sharpe. 'He's saying what your man was saying. We've paid for their virtue, that's all. We must go home empty-handed.'

Pot-au-Feu grinned as the Colonel finished, swallowed his

mouthful, then waved the soldiers who barred the entrance to the Convent to make way. He gestured with his spoon at the officers. 'Go! Go!'

Dubreton glanced at Sharpe, but Sharpe did not move except to unsling the rifle from his shoulder and thumb back the flint. There was one thing unsaid, one thing that needed to be said, and even though he knew it to be hopeless he would try. He raised his voice, looking around the cloister at the men in red uniforms. 'I have a message for you. Every man here will die except those of you who give yourselves up!' They began jeering him, shouting him down, but Sharpe's voice had been trained on a parade ground. He forced the words through their noise. 'You must present yourselves to our outposts before New Year's Day. Remember that! Before the New Year! Otherwise!' He pulled the trigger.

The shot was a fluke, yet he knew it would work because he had willed it to work, because he would not leave without one small measure of revenge on the scum of this place. It was a shot from the hip, but the range was short and the target big, and the spinning bullet shattered the cooking pot and Pot-au-Feu screamed in pain as the hot sauce and meat exploded over his thighs. The fat man wrenched himself sideways, lost his balance and fell onto the tiles. The soldiers were silent. Sharpe looked round. 'New Year's Day.'

He slammed the butt of the rifle down, felt in his pouch for a cartridge and then, before their eyes, reloaded the rifle with quick professional movements. He bit the bullet out of the paper cartridge, primed the pan, closed it, then poured the rest of the powder into the barrel, followed it with the wadding, and then he spat the bullet into the greased leather patch that gripped the rifling of the barrel and made the Baker Rifle into the most accurate weapon on the battlefield. He did it fast, his eyes not on his work, but on the men who watched him, and he rammed the bullet down the seven spiralling grooves, slotted the ramrod into its brass tubes, and the gun was loaded. 'Sergeant!'

'Sir!'

'What will you do to these bastards in the New Year?'

'Kill them, sir!' Harper sounded confident, happy.

Dubreton grinned, spoke softly, his eyes on Pot-au-Feu who was struggling to his feet helped by two of the girls. 'That was dangerous, my friend. They might have fired back.'

'They're scared of the Sergeants.' Anyone would be scared of those two.

'Shall we go, Major?'

A crowd had gathered outside the Convent, men, women and children, and they shouted insults at the two officers, insults that died as the two vast Sergeants appeared with their weapons held ready. The two big men walked down the steps and pushed the crowd back by their sheer presence. They seemed to like each other, Harper and Bigeard, each one amused, perhaps, by meeting another man as strong. Sharpe hoped they never met on a battlefield.

'Major?' Dubreton was standing on the top step, pulling on thin leather gloves.

'Sir?'

'Are you planning to rescue the hostages?' His voice was low, though no enemy was in earshot.

'If it can be done, sir. You?'

Dubreton shrugged. 'This place is much further from our lines than yours. You move through the country a good deal easier than us.' He half smiled. He was referring to the Partisans who ambushed the French in the northern hills. 'We needed a full Regiment of cavalry to bring us within two miles of this place.' He tugged the gloves comfortable. 'If you do, Major, may I make a request of you?'

'Yes, sir.'

'I know, of course, that you would return our hostages. I would be grateful if you could also return our deserters.' He held up an elegant hand. 'Not, I assure you, to fight again. I

79

would like them to pay their penalty. I assume yours will meet the same fate.' He walked down the steps, looked back at Sharpe. 'On the other hand, Major, the difficulties of rescue may be too great?'

'Yes, sir.'

'Unless you know where the women are kept?'

'Yes, sir.'

Dubreton smiled. Bigeard was waiting with the horses. The Colonel looked up at the sky as if checking the weather. 'My wife has great dignity, Major, as you saw. She did not give those bastards the satisfaction of knowing I was her husband. On the other hand she sounded a little hysterical at the end, yes?'

Sharpe nodded. 'Yes, sir.'

Dubreton smiled happily. 'Strange she should be over-wrought in rhyme, Major? Unless she's a poet, of course, but can you think of a woman poet?' He looked pleased with himself. 'They cook, they make love, they play music, they can talk, but they are not poets. My wife, though, reads a lot of poetry.' He shrugged. 'Withering in my bloom, lost in solitary gloom? Will you remember the words?'

'Yes, sir.'

Dubreton peeled off a newly donned glove and held out his hand. 'It has been my privilege, Major.'

'Mine too, sir. Perhaps we'll meet again.'

'It would be a pleasure. Would you give my warmest regards to Sir Arthur Wellesley? Or Lord Wellington as we must now call him.'

Sharpe's surprise showed on his face, to Dubreton's delight. 'You know him, sir?'

'Of course. We were at the Royal Academy of Equitation together, at Angers. It's strange, Major, how your greatest soldier was taught to fight in France.' Dubreton was pleased with the remark.

Sharpe laughed, straightened to attention, and saluted the

French Colonel. He liked this man. 'I wish you a safe journey home, sir.'

'And you, Major.' Dubreton raised a hand to Harper. 'Sergeant! Take care!'

The French went east, skirting the village, and Sharpe and Harper went west, dropping over the crest of the pass, trotting down the winding road towards Portugal. The air suddenly seemed clean here, the madness left behind, though Sharpe knew they would be going back. A Scottish Sergeant-Major, an old and wise soldier, had once talked to Sharpe through the dark night before battle. He had been embarrassed to tell Sharpe an idea, but he said it finally and Sharpe remembered it now. A soldier, the Scotsman had said, is a man who fights for people who cannot fight for themselves. Behind Sharpe, in the Gateway of God, were women who could not fight for themselves. Sharpe would go back.

CHAPTER 6

'So you didn't see her?'

'No, sir.' Sharpe stood awkwardly. Sir Augustus Farthingdale had not seen fit to invite him to take a chair. Through the half open door of Farthingdale's sitting room, part of his expensive lodgings in the best part of town, Sharpe could see a dinner party. Silverware caught the light, scraped on china, and two servants stood deferentially beside a heavy sideboard.

'So you didn't see her.' Farthingdale grunted. He managed to convey that Sharpe had failed. Sir Augustus was not in uniform. He wore a dark red velvet jacket, its cuffs trimmed with lace, and his thin legs were tight cased in buckskin breeches above his tall polished boots. Above his waistcoat was draped a sash, washed blue silk, decorated with a heavy golden star. It was presumably some Portuguese order.

He sat down at a writing desk, lit by five candles in an elegant silver candelabra, and he toyed with a long handled paper knife. He had hair that could only be described as silver, silver cascading away from his high forehead to be gathered at the back by an old fashioned ribbon, black against the hair. His face was long and thin, with a touch of petulance about the mouth and a look of annoyance in his eyes. It was, Sharpe supposed, a good looking face, the face of a sophisticated middle-aged man who had money, intelligence, and a selfish desire to use both for his own pleasure. He turned towards the dining room. 'Agostino!'

'Sir?' An unseen servant answered.

'Shut the door!'

The wooden door was closed, cutting off the noise of mens' voices. Sir Augustus' eyes, unfriendly, looked Sharpe up and down. The Rifleman had just arrived back in Frenada and had not waited to straighten his uniform or wash the travel stains from his hands or face. Farthingdale's voice was precise and cold. 'The Marquess of Wellington is deeply concerned, Major Sharpe. Deeply.'

Farthingdale managed to convey that he and Wellington were on close terms, that he was vouchsafing a state secret to Sharpe. The paper-knife tapped the polished desk-top. 'My wife, Major, has the highest connections in the Portuguese court. You understand?'

'Yes, sir.'

'The Marquess of Wellington does not want our relationship with the Portuguese government jeopardized.'

'No, sir.' Sharpe resisted the impulse to tell Sir Augustus Farthingdale that he was a pompous idiot. It was interesting that Wellington had written, the letter doubtless posted north by one of the young cavalry officers who, by changing frequent horses, could cover sixty miles in a day. Wellington must be in Lisbon then, for the news could not have reached Cadiz in time for a reply to have been received. And Farthingdale was pompous because even Sharpe knew that Wellington's concern would not be the Portuguese government. His concern would be the Spanish. The story of Adrados had spread like fire on a parched plain, feeding from the sensibilities of Spanish pride, and in the New Year the British army must march back into Spain. The army would buy its food from the Spanish; use Spanish labour to bake bread and drive mules, find forage and give shelter, and Pot-au-Feu and Hakeswill had jeopardized that co-operation. The poison of Adrados had to be lanced as one small step towards winning the war.

Yet Sharpe, who guessed he had known Wellington longer than Farthingdale, knew that there would be something else about Pot-au-Feu which would deeply disturb the General. Wellington believed that anarchy was always just a rabble-rouser's shout away from order, and order, he believed, was not just an essential but the supreme virtue. Pot-au-Feu had challenged that virtue, and Pot-au-Feu would have to be destroyed.

The paper-knife was put down on a pile of paper, perhaps Farthingdale's next book of Practical Instructions to Young Officers, and one immaculate knee was crossed over the other. Sir Augustus straightened the tassel of a boot. 'You say she has not been harmed?' There was a hint of worry beneath the polished voice.

'So Madame Dubreton assured us, sir.'

A clock in the hallway struck nine. Sharpe guessed that most of the furnishings of these lodgings had been transported north just for Sir Augustus' visit. He and Lady Farthingdale had made their magnificent progress around the winter quarters of the Portuguese army and then stopped at Frenada on their way south so that Lady Farthingdale could visit the shrine of Adrados and pray for her mother who was dying. Farthingdale had preferred a day's rough shooting, but two young Captains had eagerly offered to escort his wife to the hills. Sharpe wished that Sir Augustus would show him a picture of his wife, but the Colonel did not evidently think that desirable.

'I have it in mind, Major, to lead the rescue of Lady Farthingdale?' Sir Augustus inflected the statement as a question, almost a challenge, but Sharpe said nothing. The Colonel dabbed the corner of his mouth with a finger, then inspected the fingertip as if something might have adhered to it. 'Tell me how possible a rescue is, Major?'

'It could be done, sir.'

'The Marquess of Wellington,' again the annoying circumlocution of Wellington's full title, 'wishes it to be done.'

'We'd need to know which of the buildings she's in, sir. There's a Castle, a Convent, and a whole village, sir.'

84

'Do we know?'

'No, sir.' Sharpe did not want to speculate here. That could wait till he saw Nairn.

The eyes looked at Sharpe with hostility. Sir Augustus' expression implied that Sharpe had failed utterly. He sighed. 'So. I have lost my wife, five hundred guineas, at least I'm glad to see you still have my watch.'

'Yes, sir. Of course, sir.' Sharpe unclipped the chain reluctantly. He had never owned a watch, indeed he had often been scathing about them, saying that any officer who needed a machine for telling the time of day did not deserve to wear a uniform, but now he felt that the possession of this timepiece, albeit borrowed, lent him a certain air of success and property; something proper to a Major. 'Here, sir.' He handed it to Sir Augustus who opened the lid, checked that both hands and the glass were still there, and who then slid open a drawer of the desk and put the watch away. Then the long slim fingers wiped delicately against each other. 'Thank you, Major. I am sorry this has been so fruitless an experience. Doubtless we will meet at Major General Nairn's headquarters meeting in the morning.' He stood up, his movements precise as a cat. 'Good night, Major.'

'Sir.'

Orders for Sharpe to attend the headquarters the following morning waited at his lodgings. Orders and a bottle of brandy, donated by Nairn, with a scrawled letter saying that if Sharpe had got back on time then he would need the contents of this bottle. Sir Augustus had not even offered him a glass of water, let alone a glass of wine, and Sharpe shared the bottle with Lieutenant Harry Price and let vent to his feelings about velvet-clad civilians who thought they were Colonels. Price smiled happily. 'That's my ambition, sir. A velvet coat, a young wife full of juice, and all the heroes like you saluting me.'

'May it happen for you, Harry.'

'May all the dreams come true, sir.' Price had been sewing

a patch onto his red jacket. Like most of the South Essex he wore a red coat; only Sharpe and his few Riflemen who had survived the Retreat to Corunna and then been formed into the South Essex's Light Company kept their prided Green coats. Green coats! Of course! Green bloody coats!

'What is it, sir?' Price was holding the bottle upside down, hoping for a miracle.

'Nothing, Harry, nothing. Just an idea.'

'Then God help someone, sir.'

Sharpe held the idea, and with it a second thought, and took them both to the headquarters in the morning. It had clouded in the night, light cold rain falling for most of the morning, and the table in the hallway outside the room where Nairn waited was heaped with coats, cloaks, scabbards and damp hats. Sharpe added his own to the pile, propped the rifle against the wall where an orderly promised to keep watch over it.

Nairn, Farthingdale, Sharpe and one unknown Lieutenant Colonel made up the meeting. Nairn, for once, had eschewed his dressing gown and wore the dark green facings and gold lace of one of the Highland Regiments. Sir Augustus was resplendent in the red, black and gold of the Princess Royal's Dragoons, his cavalry spurs tearing at the carpet. The Lieutenant Colonel was a Fusilier, his red coat faced in white, and he nodded warmly at Sharpe. Nairn made the introductions. 'Lieutenant Colonel Kinney. Major Sharpe.'

'Your servant, Sharpe, and it's an honour.' Kinney was big, broad faced, with a ready smile. Nairn looked at him and smiled.

'Kinney's a Welshman, Sharpe, so don't trust him further than you can throw a cat.'

Kinney laughed. 'He's been like that ever since my lads rescued his Regiment at Barossa.'

Sir Augustus coughed pointedly in protest at the Celtic badinage, and Nairn glanced at him from beneath his huge eyebrows.

'Of course, Sir Augustus, of course. Sharpe! Your story, man?'

Sharpe told it all and was only interrupted once. Nairn looked at him incredulously. 'Took her bodice off! Threw her at you?'

'Yes, sir.'

'And you did it up again?'

'Yes, sir.'

'Extraordinary! Go on!'

When Sharpe had finished, Nairn had a sheet of paper covered with notes. A fire crackled in the hearth. The rain was soft on the window. Somewhere in the town a Sergeant Major screamed at his men to form column of fours on the centre files. The Major General leaned back. 'This Frenchman, Sharpe. Dubreton. What's he going to do?'

'He'd like to mount a rescue, sir.'

'Will he?'

'They have twice as far to go as us, sir.' The French and British were wintering well apart.

Nairn grunted. 'We must do it first. A rescue, then smoke those scum out of their holes.' He tapped a piece of paper. 'That's what the Peer wants, that's what we'll give him. What would you need to rescue the women, Sharpe?'

'Sir!' Sir Augustus leaned forward. 'I was hoping I might be entrusted with the rescue.'

Nairn looked at Sir Augustus and stretched the silence out till it was painful. Then. 'That's noble of you, Sir Augustus, very creditable. Still, Sharpe's been there, let Sharpe give us his ideas first, eh?'

It was time for the first of the two ideas, a slim idea in the light of morning, but he would try it. 'We can rescue them, sir, as long as we know where they are. If we do, sir, then I only see one way. We must travel by night so we can approach unseen, lay up all day as close as we can, and attack the next night. It would have to be done by Riflemen, sir.'

87

'Riflemen!' Nairn bridled, Kinney smiled. 'Why do you think only Riflemen! D'you think no one else can fight in this army?'

'Because I saw many uniforms there, sir, but I didn't see one Rifleman. On that night anyone not in a green uniform is an enemy.'

Nairn grunted. 'But you didn't see all of his men.'

'No, sir.' Sharpe was placatory, yet all of them knew that less men deserted from the Rifles than from other Regiments. Nairn glanced at Sir Augustus' red, black and gold. 'Riflemen, then. What else?'

There was one other thing, but it would all be in vain unless Sharpe knew in which building the hostages were kept. He said as much and Nairn smiled slowly, mischievously. 'But we do know.'

'We do?' Sharpe was surprised, remembered to add, 'sir?'

'We do, we do.' Nairn grinned at them.

Kinney waited. Sir Augustus looked annoyed. 'Perhaps you'd care to enlighten us, sir?'

'My duty and my pleasure, Sir Augustus.' Nairn closed his eyes, leaned far back, and raised his right hand dramatically. His voice was declamatory. 'Line after line my gushing eyes o'erflow, Led through a something-something woe: Now warm in love!' He had raised his voice to a triumphant shout on the word 'love', now he lowered it conspiratorially, his eyes opening. '. . . Now with'ring in my bloom, Lost in a convent's solitary gloom!'

Nairn grinned impishly. 'Alexander Pope. From *Heloise and Abelard*. A sad tale of a young man gelded in his prime. That's what comes of too much love. So! They're in the Convent. She's a clever lassie, that Frenchman's wife.'

Kinney leaned forward. 'How many Riflemen?'

'Two Companies, sir?'

Kinney nodded. 'Can they hold the Convent overnight?'

Sharpe nodded back. 'Yes, sir.'

'So you'd need relief in the morning, yes?'

'Yes, sir.'

Kinney looked at Nairn. 'It's as we discussed, sir. One small group to go in and secure the ladies, and a Battalion to come up in the morning to punish the men. There's one thing worries me, though.'

Nairn raised an eyebrow. 'Go on.'

'They may be deserters, but I think we can assume they are not fools. If you go in at night.' He was looking at Sharpe, Sir Augustus' request utterly forgotten or ignored. 'If you go in, Major, don't you think they'll be expecting something of the sort? There'll be sentries, there'll be a picquet line. It's a risk, Sharpe, and though I don't mind a risk, you might find that they have enough time to take their vengeance on the ladies.'

Sir Augustus nodded, seeming to have changed his mind about the desirability of any rescue. 'I agree with Kinney.'

Nairn looked at Sharpe. 'Well, Major?'

'I had thought of that, sir.' He smiled. This was the second idea, the better idea. 'I thought of going in on Sowan's Night.'

Nairn grinned. Automatically he corrected Sharpe. 'Sowan's Nicht! I like it, man! I like it! Sowan's Nicht! The bastards will all be flat on their backs with the drink!'

Sowan's Nicht, the Scottish name for Christmas Eve, the night when any soldier could expect to get hopelessly, helplessly drunk. In England it was the night for Frumenty, a lethal drink of husked wheat grain boiled in milk and then liberally soused with rum and egg-yolks to be drunk until insensate. Christmas Eve.

Kinney nodded, smiling. 'We were the first to be caught by that trick, we might as well use it ourselves.' He was referring to the Christmas Eve of 1776 when George Washington caught the garrison of Trenton unawares, the defenders believing that no war would be waged over Christmas. Then Kinney shook his head. 'But.'

'But?' Nairn asked.

Kinney seemed to subside, the hope of repeating Washington's trick going. 'Christmas Day, sir, when you want my men to relieve Major Sharpe. It's scarce five days away, sir.' He shook his head. 'I can do it! I can have the men there, but I don't much like going empty handed. I'd have a thought to an extra ration issue, sir, and if the French are likely to be poking themselves into the place then I'd be glad of a full spare issue of cartridge.' He could be talking, Sharpe knew, of up to a thousand pounds of dried beef and over forty thousand cartridges. Kinney's face grew more dubious. 'All the mules are gone, sir. They'd take a week to get back here from winter pasture.' The mules, like the British cavalry, were mostly wintering in the plumper land near the sea.

Nairn growled to himself, made marks on his paper. 'You could get there without mules?'

'Of course, sir. But what if the French do come?'

'They're not there to fight us, are they? They're there to capture this Pot-au-Feu!'

Kinney nodded. 'And if they have a chance of killing off a prime Battalion as extra pickings?'

'Aye, aye, aye.' Nairn was disgruntled. 'I dare say you're right. New Year's Eve, Sharpe?'

Sharpe smiled. 'I'd rather Christmas Eve, sir.' He looked at Kinney. 'Would seven horse drawn wagons help? Plus a good few pack-horses? All fit, all ready to march?'

'Help? Good God, man, of course they'd help! They'd suffice! And how, pray, do you work this miracle?'

Sharpe looked back to Nairn. 'The Rocket troop, sir. I'm sure the Prince Regent would be delighted if they were found some warlike employment.'

'God's teeth, Sharpe!' Nairn smiled at him. 'Two weeks ago I promote you from Captain, now you're presuming to tell me what would please His Royal Highness!' He looked at Kinney. 'The suggestion of the Prince of Wales' pleni-potentiary pleases you then, Colonel?'

'It does, sir.'

Nairn grinned happily at Sir Augustus Farthingdale. 'It looks as if your wife will be safely in your arms within the week, Sir Augustus!'

Sir Augustus flinched slightly, but bowed his head. 'Indeed it does, sir, and I'm grateful. I would still like to go with the rescue force, sir.'

'You would, eh?' Nairn frowned, not understanding the request. 'I mean no offence, Sir Augustus, 'pon my word none at all! But might you not think that such exploits are best left to hotter heads! We cooler brains must wait in patience, write our books!'

Sir Augustus gave a thin smile. 'You mean older heads, sir?'

'Older! Wiser! Cooler! And do you truly fancy climbing a bloody hill in the dead of night, laying up all day in the freezing cold, and then keeping up with fellows like Sharpe the next night? I admire the sentiment, Sir Augustus, I do truly, but I beg you to reconsider the request.'

The thin face with its handsome mane of hair looked down towards the table. Perhaps, Sharpe thought, he was thinking of that cold day that would be Christmas Eve. Sharpe did not want the man there and he dared to mutter a comment that might help Sir Augustus to withdraw a request that Nairn could scarce refuse. 'We'll not be taking any horses, sir, none at all.'

The head snapped up. 'I can march, Major, if I have to!'

'I'm sure, sir.'

'My concern is for Lady Farthingdale. She is a delicate lady, of good family. I would not like to think of her treated . . .' he paused. 'I would like to offer her my protection, sir.'

'Good God, Sir Augustus!' Nairn stopped. The inference of Farthingdale's words was that Lady Farthingdale, having survived capture by Pot-au-Feu, would be at risk from Sharpe's men. Nairn shook his head. 'She'll be safe, Sir

Augustus, she'll be safe! You can ride up with Kinney in the morning, yes, Kinney?'

The Welsh Colonel did not look overjoyed, but he nodded. 'Yes, sir. Of course, sir.'

'And you'll be arriving at dawn, Sir Augustus!'

Sir Augustus nodded, leaned back. 'Very well. I shall ride with the Fusiliers.' He looked with his unfriendly gaze at Sharpe. 'I can be assured that Lady Farthingdale will be treated with every respect?'

The words implied an outrageous insult, but Sharpe supposed that they also implied an outrageous jealousy that perhaps an older man would feel for a younger wife. He chose to give a civil answer. 'Of course, sir.' He turned to Nairn, one question left. 'Do we have the Riflemen, sir?'

Nairn smiled, mischievously again, and in reply he pushed a letter across to Sharpe. 'Third paragraph down, Major. They're already on their way.'

Sharpe read the letter and understood Nairn's smile. The letter had been dictated by Wellington to his Military Secretary, and the General was making specific suggestions how Pot-au-Feu must be defeated. The third paragraph began; 'I would advert you to Major Sharpe, in need of employment, believing that, with two Companies of Riflemen, he might effect a rescue before the punitive Battalion arrives. To that end, and in the belief that this measure will be deemed appropriate, I have given orders that two Companies of the 60th be attached to Headquarters.' Sharpe looked up and Nairn smiled broadly. 'It was interesting to see, Major, whether we came to the same conclusions.'

'We evidently did, sir.'

'Console yourself with the thought that he did not think of using the Rocket troop. He has, however, asked the Partisans to help. A few irregular cavalry in the hills will make life easier.' Sharpe wondered if Teresa would receive that message. Might he see her at Christmas? The thought quickened him and pleased him. Nairn took the letter back and turned the page. His face was serious. 'The Partisans, though, are not to take the credit. Spain believes that British troops raped this village and defiled their church. There must be a new sermon preached in the churches, gentlemen, that British troops avenged that massacre, and that any person in Spain is safe under the protection of our flag.' He had evidently been paraphrasing the letter, for now he dropped it and smiled at Sharpe. 'You told these bastards they had till New Year's Day?'

'Yes, sir.'

'Then break your word, Major. Go and kill them at Christmas instead.'

'Yes, sir.'

Nairn looked out of the window. The rain had stopped and a great rift was spreading through the clouds, bringing back the blue sky. The Scotsman smiled. 'Good hunting, gentlemen. Good hunting.'

CHAPTER 7

The Rifle Captain looked villainous. His left eye was gone, the socket covered by a black patch that was green at the edges. Most of his right ear was missing, and two of his front teeth were clumsy fakes. The wounds had all been taken on battlefields.

He slammed to attention in front of Sharpe, saluted, and the military precision was diluted by the suspicion in his voice. 'Captain Frederickson, sir.' Frederickson looked lithe as a whip, as hard as the brass furniture on his mens' rifles.

The second Captain, burlier and less confident, allowed a smile on his face as he saluted. 'Cross, sir. Captain Cross.' Captain Cross wanted Major Sharpe to like him, Frederickson could not give a damn.

There had been elation in promotion, but now Sharpe was surprised by his nervousness. Just as Cross wanted Sharpe to like him, so Sharpe wanted to be liked by the men who had come under his command. He was being tempted to believe that if he was friendly and approachable, reasonable and kind, then men would follow him more willingly. But kindness was not the wellspring of loyalty and he knew the temptation had to be resisted. 'What are you smiling about, Captain?'

'Sir?' Cross's eyes darted to Frederickson, but the one-eyed man stared flintily ahead. The smile went.

These Captains, and their Companies, were the men whom Sharpe would lead into the Gateway of God, into a difficult night action, and that would be no place for a friendly, approachable, reasonable and kind man. They might like him eventually, but first they would have to dislike him because he imposed standards on them, because loyalty came from respect. 'What's your state?'

Frederickson answered first, as Sharpe had thought he would. 'Seventy-nine men, sir. Four Sergeants and two Lieutenants.'

'Ammunition?'

'Eighty rounds, sir.' The answer was too pat, it was a lie. British gunpowder was the best in the world and most soldiers made a few pence on the side by selling cartridges to villagers. Yet Frederickson's answer also implied that the shortfall was none of Sharpe's business. He, Frederickson, would make sure his men went into battle with a full pouch. Sharpe looked at Cross. 'Captain?'

'Fifty-eight men, sir. Four Sergeants and one Lieutenant.'

Sharpe looked at the Companies that paraded in Frenada's square. They were tired, dishevelled, waiting for dismissal. They had just marched from the Coa and were looking forward to warm billets, drink, and a meal. Half a dozen horses, the property of officers, stood in front of the green jacketed ranks. Sharpe looked up at the sun. Three hours of daylight left. 'We're taking extra ammunition. It's signed for. I'll tell your Sergeants where to fetch it.'

Cross nodded. 'Sir.'

'And we're going ten miles tonight. All officers' horses are to stay here.' He turned away, turned back by an exclamation of surprise from Captain Cross.

'Captain?'

'Nothing, sir.'

Frederickson was smiling, just smiling.

They bivouacked that night, as cold as flogged skin in winter, making shelters from branches and cooking ration beef in the small camp kettles. No Riflemen ever carried the huge Flanders Cauldrons that were the army issue and had to be carried on a mule because of their weight. It took a whole tree-trunk to warm a Flanders Cauldron and so the

Light troops of Wellington's army simply took the small cooking pots from the enemies they killed, as they took their comfortable packs, and Sharpe looked at the thirty small fires with satisfaction. His own Company was with him, a shrunken Company because the summer of 1812 had whittled his numbers down. Lieutenant Price, three Sergeants, and just twenty eight men were the South Essex's skirmishers, and only nine of the men, plus Harper, were Riflemen from Sharpe's old Company of the 95th that he had brought out of the retreat to Corunna four years before. Price shared a fire with Sharpe, looked at his Major and shivered. 'We can't go in with you, sir?'

'You're wearing a red coat, Harry.'

Price swore. 'We'll be all right, sir.'

'No you won't.' Sharpe raked a chestnut out of the fire with his knife. 'There'll be enough to do on Christmas Day, Harry. Trust me.'

Price's voice was resentful. 'Yes, sir.' Then, unable to stay gloomy for long, he grinned and jerked his head at the camp-fires. 'You've cheered them up, sir. Don't know what's hit them.'

Sharpe laughed. Two of the Lieutenants had been hobbling after a ten mile march, not used to being out of their saddles. The Riflemen were resigned. Sharpe was just another bastard who had denied them a warm bed, the chance of a warm girl, and forced them to sleep on a December night in an open field. Price swore as a chestnut burned his fingers. 'They're definitely intrigued, sir.'

'Intrigued?'

'Our lads have talked with them. Told them a thing or two.' He grinned as, at last, the skin came off the chestnut. 'Told them how long people usually live when they fight for Major Sharpe.'

'Christ, Harry! Don't lay it on too thick!'

Price munched happily. 'They're tough lads, sir. They'll be all right.'

They were tough, too. The 60th, the Royal American Rifles, a Regiment that had been raised in the Thirteen Colonies before the rebellion. They had been trained as sharp-shooters, stalkers, killers of the deep forest, but since the loss of America the Regiment's ranks had been filled by British and by exiled Germans. At least half these men were German and Sharpe had discovered that Frederickson was the son of an English mother and German father and spoke both languages fluently. Sergeant Harper had discovered the ironic nickname that Frederickson's Company had given to their Captain; Captain William Frederickson, as hard an officer as any in the army, had inevitably become Sweet William.

Sweet William crossed to Sharpe's fire. 'Speak to you, sir?'

'Go ahead.'

Frederickson squatted down, his one eye baleful. 'Is there a password tonight, sir?'

'Password?'

Frederickson shrugged. 'I wanted to take a patrol out, sir.' He did not want to ask permission. It offended Captains of the 60th to ask permission. The Regiment did not fight in Battalions like other Regiments, but was split up into Companies that were attached to the army's Divisions to strengthen the skirmish line. Companies of the 60th were the army's orphans, tough and independent, proud of their solitary status.

Sharpe grinned. There was no need to patrol this country; safe, friendly Portugal. 'You want to take a patrol out, Captain.'

'Yes, sir. Some of my men could do with some night training.'

'How long?'

The thin, eye-patched face looked at the flames, then back to Sharpe. 'Three hours, sir.'

Time enough to go back to the village they had passed in the dusk and get into the big farm on the hill behind the

97

church. Sharpe had heard the sounds too, and the sounds had made him just as hungry as Frederickson. So he wanted a password to get back past the picquet line? 'Pork chop, Captain.'

'Sir?'

'That's the password. And my price.'

The faintest grin. 'Your men say you don't approve of stealing, sir.'

'I never liked the sight of the provosts hanging men for looting.' Sharpe felt in his pouch, threw Frederickson a coin. 'Leave that on the doorstep.'

Frederickson nodded. 'I will, sir.' He stood up.

'And Captain?'

'Sir?'

'I like the middle chops. The ones with the kidney.'

The grin showed in the darkness. 'Yes, sir.'

They ate the pork the next day at dusk, hidden in a grove of oak trees, a long day's march behind them. Tonight there would be no rest, only a difficult night march across the river and up into the hills. Sharpe paraded them formally, stripped them of packs, canteens, pouches, haversacks, greatcoats and shakoes, and he watched as the Sergeants searched each man and his equipment for drink. This was one night and a day when no man could risk being drunk, and the Riflemen watched sullenly as their liquor was poured onto the ground. Then Sharpe held up a cluster of canteens. 'Brandy.' They cheered up a little. 'We'll dole it out tomorrow to see us through the cold. Once the job's done you can drink yourselves stupid.'

They climbed that night through a dark landscape of broken rocks and dismal shadows, the howl of wolves in their ears. The wolves rarely attacked men, though Sharpe had seen one leap on a tethered horse, bite a mouthful from its rump and scare off into the darkness pursued by a futile volley of musket shots. Higher and higher they climbed, going eastward, and a fitful moon deceived Sharpe about the landmarks he had memorized on his first visit to the Convent. He was going to the north of the Gateway of God and, past midnight, he turned the soldiers southwards and the going was easier because the climbing was done. He feared the dawn. They must be in hiding before Pot-au-Feu's men in the watchtower could search the upland scenery for intruders.

He took them too close, unaware until a sentry across the valley dropped a whole dry thorn bush onto a fire and the flames startled upwards, sheeting the watchtower stones with light, and Sharpe hissed for silence. God! They were close. He circled back and, just before dawn, he found a deep gully.

The gully, though too close to the Convent for comfort, was otherwise perfect. A Major, two Captains, four Lieutenants, eleven Sergeants, and one hundred and sixty-five rank and file were hidden by its deep banks. They must spend the whole day in concealment.

It was a strange way to spend Christmas Eve. In Britain they would be preparing food for the day's feast. Geese would be hanging plucked on the farmhouse walls next to hams rich from the smokehouse. Plum puddings would be trussed next to the hearths on which brawn would be boiling while, in the houses of the rich, the servants would be taking the pigs' heads from the pickle barrels and stuffing them with force-meat. Christmas pies were being made, veal and beef, while the Christmas fruit breads rose in the brick ovens, their smell rivalling the rich aroma of the new-brewed beer. Firelight would glint on bottles of home made wine, and on the great bowl that waited for the spices and hot wine of the wassail cup. Christmas was a time when a man should be in a warm house, steamy from cooking, and thinking of little else but the mid-winter feast.

Sharpe wondered if these men would resent losing their Christmas to the war, yet as its Eve passed slow and cold, he detected a pride in them that they had been chosen for their task. They had conceived a bitter hatred for the deserters and Sharpe suspected that hatred was caused partly by envy. Most soldiers thought at one time or another of desertion, but few did it, and all soldiers dreamed of a perfect paradise where there was no discipline, much wine and plentiful women. Pot-au-Feu and Hakeswill had come close to realizing that dream and Sharpe's men would punish them for daring to do what they had only dreamed of doing.

Frederickson thought Sharpe was being fanciful. He sat on the gully's side, next to Sharpe and Harper, and nodded at his men. 'It's because they're romantics, sir.'

'Romantics?' The word sounded surprising coming from Sweet William.

'Look at the bastards. Half of them would murder for ten shillings, less. They're drunkards, they'd steal their mother's wedding ring for a pint of rum. Jesus! They're bastards!' He smiled fondly at them, then lifted a frayed corner of the eyepatch and poked with a finger at the wound. It seemed to be an habitual, unthinking gesture. He wiped the finger on his jacket. 'God knows they're not saints, but they're upset about the women in the Convent. They like the idea of rescuing women.' Frederickson smiled his crooked smile. 'Everyone hates the bloody army till someone needs rescuing, then we're all bloody heroes and white knights.' He laughed.

Most of the men had slept fitfully through the morning while Price's redcoats provided sentries. Now those men were huddled in sleep while Captain Cross's picquets lined the gully's rim, their heads barely visible above the skyline. Sharpe had seen figures on the watchtower turret and, just after mid-day, three men on horseback had appeared to the east. Sharpe assumed they were a patrol, but the men had disappeared into a hollow and not reappeared for an hour. He guessed they had taken bottles with them, drunk, then gone back to the valley with some fiction of an uneventful patrol.

The cold was Sharpe's biggest worry. It had been colder during the night, but the men had been moving, while now they were immobile, unable to light any fires, and frozen by a wind that blew the length of their hiding place and brought with it an intermittent drizzle. After the patrol had gone Sharpe had started a childish game of tag, its bounds restricted by an imaginary contour halfway up the gully, its most important rule silence. It forced warmth into men and officers, and the game had run for more than two hours. Whenever an officer was in the game it became more boisterous. The tag was passed by forcing another player to the ground and Sharpe had twice been tackled with bone-crunching glee, both times repaying the tag on the same man. Now, as the light was beginning to fade, the men were sitting with their weapons, intent on the preparations for the night.

Patrick Harper had Sharpe's sword. It was a blade that Harper himself had bought, repaired, and given to Sharpe when it was feared Sharpe was dying in the army hospital at Salamanca. It was a Heavy Cavalry sword, huge and straight bladed, clumsy because of its weight, but a killer wielded with strength. The man who had shot him, the Frenchman Leroux who had brought Sharpe so close to death, had died beneath this sword. Harper sharpened the blade with long strokes of his hand-stone. He had worked the point to needle sharpness and now he held the handle out to Sharpe. 'There, sir. Like new.'

Next to Harper was his seven-barrelled gun, much admired by Frederickson. It was the only loaded weapon that would go with the first party into the Convent. The men of that party had been hand picked, the cream of the three Companies, and they would attack only with swords, knives, and bayonets. Sharpe would lead that party. Harper beside him, and the signal for the other Riflemen to come forward was a blast from the Irish Sergeant's gun. Harper picked the gun up, scratched at the touch-hole with wire, blew on it, then grinned happily. 'Mutton pie, sir.'

'Mutton pie?'

'That's what we'd be eating at home, so we would. Mutton pie, potatoes, and more mutton pie. Ma always makes mutton pie at Christmas.'

'Goose.' Frederickson said. 'And once we had a roast swan. French wine.' He smiled as he rammed a bullet into his pistol. 'Mincemeat pies. Now that's something to fill a belly. Good minced beef.'

'We used to get minced tripe.' Sharpe said.

Frederickson looked disbelieving, but Harper grinned at the eye-patched Captain. 'If you ask him nicely, sir, he'll tell you all about life in the Foundling Home.'

Frederickson looked at Sharpe. 'Truly?'

'Yes. Five years. I went when I was four.'

'And you got tripe for Christmas?'

'If we were lucky. Minced tripe and hard-boiled eggs, and it was called Mincemeat. We used to enjoy Christmas. There was no work that day.'

'What was the work?'

Harper grinned, for he had heard the stories before. Sharpe put his head back on his pack and stared at the low, dark clouds. 'We used to pick old ships' cables apart, the ones that were coated with tar. You'd get a length of eight-inch cable, stiff as frozen leather, and if you were under six you had to pick apart a seven foot length every day.' He grinned. 'They sold the stuff to caulkers and upholsterers. Wasn't as bad as the bone room.'

'The what?'

'Bone room. Some children used to pound bones into powder and it was made into some kind of paste. Half the bloody ivory you buy is bone paste. That's why we liked Christmas. No work.'

Frederickson seemed fascinated. 'So what happened at Christmas, sir?'

Sharpe thought back. He had forgotten much of it. Once he had run away from the Home and managed to stay away, he had tried to force the memories out of his mind. Now they were so remote that it seemed as if they belonged to some other man, far less fortunate. 'There was a church service in the morning, I remember that. We used to get a long sermon telling us how bloody lucky we were. Then there was the meal. Tripe.' He grinned.

'And plum pudding, sir. You told me you got plum pudding once.' Harper was loading the huge gun.

'Once. Yes. It was a gift from someone or other. In the afternoon the quality would come and visit. Little boys and girls brought by their mothers to see how the orphans lived. God! We hated them! Mind you, it was the one bloody day of the winter when they heated the place. Couldn't have the children of the rich catching a cold when they visited the poor.' He held the sword up, stared at the blade reflectively. 'Long time ago, Captain, long time ago.'

'Did you ever go back?'

Sharpe sat up. 'No.' He paused. 'I thought about it. Be nice to go back, dressed up in uniform, carrying this.' He hefted the sword again, then grinned. 'It's probably all changed. The bastards who ran it are probably dead and the children probably sleep in beds and get three meals a day and don't know how lucky they are.' He stood up so that he could slide the sword into its scabbard.

Frederickson shook his head. 'I don't think it's changed much.'

Sharpe shrugged. 'It doesn't matter, Captain. Children are tough little things. Leave them to life and they manage.' He made it sound brutal because he had managed, and he walked away from Frederickson and Harper because the conversation had made him think of his own daughter. Was she old enough to be excited by Christmas Eve? He did not know. He thought of her small round face, her dark hair that had looked so much like his when he had last seen her, and he wondered what kind of life she would have. A life without a father, a life that had come out of war, and he knew that he did not want to leave her alone to life.

He talked to the men, chatting easily, listening to their jokes and knowing their hidden fears. He had the Sergeants hand out another half dozen canteens of brandy and was touched because men offered him swigs of the precious liquid. He left his own advance party till last, the fifteen men sitting in their own group and putting the last touches to sword bayonets that were already sharp. Eight were Germans who spoke good English, good enough to understand urgent orders, and he waved them down as, with the formality of their race, they began getting to their feet. 'Warm enough?'

Nods and smiles. 'Yes, sir.' They looked freezing.

One man, thin as a ramrod, licked his lips as he ran an oiled leather cloth over his sword bayonet. He held the blade up to the last light of the day and seemed satisfied. He put the bayonet down and, with meticulous care, folded the leather and put it into an oilskin packet. He looked up, saw Sharpe's interest, and wordlessly handed the blade up to the Major. Sharpe put a thumb on the fore-edge. Christ! It was like a razor. 'How do you get it that sharp?'

'Trouble, sir, trouble. Work it every day.' The man took the bayonet back and pushed it carefully into its scabbard.

Another man grinned at Sharpe. 'Taylor wears a spike out every year, sir. Sharpens 'em too much. You should see his rifle, sir.' Taylor was obviously the showpiece of his company, used to the attention, and he handed the weapon to Sharpe.

Like the bayonet, this, too, had been worked on. The wood was oiled to a deep polish. The stock had been reshaped with a knife, giving a narrower grip behind the trigger while, on top of the butt, a leather pad had been nailed with brass-headed nails. A cheek-piece. Sharpe pulled the cock back, checking first that the gun was unloaded, and the flint seemed to rest uneasily at the full position. Sharpe touched the trigger and the flint snapped forward, almost without any pressure from Sharpe's finger, and the thin man grinned. 'Filed down, sir.'

Sharpe gave the rifle back. Taylor's voice reminded him of Major Leroy's of the South Essex. 'Are you American, Taylor?'

'Yes, sir.'

'Loyalist?'

'No, sir. Fugitive.' Taylor seemed an unsmiling, laconic man.

'From what?'

'Merchantman, sir. Ran in Lisbon.'

'He killed the Captain, sir.' The other man volunteered with an admiring smile.

Sharpe looked at Taylor. The American shrugged. 'Where are you from in America, Taylor?'

The cold eyes looked at Sharpe as if the mind behind them was thinking whether or not to answer. Then the shrug again. 'Tennessee, sir.'

'Never heard of it. Does it worry you we're at war with the United States?'

'No, sir.' Taylor's answer seemed to suggest that his country would manage quite well without his assistance. 'I hear you've a man in your Company, sir, who thinks he can shoot?'

Sharpe knew he meant Daniel Hagman, the marksman of the South Essex. 'That's right.'

'You tell him, sir, that Thomas Taylor is better.'

'What's your range?'

The eyes looked dispassionately at Sharpe. Again he seemed to think about his answer. 'At two hundred yards I'm certain.'

'So's Hagman.'

The grin again. 'I mean certain of putting a ball in one of his eyes, sir.'

It was an impossible boast, of course, but Sharpe liked the spirit in which it was made. Taylor, he guessed, would be an awkward man to lead, but so were many of the Riflemen. They were encouraged to be independent, to think for themselves on a battlefield, and the Rifle Regiments had thrown away much old fashioned blind discipline and relied more on morale as a motivating force. A new officer to the 95th or the 60th was expected to drill and train in the ranks, to learn the merits of the men he would command in battle, and that was a hard apprenticeship for some yet it forged trust and respect on both sides. Sharpe was sure of these men. They would fight, but what of Pot-au-Feu's men in the Convent? All were trained soldiers and his one hope, that appeared more slender as the cold day wore on into night, was that soon the deserters would be hopeless with drink.

Evening, Christmas Eve, and clouds covered the sky so there was no star to guide them. The Christmas hymns were being sung in the parish churches at home. 'High let us swell our tuneful notes, and join the angelic throng'. Sharpe remembered the words from the Foundling Home. 'Good will to sinful men is shewn, and peace on earth is given'. There would be no good will for sinful men this night. Out of the darkness would come swords, bayonets and death. Christmas Eve, 1812, in the Gateway of God would be screams and pain, blood and anger, and Sharpe thought of the innocent women in the Convent and he let the anger begin. Let the waiting be done, he prayed, let the night arrive, and he wanted the flare of battle within him, he wanted Hakeswill dead, he wanted the night to come.

Christmas Eve turned to darkness. Wolves prowled in the saw-toothed peaks, a wind drove cold from the west, and the men in green jackets waited, shivering, and in their hearts was revenge and death.

CHAPTER 8

A night so dark it was like the Eve of Creation. A blackness complete, a darkness that did not even betray an horizon, a night of clouds and no moon. Christmas Eve.

The men made small noises as they waited in the gully. They were like animals crouching against a bitter cold. The small drizzle compounded the misery.

Sharpe would go first with his small group, then Frederickson, as Senior Captain, would bring on the main group of Riflemen. Harry Price would wait outside the Convent until the fight was over, or until, unthinkably, he must cover a wild retreat in the darkness.

It was a night when failure insisted on rehearsing itself in Sharpe's head. He had peered over the gully's rim in the dusk and he had stared long at the route he must take in the darkness, but suppose he got lost? Or suppose that some fool disobeyed orders and went forward with a loaded rifle, tripped, and blasted the night apart with an accidental shot? Suppose there was no track down the northern side of the valley? Sharpe knew there were thorn bushes on the valley's flanks and he imagined leading his troops into the snagging spines and then he forced the pessimism away. It insisted on coming back. Suppose the hostages had been moved? Suppose he could not find them in the Convent? Perhaps they were dead. He wondered what kind of young, rich woman would marry Sir Augustus Farthingdale. She would probably think of Sharpe as some kind of horrid savage.

The line of the Christmas hymn kept going through his

head, another unwelcome visitor to his thoughts. 'Goodwill to sinful men is shewn'. Not tonight.

He had meant to go at midnight, but it was too dark for Frederickson or any of the other owners of watches to see their timepieces and it was too damned cold to wait in the interminable darkness. The men were numbed with the cold, somnolent with it, cut to the bone by the western wind and Sharpe decided to go early.

And there was light. It was a glow, hazed in the air, made by fires in the valley. The glow had been invisible from the gully, but as Sharpe led his force south, stumbling on the rough broken ground, the crest of the valley's northern edge was limned by the flame-glow in the air. He could see the slight dip in that crest which he had marked as his target, and he sensed the path that led left and right and then on towards the flames of Adrados' valley.

They carried only their weapons and ammunition. Their packs, haversacks, blankets and canteens were left in the gully. That equipment could be fetched in the morning, but this night they would fight unladen. The Riflemen would discard their greatcoats before the attack, revealing their dark-green uniforms which would be their distinguishing mark this night. Goodwill to sinful men.

Sharpe stopped, hearing noise ahead, and for a fraction of a second he feared that the enemy had a picquet line at the valley's rim. He listened, relaxed. It was the sound of revelry, cheers and laughter, the roar of mens' voices. Christmas Eve.

A bloody night to be born, Sharpe thought. Midwinter, when food was scarce and wolves prowled close to the hill villages. Perhaps it was warmer in Palestine, and perhaps the shepherds who saw the angels did not have to worry about wolves, but winter was still winter everywhere. Sharpe had always thought Spain a hot country and so it was in the summer when the sun baked the plains into dust, but in winter it could still be freezing and he thought of being born in a stable where the wind sliced like a knife between the cracks of the timber. He led them on again towards the Gateway of God, a dark line of men bringing blades in the night.

He dropped flat at the valley's rim. Thorn trees were dark on the slope before him, the valley was lit by the fires in Castle, Convent, watchtower and village, and, glory to God in the highest, there was a path leading at an angle down through the thorns.

The sound of laughter came from the Convent. Sharpe could see other men silhouetted by the fires in the Castle's big yard. It was cold.

He turned his head round and hissed at his men. 'Count!'

'One.' Harper.

'Two.' A German Sergeant called Rossner.

'Three.' Thomas Taylor.

Frederickson dropped beside Sharpe, but stayed silent as the men counted themselves off in the darkness. All were present. Sharpe pointed to the foot of the slope where the dark path between the thorns debouched onto a rough pasture land that was stippled red and black by the firelight. 'Wait at the tree-line.'

'Yes, sir.'

Frederickson's men would have only fifty yards to cover from the edge of the bushes to the door of the Convent. They would come when they heard the boom of the seven-barrelled gun, or if they heard a volley of musketry, but they would ignore a single musket shot. On a night like this, a night of drinking and celebration, the odd single shot would be nothing unusual. If Frederickson heard nothing while he counted off fifteen minutes, then he was to come anyway. Sharpe looked at the Captain whose black patch gave his face a spectral look in the darkness. He was beginning to like this man. 'Your men are all right?'

'Anticipating the pleasure, sir.' Goodwill to sinful men.

Sharpe took his own group forward. He looked once to his

right. Far off, in Portugal, a speck of light throbbed like a red star. A fire in the border hills.

The path was steep. The drizzle had made it slick and treacherous, causing one of Sharpe's men to slip and crash into a tangle of thorn branches. Everyone froze. Spines of thorn snapped and tore as the man pulled himself free.

Sharpe could see the great arched door of the Convent, a single slit of light showing where the doors were slightly ajar. Shouts and laughter came from the building, and once a crash of glass and loud jeers. There were womens' voices among the mens'. He went slowly, testing each foothold, feeling the excitement because he was so close to revenging himself for the insults of his last visit.

The door opened. He stopped, the men behind him stopped without orders, and two figures were silhouetted in the archway of the Convent. One man, with a musket on his shoulder, clapped the shoulder of the second man and pushed him out into the roadway. Clear over the sounds of revelry was the noise of the second man retching. Christmas was working its magic in the Convent. The first man, presumably the sentry, laughed from the archway. He stamped his feet, blew on his hands, and Sharpe heard him shout for the sick man to come inside. The door closed on them.

The slope was gentler now and Sharpe risked a glance behind and was shocked by how naked and visible his men appeared to be. Surely they must be seen! Yet no one had shouted an alarm from the valley, no shot had stabbed the night, and then he was at the edge of the bushes and he brought his men to a halt. 'Taylor and Bell?'

'Sir?'

'Good luck to you.'

The two Riflemen, greatcoats hiding their uniforms, went forward towards the Convent. Sharpe would have liked to have done this piece of work, but there was a danger that the sentry might recognize him or Harper. He must wait.

He had chosen both men carefully, for to kill a man silently with a bare blade was no job for a keen beginner. Bell had learned his skills in the London streets, Taylor across the other side of the world, but both men were confident. Their job was simply to kill the sentry or sentries in the entrance-way.

They made no attempt to hide their approach. Their feet dragged on the roadway, their voices slurred as if with drink, and Sharpe heard foul oaths from Bell as the Rifleman stepped in the vomit at the foot of the steps. The door opened, and the sentry looked out. The door was pushed wider open and a second man stood there, musket slung. 'Come on! It's bloody cold!' A brazier flamed behind them.

Taylor sat down on the bottom step and began singing. He held a bottle up that had been provided by Sharpe. 'Got a present for you.' He sang the words over and over, laughing at the same time.

Bell bowed to them. 'A present!'

'Christ! Come on!'

Bell gestured at Taylor. 'He can't walk.'

The bottle was still held up. The two sentries came down the steps good-naturedly and one reached for the bottle and never saw the right hand pull the honed blade from inside the greatcoat, swing, and the sentry's right hand was touching the bottle as Taylor's blade went in under the armpit, travelling slightly upwards, straight to the tangle of heart and arteries. Taylor still held the bottle, but now he supported the dead weight of the man as well.

Bell grinned at the second sentry just as alarm touched his face and the Londoner was still grinning as his blade cut any shout from the man's throat. Sharpe saw the body lurch, saw it held, saw the two Riflemen taking the corpses into the shadows. 'Come!'

He took the rest of his men forward. Frederickson was at the foot of the slope now, beginning the slow count towards fifteen minutes or the sound of the shot that would signal vengeance for Adrados.

The Convent steps were messy with the blood of Bell's victim and Sharpe's boots made dark footprints in the entrance tunnel beside the brazier. He walked alone into the upper cloister, stepping into the shadows of the arched walkway, and the cloister seemed to be deserted. The shouts, the laughter, both came from the inner cloister, but as he waited, his eyes searching the courtyard, he heard moans and small voices from the darkness. The tunnel ahead of him, the passage through which he and Dubreton had been escorted to see the woman branded with the word 'puta' was empty, the door and grille open. He held out his left hand and clicked his fingers and then led his men under the dark of the cloister's walkway, going slowly. Their boots seemed to be loud on the stones. The brazier touched light on the tiles about the raised pool.

The chapel door was open and, as Sharpe passed, a hand shot out and grasped his left shoulder. He swung on the hand, right fist already moving, then stopped. A woman stood there, swaying and blinking, and behind her there were candles beyond the open door in the grille. 'Coming in, darling?' She smiled at Sharpe, then staggered against the door.

'Go and sleep it off.'

A man's voice, speaking in French, called from inside the chapel. The woman shook her head. 'He's no bloody good, darling. Brandy, brandy, brandy.' A child, not three years old, came and stood beside her mother and peered up solemnly at Sharpe, sucking its thumb. The woman squinted at Sharpe. 'Who are you?'

'Lord Wellington.' The French voice shouted again and there was the sound of movement. Sharpe pushed the woman inside the door. 'Go on, love. He's feeling better now.'

'A chance would be a fine thing. Come back, yes?'

'We'll be back.'

He led his men, grinning broadly, round the further corner and down to the passageway that led to the inner cloister. Footsteps echoed in it as he approached and then a child burst from the archway, pursued by another child, and they ran into the upper cloister and shrieked with laughter and excitement. A voice yelled at them from a storeroom. The drunks seemed to be sleeping it off in this upper level.

Sharpe motioned his men to wait in the passageway and walked out onto the upper cloister level where he had stood and talked with Madame Dubreton. He stayed in the shadows and he stared down into the eye of chaos. This was the anarchy that Wellington feared, the short step from order, the abandonment of hope and discipline.

Flames lit the deep cloister. A great fire burned on the broken stones, above the wreckage of the delicate canals, and the fire was fed by thorn trees and by planks that had been torn from the great windows of the hall on the northern side of the cloister. The windows ran from the ground level, past the upper walkway, to delicate arches beneath the gallery, and now that the protective planks had been prised from the stonework the window spaces gave free entrance between courtyard and hall. Their glass was long gone. Men and women came and went between the two areas and Sharpe watched from above.

He had run from the Foundling Home before his tenth birthday and he had gone into the dark close alleys of London's slums. There was work there for a nimble child. It was a world of thieves, body-snatchers, murderers; of drunkards, cripples, and of whores who had sold themselves into disease and ugliness. Hope meant nothing to the inhabitants of St Giles. For many their longest journey in this world was a mile and a half along the length of Oxford Street, due west, to the three-sided gibbet at Tyburn. The countryside, just two miles north up the Tottenham Court Road, was as remote as paradise. St Giles was a place of disease, starvation, and a future so dark that a man measured it in hours and took his pleasures accordingly. The gin-shops, the gutter, the floors of the common lodging houses were the places where men and women dissolved their desperation in drink, coupling, and finally in death that tipped most into the open sewer along with the night's harvest of dead babies. Without hope there was nothing but desperation

And these people were desperate. They must have known that revenge was coming, perhaps in the spring when the armies stirred from winter torpor, and until it came they numbed their desperation. They had drunk and were still drinking. Food lay on the broken stones, men lay with women, children picked their way through the couples to find bones that still had chewable meat or wineskins whose spigots they would suck on desperately. Close to the fire some of the bodies were naked, asleep, while further away they were covered in blankets and clothes. Some moved. One man was dead, blood black on his opened stomach. The noise was not from here, but from the hall and Sharpe could not see what was prompting the sound. He thought of the minutes ticking by, of Frederickson counting in the cold thorns.

He turned to the passageway and kept his voice low. 'We're going round the cloister, lads. Walk slowly. Go in twos and threes. There's a view you'll like as you go round.'

Harper walked just behind Sharpe, both men clinging to the shadows by the wall. The huge Irishman watched the couples by the fire and his voice was cheerful. 'Just like the officers' mess on a Friday night, eh?'

'Every night, Patrick, every night.'

And what, he wondered, was to stop his own men going to join those in the courtyard? To be offered drink and women instead of work and discipline was the avowed dream of every soldier, so why did they not just go now? Kill him and Harper and take their freedom? He did not know the answer. He just knew that he trusted them. And where, more importantly, were the hostages kept? He pushed open the doors that he passed, but the rooms were either empty or inhabited by sleeping people. None were guarded. Once a man growled in protest from the darkness and two women giggled. Sharpe closed the door. The flames of the great fire were warm on the left side of his face.

He turned the corner and now he could see into the great hall. A hundred men and as many women crowded the floor. There was a kind of platform at the far end, a raised dais, and a staircase went from the dais to a gallery above that spanned the width of the hall. Sharpe could see two doorways leading from the gallery into corridors or rooms behind. There was easy access to the gallery through the tall, empty windows. A man could simply step from the cloister onto the gallery.

The men and the women were shouting, the shouting orchestrated from the dais. There sat Hakeswill. He had a chair that rose high above his head, like a throne, a chair with decorated armrests. He was dressed in the priest's finery, the robes too short for him so that his boots were visible almost to his knees. Beside him, leaning on the armrest, Hakeswill's hand about her waist, was a small, thin girl. She was dressed in brilliant red, a white scarf about her waist, long black hair falling below the scarf.

A woman stood on the dais. She was grinning. She was dressed in a shift over which she wore a vest and a shirt. She had a dress in her right hand and, to the crowd's roar, she hurled the dress towards a man in the crowd who caught it and waved. Hakeswill held up his hand. The face twitched. 'Shirt! Come on, then! How much? Shilling?'

It was an auction. She had sold the dress, presumably, and Sharpe saw two small grinning children picking up coins from the floor beneath the dais and carry them to an upturned shako. The shouts came from the hall, two shillings, three, and Hakeswill whipped them up and his eyes looked into the hat to see the takings.

They cheered and screamed as the shirt came off.

The vest went for four shillings. The coins rattled on the stones. Sharpe wondered how many minutes had passed.

The yellow face grinned. The hand jerked up and down on the small girl's ribcage. 'Her shift! Make it good. Ten shillings?' No one answered. 'You lousy bleeders! You think she's not as pretty as Sally? Christ! You paid her two quid, now come on!' He beat them up, higher and higher, and to a great cheer and thrown coins she peeled herself naked for one pound and eighteen shillings. She stood there grinning, hand on hip, and Hakeswill lurched upright and sidled towards her, his gold and white robes ridiculous in the flamelight, and his blue bright eyes leered at the people in the hall as he slid his right arm across the woman's shoulders. 'Now then. Who wants her? You're going to pay! Half to her, half to us, so come on!'

Bids came and to some the woman stuck out her tongue, others she laughed, and Hakeswill egged them on. A consortium of Frenchmen bought her in the end, their price four pounds, and they came to fetch her and the crowd cheered louder as one of them carried the woman sitting on his shoulders towards the fire in the courtyard.

Hakeswill calmed them with long arms. 'Who's next?'

Names were shouted, women pushed forward by their men. Hakeswill drank from a bottle, his face twitched on its long neck, and the small girl still clung solemnly to him. A group of men began chanting. 'A prisoner! A prisoner!' The chant was taken up, shortened. 'Prisoner! Prisoner! Prisoner!'

'Now, lads, now! You know what the Marshal says!'

'Prisoner! Prisoner! Prisoner!' The women were screaming with the men, spitting the words like bile from their mouths. 'Prisoner! Prisoner! Prisoner!'

Hakeswill let them chant, his eyes knowing on them. He raised a hand. 'You know what the Marshal says! They're our precious little ones, the prisoners! We can't touch them, oh no! That's the Marshal's orders. Now! If the bastards come! Ah. Then you can have them, I promise.' The crowd roared at him, protesting, and he let them roar before he held up the hand again. The thin girl clung to him, her left hand tight on the embroidered vestment. 'But!' the crowd silenced slowly. 'But! As it's Christmas we might have a look at one. Yes? Just one? Not to touch! No, ño! Just to check she's all there? Yes.'

They roared their approval and the yellow face with its lank, grey hair twitched at them while the toothless mouth gaped in silent laughter. People drifted in from the court-yard, attracted by the new noise. Sharpe turned and saw the faces of his men pale in the cloister, anxious, and he wondered how long they had been. It must be near the quarter hour.

Hakeswill's left hand was twined in the long black hair of the girl. He twisted it and pointed at a man. 'Go and tell Johnny to fetch one.' The man started towards the staircase that led from the dais, but Hakeswill stopped him as he was climbing onto the platform. He turned to his audience, his face grinning. 'Which one do you want?'

The crowd erupted again, but Sharpe had seen enough. The hostages were behind one of the two doorways that led from the gallery. He turned to his men and his voice was urgent, drowned to all but them by the cacophony in the hall. 'We go to the gallery. We walk as far as the windows. Drop your coats here.' His own greatcoat was unbuttoned. 'Even numbers go into the right doorway, odd numbers go into the left. Sergeant Rossner?'

'Sir?'

'Take two men and keep the bastards from the stairs. First man to find the hostages, shout! Now enjoy this, lads.'

Sharpe walked down the northern side of the cloister, sure that he must be visible because the windows into the hall made it seem as if the pavement was suspended in mid-air. He put one hand on Harper's sleeve. 'Fire as we go in, Patrick. Straight into the bloody hall.'

'Sir.'

Their boots were loud. Their uniforms, divested of coats, green in the firelight. The voices screamed and chanted below drowning the sound of the Riflemens' boots. Nemesis was coming to Adrados.

One window, two windows, three windows, and Hakeswill's voice, sounding close, shouted above the din. 'You can't have the Portuguesy! D'you want the English bitch? The one married to the Froggy? D'you want her?'

They screamed assent, the voices bellowing in excitement, and Sharpe saw two armed men walk from the right hand doorway and cross to the gallery's balustrade. One glanced at the men on the cloister, thought nothing of what he saw and leaned beside his companion to grin down at the bedlam below. The man who had been sent to fetch one of the hostages began climbing the stairs.

Sharpe touched Harper's arm again. 'Take the two on the gallery.'

'Yes, sir.'

The Riflemen were bunched now. Sharpe looked at them. 'Draw swords.' Some would fight with the sword-bayonets fixed on their rifles, some would prefer to use them as short stabbing weapons. He nodded at Harper. 'Fire.'

Harper filled the window space, the gun squat in his hands, his face broad and hard, and then he touched the trigger and the explosion of the seven barrels echoed in the hall and the two armed men were thrown sideways, ragged and twitching, while Harper was thrown back by the massive kick. Sharpe's sword was in his hand, he went through the smoke in the window space, and the long blade was red steel in the firelight.

The Riflemen followed him, screaming like the devils of hell come to this feast as Sharpe had ordered them to scream, and Sharpe led the way towards the right hand door, all waiting done, all nervousness dispelled because the fight was on and there was nothing now but to win. This was the

Sharpe who had saved Wellington's life at Assaye, who had hacked through the ranks to take the Eagle with Harper, who had gone, maddened, into the breach at Badajoz. This was the Sharpe whom Major General Nairn had only been able to guess at as he looked at the quiet, dark-haired man across the rug in Frenada.

A man appeared in the doorway, startled, his musket raised with bayonet fixed. It was a French musket and the man raised it higher in desperation as he saw the Rifle officer, but he had no hope, and Sharpe shouted his challenge as the right foot stamped forward, the blade followed, twisted, steel running with light reflected from the candles in the passageway beyond, and the sword was in the Frenchman's solar plexus and Sharpe twisted it again, kicked at his victim, and the blade was free and he could step over the screaming, dying man.

God, but there was joy in a fight. Not often in battle, but in a fight when the cause was good, and Sharpe was in the passageway, the tip of his sword dark, and he could hear the Riflemen behind him, and then a door opened spilling more light and a man peered nervously out, foolishly out, because Sharpe was on him before he understood that revenge had come and the great cavalry sword slid beneath his jawbone and he gagged, jerked back, and Sharpe was in the doorway and again the sword came forward and the man clutched at the blade which was in his throat and Sharpe could smell the foul smell that a sword drew from a man, and then his weapon was free and he was in the room with two men who fumbled with muskets, shook their heads in fear, and Sharpe bellowed at them, jumped the dead man, and the sword was a flail above the table that separated him from his enemies. Blood flew from the sword tip as it circled, and then it bit, and Sharpe could see a Rifleman going the other way about the table, a grin of maniacal joy on his face, and the second enemy backed away, back until he was hard against another door, and the Rifleman drove rifle and sword-bayonet in a blow that would have pierced stone so that the blade tip buried itself hard in the wood of the door. The enemy folded over it, bubbling and crying, and a second Rifleman, a German, finished him off with far less force and more efficiency.

The man Sharpe's sword had hit in the face screamed beneath the table. Sharpe ignored him. He turned to the room of Riflemen. 'Load! Load!'.

Three men in a room, armed, guarding a door. This had to be a guardroom. He reached past the pinned, bleeding figure, and tried the handle to the door. It was locked. Behind him he could hear shouts, the banging of muskets, but he ignored it. He pressed the catch, twisted, and the rifle came free of the bayonet that still nailed the dead man to the door, and then he had space to stand in front of the door, raise his heel, and smash it forward. The door shuddered. He did it again, a third time, and then the door banged open, wood splintering at the old lock, and the corpse was still attached to the wood by the twenty-three inch bayonet as it swung open and Sharpe entered.

Screams, screams of fear, and Sharpe stood in the doorway, his sword bloody, his cheek smeared with the blood of the man he had killed in the guardroom door, and he saw the women huddled against the far wall. He lowered his sword. The blood was fresh on his green uniform, glistening in the candlelight, dripping onto the rug that furnished this prison room. One woman was not hiding her face. She was protecting another woman whose face was buried in her side, beneath the encircling, protective arm, and the face was proud, thin, topped by the piled blonde hair. Sharpe made a half bow. 'Madame Dubreton?'

Two Riflemen crowded in behind Sharpe, curious, and he turned on them. 'Get out! There's a fight! Join it!'

Madame Dubreton frowned. 'Major? Major Sharpe, is it?'

'Yes, Ma'am.'

'You mean?' She was still frowning, still disbelieving.

'Yes, Ma'am. This is a rescue, Ma'am.' He wanted to leave them, to go back and see how his men were faring, but he knew these women must be terrified. One of them was sobbing hysterically, staring at his uniform, and Madame Dubreton snapped at her in French. Sharpe tried a smile to lessen their shock. 'You will be returned to your husbands, Ma'am. I'd be grateful if you would translate that for me. And if you'd excuse me?'

'Of course.' Madame Dubreton still looked as if she were in shock.

'You are safe now, Ma'am. All of you.'

The woman whose face had been hidden in Madame Dubreton's side pulled herself free. She had black hair, lustrous hair, and she pushed it away from her face as she turned hesitatingly towards Sharpe.

Madame Dubreton helped her upright. 'Major Sharpe? This is Lady Farthingdale.'

Lucky Farthingdale was the thought of a half second, then utter disbelief, and the girl with the black hair saw Sharpe, her eyes widened, and then she screamed. Not in terror, but in some kind of joy, and she leaped across the room, running to him, and her arms were about his neck, her face pressed against his bloodied cheek, and her voice in his ear. 'Richard! Richard! Richard!'

Sharpe caught Madame Dubreton's eyes and he half smiled. 'We've met, Ma'am.'

'So I see.'

'Richard! God, Richard! You? I knew you'd come!' She pulled back from him, keeping her arms about his neck, and her mouth was as hopelessly generous as he had ever remembered, and her eyes as tempting as a man could want, and even this ordeal had not taken the mischief from her face. 'Richard?'

'I have to go and fight a battle.' The noise was loud outside, orders and shots, screams and the clash of steel.

'You're here?'

CHAPTER 9

He left one man guarding the hostages. Two each stood post in the passageways, the rest protected the stairway and the entrance to the gallery through the windows opening to the cloister. Smoke already clotted the gallery, Riflemen were slamming ramrods into fired barrels, others crouched waiting for a target. Harper was reloading the seven-barrelled gun. He looked up at Sharpe, grinned quickly, and held up four fingers. Sharpe raised his voice.

'We've got the women, lads!'

They cheered, and Sharpe made a swift count. All his men were there, all seemingly unwounded. He watched a Rifleman bring his gun into his shoulder, aim swiftly, and a bullet spun into the cloister. There was a yelp from the far side, then a ragged volley of muskets, the balls going high. One struck an iron ring, suspended as a chandelier, old and rusty on its chains, and the four yellow candles fluttered as the ball struck. Sharpe moved to the stairhead.

Three bodies lay on the stairs, thrown back by rifle fire. The German Sergeant, Rossner, his face blackened by the powder from his rifle pan, looked happily at Sharpe. 'They run, sir.'

They did, too. The deserters and their women were screaming and shouting, pushing and scrambling, going into the courtyard of the cloister. Sharpe looked for Hakeswill, but the big man in his priest's vestments had disappeared in the crush. Rossner gestured with his rifle down the stairs. 'We go down, sir?'

'No.' Sharpe was worried about Frederickson's men. He

would rather that the main force of Riflemen found the advance party concentrated, so that no one shot a man of his own side in the confusion and the shadows. He went back to the windows where Harper waited hopefully with the big gun reloaded. 'Frederickson?'

'Not yet, sir.'

Someone was shouting in the courtyard, bellowing for order, someone who had, perhaps, realized that the attackers were few in number and that a concentrated counter-attack could overwhelm them. Sharpe stared at the far side of the upper cloister. He could see no men there in the firelight, the rifles had made it an unhealthy place, but then it was suddenly filled with running figures, shouting for aid, and Sharpe pushed down a rifle that was brought up to fire. 'Hold it!'

Women and children were fleeing, which meant Frederickson's men must be in the outer cloister, and Sharpe bellowed at the men who guarded the windows. 'Watch out for Captain Frederickson!'

Then there were dark figures in the entrance way of the upper cloister, figures that took immediate cover as they emerged into the wide-open space of the cloister, and Sharpe shouted again. 'Rifles! Rifles! Rifles!' He stepped through the window, out onto the cloister where the firelight illuminated his uniform. 'Rifles! Rifles!' A musket flamed below, the ball ricocheting off the balustrade into the night. 'Rifles! Rifles!'

'See you, sir!' A man with a curved sabre standing across the cloister. Riflemen were going left and right, clearing the upper gallery, and Frederickson came with them towards Sharpe.

Sweet William looked dreadful. He had taken the patch from his eye, and the false teeth from his mouth. It was a face from a nightmare, a face that would terrify any child, but it was a face that was smiling as he approached Sharpe. 'Do we have them, sir?'

'Yes!'

Frederickson's sabre was bloodied. He flexed it, wanting

124

to use it again, and watched as his men burst open doors and shouted at men and women to surrender. One man hopped down the cloister, his right leg in his trousers, his left leg caught at the ankle, and he turned ludicrously as Riflemen blocked his way only to find Riflemen behind him. He rolled over the balustrade, dropped into the courtyard, and hobbled away towards an archway on the far side.

One of Frederickson's Lieutenants blew long blasts on his whistle, then shouted over the cloister. 'All secure, sir!'

Frederickson looked at Sharpe. 'Which way down?'

'In there.' Sharpe pointed at the gallery. There had to be another way down, but he had not seen it. 'One section to guard the gallery.'

'Sir.' Frederickson was already moving, his mutilated face eager for more fighting. Sharpe followed him and slapped Harper on the shoulder. 'Come on!'

Now it was a romp, a riot, a headlong charge down the stairs, a yelling pursuit of the enemy who had crowded through the archway across the cloister, a sabre-hacking, sword-swinging fight at the arch itself, a crash as the seven-barrelled gun cleared the few defenders from the room within, and the cloister echoed to the cries of children, the shouting of their mothers, and Riflemen rounded them up, herded them, and dragged men from hiding places.

Sharpe went through the arch, through the room, and he seemed to be in some kind of dark crypt, damp and freezing, and he shouted for light. A Rifleman brought one of the straw and resin torches that burned in the outer room and it showed a huge, empty cave, another entrance opposite. 'Come on!'

There was a current of air blowing towards them, shivering the torch flame, and Sharpe knew these rooms must lead to the blanket covered hole that looked out onto the lip of the pass. If there was a gun there, and he knew the Spanish garrison had possessed four guns, then there would be powder there, and a defender could just be lighting a fuse that would bring flame and destruction billowing into this crypt. 'On! On! On!' He led the way, sword out, boots pounding on the cold stones, and the flame-light showed that he had charged into a strange passageway and that his shoulders were brushing against curiously rounded yellow-white stones that reached from floor to ceiling.

The gun was there, abandoned by Pot-au-Feu's men, pointing at the gaping hole that had been prised out of the Convent's thick wall. The rammer leaned against the dirty barrel, next to it a powder scoop and a ripper or 'wormhead', the giant corkscrew used to pull out a damp charge. Sharpe could see roundshot, canister, both piled up against the curious white walls that opened up into the space where the gun had been put.

A priming tube was in the gun's vent, suggesting that the cannon was loaded, but Sharpe ignored it, went to the opening from which the blanket had been torn aside, and listened. Boots scrambling on the turf and rocks outside, the gasping and crying of women and children, the shouts of men. Those who had escaped from the Convent were going for the Castle. Torches flared on the battlement.

'Can we fire it?' Frederickson was fingering the priming tube, a quill filled with fine powder that flashed the fire down to the charge in its canvas bag.

'No, there are children out there.'

'God save Ireland!' Harper had picked up one of the whitish rounded stones that had fallen behind the gun. He held it as if it would kill him, his face screwed in distaste. 'Would you look at this? Good God!'

It was a skull. All the 'stones' were skulls. The man with the torch pressed closer until Frederickson barked him back because of the powder barrels, but in the smoky light Sharpe could see that the piled skulls walled in a great pile of other human bones. Thigh bones, ribs, pelvises, arms, small curled hands and long feet bones, all piled in this cellar. Frederickson, his face more ghastly than any skull, shook his head in wonderment. 'An ossuary.'

'A what?'

'Ossuary, sir, a bone house. The nuns. They bury them here.'

'Jesus!'

'They strip the flesh off first, sir. God knows how. I've seen it before.'

There were hundreds of the bones, perhaps thousands. To make a space for the trail of the gun Pot-au-Feu's men had broken into the neat pile and the skeletons had tumbled down onto the floor, the bones had been shovelled to one side, and Sharpe could see a fine white powder littered with shards where men had stepped on the human remains. 'Why do they do it?'

Frederickson shrugged. 'So they're all together at the resurrection, I think.'

Sharpe had a sudden image of the mass graves at Talavera and Salamanca heaving on the last day, the dead soldiers coming to life, their eye sockets rotten like Frederickson's, the earth shedding off the dead ranks coming from the grave. 'Good God!' There was a pail of dirty water under the gun, ready for the sponge, and a rag beside it. He stooped and cleaned off his sword before pushing it home in the scabbard. 'We'll need six men here. No one's to fire the gun without my order.'

'Yes, sir.' Frederickson was cleaning the sabre, pulling the curved blade slowly through the wet rag.

Sharpe went back through the pathway of skulls, following Harper's broad back. He remembered walking across Salamanca's battlefield in the autumn, before the retreat to Portugal, and there had been so many dead that not all had been buried. He could remember the hollow sound as a horse's hooves had clipped a skull which had rolled like a misshapen football. That had been in November, not even four months after the battle, yet already the enemy dead had been flensed white.

He walked into the cloister, a place of the living, and the

fire showed disconsolate prisoners hedged by sword-bayonets. A child cried for its mother, a Rifleman carried a tiny baby deserted by its parents, and the women screamed at Sharpe as he appeared. They wanted to leave, it was not their doing, they were not soldiers, but he bellowed at them to be quiet. He looked at Frederickson. 'How's your Spanish?'

'Good enough.'

'Find whatever women were captured up here. Give them decent quarters.'

'Yes, sir.'

'The hostages can stay where they are. They're comfortable enough, but make sure you've half a dozen reliable men to protect them.'

'Yes, sir.' They were walking across the courtyard, stepping over the small canals. 'What about this scum, sir?'

Frederickson stopped beside the deserters who had been captured. No Hakeswill there, just three dozen sullen frightened men. Sharpe looked at them. Two-thirds were in British uniform. He raised his voice so that all the Riflemen in the courtyard and on the upper gallery could hear him. 'These bastards are a disgrace to their uniforms. All of them. Strip them!'

A Rifle Sergeant grinned at Sharpe. 'Naked, sir?'

'Naked.'

Sharpe turned round and cupped his hands. 'Captain Cross! Captain Cross!' Cross had been detailed to capture the outer cloister, the chapel, and the storerooms.

'He's coming, sir!' A shout from above.

'Sir?' Cross leaned over the balustrade.

'Wounded? Killed?'

'None, sir!'

'Give the signal for Lieutenant Price to come up! Make sure your picquets know.'

'Yes, sir.' The signal was a bugle call from Cross's bugler.

'And I want men on the roof! Two hour duty only.'

'Yes, sir.'

'That's all, and thank you, Captain!'

Cross's face smiled at the unexpected compliment. 'Thank you, sir!'

Sharpe turned to Frederickson. 'I need your men on the roof, too. Say twenty?'

Frederickson nodded. There were no windows in the Convent so any defence would have to be made over the parapet of the roof. 'Loopholes in the walls, sir?'

'They're bloody thick. Try if you like.'

A Lieutenant came up, grinning broadly, and handed Frederickson a slip of paper. The Rifleman twisted it towards the firelight and then looked at the Lieutenant. 'How bad?'

'Not bad at all, sir. They'll live.'

'Where are they?' The missing teeth made Frederickson's voice sibilant.

'Store-room upstairs, sir.'

'Make sure they're warm.' Frederickson grinned at Sharpe. 'The butcher's bill, sir. Bloody light. Three wounded, no dead.' The grin became wider. 'Well done, sir! By God, I didn't know if we could do it!'

'Well done, yourself. I always knew we could.' Sharpe laughed at the lie, then asked the question he had been wanting to ask ever since Frederickson had appeared in the Convent. 'Where's your patch?'

'Here.' Frederickson opened his leather pouch and took out the teeth and the eye-patch. He put them back in place, looking human again, and laughed at Sharpe. 'I always take them off for a fight, sir. Scares the other side witless, sir. My lads reckon my face is worth a dozen Riflemen.'

'Sweet William at war, eh?'

Frederickson laughed at the use of his nickname. 'We do our best, sir.'

'Your best is bloody good.' The compliment felt forced and awkward, but Fredrickson beamed at it, had needed

Sharpe's praise, and Sharpe was glad he had said it. Sharpe turned away to look at the prisoners who were being forcibly stripped. Some were already naked. It would be hard to escape on a night like this without clothes. 'Find somewhere for them, Captain.'

'Yes, sir. What about them?' Frederickson nodded towards the women.

'Put them in the chapel.' Whores and soldiers were an explosive mix. Sharpe grinned. 'Find some volunteers and they can have a storeroom apiece. That's the lads' reward.'

'Yes, sir.' Frederickson would make sure some of the women volunteered. 'That all, sir?'

My God, no! He had forgotten the most important thing! 'Your four best men, Captain. Find their liquor store. Any man who gets drunk tonight sees me in the morning.'

'Yes, sir.'

Frederickson left and Sharpe stood close to the fire, enjoying its warmth, and wondered what else had to be done. The Convent could be defended from the roof, its door well guarded, and the prisoners had been taken care of. A dozen of the deserters were wounded, three would never recover, and he must find a place for them. The women were disposed of, the children too, and the upper cloister would be like a brothel all night, but that was only fair to his men. A Christmas present from Major Sharpe. The liquor would be locked up. He must find food for his men.

The hostages. He must reassure them, make certain of their comfort, and he stared up at the hall gallery and laughed out loud. Josefina! Good God alive! Lady Farthingdale.

The last time he had seen Josefina she was living in comfort in Lisbon, her house terraced above the Tagus and filled with sunlight reflected from the river and framed by orange trees. Josefina Lacosta! She had jilted Sharpe after Talavera and run off with a Cavalry Captain, Hardie, but he had died. Josefina had run for Hardie's money, abandoning

Sharpe's poverty, and she had always wanted to be rich. She had succeeded, too, buying the house with its terrace and orange trees in the rich Lisbon suburb of Buenos Ayres. He shook his head, remembering her two winters ago, when her house had been a languorous place where rich officers congregated and the richest vied for Josefina. He had seen her at a party, a small orchestra sawing away at violins in the corner, Josefina gracious as a queen among the dazzling uniforms that fawned on her, wanted her, and would pay the highest price for one night of La Lacosta. She had put on weight since Talavera and the weight had only made her more beautiful, though less to Sharpe's taste, and she had been choosy; he remembered that. She had turned down a Guards Colonel who had offered her five hundred guineas for a single night, and had rubbed salt in that wound by accepting a handsome young Midshipman who only offered twenty. Sharpe laughed again, attracting a curious glance from a Rifleman who herded the deserters to their naked, cold prison. Five hundred guineas! The price Farthingdale had paid for her ransom! The most expensive whore in Spain or Portugal. And married to Sir Augustus Farthingdale? Who called her delicate! God in his heaven! Delicate! And with the highest connections? That was true, though not in the way Farthingdale had meant it, but then perhaps he was right. Josefina had been married and her husband, Duarte, had gone to South America at the beginning of the war. He had been of good family, Sharpe knew, and he had some sinecure with the Royal Portuguese family; Third Gentleman of the Chamberpot or some such nonsense. And how had Josefina snared Sir Augustus? Did he know of her past? He must. Sharpe laughed again out loud and turned towards the staircase they had discovered in the cloister's south-west corner. He would pay his respects to La Lacosta.

'Sir?' It was Frederickson, emerging from a doorway. He held a hand up, motioning Sharpe to wait, while in his other he held his watch to the light of a torch.

'Captain?'

Frederickson said nothing, just kept his hand up, stared at his watch, then, a moment later, he snapped the cover shut and smiled at Sharpe. 'A happy Christmas to you, sir.'

'Midnight?'

'The very hour.'

'And to you, Captain. And your men. A tot of brandy all round.'

Midnight. Thank God he had come early, or else Madame Dubreton would have been the butt of Hakeswill's cruel game. Hakeswill. He had escaped, over to the Castle, and Sharpe wondered whether the deserters would still be there in the morning, or would they, knowing the game was up, flee in the dawn? Or perhaps they would try to retake the Convent while Sharpe's men were still unfamiliar with the battleground.

It was Christmas Day. He stared up into the total darkness beyond the sparks that were whirled upwards by the fire. Christmas. The celebration of a Virgin giving birth, yet it was more than that, much more. Long before Christ was born, long before there was a church militant on earth, there had been a feast at midwinter. It celebrated the winter solstice, December 21st, and it was the lowest point of the year when even nature seemed dead and so mankind, with glorious perversity, celebrated life. The feast promised spring, and with spring would come new crops, new life, new births, and the feast held out the hope of surviving the barrenness of winter. This was the time of year when the flame of life burned lowest, when the dark nights were longest, and on this night Sharpe might be attacked in the Convent by Pot-au-Feu's desperate men. At this time of the winter solstice the dawn could be a long, long time coming.

He watched a Rifleman scramble onto the roof and, as he leaned down to take his gun from a colleague, the man laughed at some joke. Sharpe smiled. They would endure.

CHAPTER 10

Christmas morning. In England people would be walking frost-bright roads to church. In the night Sharpe had heard a sentry softly singing to himself 'Hark the Herald Angels Sing'. It was the Methodist Wesley's hymn, but the Church of England had nevertheless printed it in their Prayer Book. The tune had made Sharpe think of England.

The dawn promised a fine day. Light flared in the east, seeped into the valley and showed a landscape mysterious with ground fog. The Castle and Convent stood like towers at the entrance to a harbour containing white, soft water that flowed gently over the lip of the pass and spilt slowly towards the great mist-filled valley to the west. The Gateway of God was white, weird, and silent.

There had been no attack from Pot-au-Feu. Twice the picquets had fired in the night, but both were false alarms and there had been no rush of feet in the darkness, no makeshift ladders against the convent walls. Frederickson, bored with the enemy's quiescence, had begged to be allowed to take a patrol across the valley and Sharpe had let them go. The Riflemen had sniped at the Castle and watch-tower, causing anger and panic in the defenders, and Frederickson had come back happy.

After the patrol's return Sharpe had slept for two hours, but now the whole garrison stood to its arms as the dawn turned from grey danger into proper light. Sharpe's breath misted before his face. It was cold, but the night was over, the hostages were rescued, and the Fusiliers would be climbing the long pass. Success was a sweet thing. On the ramparts of

133

the Castle he could see Pot-au-Feu's sentries, still at their post, and he wondered why they had not fled against the wrath they knew must be coming. The sun touched the horizon, red-gold and glorious, smearing the white mist pink, daylight in Adrados. 'Stand down! Stand down!'

The Sergeants repeated the call about the rooftop and Sharpe turned towards the ramp Cross had built and thought of breakfast and a shave.

'Sir!' A Rifleman called to him from twenty paces away. 'Sir!' He was pointing east, direct into the brilliance of the new sun. 'Horsemen, sir!'

God damn it, but the sun made it impossible. Sharpe made a slit with his fingers and peered through and he thought he saw the shapes riding on the valley's side, but he could not be certain. 'How many?'

One of Cross's Sergeants guessed three, another man four, but when Sharpe looked again the shapes had gone. They had been there, but not now. Pot-au-Feu's men? Scouting an eastward retreat? It was possible. Some of the prisoners had spoken of raiding Partisans, seeking vengeance for Adrados, and that was possible too.

Sharpe stayed on the roof because of the horsemen, but the dawn showed no more movement in the east. Behind him there were warning shouts as men carried bowls of hot water from the makeshift kitchens. The men not on guard started shaving, wishing each other a Happy Christmas, teasing the women who had elected to join their conquerors and who now mixed with the Riflemen as if they had always belonged. This morning was a fine morning for a soldier. Only the detail who had to climb the hill to fetch the packs from the gully were grumbling about work.

Sharpe turned to see them leave and was intrigued by a strange sight in the courtyard of the upper cloister. A group of Riflemen were tying strips of white cloth to the bare hornbeam that had broken through the tiles. They were in fine spirits, laughing and playful, and one man was hoisted piggy-back onto a comrade's shoulders so he could put an especially large ribbon on the topmost twig. Metal glinted on the bare twigs, buttons perhaps, cut from captured uniforms, and Sharpe did not understand it. He went down the narrow ramp and beckoned Cross to him. 'What are they doing?'

'They're Germans, sir.' Cross gave the explanation as if it answered all Sharpe's puzzlement.

'So? What are they doing?'

Cross was no Frederickson. He was slower, less intelligent, and far more fearful of responsibility. Yet he was fiercely protective towards his men and now he seemed to think that Sharpe disapproved of the oddly decorated tree. 'It's a German custom, sir. It's harmless.'

'I'm sure it's harmless! But what the devil are they doing?'

Cross frowned. 'Well it's Christmas, sir! They always do it at Christmas.'

'They tie white ribbons on trees every Christmas?'

'Not just that, sir. Anything. They usually like an evergreen, sir, and they put it in their billet and decorate it. Small presents, carved angels, all kinds of things.'

'Why?' Sharpe still watched them, as did men of his own Company, who had not seen anything like it.

It seemed that Cross had never thought to ask why, but Frederickson had come into the upper cloister and heard Sharpe's question. 'Pagan, sir. It's because the old German Gods were all forest Gods. This is part of the winter solstice.'

'You mean they're worshipping the old Gods?'

Frederickson nodded. 'You never know who's in charge up there, do you?' He grinned. 'The priests say that the tree represents the one on which Christ will be crucified, but that's bloody nonsense. This is just a good old-fashioned offering to the old Gods. They've been doing it since before the Romans.'

Sharpe looked at the tree. 'I like it. It looks good. What happens next? Do we sacrifice a virgin?'

He had spoken loud enough for the men to hear him, to laugh, and they were pathetically pleased because Major Sharpe had liked their tree and had made a joke. Frederickson watched Sharpe go into the inner cloister and the one-eyed Captain knew what Sharpe did not know; he knew why these men had fought last night instead of deserting to their comfortable, lascivious enemy. They were proud to fight for Sharpe. It made a man good to match up to high standards, and when those standards led to victory and approval then the men would follow always. God help the British army, Frederickson thought, if the officers ever despised the men.

Sharpe was tired, cold, and he had not shaved. He walked slowly around the upper cloister, down the stairs, and found the large, chill room where Frederickson had put the naked prisoners. Three Riflemen guarded them and Sharpe nodded to a Corporal. 'Any trouble?'

'No, sir.' The Corporal spat tobacco juice through the doorway. The door had gone and the three rifles looked over a crude barrier of charred timbers. 'One of 'em got all upset, sir, 'bout an 'our ago.'

'Upset?'

'Yessir. 'E was 'ollering an' shoutin', sir, makin' aggravation. Wanted clothes 'e said. Said they wasn't animals an' all that kind of rubbish, sir.'

'What happened?'

'Cap'n Frederickson shot 'im, sir.'

Sharpe looked at the Corporal curiously. 'Just like that?'

'Yessir.' The man smiled happily. ''E don't take no nonsense, the Cap'n, sir.'

Sharpe smiled back. 'Nor should you. If anyone else gives you trouble, just do the same thing.'

'Yessir.'

Frederickson had been busy, and evidently still was for a cheer came from his Company that manned the roof about the inner cloister. Sharpe climbed the stairs again, then the ramp that went from the upper gallery. There he saw why the men had cheered.

A flag had been raised. It was a makeshift flagpole, nailed together, and because there was not a breath of wind on this cold, Christmas morning, Frederickson had ordered a cross-piece hammered into the staff on which the flag had been hung. It was the signal which would tell the Fusiliers that the rescuers had succeeded, that they could climb the pass, and Sharpe had assumed that he would simply hang the flag over the edge of the building. The flagpole was a much better idea.

Frederickson had come to this part of the roof and looked up at the flag. 'Doesn't look the same, sir.'

'The same?'

'The Irish bit.'

When the Act of Union had been passed, indissolubly joining Ireland to England as one nation, a diagonal red cross had been added to the Union flag. For some people, even after eleven years, it still looked strange. For others, like Patrick Harper, it was still offensive. Sharpe looked at the Captain. 'I hear you shot a prisoner.'

'Was I wrong?'

'No. You just saved a Court-Martial ordering the same thing.'

'It seemed to pacify them, sir.' Frederickson said it mildly, implying he had done the prisoners a service.

'Have you slept?'

'No, sir.'

'Get some. That's an order. We might need you later on.'

Sharpe wondered why he had said that. If all went to plan the Fusiliers would relieve him within hours and the Rifles' job would be done. Yet an instinct needled him. Perhaps it was those strange horsemen in the dawn, or perhaps it was nothing more than the unaccustomed responsibility of lead-ing nearly two hundred men. He yawned, rubbed the bristles on his chin, and hunched himself closer inside the greatcoat.

A cat walked on the tiles of the shallow-pitched roof, disdaining the Riflemen who crouched beneath the low stone parapet. It walked to the ridge of the tiles, sat, and began to wash its face with cuffing paws. Its shadow was long on the pink tiles.

Across the valley the shadow of the watchtower stretched towards the Castle. The two buildings were five hundred yards apart, the watchtower a good hundred and fifty feet higher, and between the two was a small, steep, thorn-covered valley. The mist was clearing from the smaller valley, showing the bare thorns touched with frost, revealing a small sparkling stream. Men still guarded the Castle and watchtower, and that was strange. Did Pot-au-Feu think that once the hostages were rescued his enemies would simply march away?

To the west the hills of Portugal were touched by the flame gold of the sun, their valleys black and grey, streak-ed with white mist, while the horizon was still smoky with night. The landscape looked crumpled, as if it needed to stretch and waken up. In the far valleys it would still be night.

Sharpe walked along the rooftop until he was at the northern parapet, lightly guarded, and he sat on the tiles and looked left towards the pass. No sign of the Fusiliers, but it was early yet.

'Sir?' A German voice behind him. 'Sir?'

He turned. The man was offering him a cup of tea. The Germans had taken the habit from the British and, like them, carried the leaves loose in their pockets. One good rainstorm could ruin a week's supply. 'Yours?'

'I have more, sir.'

'Thank you.'

Sharpe took it, cradled it in his gloved hands, and watched the German go back towards the flag. The cloth was beaded with moisture. The sun shone through the thin material. Something to fight for.

The mist still flowed soft down the pass, spilling like water, and Sharpe sipped the hot tea and was grateful to be alone. He wanted to stare at the great unfolding beauty of the dawn, the light spreading across Portugal beneath a sky that was vast and streaked with the cloud remnants of the night. More cloud threatened in the north, dark cloud, but this day would be fine.

He heard the footsteps on the roof and he did not turn round for he did not wish to be disturbed. He looked to his right, pointedly away from the footsteps, and watched the work-party coming down the steep path between the thorns with the packs tied to their rifles.

'Richard?'

He turned back, scrambling to his feet. 'Josefina.'

She smiled at him, a little nervous, and her face was swathed by the silver-fur of her dark green cloak hood. 'Can I join you?'

'Yes, do. Aren't you cold?'

'A bit.' She smiled at him. 'Happy Christmas, Richard.'

'And to you.' He knew the Riflemen on the huge, wide roof would be looking at them. 'Why don't you sit.'

They sat two feet apart and Josefina drew the thick, furred cloak about her. 'Is that tea?'

'Yes.'

'Can I have some?'

'And live, you mean?'

'I'll live.' She held a hand out of her cloak and took the tin mug from him. She sipped, made a face. 'I thought you might come back last night.'

He laughed. 'I was busy.' He had been to see the hostages to find three Lieutenants paying court to them. Sharpe had not stayed long, only long enough to hear assurances that they had not been harmed, and to assure them that they would be returned to their husbands. All of them, curiously, had been concerned about the fate of the men who had held them hostage, and Sharpe had taken a list of names of those

139

men who had been kind to the women. He had promised he would try and save them from execution. He grinned at Josefina and took the tea back. 'Would I have been welcome?'

'Richard!' She laughed, her nervousness gone because Sharpe's voice indicated approval of her. 'Do you remember when we met?'

'Your horse had lost a shoe.'

'And you were all grumpy and disagreeable.' She held a hand out for the tea. 'You were very earnest, Richard.'

'I'm sure I still am.'

She made a face at him, blew on the tea, and sipped at the cup. 'I remember telling you that you'd become a Colonel and be horrid to your men. It's coming true.'

'Am I horrid to them?'

'The Lieutenants are frightened of you. Except for Mr Price, but then he knows you.'

'And no doubt wanted to know you?'

She smiled happily. 'He tried. He's like a puppy. Who's the frightening Captain with one eye?'

'He's an English Lord, he's terribly rich, and he's very very generous.'

'Is he?' She looked at him, interest quickening in her voice, and then she saw he was teasing. She laughed.

'And you're Lady Farthingdale.'

She made a shrugging motion beneath her cloak as if to indicate that it was a strange world. She sipped the tea, then offered it to Sharpe. 'Was he worried about me?'

'Very.'

'Truly?'

'Truly.'

She stared at him with interest. 'Was he truly very worried?'

'He was truly very worried.'

She smiled happily. 'How nice.'

'He thought you were being raped daily.'

'Not once! That strange "Colonel" Hakeswill made sure of that.'

'He did?'

She nodded. 'I told him that I'd come here to pray for my mother, which was sort of true.' She laughed. 'Not really, but it worked for Hakeswill. No one could touch me. He used to come and talk to me about his mother. Endless talks! So I kept telling him that mothers were the most wonderful things in the world, and how lucky his mother was to have a good son like him, and he couldn't hear enough!' Sharpe smiled. He knew of Hakeswill's devotion to his mother, and he knew that Josefina could not have stumbled on a better protection than to appeal to that devotion.

'Why did you come here?'

'Well, my mother is ill.'

'I didn't think you liked her.'

'I don't. She doesn't approve of me, but she is ill.' She took the tea from Sharpe, finished it, and put the tin mug on the parapet. She looked at the Rifleman and grinned. 'The truth is I wanted to go away for a day.'

'By yourself?'

'No.' She drew the word out reprovingly, suggesting he knew her better than that. 'With a delicious Captain. But Augustus insisted another one came along as well, so it would all have been very difficult.'

Sharpe grinned. Her eyelashes were impossibly long, her mouth indecently full. It was a face that promised every comfort. 'I can understand why he worries about you.'

She laughed at that, then shrugged. 'He's in love with me.' She made the word 'love' ironic.

'And you with him?'

'Richard!' She reproved him again. 'He's very kind, and he's very, very rich.'

'Very, very, very rich.'

'Even richer.' She smiled. 'Anything I want! Anything! He tries to be strict with me, but I won't let him. I locked the

141

door on him for two nights and I haven't had any trouble since.'

Sharpe twisted round and was thankful that no one seemed to need his presence. The sentries crouched or paced the roof, the sound of knives and canteens came from the breakfasts in the cloisters, and there was still no sign of the Fusiliers. He looked back at her and she smiled. 'I really am glad to see you, Richard.'

'You'd have been glad of any rescuer.'

'No. I'm glad to see you. You always make me tell the truth.'

He smiled. 'You don't need me to do that.'

'You need friends.' She smiled quickly. 'You really know me, don't you, and you don't disapprove of me.'

'Should I?'

'They usually do.' She was staring at the hillside. 'They all say differently, and they all make wonderful speeches, but I know what they think. I'm popular, Richard, just as long as I keep this.' She pointed to her face.

'And the rest of it.'

'Yes.' She smiled at him. 'It still works.'

He smiled back. 'Is that why you married Sir Augustus?'

'No.' She shook her head. 'That was his idea. He wanted me to be his wife so I could go everywhere with him.' She laughed, as if Sir Augustus had been stupid. 'He wanted me to go north to Braganza, and we sailed to Cadiz, and he couldn't have me going to dinners as his whore, could he?'

'Why not? Lots of men do.'

'Not to those dinners, Richard. Very pompous.' She made a face.

'So you married him so you could go to pompous dinners?'

'Marry him!' She looked at Sharpe as though he were mad. 'I'm not married to him, Richard! You think I'd marry him?'

'You're not . . . ?'

She laughed at him, her voice attracting the attention of

the sentries. She lowered it. 'He just wants me to say that I'm married to him. Do you know what he pays me for that?' Sharpe shook his head and she laughed again. 'A lot, Richard. A lot.'

'How much?'

She ticked the things off on her fingers. 'I've got an estate near Caldas da Rainha; three hundred acres and a big house. A carriage and four horses. A necklace that would buy half of Spain, and four thousand dollars in a London bank.' She shrugged. 'Wouldn't you say yes to an offer like that?'

'I don't think anyone would ask me.' He looked at her incredulously. 'You're not Lady Farthingdale?'

'Of course not!' She smiled at him. 'Richard! You should know me better than that! Anyway, Duarte's still alive. I can't marry anyone else while I'm still married to him.'

'So he suggested that you call yourself his wife? Is that it?'

She shrugged. 'Something like that. He wasn't very serious, but I asked him what he'd pay for it, and once he told me I went along.' She smiled to herself. 'I mean he was already paying me so that no one but him got in the saddle, so why not pretend to be married? It's as good as marriage, isn't it?'

'I'm sure your priest would agree,' Sharpe observed ironically.

'Whoever he is.'

'And no one suspects?'

'They don't say anything, at least not to Augustus. He told everyone he'd married me, why shouldn't they believe him?'

'And he doesn't think anyone's suspicious?'

'Richard, I told you.' She sounded almost exasperated. 'He's in love with me, he really is. He can't get enough of me. He thinks I was created by the moon goddess, at least that's what he said one night.' Sharpe laughed, and she smiled. 'He really does. He thinks I'm perfect. He's always saying that. And he wants to own me, every part of me, every hour, everything.' She shrugged. 'He pays.'

'And he doesn't know about anyone else?'

'The past, you mean? He's heard. I told him it was all rumour, that I had entertained officers, but why shouldn't I? A respectable married woman in Lisbon, perhaps a widow, I was allowed to take tea with an officer or two.'

'He believes that?'

'Of course! That's what he wants to believe.'

'How long will it last?'

'I don't know.' She made a face at the hillside. 'He's nice. He's like a cat. He's very clean and very delicate and very jealous. I miss, well, you know.'

Sharpe laughed. 'Josefina!' It was an incredible story, but no more so than dozens he had heard of the shifts men and women resorted to in Cupid's service. She watched him laugh.

'I'm happy, Richard.'

'And rich.'

'Very.' She smiled. 'So you're not to tell him I told you all this, understand? You're not to tell him!'

'I won't say you told me.'

'You'd better not. Another two months and I'll have enough to buy some property in Lisbon. So I've told you nothing!'

He knuckled his forehead. 'Yes, Ma'am.'

'Lady Farthingdale.'

'Yes, Milady.'

She laughed. 'I'm getting to like being called that.' She clutched the cloak tighter at her throat. 'So tell me about you.'

He grinned, shook his head, and was trying to think of something non-committal to say when there was a bellow from across the roof. 'Sir! Major Sharpe, sir!'

He turned, getting to his feet. 'What?'

'Those horsemen, sir. Saw them again. They've gone now.'

'You're sure?'

'Yes, sir.'

'What were they?'

'Dunno, sir, except . . .'

'Except what?' Sharpe shouted.

'Can't be sure, sir, but I thought they could be bloody French. Only three of them, sir, but they did look Frenchie.'

Sharpe understood the man's doubt. French Cavalry rarely moved except in large formations and it sounded strange that just three enemy cavalry could be in this high valley. 'Sir?' The man called again.

'Yes?'

'Could be the deserters, sir. They've got Frenchie uniforms.'

'Keep looking!' The man was probably right. Three French cavalrymen from Pot-au-Feu's band were merely scouting the valley to the east and south. Pot-au-Feu surely was leaving. Sharpe turned to Josefina. 'Time to go. Work to do.' He held out his hand and helped her up. She looked at him with a hint of worry.

'Richard?'

'Yes.' He presumed she was worried about the possibility of French troops in the high valley.

'Are you glad to see me?'

'Josefina.' He smiled. 'Yes, of course.'

They walked along the flat space between the parapet and the tiles, Riflemen making way for them and giving Josefina admiring looks. Sharpe stopped beneath the spread flag and stared westward into the shadows of the pass where the mist was shredding itself into decaying wisps. There was a slight movement among the grey rocks far down, a movement scarcely visible, but enough to prompt a shout from another sentry.

'Sir!'

'I've seen them, thank you!'

The Fusiliers were in sight. Sharpe looked from them up to the beaded, frail flag and he wondered why the instinct persisted that he might yet have to fight for it. He pushed the thought away, handed Josefina to the head of the ramp, and raised his voice so that the Riflemen could hear him. 'Your husband will be here within the hour, Milady.'

'Thank you, Major Sharpe.' She bowed slightly towards him then, in a superb gesture, waved an arm around the whole Convent, a gesture that embraced all the watching Riflemen. She raised her voice. 'And thank you to all of you. Thank you!'

They all looked pleased, bashful and pleased, and Sharpe nudged a Sergeant beside him. 'Three cheers for her Ladyship?'

'Oh yes, sir, of course, sir.' The Sergeant beamed at the men. 'Three cheers for her Ladyship! Hip, hip, hip!'

'Hooray!' They bellowed it twice more, startling the cat on the roof tiles, and Josefina acknowledged it graciously. She nodded to them all, finishing with Sharpe and he could have sworn that she gave him a wink as her head inclined.

He went back to the flag, grinning. It was a morning of surprises. A Christmas tree for Christmas day, Josefina for Sir Augustus Farthingdale, and in the east three horsemen to trouble Christmas morning. The shadows in the pass resolved themselves into a skirmish line that climbed towards the Gateway of God, the Companies in column behind it. Sharpe looked up at the flag and his instinct still told him that trouble was in the windless air, that this Christmas held other surprises yet to come.

CHAPTER 11

Lieutenant Colonel Kinney sent his Fusiliers in open order for the last few yards of the scramble uphill. There was still a possibility that Pot-au-Feu might open fire with his captured Spanish guns, though the prisoners taken in the night swore that two of the cannon were in the watchtower while the third remaining in the deserters' hands was mounted on the east wall of the Castle and unable to bear on the pass. Kinney nevertheless took no chances.

Sharpe experienced a sudden regret because he was no longer the senior officer in the Gateway of God. Kinney now outranked him, Sir Augustus Farthingdale too, and Sharpe presumed that the single Major of the Fusiliers was also his superior. Kinney slid from his horse at the Convent gate and held a hand out to Sharpe, ignoring the salute. 'Well done, Major, well done!'

Kinney was generous in his praise, embarrassingly so, effusive about the difficulties of a night march, a silent approach, and an assault on a building that incurred no serious casualties among the attackers. Sharpe introduced Frederickson, Cross and Price, and Kinney spread his praise liberally among them all. Sir Augustus Farthingdale was less forthcoming. He dismounted stiffly, helped by his servant, and twitched the silk scarf that was tucked into the high collar of his cavalry cloak. Beneath the cloak he slapped a riding crop against his boots. 'Sharpe!'

'Sir.'

'So you were successful!'

'Happily yes, sir.'

Farthingdale grunted, sounding far from happy. His aquiline nose was red from the cold, the mouth more peevish than usual. The crop still slapped against the leather. 'Well done, Sharpe. Well done.' He managed to make the praise sound grudging. 'Lady Farthingdale well, is she?'

'Perfectly, sir. I'm sure she'll be relieved to see you.'

'Yes.' Farthingdale fidgeted, his eyes looking without interest at the Castle and the village. 'So what are you waiting for, Sharpe? Take me to her.'

'Of course, sir. I'm sorry, sir. Lieutenant Price?' Sharpe nominated Price as Sir Augustus' guide to his 'bride'. Sir Augustus turned at the Convent steps, removed the bicorne hat from his sleek silver hair, and nodded at Kinney. 'Carry on, Kinney!'

'Does the man think I'm planning to go to sleep?' The comment was made loud enough for Sharpe to hear. Kinney had obviously had a difficult time with Sir Augustus during the long night march and now the Welshman kicked at a stone, sending it skittering against the Convent wall. 'God damn it, Sharpe, but she must be a remarkable woman to bring Sir Augustus all this way?'

Sharpe smiled. 'She's a beauty, sir.'

Kinney looked east where his Battalion were forming up well out of canister range from Castle or watchtower. 'What do we do now, eh?' The question was not aimed at Sharpe. 'Let's clear the beggars out of the village, then look at the Castle.'

'The watchtower, sir?'

Kinney turned towards it. The two guns in the watchtower, if they existed, could fire into the flank of any attack made on the fallen east wall of the Castle. If there was to be a fight at the Castle, then the watchtower would have to be taken first. Kinney scratched his cheek. 'You think the buggers will fight?'

'They haven't run away, sir.'

Pot-au-Feu must know that his escapades were over. His

148

hostages were gone, the Convent was taken, and now a Battalion of British infantry was in his valley. The sensible thing, Sharpe thought, was for the deserters to run again, to flee eastwards or northwards, but they had stayed. Pot-au-Feu's troops were visible on the Castle ramparts and in the earthworks at the foot of the watchtower. Kinney shook his head. 'Why have they stayed, Sharpe?'

'Must think he can beat us, sir.'

'Then the man must be disabused.' Kinney dwelt lovingly on the last word. 'I don't fancy any of my men dying today, Major. It would be a terrible tragedy on Christmas Day.' He sniffed. 'I'll roust the village with bayonets, then I'll have a chat with our man at the Castle to see if he wants to surrender. If he wants to do it the hard way . . .' He looked at the watchtower. 'I'd be grateful, in that case, for the loan of a Rifle Company, Major.'

It was kind of Kinney to wrap an order in such politeness. 'Of course, sir.'

'Let's hope it won't come to that. By then young Gilliland should have arrived.' The Rocket Troop was an hour behind the 113th, delayed by a loosened wheel-rim. Kinney smiled. 'Two of those fireworks up their backsides might persuade them to throw themselves on our tender mercies.' Kinney called for his horse, grunted as he pulled his considerable weight into the saddle, then grinned down on Sharpe. 'They probably haven't run, Sharpe, because they're all blind drunk. Well then! To work! To work!' He gathered his reins, then stopped, staring over Sharpe's head. 'My word! My word!'

Josefina was in the Convent gateway, being handed down by a Sir Augustus Farthingdale who looked quite different. The peevishness was gone, replaced by a simpering attention to the gorgeous woman who dazzled Kinney with her smile. There was a wealth of pride in Farthingdale's voice, the pride of possession. 'Colonel Kinney? The honour of meeting my lady wife? My dear, this is Colonel Kinney.'

Kinney removed his hat. 'Milady. We would have marched half way round the globe to rescue you.'

Josefina rewarded him with parted lips, dipped eyelashes, and a pretty speech that complimented both Kinney and his troops. Sir Augustus watched it with pleasure, enjoying the admiration in Kinney's eyes, approving as his 'wife' walked with small steps to pet Kinney's horse. When she was away from his side he plucked at Sharpe's sleeve. 'A word with you.'

Had she told him that Sharpe had known her? It seemed unbelievable, but Sharpe could think of no other explanation why Sir Augustus should draw him aside, out of Josefina's earshot. The Colonel's face was furious. 'There are naked men in there, Sharpe!'

Sharpe almost smiled. 'Prisoners, sir.' He had ordered a work-party of deserters to continue the hard slog of boring loopholes in the huge walls.

'Why the hell are they naked?'

'They disgraced their uniforms, sir.'

'Good God, Sharpe! You let my wife see this?'

Sharpe bit back a retort that Josefina had probably seen more naked men than Sir Augustus ever had, instead he gave a mild answer. 'I'll see that they're covered, sir.'

'You do that, Sharpe. Another thing.'

'Sir?'

'You haven't shaved. You're hardly in a position to talk about disgracing uniforms!' Farthingdale turned abruptly, and his face changed to an indulgent smile as Josefina approached. 'My dear. Do you really want to stay out in this cold?'

'Of course, Augustus. I wish to see Colonel Kinney's men punish my oppressors.' Sharpe almost smiled again at the last word, but she had chosen it well for Sir Augustus. He straightened up, looking fierce, and nodded.

'Of course, my dear, of course.' He looked at Sharpe. 'A chair for her Ladyship and some refreshment, Sharpe.'

'Yes, sir.'

'Not that there'll be much of a fight.' Sir Augustus was talking to Josefina again. 'They won't have the stomach for a fight.'

An hour later it seemed as if Sir Augustus was right. The deserters who had stayed in the village fled with their women and children as Kinney's Light Company went in from the north. They fled, unmolested, across the valley floor and threaded the thorn bushes towards the watchtower. Two dozen were on horseback, muskets slung on their shoulders and sabres visible at their sides. Madame Dubreton and the other two hostages from the French army came out for a while, took tea with Josefina, but the cold drove them back into the Convent that had been their prison. Sharpe had asked Madame Dubreton what she had thought when she saw her husband in the upper gallery of the inner cloister.

'I thought I would never see him again.'

'You showed no recognition. That must have been hard.'

'For him as well, Major, but I would not give them that satisfaction.'

He had talked to her, while Price had tried to charm Josefina, of the difficulties of living as an Englishwoman in France, but she had shrugged the difficulties away. 'I am married to a Frenchman, Major, so my loyalty is obvious. Not that he requires me to feel enmity for my own country.' She smiled. 'In truth, Major, the war affects us little. I imagine it must be like living in Hampshire. The cows get milked, we go to balls, and once a year we hear of a victory and remember that there's a war.' She had looked down at her lap, then up again. 'It's difficult with my husband away, but the war will end, Major.'

Pot-au-Feu's war was ending now. With the village cleared of the enemy, Kinney lined his Battalion in the crisp wintry sunlight, and then he rode forward, two officers at his side, walking the horses slowly towards the Castle. Sharpe walked up the valley so he could see the broken east wall, and

Frederickson came with him. The Captain nodded towards the three horsemen. 'Calling for a surrender?'

'Yes.'

'I can't think why the bastards haven't run for it. They must know what's waiting for them.'

Sharpe did not reply. The thought worried him too, but perhaps Kinney was right. Perhaps they were too drunk to know what was happening, or perhaps the survivors of Pot-au-Feu's band preferred to throw themselves on the mercy of the British army rather than face a cold winter in these hills that would be infested with vengeful Partisans. Or perhaps Pot-au-Feu simply did not want to leave. The prisoners, questioned in the night, had said that the fat Frenchman had set himself up in mock state in the Castle, lording it like a mediaeval baron, imparting justice and reward on his followers. Perhaps Marshal Pot-au-Feu's fantasy was strong enough to persuade him, and his followers, that the Castle could resist assault. Whatever the reason, he had stayed, and his men had stayed, and now Kinney with his two officers reined in eighty yards from the fallen east wall, the rubble of which made a chest high barrier that guarded the great courtyard.

Kinney was standing in his stirrups, his hands cupped in front of his face. A group of men stood on the rubble and Sharpe saw one of them beckon the horsemen closer. 'They can't hear.'

'Jesus!' Frederickson was frustrated. He did not approve of this parley with a dishonourable enemy. He fidgeted with the frayed edge of his eye-patch and obviously wanted to lead his Riflemen against the enemy who still beckoned Kinney closer.

Kinney, in exasperation, kicked back with his heels and his horse trotted forward. He stopped fifty yards from the enemy, within musket range, and shouted again. Then he seemed to wrench at his reins, lean to his right to help the horse turn, for he had seen the movement to his left, the uncovering of the gun embrasured at the broken end of the eastern wall, but he was too late.

Sharpe saw the smoke first, growing from the stub of wall, and then the bang came, a flat sound, echoing round the valley like dying thunder, and the sound had the distinctive crack of a splitting canister fired from a cannon. The tin can had burst in the muzzle-flame of the gun, spreading its musket-balls in a widening cone that centred on Lieutenant Colonel Kinney. Horse and man went down, knocked sideways, and while the horse vainly thrashed and tried to regain its feet, the man lay still in the torn spray of his blood. Sharpe whirled on Frederickson. 'Get your Company over to the Fusilier Light Company! You'll be attacking the watchtower!'

'Sir!'

Sharpe looked at his own men, lazing by the Convent wall. 'Sergeant!'

Farthingdale was out of his chair, calling for his horse, then for Sharpe. 'Major!'

'Sir?'

'I want your men in front of the Castle! Skirmish order!'

Frederickson, already running, heard Farthingdale and stopped, looking back at Sharpe. Sharpe looked at the Colonel who was swinging himself into his saddle. 'Not the watchtower, sir?'

'You heard me, Major! Now move!' Sir Augustus touched spurs to his horse and it took off towards the silent, stunned Battalion that was lined across the road leading from the village. Sharpe pointed towards the Castle. 'Skirmish order! My Company left of the line, Captain Cross in the centre, Captain Frederickson to the right! Move!'

Now why in the name of all that was holy had Pot-au-Feu prompted this fight? Did he really think he could win? As Sharpe ran across the hard pasture land of the valley he saw the two officers who had ridden behind Kinney lift the Colonel from the ground. One of them despatched the Colonel's horse with a pistol shot. The enemy ignored the two officers, content, perhaps, with a Colonel's death, but why had they done this? They must think they could beat a Battalion in a straight fight, and then Sharpe forgot about Pot-au-Feu's motives because the first musket balls were twitching at the grass and soil about his feet. Smoke was lingering in tiny clouds above the thorn bushes that grew between the Castle and watchtower, and Sharpe shouted for Lieutenant Price. 'Keep those bastards busy, Harry. Use the muskets and four rifles.'

'Aye aye, sir.' Price spread his arms wide. 'Spread out! Spread out!' He took the small whistle from his cross-belt and blew the signal.

Frederickson and Cross both used buglers to relay orders on the battlefield. Their lads, neither more than fifteen, were blowing as they ran, the notes ragged and broken, but the calls unmistakable ordering the Companies to form the skirmish chain. Sharpe anchored them a hundred yards from the broken wall, out of effective musket range, and he ordered Cross's bugler to play the single note, the sustained G, that told the Riflemen to lie down. 'Now the "open fire", lad.'

'Yes, sir.' He took a breath, then the glorious run of three notes climbing a full octave, repeated till the Rifles were cracking down the line and the bullets were forcing Pot-au-Feu's defenders into hasty cover.

Sharpe looked to his left. Price was keeping the scattered enemy in the thorn bushes busy, the Lieutenant walking up and down behind his men, looking for targets. To Sharpe's front the Castle seemed suddenly bare of defenders, driven behind the castellations or the rubble by the Rifles' accuracy. Behind him he could hear orders being bellowed at the Fusiliers. God damn it, but Farthingdale was proposing an immediate assault. The cannon, hidden in the short length of standing east wall, would only be vulnerable to fire from the right of Sharpe's line and he called Cross's bugler to him again. 'My compliments to Mr Frederickson, and ask him to keep an eye on the cannon.' 'Keeping an eye' was an unfortunate way to phrase it, but that did not matter, nor did it matter that Frederickson would doubtless not need to be reminded.

The Rifle fire had slackened to an occasional burst whenever a defender showed his head, and Sharpe listened to the Lieutenants shouting at their men to call out their targets and not to waste shots. Behind them, way back at the village, Sir Augustus was forming the Fusiliers into two columns, four files wide, that were aimed like human battering rams at the broken wall. Sergeant Harper, exercising the privilege of his rank, stood up and joined Sharpe. Only sporadic musket shots came from the hillside, and the range was too great to concern either man. The big Irishman grinned sheepishly at Sharpe. 'Sir?'

'Sergeant?'

'You wouldn't mind me asking, sir, but would that have been Miss Josefina in the Convent?'

'You recognized her?'

'Hard to forget, sir. She's growing into a rare looking woman.' Harper liked his women plumper than Sharpe. 'Is she the Lady Farthingdale?'

Sharpe was tempted to tell Harper the truth, but resisted the temptation. 'She's doing well for herself.'

'She is that. I'll say hello to her.'

'I wouldn't do it while Sir Augustus is about.'

The big face smiled. 'Like that, is it? Would she mind?'

'Not at all.' Sharpe looked towards the Convent. He could see a few Riflemen on the roof, left there as guards for the women and on the prisoners, and he could see the dark green of Josefina's cloak a few yards from the gate. Was she the reason for this precipitate attack? Was Sir Augustus so eager to prove his virility to his young 'bride' that he would throw the Fusiliers into the Castle before the watchtower guns were silenced? Perhaps he was right. There had been no shots from any gun on the hill.

The Fusilier Colours were taken from their leather cases, unfurled, and the flags were carried between the polished halberds of the Sergeants whose job was to protect them. Each halberd was a giant axe, the steel burnished to shine like silver, and the sight of the standards amidst the glittering blades would move any soldier. The panoply of war. Sir Augustus, in front of the Colours, removed his hat, waved it, and the two half-Battalion columns broke into the quick march.

Sharpe cupped his hands. 'Fire! Fire!' It did not matter that there were few targets. What mattered now was to send the Rifle bullets singing about the defenders' ears, discouraging them, making them fearful even before the two columns burst over the rubble of the shattered wall. Cross's bugler came stumbling and panting back from his errand and Sharpe made him sound the advance and took the line forward twenty yards before he sounded the halt. 'Fire! Let them know we're here!'

The rubble of the eastern wall beckoned the two columns forward. It could be easily climbed, its breast-high stones were fallen into a gentle ramp on which Sharpe could see his mens' rifle bullets kicking up spurts of whitish dust. He imagined the two columns of the Fusiliers flowing over the wall into the courtyard, their anger fired by Kinney's death, so why, why in God's name, had Pot-au-Feu invited this attack?

The rifles were drowned by a double explosion from the watchtower hill and Sharpe turned to see the jets of burgeoning smoke mark the position of the two guns in the earthworks beneath the tower. The roundshot rumbled, struck the ground short of the columns and bounced over their heads. The Fusiliers jeered and their officers shouted for silence. Bayonets were bright in the ranks.

Sergeants shouted dressing at the men, ordered their marching, and some of the red jackets with white facings were clean and bright, showing that new recruits were fighting on this Christmas morning. The guns fired again.

The barrels were hotter, or else the elevating screws had been touched a fraction, and this time the first bounce of the balls was in the nearer column and Sharpe saw the files swiped sideways, blood splashing behind, and one man pitched forward, musket dropping, and then crawled from the column and collapsed.

'Close up! Close up!'

'Faster!' Farthingdale waved the hat.

Perhaps he was still right, Sharpe thought. The guns could do little damage in the time it would take for the columns to reach the Castle. They might kill a dozen men, wound as many again, but that would not stop the attack. He looked at the Castle. Musket smoke spouted from almost every embrasure, his Riflemen had targets now, and no bullets struck the slope of the broken wall. He ordered the skirmish line another ten paces forward.

No bullets striking the rubble. He looked again. Nor was there musket smoke above the wall. His men had switched their fire to the men who fired at the attack, and no men fired from the wall which meant it was undefended. Undefended! No men were there, and then Sharpe cursed and began a stumbling run over the uneven ground towards the columns that were close to his skirmish line.

A cannon fired from the watchtower, high this time, so the ball struck between the columns and bounced up and over. The Sergeants called the marching time, their mouths huge, and the officers rode or walked beside their companies with swords drawn. The second gun fired, smashing the nearer column again, plucking men out of the ranks so that the men behind stepped over the carnage and closed files, and still the columns came on. The gun echo died in the valley. The Rifles cracked ahead, muskets spattered from the ramparts, and the leading men of the columns were in the lingering smoke of the skirmish lines first position.

Sharpe pushed unceremoniously through the ranks of the nearer column. He waved at Sir Augustus, proud on his nervous horse. 'Sir! Sir!'

Farthingdale's sabre was drawn. His cloak was peeled back to show the red, black and gold of his uniform. He had purchased his way to a Colonelcy, never having fought, always being the political soldier in the palaces and parliaments of power. 'Sir!'

'Major Sharpe!' He sounded cheerful. He was leading an attack before the eyes of his lover.

'The wall's mined, sir!'

The peevishness was back in his face. He looked at Sharpe in annoyance, thinking, reining in his restless horse. 'How do you know?'

'No one's defending it, sir.'

'They're deserters, Sharpe, not a damned army!'

Sharpe was walking alongside the prancing horse. 'For God's sake, sir! It's mined!'

'God damn you, Sharpe! Out of my way!' Farthingdale let his horse have its head and it leaped ahead, and Sharpe stood there, impotent, while the two columns marched stolidly past. Two hundred and seventy men in each column, bayonets glittering by their faces, marching for the easy-looking wall that Sharpe knew had been left as a temptation for just such an attack as this. God damn it! He looked behind him. The grass had been trampled flat and pale by the two columns, littered by the small knots of bleeding and dead men where the cannon fire had struck. The guns fired again and Sharpe pushed through the column and headed back for his men. Pray God he was wrong.

Cross had pulled his Company aside to let the columns through and Sharpe could see the Colours held high and he knew that the Ensigns, not yet out of boyhood, would be proud of this moment. Kinney had not brought the band's instruments with him, or else the musicians would be playing the attack forward until the fighting made them take up their secondary job, that of caring for the wounded. Farthingdale waved them on, cheered them on, and at last the Fusiliers were allowed to cheer themselves as they broke into a run for the last few yards.

The cannon on the eastern wall was unmasked, fired, and

the head of the further column was torn ragged by the flailing canister. One man crawled on the grass, his white trousers soaking red, his head shaking because he did not know what had happened.

'On! On! On!' Sir Augustus Farthingdale had stopped his horse, let the Colours go past him, and now he urged the columns onto the eastern wall. Smoke from the cannon drifted over the rubble.

Let me be wrong, Sharpe prayed. Let me be wrong.

The first men onto the rubble broke ranks. They spread out as each chose a path on the uneven stones. Their muskets were held ready for the killing thrust of the bayonet.

'On! On!' Farthingdale was up in his stirrups, sabre flailing the air, and Sharpe cursed the man for he knew that this display had been put on for Josefina. Musket bullets struck in the columns, making a flurry like a stone dropped into a water-current, the men reclosing about the disturbed patch. 'On! On!'

They ran at the rubble, packing it, spreading up it, cheering as they breasted it and saw the courtyard in front of them, and again Sharpe prayed he was wrong, and then he saw that the first men were over the stones and he felt a flood of relief because they would not die in the flaming horror of an exploding mine on Christmas Day in the morning.

The jet of smoke seemed to leap from the base of the stones towards Farthingdale and his horse, leaping like a striking snake, and the horse reared, throwing Farthingdale backwards, and then the smoke was coming from every crevice of the stones and Sharpe shouted in helpless warning.

The broken wall heaved upwards, turned into flame and boiling dark smoke so that it was like premature night where the Fusiliers were hurled up and back by the packed powder beneath the stones. The explosion rumbled, then cracked into defiant thunder that rolled between the thorn-clad hills, and the wall heaved up, out, and the men who had not reached the broken barrier stopped in fear.

The gun on the wall fired again and then there was cheering from the Castle, from the hill by the watchtower, and Pot-au-Feu unleashed every musket onto the motionless columns. Flames licked among the smashed barrier beneath the smoke. Musket flashes showed where the enemy was hunting the survivors who had been first into the courtyard.

'Back! Back!' Someone shouted it, all accepted it, and the two columns went back from the smoke, the musket noise, and then Price screamed at Sharpe. 'Sir!'

Men were filing down between the thorn bushes to attack the stricken Battalion on its flank.

'Form on the column!' Sharpe bellowed. Cross's bugler blew the three notes that meant 'form' and Sharpe pushed men towards the red-coated ranks.

A Fusilier Captain, wild-eyed and confused, was shouting at his men to go back. Sharpe yelled at him to stand fast. Six companies at least were unaffected by the mine, and there was still a chance of hurling them into the courtyard, but the Fusiliers obeyed the voices of their own officers. 'Back!'

The men from the thorn bushes were making a rough skirmish line to attack the retreating Battalion and there was some satisfaction, not much, in seeing the Riflemen hurl them back with well-aimed shots, and then Sharpe heard the clash of steel from beyond the smoke, the sound of more shots, and he knew that there were Fusiliers trapped in the courtyard of the Castle. Those men must not die, or worse, become new hostages to Hakeswill's cruel vices. Sharpe threw his unfired Rifle at Hagman, drew his sword, and turned to where the dark smoke still clung to the blood-streaked stones. He would get those men out, and then they would take this Castle in the proper way, the professional way, and he turned as he heard footsteps beside him on the grass. 'What are you doing?'

'Coming with you.' Harper's voice brooked no argument.

It was Christmas Day, and they were going to war.

CHAPTER 12

Going through the acrid curtain of smoke, between the licking flames that consumed the scraps of powder barrel, was like passing into a different world. Gone was the clean air and cold grass of the valley, instead it was a world of broken stone, slick with blood, littered by scraps of unrecognizable burned flesh; a courtyard where the survivors of the mine were being hunted across a cobbled yard.

Sharpe saw Harper go down and he checked in fear for the Sergeant, then saw the huge Irishman tugging the shaft of a halberd clear from a body. The blade swung up into the smoke, a great axe of silver light, and Harper screamed his war shout in his native Gaelic. Sharpe had seen this moment before, the instant when the normally placid Sergeant seethed with the anger of Irish heroes, careless of his safety, caring only to fight in a manner that might be enshrined in the plaintive Irish songs that kept alive the heroism of a nation.

Within the courtyard was a new, low wall, easily jumped, that was Pot-au-Feu's defence line inside the Castle. Men were running to the wall, laughter on their faces, muskets ready to fire at the Fusiliers who were dazed in the smoke. Some of Pot-au-Feu's men had leaped the wall and hunted survivors with bayonets. A few of the Fusiliers had bunched together, a Sergeant commanding them, and they held their bayonets out and died as the musket balls flamed across the puny wall.

Then Harper came out of the smoke.

To the defenders in the courtyard it must have seemed as if a creature from myth had come out of the explosion's darkness, a huge man, drunk with battle, an axe head swinging from his hands, and he ran at the wall, jumped, and the steel blade clove the smoke and bit wet into the defenders.

'Fusiliers! Fusiliers!' Sharpe shouted. He slipped, his right heel greased by a smear of blood, and the fall saved him from a Frenchman's bayonet that came from his left. Sharpe rolled on the ground, swung the huge sword and saw a sliver of wood slice from the musket above him. He lashed out with his left foot, caught the man on his kneecap, and then the man was staggering and Sharpe was on his feet, and the sword finished the Frenchman off. 'Fusiliers! To me!'

He tugged at the sword blade, kicked the body, and the weapon came reluctantly free. 'Fusiliers!'

God, this was a bad place! It was only the presence of some of the enemy around the survivors that stopped Pot-au-Feu's muskets sweeping the courtyard clean. Four men lay at Harper's feet, others had gone back from the fury in the huge man, from the great blade that swung from his powerful arms, and Sharpe saw a man take careful aim with his musket. 'Patrick!'

The halberd was thrown, the fluke of its axe head burying itself in the man's forehead, and Harper came back over the wall unslinging his seven-barrelled gun.

'Save it, Patrick! To me! To me!'

The Sergeant was hustling his men towards Sharpe. Three wounded were being helped, another man had both Colours of the Fusiliers bundled carelessly under his arm. The shafts were broken and splintered.

'This way!' Sharpe turned and kept the movement going in a backswing of his sword that drove back a man in Portuguese uniform who was charging from the rubble. The man seemed crazed, mad with fighting, and Sharpe saw other figures on the broken wall where the smoke clung and was thick with the smell of roasted flesh. Sharpe concentrated on the one man, letting all his anger flow into the lunge

162

of the twisting sword, and he saw the brown uniform fold over the great blade and he was twisting it free even as he knew that they were surrounded.

A musket ball slammed into the stones by his left foot, another plucked at the tail of his jacket, and a third spun a Fusilier clear round, dying before he hit the ground, and Sharpe could see men thick on the stones, scrambling towards them, and he knew that he could never get the wounded across the barrier. He twisted round again. He would not die here! Not at the hands of these scum on this day!

They expected him to stand and fight or else to run over the stones, so he must do something else, and he must decide in an instant or else they would all be dead or worse. Pot-au-Feu did believe he could win! He was proving it to his men, and they were rewarding him by fighting with a fanaticism that was partly born of the knowledge that they were doomed if defeated.

To his right was the gate-tower, huge and massively turreted. There had to be a doorway into it and Sharpe was moving, yelling, and the Fusiliers changed direction and Sharpe led them with his sword and the deserters backed off because they had not expected this and the sword swept at them. He stepped over a red-jacketed body, its mouth open and red, and then the sword took a man in the back and Harper seized the fallen musket, squeezed the trigger, and Sharpe was on the low wall, across it, yelling as if the fiend was inside him, beginning to enjoy this crazy charge into the heart of the enemy's defence, and there was the doorway, small and black, off to his right. 'There! Go! Go! Go!'

The Sergeant led them, dragging a wounded man despite his screams of pain, and Sharpe seized Harper's elbow, turned him, so the two of them would be the rearguard as the Fusiliers scrambled into the desperately small doorway. A backswing to knock a musket and bayonet into the air, withdraw, lunge, and shout in triumph because another bastard was down, and then the shout across the court-yard.

'Get them!'

Hakeswill's voice. The musket balls flattened on the gate-tower, pecked at the cobbles, and Sharpe went backwards. 'Get inside!' Thank God for the smoke in the courtyard, the hiding smoke, but then there was a crude line visible that came towards them, mouths open, bayonets ahead of them and Harper went onto one knee and the great gun was in his shoulder. 'Get back, sir!'

The kick of the seven-barrelled gun almost threw Harper into the doorway. The centre of the attacking line was snatched away, the shot echoed huge in the Castle, and Sharpe grabbed Harper's collar and hauled him backwards. The Sergeant rolled clear inside the doorway and shook his head. 'God save Ireland.'

'Stairs, sir!' The Fusilier Sergeant pointed at a winding stairway.

'Door!'

Harper slammed it. It looked rotten and frail, nail heads half falling from the once stout planks. There was a bar for it and Sharpe dropped it into place as a musket ball splintered a hole by his right wrist.

The Fusilier Sergeant was hesitating at the bottom of the curving stairs. 'Buggers are up there, sir.'

Sharpe told him what he thought of the defenders upstairs, then led the way with his sword outstretched. Going up the tight, spiral staircase Sharpe understood the cleverness of the old Castle builders for the steps, in this direction, turned in a clockwise direction. Sharpe's sword arm, like most mens', was his right arm, and it was blocked and hampered by the central stone shaft that supported the inner side of each step. A defender, going backwards up the stairs, would have far more freedom for his right arm. So far no one challenged his ascent.

He was going slowly, carefully, scared of each step. Below

him he could hear the thumping as musket butts hammered at the door. It could not hold. Then one of his wounded screamed horribly and Sharpe remembered a glimpse of a shattered thigh-bone sticking clean from the torn flesh and he knew the man was being dragged up the steps. Poor bastard, Christmas Day 1812, and the thought gave him such anger that he abandoned his caution and ran up the steps, shouting, and he burst into a spacious room where men, far more frightened than he, waited to see what came out of the doorway. They did not know if it would be friend or foe and they hesitated long enough for the sword to take one and the other two ran back to an open door that looked onto the northern ramparts. Sharpe slammed the door shut, barred it, then turned to look at their refuge.

It was a large, rectangular chamber lit by two arrow slits that looked out at the valley. Two huge and broken wind-lasses were in the room, long decayed, and a rusted pulley on the ceiling showed where once a portcullis had been raised and lowered by guards in this room. Another circular stair-case led upwards from a doorway and Sharpe knew it must lead to the turret's top from which Pot-au-Feu's men had fired on the attack.

Harper was loading his seven-barrelled gun, a long pro-cess, while the Fusiliers dragged the wounded into the chamber. Sharpe grabbed the Sergeant's tunic. 'Two men for each doorway, muskets loaded.' He looked at the windlasses. The great drums were still there, the wood rotten and dusty. 'Try and block the stairway with one of them.'

A shot echoed up the stairway, then another, then a splintering crash as the door was pounded down. Sharpe grinned at the Sergeant. 'Don't worry. They'll be cautious coming up here.'

Two Fusiliers tugged at the nearest windlass, snapping bits of wood from its decrepit frame, but achieving nothing. Harper gave one his seven-barrelled gun and a handful of the pistol cartridges he fed it with. 'Load that, son. Just like a bloody musket. Now stand back.'

He wrapped the huge arms about the vast wooden drum, tested his strength tentatively against the force of the anchors that held the axle to the huge beam beneath, and then the arms tightened, the legs pushed, his face was distorted with the effort, and still the drum would not move. One of the men guarding the staircase primed his musket, hastily levelled it, and fired down into the winding stair. A shout from below. That would slow them.

Harper tugged at the drum, swore at it, jerked it rhythmically so that his muscles tore at the ancient brackets. He pulled again, sinews like the ropes that had once raised the portcullis through the slit in the floor, and Sharpe saw a rusted angle-iron snap, heard the splintering of dry wood, and Harper's legs straightened as the drum rose ponderously clear, shedding old dust, and the Irishman carried it, gait as clumsy as a dancing bear, the burden looking like a hogshead of beer in his grasp and he grunted at the two guards to stand aside. He let it go into the stairway, it fell, crashing and bouncing, and then jammed itself into the bend. He wiped his hands and grinned. 'A present from the Irish. They'll have to burn the bastard out of there.' He went back to his seven-barrelled gun, finished the loading, and grinned at Sharpe. 'Next floor, sir?'

'Did I ever tell you you're a useful man to have around?'

'Tell my Ma, sir. She wanted to throw me back I was so little.' One of the Fusiliers laughed almost hysterically. His jacket was fresh and bright, a recruit, and Harper grinned at him. 'Don't worry, lad, they're far more scared of you than you are of them.' The boy was guarding the door onto the northern rampart, a rampart that had been clear of the enemy for no attack threatened from that side.

Sharpe went to the doorway that led to the turret's top and peered cautiously inside. An empty stair going up. A voice swore in the other staircase, a bayonet scraped on the wood of the blockage, but Sharpe had no fears now of an attack from below. He was frightened of this stairway, though. The men at the top would know by now that there was an enemy below. He was tempted to leave them there, but he knew that he could defend the summit of the gate-tower far more easily than this room. 'I'll go first.'

'With respect, sir, the gun's handier.' Harper hefted the seven barrels. It was true, but Sharpe could not let someone else lead.

'You follow.'

The staircase was like the first, bending inconveniently to the right, and Sharpe pushed away the inconsequential thought that Captains of the past must have sent their left-handed swordsmen first into stairways like this. He was frightened. Each step added to the fear, each step revealing another stretch of dark, blank wall. A single man with a musket would have no difficulty in killing him. He stopped, listening, wishing he had thought to remove his boots so that their ascent would be quieter.

Beneath him he heard muskets, a shout, and then the calm voice of the Fusilier Sergeant. The man could easily defend the chamber for a few minutes, but Sharpe half expected his small party to be marooned in this Castle for hours. He had to have the turret top and he thought of the defenders waiting up these stairs and he wished devoutly that he did not have to climb them. He could hear Harper fidgeting and grunting behind him and he shushed him irritably.

The Irishman pushed something at him. 'Here, sir.'

It was his green jacket. Sharpe understood. Hang the jacket on the sword tip because the defenders, nervous themselves, were just waiting for something to appear in the gloom of the stairway. Harper grinned and motioned with his gun, telling Sharpe to stay close to the shaft of the staircase so the Sergeant could fire past him and trust to the ricocheting of the seven bullets. Sharpe pushed the bloody tip of the sword into the collar of the jacket and, in the half-light, he could see the laurel wreath badge that was sewn onto the sleeve. Sharpe wore one himself, the coveted badge that said a Rifleman had gone first into a defended breach, yet Badajoz seemed so long ago now, the utter fear of it just a dulled memory, while the fear of this moment was so huge and paralysing. Death was so channelled and directed by this staircase, yet Sharpe had learned that the steps a man feared most were the ones that had to be taken. He climbed.

The jacket was ahead of him, a dark shape in the gloom, and he tried to remember how tall the gatehouse was, and how many steps it would take to reach the top, but he was confused. The turning of the stair had taken away his sense of direction, the fear turned each scrape of his boots' soles on the cold stone into a jab of alarm as he imagined the bullet striking from above.

The sword blade jarred on the central pillar. The jacket jerked with each step. It was a pathetic ruse, looking nothing like a man, but he told himself that the defenders would be nervous too. They were rehearsing in their minds what kind of attack would burst up these stairs, they were imagining death too on this Christmas Day.

The volley, when it came, was sickeningly close, and the bullets snatched at the jacket, billowed it, tore it, and Sharpe involuntarily ducked for the staircase seemed full of shrieking metal striking stone, and then the seven-barrelled gun exploded next to his ear, deafening him, and Sharpe screamed a challenge that he could not hear, twitched the jacket free of the sword point and charged up the stairs.

The jacket saved his life. He had thought only to discard it, to free the blade, but his right foot stepped on it, threw him painfully forward and tumbled Harper behind him. The Irishman crushed the breath from Sharpe, drove his ribs against the corners of the steps, and as they fell so the second volley, saved for this moment, flamed over their heads. Harper felt the hot breath of the guns, knew that the shots had missed, and he clawed his way forward over Sharpe's body and used the massive gun as a club in the doorway of the small turret that carried the staircase onto the tower's top.

Sharpe followed, his head ringing with the explosion of the seven-barrelled gun, and on the confined roof space his sword was the better weapon. The fear would have its outlet now, like a clawed animal released from a stinking cage, and he killed with the blade. He could hear nothing, only see the enemy who went back before him and he knew these men had drawn his nerves steel tight, had forced fear on him in a small place, and he killed with the efficient skill of his sword arm.

Six men cowered in a corner of the turret, weapons discarded, hands held up in supplication. Those the Riflemen ignored. Three men still fought, and those three died. Two with the sword, the third Harper picked up bodily and heaved into the courtyard, his dying scream being the first sound that penetrated Sharpe's fuddled, deafened ears.

He lowered the sword, his eyes grim on the terrified men who pressed back against the castellations. He breathed deep, shook his head. 'Jesus.'

Harper took the two bodies at the stairhead, one at a time, and hurled them after the other man. He looked at his officer. 'Stairways cleared and Castles taken. We should go into business, sir.'

'I didn't enjoy that.'

'Nor did they.'

Sharpe laughed. They had done it, they had taken the turret's top and he wondered who had last climbed those stairs in a fight and how many years before. Had it been before gunpowder? Had the last man to come into the sunlight of this rampart been in uncomfortable armour, swinging a short mace that would crush in the confined deathtrap of the winding stair? He grinned at Harper, slapped his arm. 'Well done.'

Whoever had been last up these stairs, fighting up, had

done exactly what Sharpe did now. He shouted down the stairway, shouted loud, and waited for the man to bring what he wanted. Bullets fluttered about their heads from the Castle's keep, but Sharpe ignored them. He shouted again, impatient, and here they were, staffs broken, but it did not matter.

On the old battlements, facing east, facing the Fusiliers and the Rifle Companies, Sharpe hung the Colours. They were discoloured by smoke, torn by explosion and bullet, but they were the Colours. Banners hanging from a Castle wall, the boast of a fighting man, banners hung by Sharpe and Harper. The gatehouse was taken.

CHAPTER 13

It had been a piece of pure bravado to hang the Colours on the gate-tower, each one fixed by driving an enemy bayonet through the flag and into the crumbling mortar of the battlements. It crossed Sharpe's mind that he and Harper had saved these Colours from Sir Augustus' impetuosity, from the man's stupidity, and Sharpe looked down at the place where Farthingdale had fallen. Smoke still drifted there, and then Sharpe swore and ducked as a bullet from the valley chipped at the stone by the flags. Someone down there thought the Colours had been captured, that the enemy was flaunting them.

'Sir?' Harper pointed north towards the Convent.

The Rocket Troop had arrived. The fight at the eastern wall had meant their passage of the pass, close to the Castle's northern wall, had been undisturbed. Now the wagons were parked on the road leading to the Convent, the troopers watching curiously the confusion of the failed attack.

Who was in charge down there? Was Sir Augustus alive? Sharpe had assumed Kinney's death, certainly the Welshman was hard hit, so who was giving the orders to the Companies that had escaped the explosion? Bullets made the air above the gate-tower a deadly place, bullets fired from both sides, from keep and from valley. Sharpe sat down and watched Harper load the seven-barrelled gun. 'We wait.' There was nothing Sharpe could do from the high turret. He had plucked some Fusiliers from the chaos, saved the Colours, and now they would have to sit it out until the Castle fell. He wished he had eaten some breakfast.

Sharpe had raised the Colours in bravado, but to the Fusiliers they were a taunt of failure. They did not see that it was Riflemen on the high battlement, they only saw their pride, their Colours, tacked to an enemy fortress. Men did not fight for King and Country so much as they fought for those squares of fringed silk, and the Fusiliers, recovering their order, saw the flags and no power on earth was going to stop them attempting to recover them. Six Companies had been untouched by the explosion, two others hardly affected, and now they turned, charged, and Frederickson launched his Riflemen ahead of them.

No one noticed that the guns in the watchtower had ceased firing. The battle was no longer being directed, it was now an expression of anger.

The bullets had stopped flickering about the gate-tower and Sharpe risked a look, saw the surge of men coming from the valley and turned back. 'Muskets!' He pointed to the guns that had belonged to the half-dozen prisoners who still cowered against the stones.

Harper raked the muskets towards them, selected four that were still loaded, and raised his eyebrows towards Sharpe.

'The cannon.'

The gun on the eastern wall, hard by the keep, was still the one weapon that could hurt the attack. It was a long shot for a musket, but the balls flying about the gunners' ears would at least discourage them. Sharpe levelled an unfamiliar French musket over the wall. It felt clumsy. He could see the gunners behind their embrasure, one holding the portfire which would spark the priming tube and slam the canister from the muzzle, and he aimed a little above the man's head and pulled the trigger. The gun hammered his shoulder, smoke blotted out his view, and then Harper's musket sounded in the next embrasure. Sharpe took the second musket, cocked it, and waited till the smoke of the first shot had thinned a little. Damn this still air!

The gunners had ducked, were looking wildly about for the source of the shots. Sharpe grinned, aimed lower, and once more a flint sparked on steel, priming exploded in his face, the burning powder stinging his cheek, and again the smoke obscured his view. Then there were cheers from the rubble, shouts of alarm from the courtyard, and Sharpe and Harper stood up and watched the scene from above.

Pot-au-Feu had no defence against this second attack. He had pinned all his hopes on the destructive power of the mine added to the desperation of his men, and now his defence collapsed. Sharpe saw, with satisfaction, the gunners leaving the cannon unfired, scrambling for the safety of the keep, and their example was being followed by the rabble in the courtyard. Red uniforms were flooding over the rubble, a line of green Riflemen ahead of them, and the Fusiliers were in no mood for mercy. They took the slim, seventeen-inch bayonets to the enemy, stabbed, and the blades came back reddened while Pot-au-Feu's men clamoured and fought to gain the safety of the single arched door that led into the keep.

A bugle was playing, a double note in the centre of each call that drove men to the charge, and Frederickson's Riflemen with their longer bayonets drove more fugitives towards the stable block beneath the western ramparts. They jumped the low wall, shouted their challenges, and the enemy ran.

Bayonets were not used often on the battlefield, at least not to kill. The force of the weapon was in the fear it provoked and Sharpe had witnessed dozens of bayonet charges when the blades never reached the enemy. Men would turn and run rather than face the edged steel. Yet here, in the confines of the courtyard, the Riflemen and Fusiliers had trapped an enemy with no space to run. They killed, as they had been trained to kill, and it took time before individual soldiers saw that some of the deserters were surrendering, and then the attackers began defending the unarmed prisoners against the fury of other men who still hunted with dripping blades.

Sharpe saw Frederickson, his patch and teeth removed, sending troops up the staircase which led, beside the stable block, to the western wall. The Castle was falling.

'Let's go down.'

Two more Fusiliers had come to the turret's top and Sharpe left them guarding the prisoners. He and Harper clattered down the staircase, mundane now that it was not a place of stifling fear, and they came into the large room where the wounded moaned and the Fusilier Sergeant turned a worried face to Sharpe. 'Our lads, sir?'

'Yes. Keep shouting down the stairs. They'll know your name, won't they?'

'Yes, sir.'

Sharpe opened the door that led to the northern wall. The rampart was empty. At its far end the firestep entered a tunnel in the north-western turret before turning left onto the western wall. As he watched he saw a figure appear in the turret, drop to one knee and bring up a rifle. Sharpe stepped into the sunlight. 'Don't shoot!'

Thomas Taylor, the American, jerked his rifle safely upwards. He grinned, knowing he had frightened Sharpe, then called over his shoulder. Frederickson appeared, sabre in hand, and his face showed astonishment and then pleasure. He ran down the rampart. 'Was that you on the top?'

'Yes.'

'Christ! We thought it was enemy. Jesus! I thought you were dead, sir!'

Sharpe looked at the courtyard where Pot-au-Feu's men made a desperate defence at the gateway to the keep. Otherwise it was chaos as Fusiliers took prisoners, searched them, and shouted triumphantly over their booty. 'Who's in charge?'

'Damned if I know, sir.'

'Farthingdale?'

'Haven't seen him.'

Sharpe could imagine what would happen if the Fusiliers

174

reached the liquor that Pot-au-Feu undoubtedly had within the keep. He gave orders to Frederickson, shouted more to Captain Cross whose Riflemen now lined the eastern wall, and turned to Harper. 'Let's see if we can find that bloody gold we delivered.'

'God! I'd forgotten it!' The Sergeant grinned. 'After you, sir.'

There was no resistance at the doorway that led from the ramparts into the keep. The Riflemen were already through, spreading out into the floors built about the keep's central courtyard. Prisoners were dragged from hiding places, booted down steep winding stairs, and Sharpe could hear the screams of women and the cries of frightened children. Then, looking through a crumbled and widened arrow slit at the southern side of the keep, he swore.

'Sir?'

'Look.'

It was his fault. One patrol of Rifles in the early morning would have discovered that there was an escape into the hills direct from the keep. Sharpe could not see it, but he guessed that the stones had fallen from part of the lower wall, and he could see the remnants of Pot-au-Feu's band scrambling through the thorns to the clearer turf of the hilltop. Scores of them; men, women and children, all escaping. He swore again. This was his fault. He should have scouted to the south.

Harper swore too, then pointed through the arrow-slit. 'More lives than a basketful of bleeding cats.'

Hakeswill, mounted on a horse, the long neck easily visible as he spurred the horse onto the hilltop. Harper climbed out of the embrasure. 'Won't get far, sir.'

Most would not get far. The winter and the Partisans would see to that, but Hakeswill had gone, slipped out into the world where he would plan more evil. Harper still tried to gloss over the failure. 'We must have got half of them, sir. More!'

'Yes.' It was a success, no doubt of that. Adrados would be seen to be avenged, the hostages had been rescued, the women captured on the Day of the Miracle had been saved, the priests who had preached Britain's calumny from their pulpits would have to eat humble pie. It was a success. Yet Sharpe could see his enemy on the hilltop, an enemy who paused, turned in his saddle, then rode over the crest. 'They'll have taken the bloody gold with them.'

'Like as not.'

Shouts, musket shots, the noises of hunters and hunted still came from the castle rooms. Redcoats were running through the floors now, looking for loot or women, and Sharpe and Harper elbowed them aside as they went downstairs into the courtyard. A bellow attracted them and they saw Frederickson, sabre still drawn, threatening Fusiliers. He saw Sharpe and grinned. 'Liquor's in there, sir.' He jerked his ghastly face at a door behind him. 'Enough to get London drunk.'

Prisoners were herded into the corners of the yard, a repetition of the scene last night in the Convent, and Sharpe watched as Fusilier officers took control of their men. It was over, all done, a Christmas Day's work. He looked at Frederickson who was marking the fight's end by donning his eye-patch. 'Anything else interesting?'

'You should look in the cellars, sir. Something nasty in the dark.'

The darkness was lifted by straw torches carried by curious men into the dungeons of the Castle. It was a miserable place. One vast room, low vaulted, wet and freezing, and Sharpe pushed through the crowd of Fusiliers and stopped at the edge of the horror. He saw a Sergeant. 'Don't just stand there! Get a detail of prisoners. Get rid of this!'

'Yes, sir.'

'Hakeswill?' Harper asked.

'Who knows? We can find out if any of the bastards will tell the truth.' Someone had been busy. The band of deserters at the Gateway of God had not been over brotherly. There had been punishment here, too, and the punishment was worse than any the army ever handed out. It stank in the cellar. Men had been mutilated here and Sharpe, looking into the grisly shadows, saw that women had been brought to this place of punishment as well. The bodies looked as though a madman had attacked them with an axe, then left them as rat food, and only one body, naked and stiff, was whole. It appeared to be untouched and Sharpe, curious, walked so he could see the man's head. 'Hakeswill did this.'

'How do you know?'

Sharpe tapped a fingernail against the skull. It sounded metallic. 'He's been killed with a flat headed nail.'

'What? Hammered in?'

'Not exactly. I saw him do it before. In India.' Sharpe told Harper the story and the Fusiliers listened. He told of being captured by the troops of the Sultan Tippoo and how he had been taken to the prison cells in Seringapatam and had watched, through the half-moon windows that looked out at ground level, the torture of British prisoners. Perhaps torture was too strong a word, for the men had died swiftly enough. The Tippoo Sultan, for his own pleasure and the pleasure of his women, employed Jetties, professional strong-men, and Sharpe had watched as men from the 33rd had been dragged over the sand to where the muscled men waited. The heels of the prisoners had left scuff marks, he remembered. They killed in two ways that day. The first was to clamp their massive forearms either side of the victim's head and, on a signal from the Tippoo, they would take a breath then jerk the head through half a circle. Another Jettie would hold the body still and, whatever the resistance of the prisoners, their necks would be wrung swift as a chicken.

The other method was to place a flat-headed nail on the victim's skull and then, with one massive blow of the palm, drive the nail six inches into the skull. That killed quickly too, if the job was not botched, and Sharpe remembered telling Sergeant Hakeswill what he had seen, the Sergeant listening with the other men about the bivouac fire. Hakeswill had tried it on Indian prisoners, practising until he had got it right. Damn Hakeswill. Sharpe had damned the Sultan Tippoo too, and he had killed him later when the British troops were assaulting the citadel of Seringapatam. Sharpe could still remember the look on the fat little man's face when one of his prisoners had come from the wrong end of the Water Tunnel where the Sultan was firing his be-jewelled fowling pieces at the British. That was a good memory, spoilt only by the ruby that Sharpe had cut from one of the pudgy, dead fingers. He had given that ruby to a woman in Dover, a woman he thought he loved more than life itself, and then she had run off with a bespectacled schoolteacher. He supposed she had been sensible. Who needs a soldier for a husband?

A burst of cheering startled him from the top of the dungeon steps, cheers and jeers, laughter and catcalls, and he left the bodies in their crusted horror and went up the steps to see what was causing the commotion.

Fusiliers and Riflemen had formed a rough corridor down which they propelled a prisoner with their musket and rifle butts. The prisoner made small, futile, placatory gestures with plump hands and he smiled left and right, bowed, then yelped as another musket butt prodded him in his ample buttocks. Pot-au-Feu. He was still dressed in his ludicrous Marshal's uniform, missing only the enamelled gold cross that had hung about his neck. He saw Sharpe and dropped to his knees, pleading in his deep voice while the enemy laughed about him. A Fusilier behind him raised a musket and aimed at the neck beneath the white-plumed hat. 'Put that down! Did you find him?'

'Yes, sir.' The man dropped the musket. 'He was in the stables, sir, hiding under a tarpaulin. Reckon he was too fat to run, sir.'

Sharpe looked at the fat face that babbled at him. 'Shut up!'

Silence from the quivering mass of uniformed fat. Sharpe walked round him, plucking the gorgeous hat from the cherubic white curls. 'This, lads, is your enemy. This is Marshal Pot-au-Feu.' The Fusiliers laughed. Some of them saluted the fat man whose eyes watched Sharpe as he circled. Each time Sharpe walked behind him the head jerked on its bed of chins to catch Sharpe coming round again. 'Not every day we capture a French Marshal, eh?' Sharpe tossed the hat to the man who had found Pot-au-Feu. 'I want him looked after, lads. Don't hurt him. Be very kind to him because he's going to be very kind to you.' The head jerked again, the eyes worried. 'He's really a Froggie Sergeant, this one, and he used to be a cook. A very, very good cook. So good that he's going to the kitchens now to make you a Christmas meal!'

They cheered that and watched as Sharpe pulled Pot-au-Feu to his feet. Sharpe brushed straw from the blue and gold jacket. 'Be good now, Sergeant! Don't put anything in the soup that shouldn't be there!' It was hard to connect this fat, happy-looking face with horror in the dungeons. Pot-au-Feu, understanding that he was not to be killed on the spot, was nodding eagerly at Sharpe.

'Look after him. Take him away.'

That made victory sweeter, alleviated the blunder of not blocking the escape route from the castle, to have captured the leader of this miserable band. Sharpe stood and watched the groups of prisoners being pushed together, listened to the shouts of women who pulled at their captors' arms and shrieked after husbands and lovers. It was still chaos in the yard.

A Rifle Lieutenant found him and saluted. 'Captain Frederickson's compliments, sir, and he says they've abandoned the watchtower.'

'Where is Captain Frederickson?'

'On the roof, sir.' The Lieutenant jerked his head at the keep.

'Leave three men guarding the liquor and ask the Captain to take the Company to the tower.' Sharpe did not like putting yet another burden on Frederickson, but he could hardly order a Company of the Fusiliers to the watchtower, not while he was still a junior officer to whoever was in command. That was a thought. Who was in command? Sharpe asked Fusiliers if they had seen Farthingdale, but they shook their heads, nor did they have news of Kinney. A Major Ford would be next in line for command of the Fusiliers, but Ford was missing too. 'Look for him!'

'Yes, sir.' A Sergeant of the Fusiliers backed from Sharpe's anger.

Sharpe looked at Harper. 'I could do with some lunch.'

'I'll take that as an order, sir.'

'No! I was just talking.'

Harper nevertheless followed Pot-au-Feu towards the Castle kitchens and Sharpe walked up onto the rubble of the eastern wall and smelt the smell of burned flesh. A miserable battle against a miserable enemy, and worse, a battle that need not have been fought. If the watchtower had been taken then the bodies that still littered the wide breach would not need to be here. The thought made him angry and he turned on a Captain of the Fusiliers who was clambering over the blackened stones. 'Hasn't anyone thought to bury these men?'

'Sir? Oh. I'll attend to it, sir. Major Sharpe?'

'Yes.'

The Captain saluted. 'Captain Brooker, sir. Grenadier Company.' Brooker was nervous.

'Well?'

'Colonel Kinney's dead, sir.'

'Oh, I'm sorry.' Sharpe truly was. He had liked Kinney in the short time he had known him, and he remembered the

Welshman saying what a tragedy it would be if any man was to die on this Christmas Day. 'I am sorry, Captain.'

'He was a good man, sir. Major Ford's dead too, sir.'

'Jesus!'

Brooker shrugged. 'In the back, sir. Shot.'

'Unpopular?'

Brooker nodded miserably. 'Very, sir.'

'It happens.' It did too, though no one liked to admit it. Sharpe had once heard a Captain, knowing his unpopularity, appeal to his men before battle to let the enemy kill him. They had granted him his wish.

Then Sharpe remembered. Ford had been the only Major with the Fusiliers, the second Major being on leave, and that meant Sharpe was senior officer. Except for Farthingdale. 'Have you seen Sir Augustus?'

'No, sir.'

'Are you senior Captain?'

Brooker nodded. 'Yes, sir.'

'Then I want one Company back in the Convent, and I want another sent to the watchtower, understand?'

'Yes, sir.'

'You'll find Riflemen there as well. And send someone to get those damned fools over here.' Sharpe pointed to the Rocket Troop who were wandering curiously towards the village.

'The prisoners, sir?'

'In the dungeons, once they're cleared up. Bring the ones from the Convent here, too. Strip them all.'

'Sir?'

'Strip them. Take their bloody uniforms off. They've disgraced them. And naked men find it hard to escape in this weather.'

Brooker nodded unhappily. 'Yes, sir.'

'And get these men buried! You can use prisoners. They can stay dressed if they're working outside. Do you have a surgeon with the Battalion?'

'Yes, sir.'

'Put him to work in the Convent. Move the wounded there.' Sharpe turned to look at the first two squads of Frederickson's Company going over the stones towards the watchtower five hundred yards away. Thank God for Riflemen. 'Carry on, Captain. Then come and find me. We're bound to have forgotten something.'

'Yes, sir.'

Farthingdale. Where the hell was Farthingdale? Sharpe walked through the scattered stones towards the spot where he had seen the Colonel fall, but there was no red, gold and black uniform among the dead. Nor was Sir Augustus' big bay horse lying in its own blood. Perhaps the Colonel still lived, in which case he was in command here, but where the hell was he?

A Lieutenant led another dozen Riflemen over the stones, but there were still some Greenjackets on the ramparts of the keep for a bugle suddenly startled the valley, a bugle blown from the topmost stone of the Castle, a bugle that sounded two quick calls. The first was nine notes long, the second just eight. 'We have discovered the enemy'. 'The enemy is cavalry'.

Sharpe stared at the ramparts. A face leaned out of an embrasure and Sharpe cupped his hands. 'Where?'

A hand pointed eastwards.

'What are they?'

'Lancers! French!'

Another enemy had come to the Gateway of God.

CHAPTER 14

There was one priority in Sharpe's head, just one, and he ran towards the Convent, arms waving, voice bellowing. 'Captain Gilliland! Captain Gilliland!'

He pounded over the road and saw with relief that the horses were still in the traces of the carts. 'Get them moving! Hurry!'

'Sir?' Gilliland was running from the Convent's door.

'Get this troop moving! Hurry! Into the Castle. Push that bloody cart aside, but hurry!' Sharpe pointed to the ox cart that blocked the main gate of the Castle. Gilliland was still gaping at him. 'For Christ's sake, move!'

Sharpe looked at the artillerymen spread up the valley towards the village. He cupped his hands. 'Gunners!'

He chivvied them, snapped at them, turned horses himself, and gradually the sense of urgency communicated itself to the men who had thought Christmas Day a day of rest. 'Move, you bastards! It's not a bloody funeral! Whip it up, man! Move!'

He was not fearing an attack by French cavalry. He guessed that the men on the keep had seen the advance scouts of a French force that had been sent to do what he had done last night; rescue the hostages. Now the three horsemen seen in the dawn made sense; they had been a patrol who had discovered that the work had been done for them, and doubtless the French now hoped to recover their own hostages under a flag of truce, but Sharpe still did not want them to see the strange carts and portable forge of the Rocket Troop. Perhaps he was right, and there would be no fight, or perhaps he was wrong. In which case the rockets, bundled inside their special cases on the long carts, would be the one surprise he could spring in this high valley. 'Move it!' Even if the French did see the carts they would have no idea of their purpose, but Sharpe wanted to take no chances. They would know there was something odd at the western end of the valley, and that something would give them caution. Surprise would be diluted.

Sharpe ran with the leading cart and bellowed at Fusiliers. 'Clear that gate! Hurry!'

Frederickson, reliable Frederickson, pushed past the men struggling with the cart. 'Lancers, sir. Green uniforms, red facings. There's only a dozen.'

'Green and red?'

'Imperial Guard, I think. Germans.'

Sharpe looked towards the village, but could see nothing. The valley floor fell beyond Adrados before turning right, turning south, and if he could not see them then they could not see the odd carts that were at last moving behind him into the Castle courtyard. German lancers. Men recruited from the duchies and small kingdoms that had allied themselves to Napoleon. There were far more Germans fighting against the Emperor than for him, but they were alike in one thing; they fought as well as any man on a battlefield. Sharpe looked for Gilliland. 'Hide your men in the stable, d'you hear me? Hide them!'

'Yes, sir.' Gilliland was appalled by the sudden urgency. His war, till now, had been a patient matter of angles and theories; suddenly death was just beyond the horizon.

'Where's your Company?' Sharpe turned back to the Rifle Captain.

'On their way, sir.' Frederickson nodded towards the Riflemen threading the thorn bushes. 'Ten minutes and they'll all be there.'

'I've ordered a Company of Fusiliers up there as well. I'll send another. Just make sure of one thing.'

'Sir?'

'Your Commission dates before theirs.'

Frederickson grinned. 'Yes, sir.' Whichever Captain had been promoted to the rank first would be in charge of the watchtower garrison, and Sharpe had no wish for this one-eyed fighter to be under anyone's command but his own. Frederickson would lie for him.

'And William?' It was the first time he had used his Christian name.

'Try Bill, sir.'

'Assume we'll have to fight eventually. That means you'll be holding that hill.'

'Yes, sir.' Sweet William went happily away with the promise not just of a fight, but his very own personal fight. Some officers hated responsibility, but the best welcomed it, wanted it, and would take it whether it was offered or not.

Now there were a dozen things for Sharpe to do. A second Company had to be despatched to the watchtower, Riflemen must be sent to the Convent, ammunition must be taken from Gilliland's carts and distributed as ready magazines about all the positions. He found Cross's bugler, then two Ensigns of the Fusiliers, and made them into his own messengers, and all the while fools came to him with problems they could have solved without his help. How was food to be taken to the watchtower? What about the packs left in the Convent? The rope that took water from the well in the keep was broken, and Sharpe snapped, cajoled, decided, and all the time watched the village for the first sight of the enemy horsemen.

Sergeant Harper, stolid and calm, walked to where Sharpe stood on the rubble of the mined wall and in one hand he carried a hunk of bread topped with meat and in the other a skin of wine. 'Lunch, sir. Bit late.'

'Have you eaten?'

'Yes, sir.'

God, he was hungry! It was cold lamb and the butter on

185

the bread was fresh and he bit into it and it tasted like heaven. A Fusilier Sergeant approached and wanted to know if the Castle gate should be blocked again, and Sharpe said no, but to keep the cart close, and then another man asked if they could bury Kinney in the very mouth of the pass where the grave would look for ever out to the green and brown hills of Portugal, and Sharpe said yes, and still the French cavalry loitered out of sight. Frederickson's men were at the tower, thank God, and Brooker had two Fusilier Companies following him, and Sharpe watched as a third Company set out for the Convent and he began to relax. A start had been made. The wine was cold and harsh.

He walked into the Castle courtyard and ordered the low wall pulled down and the stones used to block the stairway beside the stables that led to the western ramparts. He finished the lamb, licking the crumbs and grease from his hand, and then there was an imperious shout from the Castle gateway.

'Sharpe! Major Sharpe!'

Sir Augustus Farthingdale, Josefina mounted sidesaddle beside him, standing his horse in the archway.

Sir Augustus bloody Farthingdale, looking for all the world as if he was riding in London's Hyde Park. The only discrepancy was a clean white bandage that showed beneath his hat on his right temple. He was summoning Sharpe with jerks of his riding crop. 'Sharpe!'

Sharpe walked to the low wall. 'Sir?'

'Sharpe. My lady wife would like to see a rocket fired. Be so good as to arrange it.'

'That won't be possible, sir.'

Sir Augustus was not a man who liked to be crossed, and certainly not by an inferior officer in front of the love of his life. 'I think I gave an order, Mr Sharpe. I expect it to be obeyed.'

Sharpe put his right foot on the wall and the wineskin hung from the hand resting on the knee. 'If I demonstrated a

186

rocket for Lady Farthingdale, sir, then I am also demonstrating it to the French troops in the village.'

Josefina squeaked, looking excited, Sir Augustus stared at Sharpe as though the Rifle officer was mad. 'The what?'

'French troops, sir. In the village.' Sharpe looked at the ramparts of the keep and shouted. 'What d'you see?'

A Rifleman, from Cross's Company, bellowed back. 'Two squadrons Lancers, sir! Battalion of Infantry in sight now, sir!'

Infantry now! Sharpe twisted to look at the village, but still no French had pushed through the houses and come in sight. Farthingdale moved his horse forward, the hooves loud on the cobbles. 'Why the devil wasn't I told, Sharpe?'

'No one knew where you were, sir.'

'God damn it, man, I was with the doctor!'

'Nothing serious I trust, sir?'

Josefina smiled at Sharpe. 'Sir Augustus was hit by a stone, Major. In the explosion.' And Sir Augustus, Sharpe thought, had insisted on the doctor's attention when there were eviscerated, screaming men who needed it far more.

'God damn it, Sharpe! Why are they in the village?'

The question, Sharpe decided, really meant why had the French been allowed to reach the village; to which there was an obvious answer, an answer that even the author of 'Practical Instructions to the Young Officer in the Art of Warfare with Special Reference to the Engagements now Proceeding in Spain' should have known. The French were in the village because there were not enough troops to hold watchtower, Castle, and Convent, and still fight the French further east. Sharpe chose to read a different meaning into Sir Augustus's petulant enquiry. 'I imagine they've come for the same reason we came, sir. To rescue their hostages.'

'Are they going to fight?' Sir Augustus was not happy to ask the question, but he could not help himself. The author of 'Practical Instructions' had taken his material entirely from

Despatches and from the other books similar to his own, and he was not used to such close proximity to the enemy.

Sharpe pulled the plug from the wineskin's neck. 'I doubt it, sir. Their women are still with us. I expect we'll get a flag of truce within the half hour. Might I suggest we advise Madame Dubreton that she will be leaving us soon.'

'Yes.' Farthingdale was craning over Sharpe's head looking for a glimpse of the enemy. Nothing was yet in sight. 'Look after it, Sharpe.'

Sharpe looked after it, and he also sent Harper with a request to Gilliland for the loan of a saddle horse. He had no intention of letting Sir Augustus do all the talking with the enemy, and Sharpe's trust in the senior officer was not bolstered when he at last took an interest in Sharpe's preparations. He watched the soldiers dismantling the low wall and frowned. 'Why did you order that?'

'Because it's useless as a defence, sir. And anyway, if it comes to a fight I'd rather they got into the courtyard.'

Farthingdale was speechless for a moment. 'Into the courtyard?'

Sharpe wiped wine from his lips, restoppered the bottle, and smiled. 'A rat-pit, sir. Once inside they're trapped.' He made himself sound more confident than he felt.

'But you said they wouldn't fight.'

'I don't suppose they will, sir, but we should prepare against the possibility.' He told Farthingdale of his other precautions, of the garrison in the watchtower, and kept his voice polite. 'Is there anything else you'd want done, sir?'

'No, Sharpe, no. Carry on!'

Bloody Farthingdale. Major General Nairn, with his engaging indiscretion, had told Sharpe that Farthingdale had hopes of high command. 'Nothing dangerous, mind you, Christ no! One of those fancy rooms in the Horse Guards with chocolate soldiers saluting him. Thinks if he writes the right book then they'll give him the whole army to smarten up.' Nairn had looked gloomy. 'They probably will, too.'

Patrick Harper appeared from the stables leading two horses. He passed close to Sir Augustus and stopped by Sharpe. 'Horse, sir.'

'I see two.'

'Thought you might like company.' Harper's face was tight with annoyance. Sharpe looked at him curiously.

'What is it?'

'D'you hear what the man's saying?'

'No.'

'"My victory." He's telling her that he won here, so he is. Telling her that *he* took the Castle. And did you see her? She didn't even recognize me! Not so much as the time of day!'

Sharpe grinned, took the reins, and pushed his left foot into a stirrup. 'She has a fortune to protect, Patrick. Wait till he's gone, she'll say hello.' He pulled himself up. 'Wait here.'

He hid his annoyance from Harper, but he was affronted just the same. If Sharpe ever wrote a book like 'Practical Instructions', which he would not, then there would be one piece of advice repeated page after page. Always give credit where it is due, however tempting to take it for yourself, for the higher a man rises in the army the more he needs the loyalty and support of his inferiors. It was time, Sharpe decided, to puncture Sir Augustus' self-esteem. He pulled the horse round, walked it to where Farthingdale was pointing up at the Colours and describing the morning as a very satisfying little fight.

'Sir?'

'Major Sharpe?'

'I thought you should have this, sir. For your report.' Sharpe held out a scruffy, folded scrap of paper.

'What is it?'

'The butcher's bill, sir.'

'Ah.' A hand, gloved in fine leather, twitched the paper away and tucked it into his sabretache.

'Aren't you going to look at it, sir?'

189

'I was with the doctor, Sharpe. I've seen our wounded.'

'I was thinking of the killed, sir. Colonel Kinney, Major Ford, one Captain, and thirty-seven men, sir. Most of those died in the explosion. Wounded, sir. Forty-eight seriously, another twenty-nine not so serious. I'm sorry, sir. Thirty. I'd forgotten yourself.'

Josefina giggled. Sir Augustus looked at Sharpe as though the Major had just crawled out of a particularly malodorous sewer. 'Thank you, Major.'

'And my apologies, sir.'

'Apologies?'

'I haven't had time to shave.'

Josefina laughed outright and Sharpe, remembering that she had always liked her men to fight, gave her a look of anger. He was not her man, and he was not fighting for her, and then whatever he might have said was interrupted by a trumpet call, insistent and faraway, the tones of a French cavalry instrument.

'Sir!' The Rifleman on the keep. 'Four froggies, sir! One of 'em's got a white flag, sir. Coming this way!'

'Thank you!' Sharpe was tugging at the slings of his sword. He was not elegant on horseback, not like Sir Augustus, but at least the huge cavalry sword could hang properly at his side instead of being hitched half way up his ribs by shortened slings. He rebuckled the leather straps and looked about the courtyard. 'Lieutenant Price!'

'Sir?' Harry Price was tired.

'Look after Lady Farthingdale till we return!'

'Yes, sir!' Price seemed suddenly awake.

If Sir Augustus was peeved at this usurpation of his authority then Sharpe gave him no time to protest, nor did Sir Augustus choose to countermand the order. He followed Sharpe's horse through the shadowed sloping cobbles of the gateway, out onto the track and then right onto the grass where Sharpe let his horse have its head.

The trumpet was still calling, demanding a response from

the British positions, but at the appearance of the three horsemen the notes died to an echo. In front of the French officers was a Lancer, a white strip of cloth tied beneath his lance-head, and Sharpe remembered the white ribbons that decorated the hornbeam in the Convent and he wondered if the German Lancers who fought for Napoleon also worshipped their old forest Gods at Yuletide; the old pre-Christian name for the winter feast.

'Sir!' Sergeant Harper spurred up on Sharpe's left. 'Do you see, sir? The Colonel!'

It was, too, and at the same moment Dubreton recognized Sharpe and waved. The French Colonel touched spurs to his horse, went past the Lancer, splashed through the small stream and cantered towards them. 'Major!'

'Sharpe! Hold back!' Farthingdale's protest was lost as Sharpe also put his heels back and the two horsemen raced together, circled, then reined in so that the horses were alongside each other and facing different directions. 'Is she safe?'

Dubreton's eager request was in stark contrast to his studied calm when they had met before in the Convent. Then the Frenchman had been able to do nothing for his wife, now it was different.

'She's safe. Quite safe. Not even touched, sir. Can I say how glad I am?'

'God!' Dubreton shut his eyes. The bad dreams, the imaginings of all those drear nights seemed to flow out of him. He shook his head. 'God!' The eyes opened. 'Your doing, Major?'

'The Rifles, sir.'

'But you led them?'

'Yes, sir.'

Farthingdale reined in a few paces behind Sharpe and on his face was a look of fury because the Rifleman had offended decorum by racing ahead. 'Major Sharpe!'

'Sir.' Sharpe twisted in his saddle. 'I have the honour to

name Chef du Battalion Dubreton. This is Colonel Sir Augustus Farthingdale.'

Farthingdale ignored Sharpe. He spoke in what, to Sharpe's ears, sounded like fluent French, and then the other two French officers arrived and Dubreton made the introductions in his equally flawless English. One was a German Colonel of Lancers, a huge man with a red moustache and curiously gentle eyes, while the other was a French Colonel of Dragoons. The Dragoon Colonel wore a green cloak over his green uniform, and on his head was a tall metal helmet that had a cloth cover to stop the sun reflecting from the polished metal. He had a long straight sword and, unusual for a Colonel, a cavalry carbine rested in his saddle's bucket holster. A fighting Regiment, the Dragoons, hardened by chasing elusive Partisans through a hostile countryside, and Sharpe saw the Frenchman's disdain when he looked at the fastidious Sir Augustus. Behind the officers the Lancer picked at the knot of the white cloth.

Dubreton smiled at Sharpe. 'I owe you thanks.'

'No, sir.'

'But I do.' He looked at Harper, modestly holding back, and raised his voice. 'I'm glad to see you well, Sergeant!'

'Thank you, sir. Kind of you. And your Sergeant?'

'Bigeard's in the village. I'm sure he'll be glad to see you.'

Farthingdale interrupted in French, his voice implying annoyance at the civilities. Dubreton's replies were in English. 'We came, Sir Augustus, on the same mission as yourselves. May I express our pleasure at your success, my personal thanks, and my regrets that you have suffered casualties?' The stripped bodies of the dead waited white and cold beside the deepening graves.

Sir Augustus stayed talking in French, Sharpe suspected to exclude him from the discussion, while Dubreton, perhaps wishing the opposite, obstinately made his replies in English. The patrol Sharpe had half glimpsed in the dawn had been Dubreton's scouts, brave men who had volunteered to ride into the valley pretending to be deserters and who would have somehow escaped back before nightfall to guide the rescue party into the valley. They had seen the Riflemen, seen the flag hoisted, and had prudently withdrawn. 'They were disappointed, Sir Augustus!'

The Frenchwomen were to be handed over immediately, that Sharpe gathered from Dubreton's words, and then the conversation grew sticky and awkward because Sir Augustus was not able to answer the Frenchman's questions about the whereabouts of the French deserters. Farthingdale was forced to turn to Sharpe for help. Sharpe smiled ruefully. 'I'm afraid many escaped.'

'I'm sure you did everything possible, Major.' Dubreton said it tactfully.

Sharpe glanced at the two other Colonels. Two Regiments of Cavalry? It seemed a lot for this rescue attempt, but their presence had given him another idea. The Dragoon Colonel was looking at Sharpe's great sword that hung beside the cavalry sabre that was attached to his borrowed saddle. Sharpe grinned. 'Our weakness, Colonel, was in cavalry. We chased them out of the Castle, but we can't do much about rounding them up in the hills.' He looked southwards. 'Not, I think, that they'll have got very far.'

Dubreton understood. 'They went south?'

'Yes.'

'How long ago?' Sharpe told him and Dubreton's face was mischievous. 'We have cavalry.'

'I'd noticed, sir.'

'I think we could help.'

Sir Augustus, seeing things run away from his careful control, pushed his horse forward. 'Are you suggesting the French chase our fugitives, Sharpe?'

Sharpe turned an innocent face onto the Colonel. 'That seems to be why they're here, sir. I can't really see how we can stop them.'

Dubreton cut in smoothly. 'I would suggest, Sir Augustus,

that we fight together under a truce. We will not attempt to disturb your occupation of the Castle, the Convent or the watchtower. You, in turn, will allow us to bivouac in the village. In the meantime our cavalry will drive the fugitives back to this valley where the infantry can wait for them.'

'His Majesty's Army is quite capable of managing its own affairs, Colonel.' Farthingdale was appalled at the suggestion.

'Of course it is.' Dubreton glanced once at the bodies, back to Sir Augustus. 'The truth is, Sir Augustus, that our Dragoons started their sweep an hour ago.' He smiled deprecatingly. 'If you prefer that we should fight for the honour of capturing them then I assure you that the Emperor's army is also quite capable of managing its own affairs.' That was a couple of fine aces to lay on the table. Sir Augustus took refuge in questions.

'You've begun? A truce, do you say?'

Dubreton smiled patiently. 'We have begun, Sir Augustus. Shall we say we anticipated your generous help? And why not a truce? It's Christmas Day, there always used to be a Truce of God on such a day, so why not for us? Can I suggest till midnight tonight? Perhaps we can discuss what happens after that at dinner tonight. You will do us the honour of being our guests?'

'Till midnight?' Sir Augustus made it another question, buying more time for his thoughts to probe every suspicion that he had of this proposal, but Dubreton pretended to mistake the inflection.

'Splendid! We are agreed! Till midnight, then, and you will be our guests?'

Sharpe smiled at the deftness of Dubreton's handling of Sir Augustus. 'I'm sure we can accept with pleasure, sir, on one condition.'

'A condition? For dinner?'

'That we supply the cook, sir.'

Dubreton laughed. 'You supply the cook? You offer that to a Frenchman! You Riflemen are braver than I thought.'

Sharpe enjoyed his next words. 'Pot-au-Feu, with our compliments.'

'You have him?'

'In our kitchens. If I'm eating with you tonight, then I'd rather he was in yours.'

'Splendid, splendid!' Dubreton looked at Sir Augustus. 'We are agreed then, Sir Augustus?'

Farthingdale was still suspicious, far from happy, but he was being forced to take guidance from the one man who did understand the enemy and how to fight them. Sharpe. More important, Sharpe understood when not to fight. Sir Augustus inclined his handsome, thin head. 'We are agreed, Colonel.'

'Do I have your permission to ride to the Convent?'

Farthingdale nodded.

Dubreton spoke briefly to the cavalrymen, watched them spur towards the village, then walked his horse between Sharpe's and Sir Augustus' and once again the conversation dropped into French. It sounded polite, the small talk of enemies on a sunlit Christmas Day and Sharpe dropped back so that he was alongside Harper. He grinned at the big Irishman. 'We've got new allies, Patrick. The French.'

'Yes, sir.' Harper took pride in showing no surprise. 'Whatever you say, sir.'

CHAPTER 15

Christmas afternoon was as festive as any man could have wished. At first the Fusiliers were disbelieving, then delighted, then they had mixed happily with Dubreton's Battalion as they formed a rough cordon that waited for the fugitives to be chased from the hills. Within an hour no Frenchman was wearing a French shako, all wore British, and men exchanged uniform buttons, liquor, food, tobacco, and sought out translators so they could exchange memories of shared battles.

A half hour after that, the first fugitives appeared. It was mostly women and children who came first, those who had little to fear from capture, and the women sought out troops of their own side and begged them for protection. Behind them there was an occasional faraway sound of a Dragoon's carbine chivvying a laggard.

Sharpe missed it all. For the first forty-five minutes he was with Harper in the Convent. It was impossible to move the gun without the French seeing their efforts, so Sharpe abandoned his hopes of mounting it in the Convent gateway. Instead he explored the cellars, climbing into a dirty, damp space beneath the floors of the chapel and store-rooms, and then he left Harper and a work party busy with materials captured from Pot-au-Feu. Sharpe would prepare a surprise or two in case they were needed.

Then he cut over the field, between the fraternising troops, and guided the horse slowly along one of the twisting paths that climbed to the watchtower. The thorns were thick, good protection, but the hill was far from the support of any troops in the Castle. Frederickson waved to him from the tower's summit as Sharpe dismounted, gave the reins to a Rifleman, then stood for a few seconds and looked at the position. It was good. The Spaniards had built earthern ramparts that faced the valley, and behind the ramparts were two of the four-pounder guns that dominated the steep slope of the hill to the north. To the west and to the east the slope was just as severe, just as thickly tangled with thorns, only to the south was the slope more gentle. Cursing Riflemen were hacking out another pit, readying it for one of the guns, and Sharpe saw with approval how Frederickson had ordered thorn bushes cut and placed on the southern slope as a barrier. One company of Fusiliers was still hacking at bushes, while the other formed a cordon to ward off Pot-au-Feu's returning men.

Sharpe climbed the steps inside the tower, emerged onto the turret, and greeted Frederickson. The Rifle Captain was cheerful. 'I hope the bastards make a fight of it, sir!'

'You do?'

'I could hold this place through Armageddon.'

'You may have to.' Sharpe grinned and rested his telescope on one of the crumbling ramparts. He stared long and hard at the village, seeing little, then panned it right where the valley wound about the hill before turning east again and disappearing. 'How many have you seen?'

Frederickson fished a piece of paper from his pocket and handed it wordlessly to Sharpe. 'Lancers, 120. Dragoons, 150. Infantry, 450.' Sharpe grunted and gave it back. 'Bit unbalanced, isn't it.' He stared eastward, the view magnificent, and he remembered now how the guns had ceased firing from the watchtower during the battle. The men up here must have seen the approaching French and taken fright, and doubtless the keep's defenders had seen them, too, and spread panic amongst Pot-au-Feu's men. The victory this morning, ragged as it already was, was diminished because the arrival of the French had dispirited the enemy. He looked where the turn of the valley carried the road out of sight. 'I wonder what's round the corner.'

'I wondered about that, too. I sent a patrol up there, but we were turned back. It was very polite, but it was very firm. *Vamos.*'

'So they must be hiding something.'

Frederickson scratched beneath the eye-patch. 'I don't trust the bastards one inch.' He sounded cheerful.

'Nor me. Have you seen any supplies?'

Frederickson shook his head. 'Not a thing.'

'There's more of them round the bloody corner.' The French infantry had to eat, the horses of the cavalry would need forage, and so far Sharpe had seen no sign of the French supplies. To the south east, where the road turned away, he could see a group of Lancers trotting on the grass. 'Did they turn you away?'

'That's them. Crawling all over that area.' Frederickson shrugged. 'Nothing I can do it about it, sir. No patrol of mine can outrun those bastards.'

'Send two men out tonight.'

'Yes, sir. I hear we're invited to dinner.'

Sharpe grinned. 'You're too ill to go. I'll make your excuses for you.' He talked for ten minutes, feeling the bitter cold seep back as the sun sank, and then he turned to go. He paused on the top step of the turret. 'You don't mind missing dinner?'

'You'll make it up to me.' Frederickson sounded happy, the more Sharpe had talked the more imminent a fight seemed for the morrow, and tonight, while Sharpe dined, Frederickson had preparations to make, surprises to prepare.

Farthingdale had approved of all Sharpe's efforts to prepare a defence of the Gateway of God, but his motive, Sharpe knew, was not because he feared an attack. Sir Augustus had sententiously quoted from his own book. 'Busy troops, Sharpe, are troops not liable to make mischief.'

'Yes, sir.'

Now, riding back to the Castle, Sharpe wondered if again he was letting his imagination run wild. He was convinced that tomorrow he might have to fight, yet there were no real reasons for thinking that. The French had reason to be in the valley, just as the British did, and within minutes the job both sides had come to do would be finished and there would seem no reason why either side should stay in the Gateway of God. Except. Except instinct. Farthingdale had mocked that instinct, accusing Sharpe of wanting a fight, and refusing to allow a Fusilier Lieutenant to be sent with a message across the border. 'Making an alarm over a handful of cavalry and a small battalion! Don't be ridiculous, Sharpe!' Farthingdale had withdrawn to his rooms, the same ones that Pot-au-Feu had inhabited, and Sharpe had seen Josefina appear on a balcony that some late owner of the Castle had built high on the keep and facing west. The room and balcony would have a magnificent view.

Back in the Castle yard Sharpe relinquished the horse and asked a Rifleman to fetch him hot water. He stripped off his uniform jacket, peeled the overalls to his waist, then pulled off the dirty shirt. Daniel Hagman gave Sharpe a toothless smile and picked up the jacket. 'Want me to brush it, sir?'

'I'll do it, Dan.'

'God help us, but you're a bloody awful Major, sir.' Hagman was the oldest man in Sharpe's Company, nearing fifty, and his age and loyalty gave him a freedom with Sharpe. 'You have to learn to have things done for you, sir, like the nobs.' Hagman began scraping at a bloodstain. 'You're eating with the quality, sir, and you can't go looking like a tinker.'

Sharpe laughed. He took his razor from the pocket in his overalls, unfolded it, and looked with displeasure at its thin blade. He must get a new one. He stropped it half-heartedly on his boot, splashed water on his face, then, not bothering to find any soap, began shaving. 'You still got my rifle, Dan?'

'I have, sir. Do you want it?'

'Not if I'm eating with the quality.'

'You'll probably get a knife and fork, sir.'

'Probably, Dan.'

'Squire used to eat with a fork.' Hagman was from Cheshire, only in the army because he had finally lost his lifelong battle with the Squire's gamekeepers. He spat on Sharpe's jacket and rubbed vigorously. 'Can't see the call for a fork, sir, I can't. Not after the good Lord gave us fingers.'

The Fusiliers lit a fire in the courtyard, the flame catching on straw fetched from the stable, the sudden flames accentuating the dusk. Sharpe wiped his face on his shirt, pulled it back on, and slowly did up the straps of his captured French overalls. Hagman beat the jacket on the ground to rid it of the last scraps of dust and held it out. 'Smart as a whip, sir.'

'That'll be the day, Dan.' Belt, crossbelt, ammunition pouch, sash, and sword completed Major Sharpe. He bashed out a dent in his shako as Hagman nodded towards the keep. 'Here comes his Lordship, sir. Had us running up and down the bleeding stairs all afternoon with timber for his bleeding fire, food for his lady. She the lady you knew at Talavera, sir?'

'That's the one.'

'Does he know he's not the first one to fire that musket?' Sharpe smiled. 'No.'

'What you don't know, don't fret you.' Hagman hurried away as Sir Augustus headed for Sharpe.

'Sharpe!' That indignantly voiced syllable was becoming the bane of Sharpe's life.

'Sir?'

'I expect our party to be ready to leave in one hour. Do you understand?'

'Yes, sir.'

'Her Ladyship is accompanying me. Will you tell all officers that I expect them to remain sober and dignified. There are appearances to be kept up.'

'Yes, sir.' Sharpe suspected the admonition was aimed at him. Farthingdale did not believe Sharpe to be a gentleman, and therefore that he was prone to drunkenness.

'Sir!' A shout from the gateway.

'What is it?' Farthingdale frowned at the interruption.

'French officer coming, sir. With a detail.'

'How many?' Sharpe asked.

'Dozen, sir.'

Sharpe would not have let them in, would have gone out of the gate so that the French would not have a chance to gauge the paltry defences of the Castle, but Farthingdale shouted at the sentries to let the Frenchmen pass. Sharpe glanced at the stable and waved the Rocket Troop out of sight. It was possible, he conceded, that Dubreton already knew of their existence. The soldiers of both sides had mixed freely, talked openly, and Sharpe's only hope of keeping the rockets a surprise lay in the incredulity of the ordinary enemy soldier and the difficulties of translation.

The hooves of the French horses sparked on the cobbles of the archway, echoed loud from ancient stone, and then Dubreton led them into the courtyard. The sun was scarlet and glorious, low in the Christmas sky, its light lustrous on the flank of the Frenchman's horse. He smiled at Sharpe. 'I owe you a favour, Major Sharpe.' His horse stopped, edged away from the sudden crackle of wood on the fire. Dubreton soothed it. 'I have come to repay my debt in part, a very small part, but I hope it pleases you.'

He turned and beckoned to the Dragoons behind him who split apart, revealing Sergeant Bigeard uncomfortable and vast on horseback. Sharpe smiled. Bigeard's right hand was twisted in dirty grey hair, the hair of Obadiah Hakeswill.

Sharpe smiled at the Frenchman. 'I thank you, sir.'

Obadiah Hakeswill, captured and helpless, still dressed in the borrowed finery of a British infantry Colonel. Sergeant Bigeard nodded a greeting at Sharpe, released his grip of Hakeswill's hair and booted him forward.

There was joy in this moment, such joy, the joy of nineteen years hatred come to this place, this hour, this helplessness of a man who had spent his life tormenting the weak and working evil. Obadiah Hakeswill, a prisoner, the yellow face twitching on its elongated neck, the bright blue eyes still darting about the courtyard as if hoping for some escape. Sharpe walked slowly forward, and still the eyes looked for a way out of this place, but then the eyes snapped to Sharpe because there was the sound of a sword scraping from a scabbard.

Sharpe smiled. 'Private Hakeswill. You lost your Sergeantcy, did you know?' The head twitched, the eyes blinked, and Sharpe waited till Hakeswill was still. 'Shun!'

Automatically, a lifetime of soldiering behind him, Hakeswill slammed upright, hands at his side, and at the same instant, catching the fire of the sinking sun, the long sword went to his throat. The blade was held at Sharpe's full arm's length, its tip barely quivering at Hakeswill's adam's apple. Silence.

Men in the courtyard sensed the anger from the two men. Fusiliers and Riflemen stopped, turned, and watched the sword.

Only Farthingdale moved. He stepped forward, his eyes horribly caught by the level, unmoving sword, and he feared the sudden rush of bright blood in the sunset. 'What are you doing, Sharpe?'

Sharpe spoke softly, each word clear and slow. 'I was thinking of skinning the bastard alive, sir.' His eyes stayed on Hakeswill.

Farthingdale looked at Sharpe and the setting sun lit the left side of the scarred face, a face implacable and frightening, and Farthingdale felt the fear. He feared cold-blooded death, and he feared that one word from him might provoke it. His protest, when it came, sounded feeble even to his own ears. 'The man must be tried, Sharpe, by a Court-Martial. You can't kill him!'

Sharpe smiled, still looking at Hakeswill. 'I said I'd skin him alive, not dead. Do you hear that, Obadiah? I can't kill you.' He suddenly raised his voice. 'This is the man who can't be killed! You've all heard of him, well here he is! Obadiah Hakeswill. And soon you'll see a miracle. You'll see him dead! But not here, not now! In front of a firing squad.'

The great blade stayed where it was. The French Dragoons, who had spent too many aching hours strengthening their sword arms by doing just what Sharpe was doing, appreciated the strength of a man who could hold a heavy cavalry sword at full stretch for so long, and keep it so still.

Hakeswill coughed. He sensed death retreating from him and he looked at Farthingdale. 'Permission to speak, sir?' Farthingdale nodded and Hakeswill screwed his face into a smile. The red light of sun and fire was reflected onto his yellow skin by the sword. 'Welcome a Court-Martial, sir, welcome it. You gentlemen are fair, sir, I know that, sir.' He was at his most obsequious.

Farthingdale was at his most patronizing. Here, at last, was a soldier who understood how to address his superiors. 'You shall have a fair trial, I promise you that.'

'Thank you, sir. Thank you.' Hakeswill would have knuckled his forehead except that the sword still terrified him.

'Mr Sharpe! Put him with the other prisoners!' Farthingdale felt he had defused the situation, was in command again.

'I will, sir, I will.' Sharpe still looked at Hakeswill, his eyes had not moved since the sword was drawn. 'What uniform is that, Private?'

'Uniform, sir?' Hakeswill pretended that he had never noticed the rank of his uniform. 'Oh this, sir! I found it, sir, found it.'

'You're a Colonel, are you?'

'No, sir. Course not, sir.' Hakeswill looked at Sir Augustus and gave him the full benefit of his rotting grin. 'I was forced to wear it, sir, forced! After they forced me to join them, sir!'

'You're a bleeding disgrace to that uniform, aren't you?'

The blue eyes came back to Sharpe. 'Yes, sir, if you say so, sir.'

'I do, Obadiah, I do.' Sharpe smiled again. 'Take it off.'

Dubreton smiled and tossed a translation over his shoulder. Bigeard and the Dragoons grinned, settled forward on the pommels of their saddles.

'Sir?' Hakeswill appealed to Farthingdale, but the sword tip was pressed against his throat.

'Strip, you bastard!'

'Sharpe!' That damned syllable.

'Strip! You poxed bastard! Strip!'

The sword blade flickered, left and right, starting blood from the skin over Hakeswill's adam's apple, and the gross, lumpen man tore at the red officer's sash, pulled at his belts, at the empty scabbard, and then scrambled out of the red jacket and dropped it on the cobbles.

'Now trousers and boots, Private.'

Farthingdale protested. 'Sharpe! Lady Farthingdale is watching! I insist this stops!'

Hakeswill's eyes looked towards the balcony and Sharpe knew that by standing at the very end of the platform Josefina could see into the courtyard. Sharpe kept the sword steady. 'If Lady Farthingdale doesn't like the view, sir, I suggest she goes inside. In the meantime, sir, this man has disgraced his uniform, his country, and his Regiment. For the moment I can only take one of those things away from him. Strip!'

Hakeswill sat, pulled off the boots, then stood to remove the white trousers. He shivered slightly, dressed only in the long white shirt that was buttoned from neck to knees. The sun had dipped beneath the western ramparts.

'I said strip.'

'Sharpe!'

Sharpe hated this yellow-skinned, lank-haired, twitching man who had tried to kill his daughter, to rape his wife, this man who had once flogged Sharpe so that the ribs showed through the torn flesh, this man who had murdered Robert Knowles. Sharpe wanted to kill him here and now, in this courtyard with this blade, but he had long ago sworn that justice would be seen to kill the man who could not be killed. A firing party would do that thing, and then Sharpe could write the letter he had long wanted to write to Knowles' parents and tell them their son's murderer had met his end.

Hakeswill looked up at Josefina, back to Sharpe, then stepped back two paces as if he could escape the sword. Bigeard lashed out with his foot, throwing him forward, and Hakeswill looked at Sir Augustus. 'Sir?'

The sword arm moved at last. Up, down, across, and the shirt was torn, blood seeping from the shallow cuts. 'Strip!'

The hands tore at the shirt, ripping it, bursting buttons free, and Hakeswill stood there, the tatters of pride at his feet, and on his face a hatred that was strong as life itself.

Sharpe hooked the shirt towards him, wiped the tip of the blade, then rammed it into the scabbard. He stepped back. 'Lieutenant Price!'

'Sir?'

'Four men to put Private Hakeswill into the dungeon! I want him tied up there!'

'Yes, sir!'

The courtyard seemed to relax. Only Hakeswill, mis-shapen and naked, was tense with anger and hate. Riflemen pulled him away, the same Riflemen he had stripped of their greenjackets before the assault on Badajoz.

Dubreton gathered his reins. 'I think, perhaps, you should have killed him.'

'Perhaps, sir.'

Dubreton smiled. 'On the other hand we have not killed Pot-au-Feu. He's hard at work preparing your dinner.'

'I look forward to it, sir.'

CHAPTER 16

German voices, singing carols, faded behind them as they rode horses slowly towards the village. Eight officers and Josefina were dining with the French.

The torches that illuminated the village street flamed inside soft haloes. There was a night mist. Sir Augustus was in a playful mood, a heavy playfulness, perhaps because Josefina was looking as sultry and beautiful as artifice could make her. He looked across her at Sharpe. 'Perhaps they'll serve you frog's legs, Sharpe!'

'One can only hope, sir.'

There would be a hard frost tonight. To the south and overhead the stars were visible through the fine mist, Christmas stars, but the northern sky was dark, spreading south, and Sharpe could smell bad weather in the air. Pray God it would not be snow. He did not relish struggling from the Gateway of God, guarding the British, Portuguese and Spanish prisoners who were crammed into the Castle's dungeon, struggling with them and Gilliland's carts down the snow covered pass. Then, he thought, they might not be leaving in the morning. It depended on the French and their plans.

Dubreton waited for them at the door of the inn. It was a large building, far too large for such a tiny village, yet once it had served as a house for travelling men who crossed the Sierra and wanted to avoid the tolls of the southern road. The war had dulled trade, but still the building looked inviting and warm. A tricolour hung from an upstairs window, lit by two straw and resin torches, while unarmed soldiers came forward to take the horses. Farthingdale left the introductions to Sharpe. Four Captains, including Brooker and Cross, and two Lieutenants including Harry Price.

Once inside, Dubreton conducted Josefina to the room where the Frenchwomen prepared themselves. Sharpe heard delighted voices greeting their former companion in misfortune, and then he smiled as he saw the trouble that had been taken for the meal.

All the inn's tables had been pushed together, making one great table covered in white cloths, and tall candles showed more than two dozen place settings. Forks, as Hagman had feared, gleamed silver beneath the flames. Wine bottles stood open on a sideboard, ranks of them, a whole Battalion of wine, while bread, hard crusted, waited in baskets on the table. A fire burned in the hearth, its warmth already reaching to the inn's main door.

An orderly took Sharpe's greatcoat, another brought a great bowl from which steam arose and Dubreton ladled out glasses of punch. A dozen French officers waited in the room, their smiles welcoming, their eyes curious to see their enemy so close. Dubreton waited till the orderly had passed the punch around. 'I wish you gentlemen a happy Christmas!'

'A happy Christmas!'

There was a smell from the inn's kitchens that could have been a foretaste of paradise.

Farthingdale raised his glass. 'To a gallant enemy!' He repeated it in French.

'To a gallant enemy!'

Sharpe drank and his eye was caught by a French officer who, unlike the others, was not dressed as either an infantryman, a Lancer, or a Dragoon. His uniform was plain blue, very dark, without a single badge of rank or unit mark. He wore spectacles, wire bound, and his face showed the ravages of childhood smallpox. The eyes, small and dark like the man himself, caught Sharpe's and there was none of the friendliness that the other officers showed.

Dubreton returned Sir Augustus' compliment and then announced that dinner would be another half hour yet, that the orderlies would keep their glasses charged, and that his officers had been chosen for their English, mostly bad, but please would they consider themselves welcome. Farthingdale made a small response and then chivvied the British officers towards the waiting French. Sharpe, hating small talk, moved to a shadowed corner of the room and was astonished that the small dark man in his blue, plain uniform headed for him. 'Major Sharpe?'

'Yes.'

'More punch?'

'No, thank you.'

'You prefer wine?' The voice was harsh, the tone mocking.

'Yes.'

The Frenchman, whose English accent was almost too perfect, snapped his fingers and Sharpe was startled by the alacrity with which an orderly responded to the summons. This man was feared. When the orderly was gone the Frenchman looked up at the Rifleman. 'Your promotion is recent, yes?'

'I don't have the honour of your name.'

A quick smile, instantly gone. 'Ducos. Major Ducos, at your service.'

'And why should my promotion be recent, Major?'

The smile came again, a secret smile as if Ducos harboured knowledge and revelled in it. 'Because in the summer you were a Captain. Let me see, now. At Salamanca? Yes. Then at Garcia Hernandez where you killed Leroux. A pity that, he was a good man. Your name didn't come to my ears at Burgos, but I suspect you were recovering from the wound Leroux gave you.'

'Anything else?' The man had been absolutely right in everything, annoyingly right. Sharpe noticed the buzz of conversation growing in the rest of the room, the beginning of laughter, and he noticed too that all the French had given this small man a wide berth. Dubreton looked over, caught Sharpe's eye, and the French Colonel gave a tiny, almost apologetic shrug.

'There's more, Major.' Ducos waited for the orderly to give Sharpe his wine. 'Have you seen your wife in the last few weeks?'

'I'm sure you know the answer to that.'

Ducos smiled, taking it as a compliment. 'I hear La Aguja is in Casatejada, and in no danger from us, I assure you.'

'She rarely is.'

The insult went past Ducos as if it had never been uttered. The spectacles flashed circles of candle-light at Sharpe. 'Are you surprised I know so much about you, Sharpe?'

'Fame is always surprising, Ducos, and very gratifying.' Sharpe sounded wonderfully pompous to himself, but this small, sardonic Major was annoying him.

Ducos laughed. 'Enjoy it while you can, Sharpe. It won't last. Fame bought on a battlefield can only be sustained on a battlefield, and usually that brings death. I doubt you'll see the war's end.'

Sharpe raised his glass. 'Thank you.'

Ducos shrugged. 'You're all fools, you heroes. Like him.' He jerked his head towards Dubreton. 'You think the trumpet will never stop.' He sipped his glass, taking very little. 'I know about you because we have a mutual friend.'

'I find that unlikely.'

'You do?' Ducos seemed to like being insulted, perhaps because his power to hurt back was absolute and secret. There was something sinister about him, something that spoke of a power which could afford to ignore soldiers. 'Perhaps not a mutual friend, then. Your friend, yes. Mine? An acquaintance, perhaps.' He waited for Sharpe's curiosity to give voice, and laughed when he knew Sharpe would say nothing. 'Shall I give a message to Helene Leroux for you?' He laughed again, delighted by the effect of his words. 'You see? I can surprise you, Major Sharpe.'

Helene Leroux. La Marquesa de Casares el Grande y Melida Sadaba, Sharpe's lover in Salamanca, whom he had last seen in Madrid before the British retreated to Portugal. Helene, a woman of dazzling beauty, a woman who spied for France, Sharpe's lover. 'You know Helene?'

'I said so, didn't I.' The spectacles flashed their circles of light. 'I always tell the truth, Sharpe, it so often surprises people.'

'Give her my respects.'

'Is that all! I shall tell her you gaped at the mention of her name, not that that surprises me. Half the officers in France fall at her feet. Yet she chose you. I wonder why, Major? You did kill her brother, so why did she like you?'

'It was my scar, Ducos.' Sharpe touched his face. 'You should get one.'

'I stay clear of battles, Sharpe.' The smile came and went. 'I hate violence, unless it is necessary, and most battles are just brawls where nobodies make fleeting names for themselves. You haven't asked me where she is.'

'Would I get an answer?'

'Of course. She has returned to France. I fear you won't see her for a long time, Major, not till the war is over, perhaps.'

Sharpe thought of his wife, Teresa, and he thought of the guilt that he had felt when he had betrayed her, but he could not erase the blonde Frenchwoman, married to her ancient Spanish Marques, from his mind. He wanted to see her again, to see again a woman who matched a dream.

'Ducos! You're monopolizing Major Sharpe.' Dubreton cut in between them.

'I thought Sharpe the most interesting of your guests.' Ducos did not bother to say 'sir'.

Dubreton's dislike of the Major was obvious. 'You should talk to Sir Augustus, Ducos. He's written a book so he must be fascinating.' Dubreton's scorn of Sir Augustus was equally evident.

Ducos did not move. 'Sir Augustus Farthingdale? A functionary only. Large parts of his book were drawn from Major Chamberlin's of the 24th.' He sipped his punch and looked about the room. 'You have officers of the Fusiliers, one man from the South Essex, and one Rifleman, excluding yourself, Major Sharpe. Let me see now. One full Battalion? The Fusiliers. One Company of the 60th, and your own Company. You were hoping to make us think you had more men?'

Sharpe smiled. 'One Battalion of French infantry, one hundred and twenty Lancers, and one hundred and fifty Dragoons. And one functionary, Major. Yourself. We're well matched.'

Dubreton laughed, Ducos scowled, and then the French Colonel took Sharpe's elbow and led him away from the small man. 'He is a functionary, but more dangerous than your Sir Augustus.'

Sharpe looked back at Ducos. 'What is he?'

'What he wills. He's from Paris. He used to be one of Fouché's right hand men.'

'Fouché?'

'How fortunate you are not to know the name.' Dubreton took another glass of punch from a passing tray. 'A policeman, Sharpe, working behind the scenes. He is periodically disgraced and loses the Emperor's favour, but these men always come back.' He jerked his head at Ducos. 'Another fanatic, spying on his own side. For him today is not Christmas Day, it is the 5th of Nivose, year 20, and it does not matter to him that the Emperor abolished the Revolutionary Calendar. He burns with the passion.'

'Why did you bring him?'

'What choice do I have? He decides where he will go, who he speaks to.'

Sharpe turned to look at Ducos. The small Major smiled at Sharpe, revealing teeth stained red by the punch.

Dubreton ordered more wine for Sharpe. 'You leave tomorrow?'

'You must ask Sir Augustus. He's in command.'

'Really?' Dubreton smiled, then turned as a door opened. 'Ah! The ladies!'

New introductions were made all round, introductions that seemed to last five minutes, and hand after hand was kissed, elaborate courtesies made, and then, with equal elaboration, Dubreton seated his guests. He himself had reserved a chair in the centre of the table, facing the door, and he steered Sir Augustus to a place beside him with exquisite grace. Ducos immediately took the chair on Farthingdale's other side, and Sir Augustus looked in alarm for Josefina. Dubreton saw the look. 'Now, now, Sir Augustus! We have talking to do, much talking, and your beautiful wife is ever with you, whereas we only have the pleasure of your company for such short time.' He gestured with his hand to Josefina. 'Can I persuade you to sit opposite your husband, Lady Farthingdale? I trust there is no draught from the door. It is well curtained, but perhaps Major Sharpe would consent to sit beside you to protect you from the winter?'

It had been neatly done. The French had Farthingdale where they wanted him. They planned to negotiate and were giving him no place to turn. Dubreton sat next to his own wife, rubbing salt into Sir Augustus' wound, and Sharpe saw Sir Augustus looking painfully at Josefina. He wanted her close, he hated to see her away from him, and it seemed pathetic to Sharpe that a man should be so bereft because his whore was seven feet away.

Madame Dubreton smiled at Sharpe. 'We meet under happier circumstances, Major.'

'Indeed we do, Ma'am.'

'The last time I saw Major Sharpe,' she addressed the table at large and conveniently forgot the meetings they had had in the Convent since her rescue, 'he was bespattered with blood, holding a very large sword, and was extremely frightening.' She smiled at him.

'I apologize for that, Ma'am.'

'Please don't. In retrospect it was a wonderful sight.'

'It was your remembrance of Alexander Pope that made it possible, Ma'am.'

She smiled. The tiredness had gone, her face seemed to be smoother, and she and Dubreton radiated a happiness in each other. 'I always said poetry would be useful one day. Alexandre never believed me.'

Dubreton laughed, shrugged off the embarrassment of his name, and then conversation died away as a soup was served. Sharpe tasted it. It was a soup so delicious that he feared the second mouthful could not possibly live up to the promise of the first, yet it did, and seemed better, and he took more and then saw Dubreton was watching him with amusement. 'Good?'

'Magnificent.'

'Chestnuts. It's very simple, Major. Some vegetable stock, crushed chestnuts, butter and parsley. Cooking is so simple! The most difficult thing is to peel the chestnuts, but we have so many prisoners. Voila!'

'Is that all there is in it?'

A French Dragoon Captain insisted there was cream in the soup, and a German Lancer protested that cooking was never simple because he had never managed to cook anything other than a boiled egg and even then it came out hard as a Cuirasseur's breastplate, and a Fusilier Captain insisted he had seen men boil eggs by whirling them round and round in a cloth sling, taking forever, and Harold Price insisted on giving the recipe for a 'tommy', the British Army pancake, which consisted of nothing but flour and water, but still took Price two minutes to describe. Sir Augustus, feeling left out, said how astonished he was that the Portuguese ate only the leaves of the turnip and Josefina, feeling her country slighted, delicately insulted him by suggesting that only a heathen would eat any other part of a turnip, and then the soup was gone and Sharpe looked wistfully into the empty bowl.

A foot touched his, pressed, and he looked to Josefina on his left. She was speaking to a French Dragoon on her other side, a man who was leaning far forward to eat his soup so he could take glimpses into the neckline of her Empire dress. It had not been what she was wearing when Sharpe had rescued her and he stole a glance at Sir Augustus and realized that he must have brought the dress in his baggage. No wonder he hated any other man sitting next to her. The foot still pressed on his and then she turned to him, gave that hint of a wink. 'Enjoy it?'

'Delicious.'

An orderly poured him more wine, and Sharpe saw where the man's fingernails were torn and stained by loading powder and pulling back flints.

Sir Augustus leaned forward. 'My dear?'

'Augustus?'

'Are you not cold? The draught? May I have your shawl fetched?'

'Cold, my dear? Not at all.' She smiled at him, and her foot pushed up and down Sharpe's ankle.

The door from the kitchen banged open and orderlies seemed to run to the table, each man with a tray of dishes, and on each dish a single bowl. The plates were steaming hot and Dubreton clapped his hands at the table. 'Eat them quickly! They're so much better eaten fast from the oven!'

Sharpe adjusted the plate and it scorched him. The bird was sitting on a slice of fried bread, golden beneath the dark brown glaze of the roasted skin.

'Major! Eat!'

Josefina's right foot pressed hard against Sharpe's and he peeled a strip of the bird's flesh away, tried it, and the meat seemed to dissolve in his mouth. It was impossible that anything could taste better than the soup, yet this was far better.

Dubreton smiled. 'Good? Yes?'

'Quite magnificent!'

Josefina looked at him. Most of the men at the table were looking at her and in the candlelight she was extraordinarily beautiful, her lips slightly parted, the smallest worry on her face. Her foot pressed almost to the point of hurting. 'Are you sure you like it, Major?'

'I'm sure.' He pressed back, turned to Dubreton. 'Partridge?'

'Of course.' Dubreton spoke between mouthfuls. 'Butter, salt and pepper inside the bird, two vine leaves on the outside with some pork fat. You see? Simple!'

Sir Augustus, still smarting from the rebuke over turnips, cheered up. 'You should try fat bacon, Colonel! Much better than pork fat. My dear Mother always insisted on fat bacon.'

Josefina's foot was now hooked round Sharpe's ankle, pulling his leg closer. An orderly served her other neighbour wine and she moved her chair, seemingly to give him room, and then her knee was touching Sharpe's.

'Fat bacon!' Dubreton had sucked a bone clean and discarded it. 'My dear Sir Augustus! It fights the juice of the bird! And bacon burns!' He smiled at Josefina. 'You must change his habits, Milady, and insist on nothing but pork fat.'

She nodded, her mouth full, then dabbed at his lips. 'No herbs, Colonel?'

'Beautiful lady.' Dubreton smile. 'A young bird needs no herbs. An older bird? Yes, perhaps. A little thyme, parsley, perhaps a bay leaf.'

She paused with a forkful of breast-meat an inch from her mouth. 'I shall always remember to have young birds, Colonel.' Her knee rubbed Sharpe.

An orderly put more logs on the fire and somewhere in the village mens' voices sang together, while other orderlies moved round the table and gave everyone a second glass of wine, lighter red than the first, and when Sharpe moved to pick up the new glass. Dubreton stoppèd him. 'Wait, Major! That's for your main dish. Stay with your, what do you call it, claret! Stay with your claret for the moment.'

Josefina's other neighbour had shifted his chair closer so that his view was not impaired. Sir Augustus pushed half of his partridge away, uneaten, and stared unhappily across the table. Josefina was dazzling the Dragoon Captain, fingering the silver wire of his epaulette, and asking him how he cleaned it. Sharpe smiled to himself. She was superb. As untrustworthy as a cheap sword in battle, but the years had not palled her excitement or her mischief. He saw Ducos' eyes on him, the spectacles flashing on and off with candlelight as the Major chewed, and it seemed to Sharpe that Ducos smiled because he knew what was happening.

Harry Price was explaining cricket to one of the Frenchwomen, using a blend of English and outrageous French. 'He bowls la balle, oui? And he frappes it avec le baton! Comme ca!' Price made a stroke with his knife that rang loud on the edge of a wineglass. His flushed face smiled an apology at the senior officers who turned to look.

A French major egged Price on. 'The same man? He throws and hits?'

'Non, non, non!' Price drank from the wineglass. 'Onze hommes, oui? Une homme bowls et une homme frappes. Dix catch. Une homme from autre side frappes comme le man bowls. Simple!'

The French Major explained cricket to the rest of the table, making much of 'une homme' and 'le frapping', and the laughter was unforced, the room warm, and the wine good. Christmas evening with the French? Sharpe leaned back in his chair and it seemed so strange, no, more than strange, unnatural that tomorrow these same men might be trying to kill each other. Price was offering to teach the French cricket in the morning, but Sharpe's instincts warned him of a different game.

Josefina's foot was still for the moment, hooked about his

ankle while she listened to the Dragoon tell a long story about a ball in Paris. That would be to Josefina's liking. Paris would be heaven to her, a mythical city where a beautiful woman could walk for ever on soft carpets beneath crystal lights receiving the homage of dazzling uniforms. He thought to remove his foot, knowing he did not want her, but he could not summon the energy or desire to move. He looked at Farthingdale, unhappily defending his book against Ducos' surprising knowledge, and Sharpe supposed that he was flirting with Josefina because he disliked Sir Augustus so much. He did it, too, because he was weak. If Sir Augustus was not guarding her tonight Sharpe knew he would not resist the temptation. He shifted his foot a fraction and she tightened the pressure fiercely.

Dubreton leaned forward as the orderlies removed the remains of the partridges. 'You're looking warm, Lady Farthingdale. Would you like a window opened?'

'No, Colonel.' She smiled at him, her black hair curled about her face, her mastery of the men at the table absolute. There was something satisfying in having her attention, albeit hidden, though Sharpe guessed she might have extended it to any neighbour.

The kitchen doors opened again and this time a variety of dishes appeared, all hot, and orderlies put new plates before each diner. The smell was tantalizing. Dubreton clapped his hands. 'Lady Farthingdale! Sir Augustus! Ladies and gentlemen. You will have to forgive us. No goose this Christmas, no hog's head, not even a roasted swan. Alas! I tried for beef in our guests' honour, but nothing. You will have to put up with this humble dish. Major Sharpe? You will assist Lady Farthingdale? Sir Augustus? Allow me.'

There were three kinds of meat on one set of plates, next to dishes of beans that seemed to be topped with breadcrumbs, and then there were bowls of crisp, brown, roasted potatoes. Sharpe had a passion for roasted potatoes and he worked out in his head how many bowls were on the table, how many potatoes in each, and how many guests had to share them. He offered some to Josefina. 'Milady?'

'No thank you, Major.' Her knee rubbed his. Sharpe was sure that Sir Augustus must see what was happening, Josefina was so close to him now that their elbows rubbed whenever they ate. There had been a time when he had murdered for this woman and back then he would never have believed that such a grand passion could fade into mere affection.

'You're sure?'

'I'm sure.' Sharpe helped himself to her share of the potatoes as well as his own. He would hide the excess under the beans.

Dubreton helped himself last, then looked to see that everyone had a full plate. 'This should cheer your English hearts. Your Lord Wellington's favourite dish, mutton!' But mutton as Sharpe had never seen it, nothing like the yellow-brown, greasy meat that the Peer ate with such relish. Dubreton's thin face was full of pleasure. 'You roast the mutton, but only a little, and then you add the garlic sausage and the half roasted duck. Alas, it should be goose, but we have none. You cook them in the beans, then separate them.' The beans were delicious, white and swollen, and there were tiny squares of crisp, roasted pork rind among them. Dubreton speared a single bean. 'You cook the beans in water and you must throw the water away, you know that?'

The British shook their heads, looking puzzled, and Dubreton continued. 'The water of flageolots is stinking, horrid. You can tell a slattern because she does not throw it far enough from the house. However!' He held the bean up, smiled. 'You can bottle the water, yes? Then you will have a substance that will take the most stubborn stains from linen. You see how much you have to learn from us? Now eat!'

Dubreton had apologized for the main course, but the apology was needless for the food, once more, exceeded

Sharpe's experience and the potatoes, to his secret delight, were so crisp that each threatened to explode like a small shell and skid across the white table-cloth. He drank the lighter wine and he understood why Dubreton had insisted that they save it for this course, and he felt wonderfully good, relaxed, and he laughed as Harry Price complained that beans always gave him flatulence and solemnly speared each one to release the hidden gas he insisted was within. The mention of gas prompted a question from Dubreton whether it was true that London already had gas lighting, and Sharpe said it was, and Madame Dubreton wanted to know exactly where and then she sighed at the answer. 'Pall Mall! I haven't seen the Mall for nine years.'

'You will, Ma'am, again.'

Josefina leaned close to Sharpe, her hair brushing his own. 'Will you take me to London?'

'Whenever you like.'

'Tonight?' She was smiling at him, teasing him, her thigh pressing rhythmically against his.

'I didn't hear your words, my dear?' Sir Augustus, unable to contain his anger, leaned forward.

She smiled at him prettily. 'I was counting the potatoes on Major Sharpe's plate. I think he is very greedy.'

'A man needs his strength.' Ducos said, his eyes going back and forth between Sharpe and Josefina.

'Which is why you eat so little, Major?' She smiled at Ducos and it was true that the small, plain-dressed man picked fussily at his food and ate little. She leaned back towards Sharpe and put her fork over his plate. 'One, two, three, four, five, you've eaten part of that one, six.' Her knee and thigh were hard against him. She lowered her voice. 'He sleeps like the dead. Three o'clock?'

'*Qui vive?*' The shout was from outside the inn, the French challenge.

Josefina's fork was in her left hand, her right hand was beneath the table, its fingers running up the junction of green cloth and leather of his French overalls. 'Eight, nine. Ten potatoes, Major? Yes?'

'Three and a half would be better.' He said. He could smell her hair. She was hovering over his plate with the fork, deciding which potato to prong. She picked one, leaned away from him, and held the potato to his mouth. 'For your strength, Major.'

He opened his mouth, the fork came forward, and then the challenge was repeated, the door was hammered, opened, and the thick curtain was swept aside letting in a flurry of freezing air.

The diners stopped, forks halfway to their mouths, Josefina's fork an inch from Sharpe's lips, and there in the doorway stood Patrick Harper, grinning, and beside him, much smaller, her eyes dark, her hair black inside her hood, was Teresa. Sharpe's wife.

'Hello, husband.'

CHAPTER 17

She would not enter the inn, not Teresa, not while French officers were there. She hated the French with all the passion of her passionate soul. They had raped and killed her mother, she repaid them by killing as many as she could find and ambush in the border hills. Sharpe walked with her down the village street, towards the Convent, and she looked up at him. 'Forgotten how to eat, Richard?'

'She was only being playful.'

'Playful!' She laughed at him. The light of the straw torches showed her thin, strong face. There was none of Josefina's softness here, this woman had the face of a hawk; a beautiful hawk, but still a killer, a hunter, a creature of supple strength and small pity. The face was proud, the face of old Spain, mellowed only by lustrous, large eyes. The mother of his child. 'That's the whore-bitch Josefina, yes?'

'Yes.'

'And you still wear her ring, yes?'

Sharpe stopped, surprised. He had forgotten it, and Josefina had not mentioned it, but he did still wear the silver ring engraved with an Eagle that Josefina had bought for him before the battle of Talavera and before he had taken the eagle standard from the French. He looked at the ring, then up to Teresa's eyes. 'Jealous?'

'Richard.' She smiled. 'You wear the ring for the eagle, not her, I know that. Still, I suspect you think she is very beautiful, yes?'

'Too fat.'

'Too fat! You think anyone's too fat who's wider than a

ramrod.' She was facing him and she punched him lightly on the arm. 'One day I'm going to become fat, very fat, and I will see if you truly love me.'

'I love you.'

'And you think that forgives all.' She smiled at him, stood on tiptoe, and he kissed her, aware of the interested gaze of a dozen French sentries as well as Harper's looming figure twenty yards away. She frowned. 'Is that how you love me?'

He kissed her again, holding her this time, and she slid her face against his cheek and whispered in his ear, and then she pulled away to see the expression on his face.

'Truly?' He asked.

'Yes. This way.' She took him by the hand and walked with him beyond the light of the torches, out into the open field. The mist was still thin, the stars still showing hazed overhead, but the clouds had spread further south and promised foul weather. She stopped him when they were well beyond the earshot of any Frenchman in the village.

'Six Battalions, Richard. They're in a village three miles down the road.' She gestured eastwards. 'And that's not all.'

'Go on.'

'Five miles beyond them there's more. Far more. We saw five batteries of guns, maybe six. More cavalry, more infantry, and big carts. Supply carts.'

'Jesus.' He felt himself sobering fast in the cold air, under the impact of Teresa's news.

The Partisans were moving, spurred by Nairn's request, and Teresa had ridden with a dozen men north and east. With instinctive wariness she had circled towards her destination, coming at Adrados from the east, and in the Christmas dusk she had seen the French troops that were hidden in the valley and aimed like a lance towards Portugal. She guessed ten French Battalions, at least, maybe more, and Sharpe knew that those troops had not been marched into the winter hills just to subdue Pot-au-Feu.

For what, then? To conquer north Portugal, as Nairn had

suggested? That seemed a paltry ambition, a feather to lay in the scale against the leaden weight of the French defeat in Russia, but what then? Why was a French corps this far north, when the real prizes would be to recapture the border fortresses of Ciudad Rodrigo and Badajoz? If the Peer lost those towns then the campaign of 1813 would be set back by weeks, even months.

Teresa clung to his arm. 'Why do they say they're here?'

'The same reason as us. To destroy Pot-au-Feu.'

'Bastard liars.'

Sharpe shivered in the cold. He could see the fires at the watchtower and he thought of Frederickson preparing a defence, but a defence that had never been designed to beat off batteries of artillery and massed infantry.

Teresa's face was pale in the darkness. 'So what will you do?'

'It's not up to me. I'm not in command.'

'Major?'

'Yes?'

She laughed. 'A Major! Are you pleased?'

He laughed. 'Yes.'

'Patrick's pleased. He says you deserve it. I hope you're not going to run away from them.'

'Not if I can help it.' He turned and looked at the village. 'No. We won't run away, but we'll need help.'

She nodded, turning with him. 'My men are riding for help in the morning.' She named a half-dozen Partisan leaders who were within a day's ride.

'And you?'

She pulled her cloak tight about her. 'What do you want me to do?'

'Go west. Take a message to our lines. So far they don't even know there are any French in the valley.'

She nodded. 'And the message?'

'That we're holding the Gateway of God.'

She liked that, smiling in the darkness, her teeth white and even. She looked north. 'I'll go soon, tonight, before the snow.'

He wished she would wait till morning, but she was right, and Sharpe despised himself for needing her protection against his assignation at half past three. There would be no assignation, not this night, because he had a defence to prepare and a battle to fight in the dawn. Teresa seemed to sense his thoughts for she smiled at him, and her voice was teasing. 'I think the whore-bitch will be safe from you tonight.'

'I think so.'

They walked slowly towards the lights in the village street and Teresa brought out a wrapped package from beneath her cloak and handed it to him. 'Open it.'

Sharpe pulled the string open, undid the cloth wrapping, and there was a doll inside the parcel. He moved closer to the light, and smiled. The doll was a Rifleman.

Teresa seemed worried. 'You like it?'

'It's beautiful.'

'I made it for Antonia.' She wanted Sharpe to like it.

He held it into the light and he saw the care and trouble that had gone into the tiny uniform. The doll was just six inches high, yet the green jacket showed every piece of black piping, small loops intricate at the facings crossed by a thin, black crossbelt. The face was carved from wood. He lifted off the tiny black-peaked shako and saw black hair beneath.

'Wool.' She smiled. 'I was going to give it to her for Christmas. Today. It will wait.'

'How is she?'

'Lovely.' Teresa took the doll back and began to wrap it with delicate care. 'Lucia looks after her.' Lucia was Teresa's sister-in-law. 'She's very good with her. I suppose she has to be, we're not the best parents in the world.' She shrugged.

'Tell her the doll's from me, too.' He had nothing to give his daughter.

She nodded. 'It's supposed to be you.' She smiled. 'She

can have a doll and call it Father. I'll tell her it's from you as well.'

Sharpe thought of his words to Frederickson. Leave her to life. He did not want that. Antonia was his only flesh and blood, but she did not know him, nor he her, and he looked up into the mist at a blurred star and thought how selfish he was. He preferred to live on the blade-edge of danger and glory rather than raise a family in peace and security. Antonia was a child of war, and war, as Ducos had said, brought death more often than life. 'Does she speak yet?'

'A few words.' Teresa's voice was subdued. 'Mamma. She calls Ramon "Gogga", I don't know why.' She laughed, but there was little pleasure in her voice.

Antonia would speak Spanish. She had no one to call Father except her uncle, Ramon, and she was lucky in him. More fortunate in her uncle than in her father.

'Major! Major Sharpe!'

The voice hailed him from the inn door, then Dubreton stepped into the street and walked towards them. 'Major?'

Sharpe put a hand on Teresa's shoulder, waited till the French Colonel was close. 'My wife, M'sieu. Teresa? This is Colonel Dubreton.'

Dubreton bowed to her. 'La Aguja. You're as beautiful as you are dangerous, Ma'am.' He gestured towards the inn. 'It would be my pleasure to have you join us. The ladies have withdrawn, but you would be welcome, I know.'

Teresa, to Sharpe's surprise, spoke politely. 'I'm tired, Colonel. I would prefer to wait for my husband in the Castle.'

'Of course, Madame.' Dubreton paused. 'Your husband has done me a great service, Madame, a personal service. To him I owe my wife's safety. If it is ever in my power, then I will feel honoured to repay that debt.'

Teresa smiled. 'You'll forgive me if I hope it is never in your power?'

'I regret we are enemies.'

'You can leave Spain, then we need not be.'

'To be your friend, Madame, makes the idea of losing this war bearable.'

She laughed, pleased with the compliment, and to Sharpe's utter astonishment held out her hand and let the Frenchman kiss it. 'Would you call my horse, Colonel? One of your men is holding it.'

Dubreton obeyed, smiling at the odd chance that had brought him so close to a woman on whose head France had a high price. La Aguja, 'the needle', fought a bitter war against his men.

Harper brought the horse, helped Teresa into the saddle, and walked back with her towards the Castle. Dubreton watched them go and took a cigar from a leather case. He offered one to Sharpe and the Rifleman, who rarely smoked, wanted one now. He waited as Dubreton blew the spark on the charred linen inside his tinder-box into a flame, then bent down to light the cigar.

The hooves of the horse faded on the brittle, frosted earth. Dubreton lit his own cigar. 'She's very beautiful, Major.'

'Yes.'

The cigar smoke vanished into the mist. A small breeze was blowing now, a breeze to blow cannon smoke away from the guns' muzzles. The mist would clear soon, blown into scraps, and then what? Rain or snow.

Dubreton gestured Sharpe back towards the inn. 'Your Colonel demanded your presence. Not, I think, that he needs or wants your advice, I suspect he merely wanted to deprive you of your wife's company.'

'As you deprived him?'

Dubreton smiled. 'My wife, who is no fool, has even suggested that the beautiful Lady Farthingdale is not all she is supposed to be.'

Sharpe laughed, made no reply, and stood aside to let Dubreton duck under the lintel of the inn door. Once inside, Sharpe pulled the curtain close, and found the room stuffy with the smoke of cigars, tense with serious talk. The Battalion of wine bottles had been destroyed, replaced with brandy that only the junior officers were drinking with enjoyment. Sir Augustus Farthingdale was frowning, Ducos was smiling his secret smile.

Dubreton looked at Ducos. 'I'm afraid you just missed La Aguja, Ducos. I invited her to join us, but she pleaded tiredness.'

Ducos turned the smile on Sharpe and kept it on his face as he made an obscene gesture. He made a loop with the thumb and forefinger of his left hand and thrust his right forefinger repeatedly into the loop. 'La Aguja, yes? The needle. We all know what we do with needles. We thread them.'

The sword came from the scabbard so fast that even Dubreton, standing at Sharpe's elbow, could not have stopped the movement. The steel glittered in the candle light, swooped as Sharpe leaned far over the table, and the tip stopped one inch from the bridge of Ducos' nose. 'Do you wish to repeat that, Major?'

The room was utterly still. Sir Augustus yelped his syllable. 'Sharpe!'

Ducos did not move. A tiny pulse throbbed beneath the pox-scarred cheek. 'She is a foul enemy of France.'

'I asked if you cared to repeat your statement? Or give me satisfaction.'

Ducos smiled. 'You're a fool, Major Sharpe, if you think I'll fight a duel with you.'

'Then you're a fool to provoke one. I'm waiting for your apology.'

Dubreton spoke in quick French, and Sharpe guessed he ordered the apology for Ducos shrugged then looked back to Sharpe. 'I have no words base enough for La Aguja, but for the insult to you, M'sieu, I offer you my regrets.' It was said grudgingly, scornfully.

Sharpe smiled. The apology had been graceless and insufficient and he moved the sword blade, fast, and this time

Ducos did react for the steel tip had grazed his left eyebrow and struck the spectacles from his nose. He reached for them and stopped. The blade blocked his hand.

'How well do you see me now, Ducos?'

Ducos shrugged. He looked myopic and defenceless without the two, thick lenses. 'You've had my apology, M'sieu.'

'It's difficult to thread a needle when you're half blind, Ducos.' The heavy steel rapped on one lens, shattering it. 'Remember me, your enemy.' The sword blade struck on the second lens and then Sharpe leaned back, reversed the sword, and thrust it home.

'Sharpe!' Farthingdale looked with disbelief at the broken glasses. It would take Ducos weeks to replace them.

'Bravo, sir!' Harry Price was drunk, happily drunk. Even the French officers, disliking Ducos, grinned at Sharpe and thumped the table with approval.

Dubreton walked back to his chair and looked at the outraged Sir Augustus. 'Major Sharpe showed restraint, Sir Augustus. I must apologize if one of the officers under my command is both offensive and drunk.'

Ducos smouldered. There had been two insults; that he was drunk, which he was not, and that he was under Dubreton's orders, which was equally untrue. A dangerous man, Sharpe knew, and a man whose enmity could stretch far into the future.

Dubreton sat, tapped ash onto a plate, and turned to Sir Augustus. 'Do I have your decision, Sir Augustus?'

Farthingdale touched the white bandage that hid part of his silver hair. His voice was very precise. 'You wish us to leave the valley at nine tomorrow morning, yes?'

'Indeed.'

'After which you have orders to destroy the watchtower?'

'Yes.'

'Following which you will go home.'

'Precisely!' Dubreton smiled, poured brandy and offered the bottle towards Sharpe.

Sharpe shook his head. He blew out a plume of smoke. 'Why do you want us to leave the valley before you destroy the watchtower? Couldn't we watch from the Castle?'

Dubreton smiled, knowing the question to be as false as the information he had already given to Sir Augustus. 'Of course you can watch.'

Farthingdale frowned at Sharpe. 'Your interest is laudable, Major, but Colonel Dubreton has already given us good reason why it would be sensible for us to leave.'

Dubreton nodded. 'We have another three Battalions of Infantry in the next village.' He shrugged, and swirled the brandy in his glass. 'They have come as a marching exercise, a hardening of young troops, and much as I appreciate your company, Major, I fear that too many troops in the valley might be explosive.'

So Dubreton was willing to reveal part of his hand, Sharpe guessed because the Colonel had realized that Farthingdale could be scared off with numbers. Sharpe leaned back. 'You have orders to destroy the watchtower?'

'Yes.'

'Strange.'

Dubreton smiled. 'It has been used in the past by Partisans. It is a danger to us, but not to you, I would suggest.'

Sharpe tapped his own cigar ash onto the floor. He heard the laughter of the women in the next room. 'I thought these hills were little used by ourselves, yourselves, or the partisans. Four Battalions seem a strong force to destroy one small tower.'

'Sharpe!' Farthingdale had lit one of his own cigars, longer and fatter than Dubreton's. 'If the French want to make a fool of themselves by blowing up a useless tower, then it's none of our business.'

'If the French want something, sir, then it's our business to deny it them.' Sharpe's voice was harsh.

'I don't need you to tell me my duty, Major!' Sir Augustus' voice was angry. Dubreton watched silent. The hand touched the bandage again. 'Colonel Dubreton had given us his word. He will withdraw when his task is done. There is no need for a useless confrontation in this valley. You may wish a fight, Major, to burnish your laurels, but my job is done. I have destroyed Pot-au-Feu, retaken our deserters, and our orders are to go home!'

Sharpe smiled. They were not Farthingdale's orders, they had been Kinney's orders, and now Kinney was in his grave looking westward at the hills, and Farthingdale had fallen into this command. Sharpe blew smoke at the ceiling, looked at Dubreton. 'You will go home?'

'Yes, Major.'

'And you call yourselves "the Army of Portugal", yes?'

Silence. Sharpe knew he was right. The French maintained three armies in the west of Spain; the Army of the North, the Army of the Centre, and the Army of Portugal. Dubreton's home was across the border, his words had been deliberately misleading, though not enough to compromise his honour.

Dubreton ignored Sharpe. He looked, instead at Sir Augustus, and he put steel into his voice. 'I have four Battalions of infantry, Sir Augustus, and can summon more within a day. I have my orders, however foolish they may seem, and I intend to carry them out. I will begin my operations at nine o'clock tomorrow morning. I leave the choice to you whether you care to obstruct them.'

Dubreton knew his man. Sir Augustus saw the odds, and saw the French bayonets coming through the war-smoke, and he folded spinelessly in front of the threat. 'And you say we can withdraw unmolested?'

'Our truce is extended to nine o'clock in the morning, Sir Augustus. That should give you ample time to distance yourself from Adrados.'

Farthingdale nodded. Sharpe could hardly believe what he was seeing, though he had known other officers like this, officers who had bought their way to high rank without ever

231

seeing the enemy and who ran away the first moment they did. Farthingdale pushed at the table, scraping his chair back. 'We will leave at dawn.'

'Splendid!' Dubreton raised his brandy glass. 'I drink to such sense!'

Sharpe dropped his cigar butt on the floor. 'Colonel Dubreton?'

'Major?'

Sharpe had cards to play now, but in a different game, and he must play them carefully. 'Sir Augustus had led a gallant attack today, as you can see.'

'Indeed.' Dubreton looked at the white bandage. Farthingdale's peevish face looked suspiciously at Sharpe.

'I've no doubt, sir, that the story of this morning's attack will bring nothing but glory to Sir Augustus.' Farthingdale's face, in the presence of such praise, showed only more suspicion. Sharpe raised an eyebrow. 'Sadly the despatch will have to record that Sir Augustus received an injury while leading troops into the breach.' Sharpe leaned forward. 'I have known times, Colonel, when such an injury caused a serious relapse during the night.'

'We must pray that doesn't happen, Major.' Dubreton said.

'And we'll be grateful for your prayers, sir. However, if it does, then the command of the British troops will fall on my unworthy shoulders.'

'So?'

'And I will exercise that command.'

'Sharpe!' Farthingdale protested, quite rightly. 'You take too much on yourself, Major! I have made my decision, given my word, and I will not tolerate this insult. You will accept my orders!'

'Of course, sir. I apologize.'

Dubreton understood. Sharpe, too, had been protecting his honour, disassociating himself from Farthingdale's decision, and the Frenchman had caught the message Sharpe had wished to convey. He held up a hand. 'We shall pray that Sir Augustus' health lasts the night, and in the morning, Major, we will know he has happily lived if we see that you have withdrawn.'

'Yes, sir.'

They stayed a half-hour more then made their farewells. Soldiers brought horses to the door, officers pulled on cloaks or greatcoats and stood to one side to allow Josefina to mount her horse. Sir Augustus mounted beside her, pulled his hat low over the bandage, and looked at the British officers at the inn door. 'All Company officers to my quarters in a half hour. All! That includes you, Sharpe.' He raised a gloved finger to the tassel of his hat and nodded at Dubreton.

The French Colonel held Sharpe aside. 'I will remember my debt to you, Sharpe.'

'There's no debt in my mind, sir.'

'I'm a better judge.' He smiled. 'Are you going to fight us tomorrow?'

'I shall obey orders, sir.'

'Yes.' Dubreton watched the first horses leave. He brought a bottle of brandy from behind his back. 'To keep you warm on your march tomorrow.'

'Thank you, sir.'

'And a happy New Year, Major.'

Sharpe mounted and walked his horse after the receding officers. Harry Price hung back for him, fell in alongside, and when they were well out of earshot the Lieutenant looked at his tall Major. 'Are we really going tomorrow morning, sir?'

'No, Harry.' Sharpe grinned at him, but the grin hid his real feelings. Many Riflemen and many Fusiliers, Sharpe knew, would never leave the high place in the hills that was called the Gateway of God. They had had their last Christmas.

CHAPTER 18

Christmas midnight. The mist clinging to stone and grass where the breeze had not yet taken it away, and the boot-heels of sentries were loud on the Castle ramparts. Flame flared in the courtyard. From below, the greatcoat-skirts of the patrolling sentries could have been the surcoats of armoured knights; their bayonets, catching the gleam of fire, the spearpoints of men who waited for Islam to attack in the dawn.

Sharpe held Teresa close. Two of her men waited in the Castle gateway, her horse moved restlessly behind her. 'You have the message.'

She nodded, pulled away from him. 'I'll be back in two days.'

'I'll still be here.'

She punched him softly. 'Make sure you are.' She turned, mounted the horse, and pulled it towards the gateway.

'Take care!'

'We ride more at night than at day! Two days!' And she was gone through the arch, turning westward to take the news of the hidden French troops to Frenada. Another parting in a marriage that was made of too many partings, and he listened to the fading hooves and thought that at the end of two days' fighting there would be a reward.

He was late for Sir Augustus' meeting, and he hardly cared. The decision that Sharpe had made would render anything Sir Augustus had to say meaningless. Sharpe would take over. He climbed the stairway in the gate-tower,

234

laboriously cleared of the windlass, and walked the circuit of the battlements towards the keep.

Sir Augustus had a huge fire in his room, the wood crackling fiercely as the thorns burned. The chimney, the only one in the Castle, opened up on the ramparts.

Farthingdale paused as Sharpe entered. A dozen officers sat or stood in the room, even Frederickson had been fetched from the watchtower, and the eyes looked at Sharpe. Farthingdale's voice was hostile. 'You're late, Major.'

'My apologies, sir.'

Pot-au-Feu had furnished the room in barbaric splendour, rugs on walls and floor, even serving as heavy curtains, and the curtains moved to reveal Josefina. She came from the balcony, smiled at Sharpe, then leaned against the wall as Sir Augustus lifted the piece of paper in his hand. 'I will recapitulate for those who could not be here on time. We leave at first light. The prisoners will go first, suitably dressed, and guarded by four Companies of the Fusiliers.'

Brooker nodded, making notes on a folded square of paper.

'Captain Gilliland will go next. You will make space on your carts for the wounded.'

Gilliland nodded. 'Yes, sir.'

'Then the rest of the Fusiliers. Major Sharpe?'

'Sir?'

'Your Riflemen will be the rear-guard.'

Captain Brooker raised the pertinent point of what was to be done with the women and children of the prisoners, and while the Captains made their suggestions, Frederickson looked appealingly towards Sharpe. Sharpe smiled and shook his head.

Frederickson misunderstood, or else was too upset to leave matters with Sharpe, for the Rifle Captain stood up and asked Farthingdale's permission to speak.

'Captain?'

'Why are we leaving, sir?'

'The Rifles are thirsting for glory,' Farthingdale sneered, and Sharpe marked the men who smiled, for those were the men who had little taste for this fight. Farthingdale handed his piece of paper to a Fusilier, acting as clerk, who began the laborious task of copying out the orders. 'We are leaving, Captain Frederickson, because we are opposed by overwhelming force in a place where we have no reason to fight. We cannot fight four Battalions of French.'

Sharpe ignored the fact that four Battalions of French were not too many for a well-sited defence. He uncurled from the wall. 'In fact, sir, a good many more than four.'

All eyes were on Sharpe. Farthingdale looked lost for a second. 'More?'

'Within eight miles of us, sir, and probably moving up tonight, there are nearer ten Battalions, maybe more. There's also five or six batteries of artillery, and at least another two hundred cavalry. My own suspicion is that that's a minimum. I'd venture a guess at fifteen Battalions.'

The thorns crackled in the fireplace. The Fusilier clerk was staring open-mouthed at Sharpe. Farthingdale frowned. 'May I ask why you chose not to apprise me of this intelligence. Sharpe?'

'I just did, sir.'

'And may I ask how you know?'

'My wife saw them, sir.'

'A woman's report.'

'A woman, Sir Augustus, who has spent the last three years fighting the French.' That jibe went home, provoking smiles from Frederickson and a handful of other officers.

Sir Augustus snapped at the clerk to keep writing, then snapped at Sharpe. 'I hardly see how it affects these orders, Major. If anything, it would seem to underline the wisdom of them.'

'It would be interesting, sir, to know why the French are here in such force. I doubt if it's to destroy a watchtower.'

236

'Interesting, no doubt, but that is not my concern. Are you suggesting we fight them?' Sir Augustus let the sarcasm show in his question.

'Well, sir. They've probably got seven or eight thousand infantry, I suspect more. We've got, let me see, just over six hundred which includes our lightly wounded. We've also got Captain Gilliland's men, so I think we can pretty safely hold them off.'

More smiles, and Sharpe marked those too, because they were the Captains he could rely on.

Sir Augustus was enjoying himself. 'How, Major?'

'In the usual way, sir. Kill the bastards.'

'My wife is in the room, Sharpe. You will apologize.'

Sharpe bowed to Josefina. 'My apologies, Milady.'

Farthingdale hitched the tail of his jacket up to warm himself in front of the fire. He was pleased with himself, having forced Sharpe to apologize, and he was enjoying his display of authority in front of Josefina. His voice was crisp. 'Major Sharpe dreams of miracles, I prefer to put my trust in soldierly common sense. Our plain duty is to live and fight another day. Captain Brooker?'

'Sir?' Sharpe had Brooker marked as a Farthingdale supporter.

'Detail two reliable Lieutenants to carry this intelligence ahead of us in the morning. See they're well mounted.'

'Yes, sir.'

Sharpe leaned back against the wall. 'I've already sent the message, sir.'

'You take a great deal upon yourself, Major Sharpe.' Sir Augustus' voice was rich in contempt. 'Did you think the courtesy of requesting my permission was too cumbersome for your precious time?'

'My wife and her men are not subject to your permission, Sir Augustus.' Sharpe let his own hostility show, and he saw the fury snap into Farthingdale's eyes. Sharpe kept talking, softening his tone. 'I do need your permission, sir, for one other thing. I would like one observation to be recorded of this meeting.'

'Damn your observation!'

'Doubtless you will, sir, but nevertheless it is important.' Sharpe knew how to bully a bully. He was upright again, taller than anyone else in the room, a subdued anger and violence threatening the meeting. He paused, giving Sir Augustus a chance to order him into silence, and when the order did not come he threw out the lifeline he had thought about so carefully. If Sir Augustus listened, Sir Augustus could hold the pass. 'It's obvious, sir, that the French are interested in far more than the destruction of the watchtower. I suggest, sir, that their force denotes an attempt to enter Portugal, and once they are through this pass then there are a dozen routes they could take. It will take a day for our message to reach Frenada, another day for any troops to be concentrated, and by then their aim might well be accomplished. I do not know what that aim is, sir, but I do know one thing. There is one place where they can be stopped, and this is it.' Sharpe's supporters, Gilliland among them, nodded.

Sir Augustus leaned against the ornate stone chimney hood and smoothed a hand over his hair, fiddling with the black bow at the nape of his neck. 'Thank you for the lecture, Major Sharpe.' Sir Augustus was feeling more comfortable. The odds described by Sharpe had justified his decision, and he could sense the support of half the officers in the room. 'You wanted that observation recorded. So it shall be, as will mine. This may be the place to stop them, but only with adequate troops. I do not intend to sacrifice a fine Battalion to your ambition in a fruitless attempt to stop an enemy who outnumbers and outguns us. Are you really suggesting we can win?'

'No, sir.'

'Ah!' Sir Augustus feigned surprise.

'I'm suggesting we have to fight.'

'Your suggestion is noted, and refused. My decision is made. Tomorrow we leave. That is an order.' He looked acidly at Sharpe. 'Do you accept that order, Major?'

'Of course, sir, and I apologize for taking up your time.' Frederickson looked appalled at Sharpe, Farthingdale looked pleased.

'Thank you, Major.' Sir Augustus sighed. 'We were discussing the problem of the women and children. Captain Brooker?'

Captain Brooker's contribution was doomed to be unsaid. Sharpe cleared his throat. 'Sir?'

'Major Sharpe.' Farthingdale was condescending in victory.

'There was one very small matter, sir, which I would be wrong not to bring to your attention.'

'I would hate you to be in the wrong, Major.' Farthingdale provoked smiles from his men. 'Pray enlighten me.'

'It's a story, sir, and please bear with me, but it has some relevance.' Sharpe spoke mildly, leaning back on the wall, his right hand across his body to hold the pommel of his sword. 'The odds against us do seem to be overwhelming, sir, extremely so, but I am reminded of a lady I know in Lisbon.'

'Really, Sharpe! A lady in Lisbon? You say this has relevance?'

'Yes, sir.' Sharpe kept his voice humble. He glanced once at Josefina, then back to the slim, elegant man who leaned against the chimney. 'She was called La Lacosta, sir, and she always said the more the merrier.'

Frederickson laughed, as did one or two others, and their laughter smothered the gasp from Josefina. Frederickson and the other officers had no idea of whom Sharpe spoke, but Sir Augustus did. He was speechless, shock in his face, and Sharpe bored on. 'Lady Farthingdale will forgive my language, sir, but La Lacosta was a whore. She still is, and her husband, Sir Augustus, is living in Brazil.'

'Sharpe!'

'You heard me, sir. The more the merrier!' Sharpe was standing now, his voice harsh. 'Might I suggest it's time for a meeting of senior officers, sir. Majors and above? To discuss my report that I will have to submit to headquarters?'

The joy of an ace falling on green baize, the joy of the moment when the enemy skirmish line turns and runs, the joy of seeing Sir Augustus trumped, beaten, destroyed.

'A meeting?'

'In the next room, sir?' Sharpe glanced at Josefina and there was shock on her face, disbelief too that Sharpe could have used the knowledge, but Sharpe's debts to La Lacosta were long paid. He walked through the room, ignoring the puzzled looks of the assembled officers, and held the door open for Sir Augustus.

There was a straw torch in the bracket outside the door and Sharpe took it and led the way into the great hall where Pot-au-Feu had reigned in shabby state. The balcony extended to the hall and Sharpe walked onto it and ordered the two soldiers who stood there with lit pipes to make themselves scarce. He lay the torch on the balustrade and turned to look at the white face of the cavalry Colonel. 'I think we understand each other, Sir Augustus. You have committed His Majesty's troops to rescue a Portuguese whore.'

'No, Sharpe!'

'Then pray tell me what we did do?'

The fight was gone from Farthingdale, but he was not surrendering. His hands flapped weakly. 'We came to destroy Pot-au-Feu, to rescue all the hostages!'

'A whore, Colonel. A whore I knew three years ago, and I knew her well. How is Duarte, her husband?'

'Sharpe!'

'Do you want a list of others who've been there, Colonel? In that nice house with the orange trees? Or shall I simply send a letter to one of the English papers? They'd like the story of how we stormed a Convent to rescue the whore Sir Augustus Farthingdale claimed was his wife.'

Sir Augustus was trapped, caught fast. He had played with fire and the flames had burned him. Sharpe glanced into the hall to make sure no one was near. 'We have to stop them here, Sir Augustus, and I don't think you're the man to do it. Have you ever defended against a French attack?'

The head shook miserably. 'No.'

'The drums never stop, Colonel, at least not until you've beaten the bastards and they take a hell of a lot of beating. I'll tell you now. We can't hold all three buildings, we don't have the men, so I'll give up the Convent first. They'll put guns in there, and once they've taken the watchtower, which they will, they'll put guns up there as well. It's like being in a meat grinder, Colonel. The bastards are turning the handle and all you can do is hope the bloody blades don't touch you. Do you want to conduct this defence?'

'Sharpe?' It was a plea.

'No. You can leave here with your reputation intact, Colonel, and you can take the whore with you. I'll say nothing. You say that your wound is hurting you, making you faint, and you hand the command to me. Do you understand? Then, at dawn, you'll go. I'll give you four men as an escort, but you go.'

'This is blackmail, Sharpe!'

'Yes it is. And it's war as well. Now what do you want? Me to say nothing? Or shall I tell your pretty tale all about the army?'

Farthingdale accepted, as Sharpe had known he would. There was no pleasure in humiliating the man, and none at all in jeopardizing Josefina's wealth. The thin, handsome face looked pitiably at Sharpe. 'You'll say nothing?'

'On my honour.'

Clouds had spread far to the south, shrouding the moon, thickening the promise of rain or snow. Sharpe waited as Sir Augustus went back to his room to make his announcement, an announcement that regretted his health, that said he and Lady Farthingdale were moving to the Convent, that Major

Sharpe was in command. In command. A month ago he had led twenty-eight men, tonight he had near eight hundred with Gilliland's men. Some men took responsibility whether it was offered or not.

He walked back into the room when Sir Augustus and Josefina had left and he was greeted by a babble of voices. Most of the officers were confused, awed by the turn in their fortunes, fearing that Sharpe had drawn them all a very short straw, and they clamoured for detail, for explanation, and Sharpe cut through the noise.

'Quiet!'

He took the papers from the clerk's desk, the orders for withdrawal, and he tossed them onto the fire. They watched, some seeing their hopes burning in the fire.

'Our task, gentlemen, is to hold this pass for at least forty-eight hours. This is how it will be done.' He brooked no questions, no discussion, not even when he ordered a bemused Lieutenant Price to have Patrick Harper capture as many live birds as he could.

'Yes, sir.' Price shook his head in wonderment. Frederickson grinned, happy at last.

He dealt with questions at the end, dismissed them to their Companies, then pulled the rug off the window so he could stare westward at the darkness over Portugal. Teresa was down there somewhere, riding in the night.

'Sir?'

He turned. Frederickson was leaning against the wall by the door. 'Yes?'

'How did you do it?'

'Never mind. You just hold that tower for me.'

'Consider it done.' Frederickson grinned and went.

The tower. The key to the whole valley, the key to living through the next two days or else perpetual darkness. Sharpe looked at the paper ashes on the fire. He would hold the Gateway of God.

CHAPTER 19

The dawn of Saturday, December 26th 1812, was muddy, slow and inglorious.

The temperature rose in the night, the warmer air bringing rain that lashed on the cobbles of the yard, hissed in the fire and bracketed torches, and soaked the thorn bushes so that, as the light struggled through the clouds, they appeared black and shiny on the hillsides.

At first light the valley seemed empty. The rain had exhausted itself into a fine drizzle that hid the far hills of Portugal. Clouds touched the rocky peaks north and south, shrouded even the topmost stones of the watchtower. The Union flag on the Convent had been taken down in the night, and the two Colours on the gate-tower hung heavy and wet above the rain-darkened stone.

At half past seven, a few minutes after sunrise, a group of French officers appeared to the west of the village. One was a full General. He dismounted, then propped his telescope on the saddle of his horse, peered at the men on the Castle ramparts, then pushed his horse round so he could stare at the figures beneath the watchtower. He grunted. "How long?"

'An hour and a half, sir.'

The rain had fed the small stream so that the water bubbled vigorously from the spring, fell white over stones and earth, and flooded small patches in the valley. Two curlews, their beaks long and curved like sabres, strutted by the stream and pecked in the cold water. They seemed to find nothing, for they flew eastwards in search of better feeding.

At eight o'clock the drizzle had stopped and a wind was pushing at the stiff folds of the Colours.

At eight fifteen the General reappeared, a roll of bread in one hand, and he was rewarded by movement at last, Riflemen were stamping the life from the remains of a fire beneath the watchtower, then they picked up their packs, their weapons, and filed westward into the thorns. The black, spiny bushes seemed to swallow them up, hiding them from sight, but then, ten minutes later, they appeared in front of the Castle. The General stamped his feet. 'Thank God those bastards are going.' No Frenchman liked the Riflemen, the 'grasshoppers', who killed at a distance and seemed invulnerable to the musket fire of French skirmishers.

At half past eight the Colours were lowered from the gate-tower and the sentries disappeared from the Castle ramparts. They came out of the Castle gate, misshapen by their greatcoats, haversacks, packs, and canteens, and a mounted officer paraded them in ranks, the Riflemen who had come from the watchtower fell in beside them, and the whole group was marched to the road, turned westwards, and over the lip of the pass. Before the mounted officer dropped out of sight he turned, faced the French, and saluted with his sword.

The General grinned. 'So that's that. How many were there?'

An aide-de-camp snapped a telescope shut. 'Fifty redcoats, sir, twenty grasshoppers.'

Dubreton sipped his coffee. 'So Major Sharpe lost.'

'Let's be grateful for that.' The General cupped his hands about his own coffee. 'They must have gone in the night, leaving that rearguard.'

Another aide-de-camp was staring at the deserted watchtower hill. 'Sir?'

'Pierre?'

'They left the guns.'

The General yawned. 'They didn't have time to get them out. Those artillerymen marched all the way here for nothing.' He laughed. It had been Dubreton's guess that the artillerymen he had seen in the Castle had been brought to fetch the guns back from the high valley. He had further guessed that Sharpe had arranged for him to see the men so that the French might think the British had properly served artillery batteries. Dubreton felt a moment of idle regret. It would have been interesting to fight against Richard Sharpe.

The General flung the dregs of his coffee onto the roadway and looked at Dubreton. 'He broke Ducos' glasses?'

'Yes, sir.'

The General laughed, the sound uncannily like the whinnying of a horse, so much so that the horse's ears flicked back in interest at the sound. The General shook his head. 'We'll catch them up before mid-day. Make sure this Sharpe doesn't fall into friend Ducos' hands. Alexandre.'

'Yes, sir.'

'What's the time, Pierre?'

'Twenty to nine, sir.'

'What's twenty minutes in a war? Let's begin, gentlemen!' The General, a small man, clapped Dubreton's back. 'Well done, Alexandre! It would have taken us all of a day to force this pass if they'd stayed.'

'Thank you, sir.' Again Dubreton felt a moment's regret that the enemy had folded so easily, yet he knew the regret was misplaced. This operation in midwinter was horribly dependent on timing. The French would take the Gateway of God, garrison it, then send most of their force down towards Vila Nova on the north bank of the Douro. Their presence would reinforce the careful rumours that Ducos had spread, rumours that talked of an invasion of North Portugal, the Tras os Montes, the Land beyond the Mountains, and when the British reacted, as they must, by bringing their forces north, then the real operation would unwind from Salamanca. Divisions of the Army of Portugal, reinforced by men from the Army of the Centre and even one division from the Army of the South would cross the Coa, stripped of its defenders from the British Light Division, and they would capture Frenada, possibly Almeida, and hoped even to surprise the Spanish garrison of Ciudad Rodrigo. Within a week the northern road from Portugal would again be in French hands, the war of the British set back at least a year, and Dubreton had lain awake in the night, his wife sleeping peacefully, and feared that Sharpe would stay in the Gateway of God. In the small hours he had got up, dressed silently, and joined the picquet line west of Adrados. A Sergeant had greeted him then nodded towards the Castle. 'Hear that, sir?'

Carts rumbling in the night.

'Bastards are going, sir.'

'Let's hope so, Sergeant.'

Now, as daylight filled the valley, a grey light, damp and depressing, Dubreton felt a moment's regret for Sharpe. He had liked the Rifleman, recognizing in him a fellow soldier, and he knew that Sharpe wanted to make his stand in the high valley. It would have been a hopeless fight, but worthy of a soldier, and as he thought so the suspicion formed in his brain. Dubreton smiled. Of course! Suppose Sharpe wanted them to think that the British had left? He took out his own glass, borrowed the shoulder of a soldier, and searched the dark arrow slits of the Castle.

Nothing. He shifted the lens to the right, his hand slipping so that for a second he could only see the freshly turned earth of the graves in front of the east wall, and then the glass was under control and he looked at the gate-tower. Still nothing. The gate seemed unblocked. He tilted the telescope up and looked at the long dark slits above the arch and there was movement! He grinned, the sentry could sense the Colonel's excitement, and then the moment had passed. A jackdaw only, flying from the empty building, the birds taking over

246

what was normally their own domain. He closed the glass. The sentry looked at him. 'Anyone there, sir?'

'No. It's empty.'

In the rectangular room above the gateway Sharpe cursed. The Fusilier shook his head. 'I'm sorry, sir. Bloody thing got out.'

'Well don't play with the bloody baskets!'

'No, sir.'

It had taken Harper and Daniel Hagman over two hours to snare the five birds from the rocks above the Convent. Sharpe had wanted to keep them until the French were much closer, when the enemy could clearly see the birds leaving the arrow slits and draw the obvious conclusion that the building was once again deserted. Now this fool of a Fusilier had prised apart the lips of the rush basket to look at the bird, and it had exploded up at him, flying desperately about the chamber before seeing daylight and rocketing out into the valley. One wasted bird! Sharpe had only one other, the remaining three were with one of Cross's Lieutenants in the Keep.

It had been a night of frantic business, a load falling from Sharpe's shoulders when, at five o'clock, Sir Augustus Farthingdale and Josefina had ridden westward down the pass with four lightly wounded Fusiliers mounted on Gilliland's troop horses as escort. An hour later Sharpe had sent the women and children westward, herded on their way by Cross's Riflemen who had pushed them a mile down the pass and then left them to their own devices. Nearly four hundred prisoners remained in the Castle dungeons, guarded by the other lightly wounded Fusiliers. The wounded had been brought by wagon from the Convent to the Castle, carried up to the big room that looked westward and would be furthest from the French cannon-fire. The surgeon, a tall, grim man, had laid his probes, saws and knives on a table carried up from the kitchens.

Three Companies of Fusiliers were now at the watchtower, reinforcing Frederickson's seventy-nine Riflemen.

Sharpe had ensured that the best Captains were at the tower, men who could fight on the isolated hill and not look for orders that might never arrive. The weakest Captains, two of them, he had put in the Convent, and with them was Harry Price with Sharpe's old Company and eight of Cross's Riflemen. A hundred and seven men held the Convent, not counting officers, exactly half the number of Riflemen and Fusiliers who now crouched on the reverse slope of the watchtower hill. Sharpe had given the Convent one advantage. Patrick Harper was there, and Sharpe had put weak Captains into the building to make it easier for the Irish Sergeant to run the defence. Frederickson held Sharpe's right, Harper his left, and in the centre, the Castle. Sharpe had forty of Cross's Riflemen with two hundred and thirty-five Fusiliers. The Rocket Troop had gone south, hidden over the crest, the men nervous on their saddles with the strange lances in their hands.

'Sir?' An Ensign in the stairway that went up towards the gate-tower top called down to Sharpe.

'Yes?'

'One man riding to the watchtower, sir.'

Sharpe swore quietly. He had tried so hard to convince the enemy that the positions were deserted. Harper had led a group of Riflemen away from the watchtower, waited by the gatehouse as one Company of Fusiliers had conspicuously lowered the Colours and formed up outside the Castle, and then all of them had dropped beneath the lip of the pass before turning right and entering the Convent through the hole hacked for Pot-au-Feu's gun. The officer, one of the Fusilier's brighter men, had ridden south and scrambled his horse up steep slopes to join Gilliland's nervous men.

'And sir?'

'Yes?'

'One Battalion coming towards us. On the road, sir.'

That was better. It was all Sharpe could hope for, one single Battalion to check that the buildings were clear, one single Battalion that he could chop into pieces before breakfast. He climbed the stairs and the Ensign made way for him. He kept well back from the arrow slit and watched the Frenchmen come west on the road. They marched casually, muskets slung, and some still held bread in their hands from their breakfasts.

A French Captain, released by his Colonel's orders, rode ahead of the Battalion. He stared up at the Castle keep and saw a bird fly from one of the gaping holes in its stonework. A second bird appeared, big and black, and perched on the ramparts to preen itself. He grinned because the buildings were empty.

Sharpe was back in the chamber that had held the winding gear for the portcullis. He saw the Captain come easily up the road, saw the man's face look up at the arrow slit and it seemed certain that the man must see him, but the Captain's eyes went on up to the rampart. 'Now.'

The Fusilier, crouched beneath the left hand arrow slit, opened the second basket and the jackdaw cawed in anger, flapped furiously towards the light and squeezed itself through the stones and up into the air. The horse, only feet beneath, shied, and Sharpe heard the Captain soothe it.

The Captain stroked the horse's neck, patted it. 'You're frightened of a bird, eh?' He chuckled, went on patting it, and then the horse-shoes echoed loud on the stones of the tunnel that sloped up into the courtyard. He chuckled again because someone had chalked big letters on the stone of the tunnel. '*Bonjour*'.

The men in the chamber held their breath.

The Captain rode into the courtyard and saw where the rain had smudged and faded the bloodstains. The remains of a fire smoked lazily to his right in front of what appeared to be a long, low stable block. His horse was uneasy, tossing its head and moving sideways in short, quick steps. He patted it again.

One of the General's aides-de camp, a man curious about

the buildings of Spain, had ridden through the thorns to the watchtower. The thorns were thick here, the path tortuous and marked by small knots of old, faded wool left from the summer when sheep grazed these high pastures. He tied his horse to the bough of a thorn, cursing quietly as a spine scratched his hand, and then he took from his saddlebag a sketch pad and pencil. These towers, he knew, had been built against the Moors and this one was in fine condition. He strolled towards it, saw the gun in its earthen pit and saw, too, the nail that had been driven into the touch-hole. It was odd, he thought, that the British had not snipped the nail off flush with the breech, but they had left in a hurry. The gun was old, anyway, of a calibre not used by the French, so it was not much of a trophy.

He turned and watched the single Battalion march towards Castle and Convent, saw the Captain ride beneath the archway, and he looked right to where the other two Battalions were forming up in the village street. These were the new garrison of the Gateway of God, the men who would ensure that the troops who would march to Vila Nova would have a safe haven behind them for their withdrawal, and then he looked at the arched doorway to the tower. A small gasp of surprise came from his mouth. The door was round arched and decorated with a zig-zag pattern, distinctively French, and he took it as a good omen that some French knight or mason had supervised the building of this watchtower in a strange land. His pencil sketched the arch, skilful strokes shading the Norman decoration, and thirty yards away Sweet William watched him. The eye-patch and teeth were in his pocket.

The General was on horseback now, pulling his sword into place, preparing for the day's march. 'What's Pierre doing?'

'Sketching, sir.'

'My God!' His voice was amused. 'Is there a building he hasn't sketched?'

'He says he's going to write a book, sir,' said another aide-de-camp.

The General gave his strange laugh. The Battalion was turning to the left, approaching the Castle. The General pushed his canteen of wine into place, checked that the small leather case on his saddle pommel had the day's supply of paper and pencil for scribbled messages, then grinned at the aide-de-camp. 'I once knew a man who wrote a book.' He scratched his chin. 'His breath smelt.'

The aide-de-camp laughed dutifully.

And the bugle sounded from the gatehouse.

CHAPTER 20

Frederickson did not move. He had hoped that at least a Company of French Infantry would be sent to the watchtower, but there was only this single man, sketch pad in hand, whose slim, good-looking face, was turned worriedly towards the Castle.

The bugle sounded again, the notes unmistakably ordering 'Incline to the right', but this morning it told the carefully positioned British troops which of the three prepared plans was to be followed. The call was a repeated sequence of two notes that reminded Frederickson of a hunting-field call. The fox hunts would be out in England at this hour.

The aide-de-camp with his sketching pad started towards his horse, then stopped. No one threatened him. He frowned and, with his usual meticulous care, took a watch from his pocket, snapped open the lid that was engraved with a message from his father, and noted the time on the corner of the pad. Four minutes to nine. He looked quickly round the hilltop, seeing the second gun in its fresh pit facing south, but still seeing no enemy. Then he saw the redcoats in the Castle and he stood, aghast, and watched the musket smoke smear the morning.

The Captain whose horse was nervous had ridden to the great gate into the keep. The archway was blocked with stones, waist high, and he could see the empty inner courtyard beyond. His horse was still frightened by something, and that was strange, but he rubbed the neck, spoke fondly to it, and turned towards the stable-block. He could hear the boots of the leading Companies coming towards the Castle.

The Colonel of the Battalion waved grumpily to another Captain who wheeled his troops right, onto the Convent road, and then the Colonel looked back to the gatehouse. A fine building once, he thought.

The Captain put spurs to his horse and trotted back towards the Castle gate. He could at least confirm the abandonment of the Castle, and he grinned as he stroked his horse's neck, and then the horse shied again for the gatehouse was suddenly swarming with men. An officer, a Rifleman, had appeared from the gate leading to the northern ramparts, and a lad was beside him, bugle to his mouth, and the notes jerked into the valley. More men poured from a small door in the gatehouse, Riflemen, who ran into the tunnel and knelt with their weapons aimed. They seemed to ignore him, as did the other green-jacketed men who ran past the officer to the northern wall, and then there was a shout, a cheer, and a rush of feet behind him.

Redcoats were climbing from the keep, sprinting for the fallen eastern wall of the Castle, Sergeants bellowing at them, officers shouting, and the French Captain was alone in a courtyard of the enemy and he put hand to his sword and then saw the Rifle officer on the northern rampart waving to him. The wave was obvious. Dismount. Surrender. Next to the officer a Greenjacket knelt with levelled gun.

The Captain swore bitterly, dismounted, and the first guns split the morning.

Sharpe turned back. The leading French Company was thirty yards from the Castle as the rifle bullets dropped the front rank, then the second, and he glanced to his left to watch other Riflemen aiming for the officers. Rifles snapped from the turret at the gatehouse top and Sharpe saw the French Colonel thrown backwards from his horse, blood spattering his uniform, and then another volley of rifle bullets drove into the leading Company and the French officers were shouting at their men, forming them into line, and the deadly rifles on the ramparts picked the officers off and then went for the men in the single gold Sergeants' stripes.

'Keep playing, lad.' The bugler had stopped for breath.

A half-company of redcoats thundered into the gateway, lined in front of the arch, and the muskets flamed, the smoke thick in their front, and Sharpe knew that the French could not succeed in a desperate frontal charge. That had been their one hope, if their officers had lived to realize it, and now Sharpe ran back into the gatehouse, down the stairs, and out into the courtyard towards the eastern wall.

Stop them at the gate, then take them in the flank. He could hear the French shouting, hear the rattle of ramrods desperate in muskets, and then he was across the wall and the officers were shouting behind him, forming the half Battalion of Fusiliers into two ranks, a line to sweep north across the valley, and he turned to face them.

He waited as redcoats stumbled into place, checked their dressing, and Sharpe did not hurry them. This had to be perfect, for this was the one chance they would have to fight in the open valley and he did not want the Fusiliers to go forward in a hurry, their concentration broken by excitement and fear, and he waved at one gap between Companies. 'Close them up, Sergeant!'

'Sir!'

'Fix Bayonets!'

The rattle and scrape along the line. Rifles sounded by the gatehouse, the crash of muskets, then, at last, the first French replies as the dazed Battalion formed a ragged line at the crossroads.

Sharpe turned, drew the great sword. 'Forward!'

He would have liked a band at this moment, he wanted to hear the music in his ears as he went forward, the crash of a good tune such as 'The Downfall of Paris' or, better still, the Rifle's song 'Over the Hills and Far Away', but there was only the bugle still sounding. He looked left and still no more French troops were visible. He feared the cavalry and had an officer with Cross's second bugler on the keep to sound a warning if it appeared.

He looked to his front again. The Riflemen on the Convent roof were biting into the back of the French. They were panicking now, the enemy, crowding eastwards towards the village and Sharpe wanted that. He inclined the line to the left, forcing the French east, and the Riflemen from the gateway sprinted further left as the Fusiliers blocked the line of fire from the gate.

The nervousness was gone now, the hours of doubt as the night crawled by, the moments of waiting to unleash this small force against the enemy, and Sharpe felt the roadway beneath his boots and saw the French fifty yards ahead, and already he was picking his way through their dead. A musket ball went close to his head, a fluttering noise that left a tiny slap of wind, and he saw a Frenchman who had died with a look of utter astonishment on his young face. Behind Sharpe the Sergeants called. 'Close up! Close up!' They were taking casualties.

Sharpe stopped, listened to the boots behind him, heard the Rifles from the gatehouse, and the two rank line came up to him. 'Fusiliers! Present!'

The twin line of muskets, steel tipped, went to the shoulders. To the French it seemed as if the red line had made a quarter turn to the right.

'Fire!'

Flames gouted into smoke, a killing volley at short range, and the cloud spread in front of the Fusiliers obscuring their view.

'Left wheel!' This would be ragged, but this did not matter. His ears rang with the bellow of the muskets.

'Charge!'

Bayonets from the smoke, swords in the hands of officers, and Sharpe bellowed with them as he ran out of the smoke cloud and saw the French running as he had known they would run. Timing was all. This had been rehearsed in his

255

head again and again, thought through in the lonely hours, dreamed of as the rain fell on the weed strewn cobbles of the yard. 'Halt! Dress!'

A wounded Frenchman cried and crawled towards the Fusiliers. Their dead were thick at the crossroads where they had taken the single volley of musket fire at a range so close that hardly a weapon could miss. The Battalion was going back towards the village, leaderless and frightened, and Sharpe was standing close to the fallen Colonel. The man's horse was running free in the valley.

Sharpe re-lined the Fusiliers, still listening for the bugle call that would warn of the French cavalry, and he bellowed at the men to load. This was clumsy because the long bayonets skinned their cold knuckles as they rammed the shots home, but he needed one more volley from them. Gilliland! Where the hell was Gilliland?

The French officer at the watchtower saw them first, Lancers! The English had no Lancers! Yet there they were, coming across the skyline to the south, riding like the very devil down the small valley that split Castle and watchtower. They looked ragged and unprofessional, but that might have been because the horses had to negotiate the thorns, and then the French Battalion saw them and the officers and the Sergeants who still lived screamed at their men. 'Form square!' They knew what the Lancers would do to scattered infantry, knew how the long blades would tear into them and slaughter them, and the French leaders pulled at men, struck them, and formed the rallying square as the greatcoated horsemen burst out into the valley's pasture.

'Forward!' Sharpe shouted again, his sword unblooded, and the two ranks stepped and stumbled over the dead bodies of the French, past the wounded who cried for help, and the joy was on Sharpe for now he was within a few seconds of this first success.

'Left! Left! Left!' The Fusilier Captain who led the Lancers shouted at them, circled towards the Castle, waved with his sword at the place of safety. Never in any of his wildest hopes had Sharpe wanted the untrained Rocket Troop to drive the charge home. They would have died like cattle in a slaughter-house, but they had done their job. They had forced the Battalion into square, into a solid target for another volley from the muskets, and as the horsemen swerved fast, water spraying from their horses' hooves, and rode for the court-yard, Sharpe halted the line again. 'Present!'

The French knew what was coming. Some called out, pleading for quarter, and some hunched down like men anticipating a storm of wind and rain, and then the great sword fell. 'Fire!'

The splitting crash and hammer of the volley, the dirty-throated cough of the half-Battalion's muskets, and the balls converged and struck home into the huddled mass and again, 'Charge!'

The bugle sounded from the keep. 'The enemy is cavalry'. 'Back! Back! Back!'

They checked, skidded, turned, and ran as they had been told to run. A panicked rush for the eastern wall, a scramble away from the threat of French cavalry coming from the village, and at the wall they stopped, turned, and lined on the rubble that would destroy any charging horse. Then they cheered. They had done it. They had taken on a French Battalion, destroyed it, and the bodies littered the valley to prove it.

Sharpe walked back. He could see that the German Lancers were far away, unformed, and no threat. He looked towards the Convent and saw the huge figure of Harper standing on the roof. Blue-coated bodies on the road to the Convent showed where the single French Company had been pushed back. He waved to Harper and saw a raised hand in reply. Sharpe laughed.

Sharpe climbed the rubble of the wall, a rubble still marked by the explosion that had happened just yesterday. He looked at the Fusiliers. 'Who said it couldn't be done?'

Some laughed, some grinned. Behind them the artillery-men were gratefully sliding from saddles, leading their horses into the inner courtyard. They chattered noisily like men who had survived the valley of the shadow of death, and Sharpe saw Gilliland talking excitedly to the Fusilier Captain who had steered them safely to the Castle gate. Sharpe cupped his hands. 'Captain Gilliland!'

'Sir?'

'Make your men ready!'

'Sir!'

Sharpe had propped the sword against his thigh and he retrieved it, sheathed it, and looked at the Fusiliers. 'Are we going to lose?'

'No!' They roared the message defiantly across the valley.

'Are we going to win?'

'Yes! Yes! Yes!'

Pierre, the aide-de-camp, appalled and alone on the watchtower hill, heard the triple shout and stared into the valley. The survivors of the Battalion were going back to the village, pressed on their way by the Rifles that still fired from Castle and Convent, leaving behind them the Gateway of God horrid with dead and wounded. He took out his watch, clicked the lid open, and jotted down the time. Three minutes past nine! Seven minutes of butchery planned by a professional, seven minutes in which a French Battalion had lost nearly two hundred dead and wounded. A second French Battalion was parading in front of the village, their ranks opening to let the survivors through, and the German Lancers were forming in squadrons at the foot of the hill. 'Hey! Hey!'

It took a few seconds for the aide-de-camp to realize the hail was for him. The Colonel of the German Lancers tried again. 'Hey!'

'Sir?'

'What's up there?'

'Nothing, sir! Nothing!'

Some men of the defeated Battalion went back for their wounded, but the Rifles' bullets drove them back. They protested, holding up their arms to show they carried no weapons, but the Rifles fired again. They went back. Dubreton crossed to the Lancers, heard the shout and shook his head. 'It's a trap.' Of course it was a trap. Dubreton had watched Sharpe lead the half Battalion into the valley and he had hated Sharpe for his skill and admired him for the achievement, and no soldier who could gut an Emperor's Battalion in such short time would leave this hill unguarded.

The German Colonel waved at the aide-de-camp. 'He's there, isn't he?'

'So are the British.' Dubreton's eyes searched the tangles of thick thorn. 'Call him down.'

The German shook his head. 'And lose the hill? Perhaps they don't have enough men to defend it?'

'If he had half his number he'd defend it.'

The German twisted in his saddle and spoke to a Lieutenant, then looked back to Dubreton and grinned. 'A dozen men, yes? They'll search it better than that artist.'

'You'll lose them.'

'Then I'll revenge them. Go!'

The Lieutenant shouted at his men, led them into one of the winding paths, and the lances were held high so that the red and white pennons were bright against the blackness of the thorns. Dubreton watched them climb, saw how slow progress was in the thick bushes, and he feared for them. A Company of Voltigeurs came running from the village, French skirmishers sent to reinforce the climbing horsemen, and Dubreton wondered whether Sharpe had decided, after all, only to defend the two great buildings at the crest of the pass. Perhaps the German Colonel was right. Perhaps Sharpe did not have the men to hold all this ground, and the watchtower hill was horribly far from the Castle. Further, indeed, than the village was from the Castle gate.

The Voltigeurs, red epaulettes bright on blue uniforms,

disappeared into the thorns, bayonets fixed on their muskets. Sixty men took a half dozen paths and Dubreton saw them climb. The Lieutenant was almost at the top. 'We should have put a Battalion in there.'

The German Colonel spat, not at Dubreton's words, but at the Riflemen who stopped the French fetching their wounded. 'Bastards.'

'They'll make us carry a white flag. He's buying time.' Dubreton shook his head. Sharpe was a hard enemy.

The Lancer Lieutenant broke clear of the last thorns and grinned at the aide-de-camp. 'You've taken the hill, sir!' His French was broken.

Pierre shrugged. 'They've gone!'

'Let's make certain, sir.'

The Lancers spread out, blades dropped, but this was no place for a heart-stopping cavalry charge, hooves thundering on turf and blades searing at an enemy. This was a cramped, pocked hilltop surrounded by dark thorn and the horses walked slowly forward so the cavalry could peer into the deep wet spines.

Frederickson watched them. A pity, this. He had hoped for a Company, at least, not such few men, but a man must take what fate gives him. 'Fire!'

Only the Rifles fired, Rifles that outnumbered the Lancers nearly seven to one, and the big horses fell, screaming, and the lance blades toppled, and Frederickson tore himself clear of the thorns. 'Forward!'

One Lancer was alive, miraculously alive, and he stood with his lance extended and shook his head as Frederickson shouted at him in German. Then more German voices called to him, Riflemen, and the Lancer still obstinately refused to surrender but challenged them with his long weapon. He lunged at Frederickson, but the sabre easily turned the lance aside, and Sergeant Rossner hooked the Lancer's feet from underneath him, sat on the man's chest, and bellowed at him in angry German.

'Come on!' Frederickson rushed the hilltop, waving his men left and right, listening to the curses and shouts and they pulled themselves from the thorns. 'Skirmishers in front!' A musket bullet flattened itself on the tower. 'Kill those bastards!'

Frederickson was not worried by a Company of French Skirmishers. He spent his life fighting Voltigeurs, as his men did, and he left his Lieutenants to push them back while he walked to the gun facing north and pulled the nail out of the touch-hole. A sketch-book had fallen under the trail of the gun and he stooped, wiped the mud from the open page, and saw the drawing of the tower doorway.

'Captain?' A grinning Fusilier came round the tower, bayonet in the back of the aide-de-camp. The Frenchman looked terrified. He had run at the first bullets, dived into the gunpit, and then the hilltop was swarming with British troops. Now he faced the most villainous man he had ever seen, a man with one eye, the other socket raw and shadowed, a man whose top front teeth were missing, and a man who smiled wolfishly at him.

'Yours?' Frederickson asked, holding the sketch pad out.

'*Oui, monsieur.*'

The vile looking Rifleman looked at the sketch, looked back to the Frenchman, and this time Frederickson spoke in French. 'Have you been to Leca do Balio?'

'No, monsieur.'

'A very similar doorway. You'd like it. And some fine lancet windows in the clerestory. And below it, too. A Templar's church, which might explain the foreign influence.' But Frederickson could have saved his breath. The aide-de-camp had fainted clean away, and the Fusilier grinned at Frederickson. 'Shall I kill him, sir?'

'Good God, no!' Frederickson sounded pained. 'I want to talk to him!'

Rifles cracked from the top of the tower, Rifles that drove confusion in the ranks of the Lancers. The German Colonel swore, grimaced, and blood was on his thigh. He clamped a hand on the wound, looked up the hill, and swore again.

The Voltigeurs were going back, hunted through the thorns that crackled as the Rifle bullets spun through them. The French Voltigeur Captain saw more troops appear, red-coated and equipped with bayonets. 'Back! Back!'

Dubreton turned his horse and spurred back to the village. They had done everything Sharpe had known they would do, everything! They had played into his hand and now they would be forced to do the next thing Sharpe had planned. They would be forced to ask for a truce to rescue their wounded. Sharpe wanted time, and they would hand it to him on a plate!

'Colonel!' The General shouted. Behind the General an aide-de-camp was already skewering one of the white cloths from the inn onto a sword.

'Yes, sir. I know.'

The aide-de-camp unhappily spread the cloth out and Dubreton could see the stains of last night's wine. It seemed so long ago, and already his dinner guests had bloodied French pride in the grass. The next time it would not be so easy for them. Dubreton turned and spurred his horse between the ranks of the new Battalion, the aide-de-camp following him.

The firing died in the Gateway of God, the powder smoke drifting westward on the breeze, and Sharpe walked out into the pasture-land that he had spattered with the dead and waited for his enemy.

CHAPTER 21

'Major Sharpe.'

'Sir.' Sharpe saluted.

'I should have known, shouldn't I?' Dubreton was leaning forward on his saddle. 'Did Sir Augustus die in the night?'

'He found he had business elsewhere.'

Dubreton sighed, straightened up and looked at the wounded. 'The next time it won't be so easy, Major.'

'No.'

The French Colonel gave Sharpe a wry smile. 'It's no good telling you that this is futile, is it? No.' His voice became more formal. 'We wish to rescue our wounded.'

'Please do.'

'May I ask why you fired on the parties we sent forward to do just that?'

'Did we hit anyone?'

'Nevertheless I wish to register our protest.'

Sharpe nodded. 'Sir.'

Dubreton sighed. 'I am empowered to offer a truce for the time it takes to clear the field.' He looked over Sharpe's head and frowned. Fusiliers were digging at the graves which had been dug the day before.

Sharpe shook his head. 'No, Colonel.' The French could bring gun limbers and have their wounded off the field in thirty minutes. 'Any truce must last till mid-day.'

Dubreton looked to his right. The wounded who were still conscious shouted at him for help, they knew why he had come, and some, more horrible still, pulled themselves by their arms towards him. Others lay in their blood and just cried. Some were silent, their lives shattered, their future to be cripples in France. Some would live to fight again and a few of them limped on the road towards the village. The French Colonel looked back to Sharpe. 'I must formally tell you that our truce will last only as long as it will take us to rescue our men.'

'Then I must formally instruct you to send no more than ten men to their aid. Any others will be fired on, and my Riflemen will be ordered to kill.'

Dubreton nodded. He had known, as Sharpe had known, how this conference would go. 'Eleven o'clock, Major?'

Sharpe hesitated, then nodded. 'Eleven o'clock, sir.'

Dubreton half smiled. 'Thank you, Major.' He gestured towards the village. 'May I?'

'Please.'

Dubreton waved vigorously and the first men ran out from the ranks of the waiting Battalion, some holding stretchers, and then there was a bigger disturbance in the ranks and two of the strange French ambulances were galloping along the road. They were small covered carts, sprung for the comfort of the wounded, and they were the envy of the British soldiers. More men survived an amputation if their limb was removed within minutes of the battle wound, and the French had developed the fast ambulances to take the casualties to the waiting surgeons. Sharpe looked up to Dubreton. 'You had them very close, considering you were not expecting to fight.'

Dubreton shrugged. 'They were used to bring last night's food and wine, Major.' Sharpe wished he had not spoken. The last time he had met Dubreton a gift had passed between them, now they were enemies on a field. The Colonel looked at the Pioneers who were shovelling the loose earth from the graves. 'I assume, Major, that we will undertake no military works for the duration of the truce?'

Sharpe nodded. 'I agree.'

'So I assume that is not a defensive trench?'

'A grave, sir. We lost men, too.' The lie came smoothly off

his tongue. Three Fusiliers had died, and eight were wounded, but the grave was not being enlarged for the dead.

Sharpe turned to the Castle and waved, as Dubreton had waved, and the French Captain was released by the sentries on the gate. He rode into the field, trotted towards Dubreton, and he looked aghast at the carnage that had been wreaked on his Battalion. Behind him Fusiliers rolled the cart into the archway, sealing it.

Sharpe waved towards the Captain and spoke to Dubreton. 'Captain Desaix had the misfortune to be in the Castle yard when the fighting begun. He has given me his parole and undertaken not to bear arms against His Britannic Majesty, or his allies, until he has been exchanged for an officer of equal rank. Till then he is in your charge.' It was a pompous speech, but a necessary formality, and Dubreton nodded.

'It will be done.' He spoke in French to the Captain, jerking his head towards the village, and the young man spurred away. Dubreton looked back to Sharpe. 'He was lucky.'

'Yes.'

'I hope luck stays with you, Major.' Dubreton gathered his reins. 'We shall meet again.'

He turned, his spurs touched the flanks of his horse, and Sharpe watched him go. An hour and a half, a little more, and the fighting would begin again.

He stopped by the Fusilier Pioneers who scraped in the graves. A Sergeant looked up at the officer. 'Bloody horrid, sir. What do we do with them?'

The bodies had been uncovered, their nakedness horribly white and stained by earth, their wounds somehow unreal. 'They weren't buried deep, were they?'

'No.' The Pioneer Sergeant sniffed. The bodies were scarce one foot under the earth, no protection against the carrion eaters that would scrape them up and tear at the dead flesh.

Sharpe jerked his head towards the southernmost part of

the trench, the excavation nearest to the thorn covered hillside. 'Put them up there. Dig it deep. I want most of this trench free.'

'Yes, sir.'

'And hurry.'

The Sergeant shook his head. 'We could do with some help, sir.'

Sharpe knew there were enough men. 'If it isn't ready in an hour and a half, Sergeant, I'll leave you here when they attack.'

'Yes, sir.' The formal politeness barely disguised the hatred the Sergeant felt. As Sharpe walked away he heard the sound of the man spitting, but then there were bellowed orders, shouts for the Pioneers to get on with it, and Sharpe let the Sergeant be. It was a horrid job, but the Pioneers of a Battalion often got the horrid jobs, the worst of the digging and the least thanks. At least this time their work would not be wasted. Sharpe would need the trench to bury his dead in when this business was done.

He climbed to the ramparts of the keep and settled himself with his telescope and a cup of tea. He could see Frederickson's men dragging thorn bushes from the slope facing the village, some men hacking at trunks with saw-backed bayonets, others pulling at the thorns so that a wide path was being cleared up the hillside. The bushes were being taken to the southern slope, the vulnerable slope, and Sharpe wondered what cunning had devised the orders. Doubtless he would find out soon. He expected the watchtower to be the next point of attack, and he expected it to fall by mid-afternoon, and he rehearsed in his mind the plan he had to evacuate the garrison. Strictly speaking, whatever Frederickson was doing on the hill broke the terms of the truce, but the French were not meticulous in it either. Through the lens of his glass Sharpe could see the artillery coming into the village. Twelve pounders, the kings of the battlefield, big bastards to make the next hours into misery and death.

For once in the morning he wanted company, but there was no soldier he would want to talk to. Teresa, maybe, but even she would have given short shrift to his fears of defeat. Common wisdom said that an attacker needed a three to one advantage over a well-sited defence, and Sharpe's defence was as good as he could make it. Yet he lacked artillery to batter the French guns, and the French could bring far more than three attackers to each defender. There were the rockets, of course, but they would be useless against the artillery. For them Sharpe had other plans.

Futile plans, he thought, as useless as the pride and duty that had made him stay in this high place where he could not win. He could delay the French, and every hour was a victory of a sort, but the hours would be bought at the price of men. He knelt behind the rampart again, levelled the telescope, and saw eight Riflemens' shakoes lined on the topmost stones of the watchtower. Eight Battalions of French infantry in sight. Eight! Call that four thousand men and it sounded no better. He laughed silently to himself, a grim laugh, and he laughed because they had made him into a Major and his first achievement would be to lose a Battalion. What had Harry Price told him on the march from Frenada? That men did not live long when they fought for Sharpe. That was a grim epitaph, the summation of his life, and he shook his head as if to clear the pessimism from his mind.

'Sir?' A squeaking voice. 'Sir?'

The bugler walked slowly towards him, Sharpe's rifle on his small shoulder, a plate balanced precariously on one hand. 'The kitchen sent it, sir. For you.'

Bread, cold meat, and ships' biscuits. 'Have you eaten, lad?'

The boy hesitated. Sharpe grinned.

'Help yourself. How old are you?'

'Fourteen, sir.'

'Where did you get the rifle?'

'Soldier put it in your room last night, sir. I've been looking after it. You don't mind, sir?'

'No. Do you want to be a Rifleman?'

'Yes, sir!' The boy was suddenly eager. 'Another two years, sir, and Captain Cross says I can join the ranks.'

'Maybe the war will be over.'

'No.' The head shook. 'Can't be, sir.'

He was probably right. There had been war between Britain and France for as long as this boy had lived. He would be the son of a Rifleman, he would have grown up in the Regiment, he knew no other life. He would be a Sergeant by twenty, if he lived, and if the war did end he would be spat out onto the rubbish heap of the old soldiers whom nobody wanted. Sharpe looked away from him, knelt again at the parapet, and stared at the horsemen who once again had appeared at the end of the village street. A full General, no less, coming to fight Sharpe.

The General drummed his fingers on the leather writing box of his saddle. Damn this Sharpe, damn this pass, and damn this morning! He looked to the aide-de-camp who scribbled figures. 'Well?'

The Captain was nervous. 'We think half the Battalion is in the Castle, sir, maybe more. We've seen one Company on the hill, and some redcoats in the Convent.'

'Damned Riflemen?'

'Certainly a Company on the hill, sir. But they've a few in the Castle and we saw a half dozen in the Convent.'

'You mean there's more than one Company?'

The Captain nodded unhappily. 'It would seem so, sir.'

The General looked at Ducos whose eyes watered without the protection of his spectacles. 'Well?'

'So they have two Companies. One on the hill, the other split in two.'

The General did not like Ducos' nonchalance. 'Riflemen are bastards, Major. I don't like the way they're breeding over there. And tell me who those Lancers are, yes?'

Ducos shrugged. 'I did not see them.' His tone suggested that if he had not seen them, then they could not exist.

'Well I saw them! God damn it, I saw them! Alexandre?'

Dubreton shook his head. 'The English don't have lancers, and if they did they would dress them in cavalry cloaks, not infantry greatcoats. And this morning, remember, they did not charge home.'

'So?'

Dubreton shifted in his saddle, the leather creaking beneath him. 'Well. We know La Aguja is here, and I think it's unlikely she would travel alone. I think they were Partisans, given army greatcoats by the English.' He shrugged. 'They give them everything else.'

The General looked to his other side. 'Ducos?'

'It makes sense.' The voice was grudging.

'So we add fifty Partisans to the garrison. Now tell me how many British troops there are, and where?'

The Captain did not like the responsibility. His voice was unhappy. 'Sixty Rifles and a hundred redcoats on the hill, sir. Thirty and three hundred in the Castle, and thirty and one hundred in the Convent?'

The General grunted. 'Dubreton?'

'I'd agree, sir. Perhaps a few less in the Convent.'

'Guns?'

Dubreton answered. 'Our prisoners are certain of that, sir. One in the Convent which can't bear. One over the broken wall which isn't a danger till we reach the courtyard, and two on the hill.'

'And they brought gunners with them?'

'Yes, sir.'

The General sat silent. Time, time, time. He wanted to be at the river this afternoon, across by evening, and at Vila Nova by nightfall tomorrow. That was optimistic, he knew, and he had allowed himself one more day to achieve his object, but if this damned Sharpe held him up all day today, then the operation would be jeopardized. He played with an idea. 'What if we ignore them? Ring that damned Castle with Voltigeurs and march straight past them? Eh?'

It was a tempting thought. If the three Battalions that were to garrison the Gateway of God remained to continue the siege, then the rest of the force could go on into Portugal, but all of the officers knew what might happen. If the Castle was not taken by the three Battalions, then the General's retreat was blocked. There was another reason too. Dubreton voiced it. 'The pass is too narrow, sir. Those damned Rifles will kill every horse that goes through.' He imagined the light guns that were to go with the General smashed on the lip of the pass, their horses shot, the weight of barrel and carriage running the wheels over wounded animals, turning over, blocking the road beneath the pitiless aim of the Greenjackets.

The General looked left, at the high tower. 'How long to take that?'

'How many Battalions, sir?' Dubreton asked.

'Two.'

Dubreton looked at the thorns, at the steepness of the hill, and he imagined the soldiers climbing into the Rifle fire. 'Two hours, sir.'

'As little as that?'

'We'll offer them medals.'

The General gave a humourless laugh. 'So we could have the tower by one o'clock. Another hour to put guns there.' He shrugged. 'We might as well put our guns here! They can pound those bastards into mincemeat.'

Ducos' voice was a sneer. 'Why take the tower at all? Why not just take the Castle?' No one answered him, so he went on. 'We lose time with every minute! Colonel Dubreton has already given them till eleven o'clock! How many men would you lose attacking the tower, Colonel?'

'Fifty.'

'And still the Castle will have to be taken. So lose the men there instead.' The Castle was a mere blur to Ducos, but he waved at it dismissively. 'The attack *en masse*! Give medals to the first five ranks and go!'

En masse. It was the French way, the method that had brought victory to the armies of the Empire throughout Europe, the way of the Emperor, the irresistible mass. Throw the mass like a human missile at the Castle's defenders, overwhelm them with targets, terrify them with the massed drummers in the columns' centre, and push over the dead to victory. The Castle could be theirs by mid-day, and the General knew that the Convent was not the same threat, that it was less heavily garrisoned and more vulnerable to the twelve pounder shots that would crumble its walls about the British. Take the Castle, unseat the gun in the Convent, and then his troops could be marching into the pass by two o'clock, the garrison on the watchtower forgotten, ignored, treated with the contempt that it deserved. *En masse.*

He tried to work out casualties. They would be heavy in the first few ranks, perhaps a hundred dead, but that was a small price to pay for the time he needed. He could afford to lose twice that number and still not notice. The Emperor's way, and this wretched Ducos would write his report and it would be a good thing if it was said that victory was won in the Emperor's way!

'All the Battalions in the village.' He was thinking out loud. 'Fifty men in each rank, how many ranks?'

'Eighty.' The aide-de-camp said. A great rectangle of eight thousand men, drums in the centre, eighty ranks pushing irresistibly home.

Dubreton had lit a cheroot. 'I don't like it.'

The General wavered. He liked the idea, he did not want to be dissuaded, but he reluctantly looked at Dubreton. 'Tell me?'

'Two things, sir. First he's dug a trench in front of the wall. That could be an obstacle. Secondly I'm worried about that courtyard. We'll get in there and find every exit blocked. We'll be marching into a cul de sac, with Rifles on three sides.'

Ducos had a small spyglass to his right eye, the barrel

slightly contracted to compensate for his missing spectacles. 'The trench does not extend the full width.'

'True.'

'How wide is it?'

Dubreton shrugged. 'It's narrow. A man could jump it without effort, but . . .'

'But?' The General asked.

'In the column a man does not see the obstacles ahead. The first ranks will clear it, but the ranks behind will stumble.'

'Then warn them! And go in from the right! Most of the column will pass the trench!'

'Yes, sir.'

The General blew on his hands, grinned. 'And the courtyard? We'll fill it with muskets! Any damned Rifleman who shows his head will be dead! How many men do we think are there?'

'Three hundred and thirty, sir.' The aide-de-camp said.

'We're frightened of three hundred and thirty? Against eight thousand?' The General gave his horse-like laugh. 'A Legion d'Honneur to the first man into the keep. Will that do you, Dubreton?'

'I already have one, sir.'

'You're not going, Alexandre. I need you.' The General grinned at him. 'Good! We ignore the watchtower. Let them think they are important, and learn differently! We will attack en masse, gentlemen, and we will put every Voltigeur in front to keep the grasshoppers busy!' His good spirits were back. 'We'll paralyze them, gentlemen! We will do it in the way of Bonaparte!'

The wind from the east was getting colder by the minute, blowing into the faces of the Castle's defenders. The small patches of floodwater by the stream were turning gelid, the beginnings of ice, and behind the village the French Battalions took their orders that would take them in the way of the Emperor into the Gateway of God.

CHAPTER 22

'In Brittany, yes?'

The captured aide-de-camp nodded. Really this villainous Rifle Captain was not at all a bad chap, and certainly much improved by the addition of eye-patch and false teeth. He took the pencil and sketched a wild boar. 'The statues are all in the west. And you say they have the same things in Portugal?'

Frederickson nodded. 'In Braganza, exactly the same. And in Ireland.'

'So the Celts could have come here?'

Frederickson shrugged. 'Or come from here.' He tapped the sketch of the wild boar statue. 'I've heard it said they're a symbol of kingship.'

Pierre shrugged. 'In Brittany they're said to be altars. One even has a niche where a cup of blood could be put.'

'Ah!' Frederickson peered as the Frenchman shaded in the carved ledge. It had been an interesting morning. The Frenchman had agreed with Frederickson that the Plateresque architecture of Salamanca was incredible but over-elaborate. The line was lost in the detail, Frederickson said, and the Frenchman had been delighted to meet another heretic who shared that view. In truth both men hated such modern work, preferring the staunch plainness of the tenth and eleventh centuries, and Frederickson had drawn from memory the Portuguese Castle of Montemoro Velho and Pierre had questioned him closely. Now they had stretched further into history, to the strange people who had carved the stone boars, when a Rifle Sergeant stopped in front of them. 'Sir?'

Frederickson looked up from the sketch. 'Tom?'

'Two Froggie officers to the south, sir. Poking about. Taylor says they're in range.'

Frederickson looked at Pierre. 'The time?'

'Ah.' He pulled out his watch. 'A minute to eleven.'

'Tell Taylor to fire in one minute. And tell him to kill one of the bastards.'

'Yes, sir.'

Frederickson turned back to the Frenchman. 'You've seen the stone bull on the bridge at Salamanca?'

'Ah, that's fascinating.'

The Sergeant grinned and left them. In one minute Sweet William would be himself again, talking English instead of heathen French, and killing the bastards. He went back into the thorns, trying to work out which other Rifleman should shoot with Taylor and have the best chance of killing the second French officer. Sweet William always gave an extra ration of rum to any man who was proved to have killed an enemy officer.

Sharpe was standing on the rubble of the eastern wall, rubble that ended now by the shallow trench. It was less than three feet deep, too narrow, but the shovelled parapet added a foot to its effective depth. It would do. 'What's the time?'

'Eleven o'clock, sir.' Captain Brooker was nervous.

Sharpe looked at the men hidden behind the gate-house. The artillerymen were as nervous as Brooker, their bundled rockets looking like quarterstaffs at a country fair. He had made them disguise their blue uniforms with Fusilier great-coats, and they looked a motley bunch. He grinned at Gilliland and raised his voice. 'Don't be too eager! I think they'll be going for the watchtower before us!'

Two Rifles sounded in the distance, the reports muffled, and Sharpe looked in vain for the tell-tale smoke.

'That must be on the southern slope.'

'Looks as if you're right, sir.'

'Yes.' Sharpe sounded distracted.

'Shall I go?' Brooker was eager to be away from the exposed rubble. He would take a Company of Fusiliers to the valley that separated Castle from watchtower, a Company reinforced by Captain Cross with twenty Riflemen. They would cover Frederickson's retreat if the hill was swamped by French infantry.

'Wait a minute.' There had been no more firing from the watchtower, no rush of men from the northern to the southern slope. Sharpe looked back to the village. 'Ah!'

His exclamation came because the single French Battalion in front of the village was moving south, towards the watchtower, and Sharpe saw the men in the rear Companies splashing through the stream by the road. So it was to be the watchtower! He had toyed with the idea that the French might be in a hurry, and might come straight for Castle and Convent, but time, it seemed, was not their prime concern. They would do this thing properly. He could see the one Battalion moving south, he guessed from the rifle shots that another was out of sight beyond the hill, and soon Frederickson would have his hands full. He grinned at Brooker. 'Go! Good hunting!'

Brooker and Cross would leave the Castle by the great hole knocked in the southern side of the keep, the hole through which so many of Pot-au-Feu's followers had temporarily escaped. Sharpe thought with satisfaction of the presence of Hakeswill, bound in the dungeons, and then wondered what would happen to those prisoners if the French over-ran the Castle. If. It occurred to him that he had wanted to hold out two days, and very nearly a quarter of that time had passed already, yet he also knew that he had yet to be tested by the veterans who massed behind the village.

'Sir?' The bugler, still lugging Sharpe's rifle, pointed at the watchtower.

'What?'

'Can't see him now, sir, but there's a man running toward us, sir. Running like hell. A Rifleman, sir.'

What could have gone wrong? There was no firing from the hill yet, no smoke drifting on the breeze that was suddenly freezing. He had put his gloves down somewhere in the night and had forgotten where, so he blew on his hands and looked up at the clouds. They bellied low and dark, reaching down again for the summit of the watchtower, bringing a promise of snow that would make the pass treacherous and the journey of a relief force long and slow.

'There he is, sir!' The bugler pointed.

A Rifleman had burst out of the thorns where the stream ran into the valley. He glanced right at the French, saw he was in no danger, and sprinted towards the Castle. He was fit, whoever he was, running with Rifle and pouches, jumping the trench and coming to Sharpe. The man was breathing too hard to speak, but just held out a folded piece of paper. His breath made thick clouds in front of his face and he just managed to pant out the one word. 'Sir!'

There was a strange drawing of a wild boar on the paper that Sharpe did not understand, a drawing over which a message had been scrawled in dark pencil. 'You remember the F. Counter-attack at Salamanca? I can see it. Behind village. Ten Guineas says it's Coming Your Way. Skirmishers All to the West. 8 Batt's. Thought you promised *me* a fight! 2 F. Officers came too close. Bang bang. S.W.' Sharpe laughed. Sweet William.

Eight Battalions? Dear God! And Sharpe had just sent half his Riflemen and a fifth of his muskets off into the thorns. Suppose the French attacked both positions? Suppose they cut Frederickson off from the Castle? He turned. 'Ensign!'

'Sir?'

'My compliments to Mr Brooker, and he's to come back as fast as he can! Captain Cross as well.'

The Ensign ran.

'Gawd, sir!' The bugler was staring at the village.

And so he should, by God. The Battalion that had moved south had done so to make way for the troops that were to assault the Castle, troops who spilled out into the valley, shepherded by mounted officers, troops who blackened the eastern end of the pasture land.

'Oh God!'

'Sir?' The bugler was worried.

Sharpe was smiling, his head shaking in disbelief. 'Lambs to the bloody slaughter, lad. Oh God, oh God, oh God!' He turned. 'Captain Gilliland!'

'Sir?' Gilliland came out from the shadow of the Gate-tower, out into the chill breeze.

'Do you see that, Captain?'

Gilliland looked at the village, his face registering disbelief and shock. 'Sir?'

'Here beginneth the first lesson, Captain.' Gilliland did not understand Sharpe's sudden pleasure. 'You're going to see a French column, Captain. It's the biggest bloody target in the world, and you're going to tear it into shreds. Do you hear me, man?' Sharpe was grinning with delight, the cold forgotten. 'We're going to murder them! Get your troughs out!'

Thank God for the Prince of Wales. Thank God for fat Prinny and his mad father, and thank God for Colonel Congreve, and thank God for a French General who was doing what any other soldier would do in his place. Sharpe grinned at the bugler. 'You're lucky to be here, lad! You're lucky to see this!'

'I am, sir?'

Sharpe stood on the rubble, the wind stirring his black hair, and a thought crossed his mind that perhaps the French planned to punch through the gap between Castle and Convent, but he could cope with that. The rockets could be swung round to face north as easily as they faced east, and he watched the cumbersome dressing of the French ranks in front of the village and he noticed how the centre line of the first rank was well to the road's right, and he knew they were coming for him. He glanced at the watchtower. That growing mass would be a tempting target for Frederickson's gun, but Sharpe had given orders that the gun was only to be used for the hill's defence. Frederickson would have to bide his time.

He looked for the other Ensign who carried his messages, and he ordered three Companies of Fusiliers into the court-yard with all the remaining Rifles. The only problem now was the French skirmishers, a veritable cloud of them, and they must be kept decently back from the trench. He walked forward to the puny excavation.

Thirty yards were usable, and in those thirty yards Gilli-land's men were carving fifteen troughs in the parapet, troughs that aimed straight ahead, and Sharpe changed the angle so they covered the centre of the valley. He crouched behind the troughs, seeing where the rockets would go if they went in a straight line, and he saw where they would bisect the line of the attack just fifty yards ahead. He nodded. 'Perfect!'

The gunners put their metal troughs into the earth beds. They were nervous, terrified, but Sharpe grinned at them, joked with them, told them of the victory they would win, and his mood spread to them. He clapped Gilliland on the shoulder. 'Bring them out. Do it casually, a few at a time!' He had dressed the rocket troop in infantry overcoats, hiding the weapon till the very last moment.

The Riflemen were in the courtyard, staring at the solid mass of enemy, and Sharpe called them forward. He ordered them to lie down in front of the trench, their job to keep the Voltigeurs away from the rockets, and he lined the three Companies of Fusiliers on the rubble. Some would die because of the French skirmishers, but their volleys would make a killing ground in front of the Riflemen.

Two artillerymen served each trough. Others waited in reserve. One man would put the weapons on the metal cradle, the other would light the fuse, and both would duck into the trench as the propellant flamed overhead. And they would fire as fast as they could, rocket after rocket, each trough capable of five shots a minute giving over seventy missiles in a minute, missiles tipped with shells, death flaming from the trench at a target that was still being assembled at the village.

Cross was back in the courtyard, breathing heavily and looking worried. Sharpe put five of his Riflemen on the gate-tower, the rest in front of the trench, and he added Brooker's company to the Fusiliers lined on the rubble. The men looked terrified, as well they might, a double rank of four Companies was facing a French column, the instrument that had brought down kingdoms, and their only help was the spindly rockets lying in the trench, rockets that had been contemptuously dismissed as toys.

'Load!' Sharpe watched them. 'On the order to fire you will commence platoon firing! Your job is to keep the skirmishers away from the trench! Captain Brooker!'

'Sir?' Brooker's company was closest to the gate-tower.

'Watch that open flank of the trench! If those skirmishers get into the trench we're all dead. So don't let them! And don't worry about the column. That's dead already!' He grinned at them. 'You're doing this for Colonel Kinney! Let him see those bastards going to hell!'

And then the first drums sounded, the drums that had driven columns to Madrid and Moscow, that had piled Paris with captured Colours, the drums that beat the *pas-de-charge*, the rhythm that accompanied all French attacks, that stopped only with victory or defeat. Boom-boom, boom-boom, boomaboom, boomaboom, boom-boom.

And this time they were for Sharpe, just for Sharpe, a compliment from the Emperor to a man from a London Foundling Home, and he turned to face them, saw the French lurch into motion, and he laughed, mouth open to the wind, laughed because of the pride that suddenly took hold of him, swept him up, because the drums, at last, were for him.

CHAPTER 23

The General fidgeted. He had the feeling that there was some gesture he ought to make, perhaps to ride at the head of his men or stand to one side and salute them as they went forward, but he dismissed the thought irritably. The drums and the raised Colours stirred emotions that were hardly suitable for the pitiable enemy who would be crushed by this massive blow. A sledgehammer to crack a nut! He smiled, because he knew it to be true, but if the sledgehammer did the work swiftly, then it was worth it.

Time. Always damned time. He had asked the time as the first skirmishers walked forward into the open field. Quarter to mid-day. Forty-five minutes to assemble the column, which was not bad, but it was still forty-five minutes lost. Well, there would be an end to this impudent enemy by mid-day, and then he could send the Lancers into the pass, start feeding the Battalions after them, and then the cumbersome supply carts that had to carry food and ammunition for this mid-winter blow.

A Colonel of Artillery reined in beside the General. The man was silent and resentful, wanting to unleash the power of his guns on the defenders of the Castle, but the General had derided the idea. To bombard the enemy would waste more time, and he suspected that the British could shelter behind stone walls that would take his gunners hours to reduce to rubble. No, the infantry could do this swiftly, lose some men in the front ranks, then surge over the rubble of the eastern wall and open the pathway to Portugal.

On the watchtower hill Pierre accepted a drink from

Captain Frederickson's canteen and nodded towards the valley. 'I think you're about to lose.'

Frederickson grinned. 'Would you want to bet on it?'

A smile and shrug from the Frenchman. 'I am not a betting man.'

Frederickson looked at the top of the tower. 'Anything for us?' He shouted.

'No, sir.'

He looked back to the valley. The skirmishers were in loose order in front of the huge column, hundreds of damned skirmishers, and Frederickson did not like the look of them. They would threaten the fragile earthwork in which, he knew, Sharpe had hidden the rockets. He had watched the strange weapons being carried forward, watched fascinated through his telescope as the troughs were aligned, and he could see now the weak line of Riflemen who would have to fight off the Voltigeurs. They would be hard-pressed. 'Lieutenant Wise!'

'Sir?'

Frederickson sent half his Riflemen, forty men, westward. The Lieutenant was to take them until they were almost abreast of the trench and then, from the edge of the thorns, was to fire across the Voltigeurs' advance. Frederickson shouted them on their way way. 'And, kill their bastard officers!'

In the Castle Sharpe was giving the same orders to his Riflemen, and especially to the marksmen on the gatehouse. 'Officers! Go for the officers!'

Captain Gilliland, trying to control his nervousness, stood beside Sharpe on the northern end of the rubble. 'We could fire now, sir.'

'No, no, no.' The column was three hundred yards away, its noise filling the valley with the thunder of drums, and Sharpe had no faith in the accuracy of the rockets. At this range at least three quarters would miss, probably more, and he would wait. He would wait till the weapon could not miss.

But God! The Voltigeurs worried him. They outnumbered his defenders by themselves! He would wait, but while he waited the Voltigeurs would press close, and then a Rifle cracked from the gatehouse and the shot provoked a ragged volley from the French, a volley fired too far away, but the musket balls worried the air about the eastern wall and Sharpe glanced to his right and saw the fear on the faces of the Fusiliers.

And no wonder, by God. The column was marching south-west, direct at the Castle, a massive hammerblow of men driven by drums, a great block of troops a hundred feet wide and eighty yards deep, and to the watchers on the hill it seemed as if they had trampled a great swathe of pasture land flat leaving a mark like a heavy roller across the valley.

The Rifles were firing now, their smoke over the trench, their bullets snatching at the Frenchmen with swords, but still the Voltigeurs came forward. They fought in pairs, one man kneeling and firing, the other reloading, and the Riflemen were hopelessly outnumbered. The Greenjackets had to lie flat, to avoid the volleys of the Fusiliers, and a rifle was a hard weapon to load lying down. Sharpe watched the men bracing the butts on their feet, thrusting down with the ramrods, then rolling onto their bellies to aim and fire again.

And the musket balls plucked at the Fusiliers. A man screamed, his cheekbone shattered, another fell backwards in silence, his body still on the rubble, and the Sergeants began to close the files. The field was thick with skirmishers, the flashes of their muskets constant, the smoke like clouds above the grass.

'Fusiliers will advance to the trench!' Sharpe bellowed at them. To move was better than to suffer in immobility, and it would take them twenty yards nearer the enemy and give their muskets a better chance of scouring these damned skirmishers from his front.

The officers gave the orders. Not that they could march on the broken stone, but they scrambled forward and Sharpe yelled at them to dress the ranks properly, kept them busy with his orders, and then he looked left and saw the first Voltigeurs were just forty yards from the trench. 'Captain Brooker?'

'Sir?'

'You will open fire!'

'Sir! 'Talion! Level!' A pause. The slim sword swept down. 'Fire!'

Thank God for the hours of training, thank God that, for all its sometimes stupidity, the British army was the only army that trained its infantry with real ammunition. The first volley jerked four French skirmishers backwards, startled the others, and the Fusiliers went into the motions that were second nature to a soldier. Fire, load, fire, load, fire, four times a minute, biting the bullets from the paper cartridges, ignoring the enemy, seeing nothing beyond the dirty smoke that spread ragged over the trench, pouring in powder, ramming the bullet and wadding down the thirty-nine inch barrel, propping the ramrod against the body, bringing the heavy musket to the shoulder and waiting for the officer's order to fire. There was nothing to aim at, just a smoke cloud that hid God knows what horrors, a smoke cloud that sometimes twitched as an enemy bullet sprang through it, and then the platoon next in the line fired, the officer shouted, and the butt crashed back into the shoulder, the powder in the pan stung the face, and the three-quarter inch ball of lead slammed into the smoke and down the field.

And men fell. Some climbed to their feet, teeth gritted against the pain, and went on firing, while others crawled to the back, bleeding and hurt, their life going as their eyes faded, and Sharpe shouted at the Sergeants that the wounded were not to be helped. Men used the excuse of helping the wounded to escape battle, and Sharpe's voice rose clear over the platoon volleys, over the sound of the drums. 'Any man who leaves the line is to be shot. You hear me, Sergeants!'

They heard, and the wounded must bleed unaided, and

the muskets flamed and slammed back, and the platoon volleys ran like stabs of red light down the face of the half Battalion.

It was working, too. Seven hundred musket balls in a minute were making the front of the trench a savage place, and the Voltigeurs split left and right. Sharpe had gone forward, to the side of the musket volleys, and he saw through the smoke the French coming from the left and he turned. 'Captain Brooker! Left files back ten paces! Incline!'

And the right! What the hell could he do at the right? There were not enough men to fill the gap in the broken wall, and he screamed at the Riflemen. 'Watch right!'

Brooker's Company was angling their fire now, slamming shots towards the advancing column, but they could not put up enough bullets to drive the Voltigeurs back. Sharpe saw the French darting forward, kneeling, another stab of flame, and a ball clanged off the steel tip of his scabbard, making the sword wrench in its slings, and he heard the Rifles from the gatehouse and saw the man who had fired at him sink down, making small movements with one hand as if paddling the air for support, and then the Frenchman was crumpled on the turf.

And the column came. It had not far to come from the village, a three minute march at most, and the drums were louder now, the drums that were the French music of conquest, and Sharpe ran right as Brooker's men reloaded because he was worried about his right.

Smoke from the thorns, stabbing flames, French going back, shouting in alarm, and Sharpe grinned. Frederickson had sent help, and Sharpe knew he should have thought to ask for it, but it did not matter now because the Riflemen were driving the French back. A mounted Voltigeur officer spurred towards the place, shouting at his men to take bayonets into the thorns, and Sharpe guessed the man was hit by four or five bullets for he seemed to be dragged backwards off his horse, his jacket suddenly splashed with red, and the horse screamed, turned, and galloped across the Castle's front and was struck by a volley of musket fire.

Back to the left, the air filled with battle noise, with muskets, shouts, cries of pain, the scrape of ramrods, the clicking of the heavy flints backwards, the drums, always the drums. The Voltigeurs took their toll of the Fusiliers, eating at the files, throwing a man down, and the platoon volleys were replaced by men firing as fast as they could, loading, firing, their faces blackened by the powder, their mouths gritty with the stuff, their fear only governed by the drill that they had practised again and again.

An Ensign crawled from Brooker's Company, vomiting blood, his eyes giving Sharpe one last accusing look, and then he slumped, only to twitch as a French bullet thumped into his dead body.

Sharpe went back to the rubble, climbed, and he saw where Voltigeurs were close, so close to the trench, in places just twenty yards, and he glimpsed, too, in the skirling smoke, the unmoving bodies of two Riflemen, and he looked left. The column, bayonets bright, was close and still marching. He could see the mouths of the French open, knew they were shouting '*Vive L'Empereur*', and Gilliland plucked at Sharpe's sleeve. 'Now?'

'No! Wait!'

Wait while the Voltigeurs grew bolder, ran a pace or two, knelt, and another Fusilier screamed and was thrown backwards, while blood spattered the ranks and still they loaded and fired, and men cursed as flints broke and the Sergeants brought them the muskets of the dead, and still they fired.

The Voltigeurs were joining the column. It was close now, almost the time for Sharpe to unleash the rockets, and he felt the respite as the Voltigeur bugles called them back, called them to swell the ranks of this overpowering attack, as the drums kept rolling, the sticks frantically wielded by the drummer boys as if by hitting the stretched skins they could personally drive the column into the Castle.

A French Colonel died in front of the column. On the gatehouse one of Cross's men grinned. 'Four.' He bit another cartridge, began to reload.

In front of the Convent, Patrick Harper had his seventeen Rifles firing across the valley. They could not miss the column at that range, but they could not hope to stop it.

The General's fingers tapped on his writing case to the rhythm of the drums. He looked at Dubreton as the front of the column seemed to be swallowed in the musket smoke. 'That's that, Alexandre. Good training for them, eh?'

On the watchtower hill Frederickson and the captured aide-de-camp stood together. Frederickson scratched beneath his eye-patch. 'Now! Now!'

Sharpe cupped his hands. 'Riflemen back!'

He could see the column now as clear as his own men. He could see the young ones of the front rank who were trying to grow the thick moustaches beloved by the French infantry, he could see the muskets coming down for the single ragged volley that the front rank would fire before the bayonets were unleashed.

'Rocket troop!' He waited. Fifty yards. They could not miss. They had never been used on land against the enemy. One thing destroyed a column faster than any other weapon; artillery, and Sharpe was about to unleash a barrage of shells. He saw the French muskets come up for the hurried volley. 'Fire!'

The first rockets were already lying in the troughs, the linstocks touched fuses, and for a second nothing happened. The French volley, just fifty musket balls, busied the air, but Sharpe was not aware of it. He heard the first shout from the French, the first triumphant calls of victory, and then it was drowned by the rushing sound of the flaring exhausts, the smoke and sparks and flame bellowing and billowing from the trench, and they were away.

Like fire-balls hurled at unbelievable speed, like the bad dreams of a soldier, death from the ground, searing from the trench, the rockets given no chance to rise into the air, only to hurtle in front of the licking flame torch, bury themselves into the column, rockets coming from front and right, and the French who had started to run saw the sudden unbelievable smoke, a bank thicker than fog, and in the thickness was the serried rank of giant flame, leaping flame, and the rockets drove their heads into the column, file after file, rank after rank, thrusting in, scorching with their tails, shrieking noise louder than the drums, and the first shell-head exploded.

'Fusiliers! Fire! Fire! Fire!' The Fusiliers had gone back from the angry rush of flame and now stood, aghast, as they saw the weapon for the first time. Sharpe put anger into his voice. 'Fire! You bastards! Fire!'

God, but he had let them come close. He needed the volleys to pluck at the leading ranks, because the French could still win this if they had the wit to rush forward.

More rockets, the second volley, some teams quicker to load the metal troughs than others, a hasty duck as the tail flamed overhead, and then swing another twelve pound rocket into the cradle and touch fire to its tail.

'Faster! Faster!' Gilliland was almost jumping up and down in his excitement. 'Faster!'

One rocket managed to climb, screaming up into the valley's air, a streak of flame that stacked smoke behind it, and the French at the village saw it, saw the strange thing climb into the low cloud.

'What the hell?' The General could see nothing at the Castle, only a huge spread of smoke that seemed shot through with intermittent glow of flame.

'An explosion?' Ducos frowned.

A Frenchman came through the smoke, fearful and lost, his bayonet bright, and he saw the men in the trench and he knew his duty. The Riflemen, ordered to stay with the Rocket troop, saw him and two fired. The Frenchman fell back and a rocket lodged in his body, began to turn, spewing sparks and thick smoke, and a Rifle Corporal ran to it, kicked the head free, and it slithered faster and faster on the grass, disappearing into its own smoke.

The northernmost part of the column was escaping the rockets. They heard the noise, the screams, saw the explosions that seemed to come twenty yards inside the ranks, but they pressed ahead and Sharpe called the target to Brooker's Company. 'Fire!'

A small volley, but it checked them, put a barrier of dead on the grass, and then Gilliland pushed past Sharpe, hammered a trough into the grass with his boot, and an artilleryman laid a rocket into the trough. Another man struck fire onto a linstock with his pistol-grip steel and flint, and Sharpe stepped away from the terror of flame. 'How many more launchers have you got?'

'Four!'

'Get them!'

The close-packed bodies of the French soaked up the terrible force of the rockets. The missiles slammed home, slowed as they ploughed through the ranks, and then they would stop, lodged in flesh, and the flames of the propellant would make a swathe of scorching space, and then the shell, its fuse hidden in the metal tube, would spatter blood and iron fragments into the French.

No man could go into that flame-lanced cloud. The noise of the drums was drowned utterly, obliterated by the howling rush of the rockets, by the coughing explosions, and still the rockets came, still they searched further into the ranks, gouging new channels of destruction, exploding, and the French could see nothing but smoke, flames to left and right, and their ears were filled by the noise, by screams that came from dying comrades, and they went back.

More rockets had risen over the heads of the column, one drove through at head height and slammed into the open valley, over the trampled grass, and it veered left, climbed, and the French staff watched it in awe. The noise filled the valley, the smoke was stretched behind the long flame, and then the shell exploded north of the village and the fragments smashed outwards from the black smoke and the stick, burning, tumbled to earth.

Ducos watched the smoke of the explosion as if mesmerized. 'Colonel Congreve.'

'What?'

'Congreve's rocket system.' He snapped the telescope shut.

The General shook his head, looked back at the column. Its rear seemed unshaken, the ranks still formed, but he could see the explosions now, and the front of his huge column seemed to be buried in a writhing flame-filled cloud. 'They're not moving.'

Two more rockets arced over the column, struck the ground, bounced, cartwheeled, and exploded in the valley. Two more went north, climbing insanely over the Convent, but most were burying themselves in the column, twisting and flaming their way into the human target, searing noise and fire, exploding in the ranks, and the Fusiliers still fired.

'Alexandre!' The General put spurs to his horse. He could not watch while his men died, and he spurred into a gallop down the road and shouted at Dubreton. 'What the hell are rockets?'

'Artillery!'

The General swore, again and again. He could hear the weapons now, and he could hear, too, that the drums had stopped. He could hear shouting and screams, the sound of panic, and he knew that at any second the carefully disciplined ranks would dissolve into a panicked mob. 'Why in God's name would they bring them here?'

Dubreton shouted the horrid truth back. 'They knew we were coming!'

'Keep firing!' Sharpe yelled at his men. 'You're beating the bastards! Fire! Fire!'

Science at war. Death pushed by fire, and still the rockets

shook themselves clear of the troughs, dropped to the grass, slid in front of the flame, faster and faster, rose a few inches and leaped towards the enemy. Some went at knee height, cutting down file after file, others cannoned off men and angled through the French mass, and the French ran. They broke, the explosions and the flames seemingly filling the valley so that they lived in a place that was mysterious death and thick smoke and jagged shell fragments and always the roaring things from hell that came at them faster than lightning and dinned the eardrums and killed and killed and killed.

'Keep firing!'

Frederickson's men were out of the thorns now, loading and firing, aiming at any officer who seemed to be controlling a group of men, and the Fusiliers hammered their volleys into the obscuring smoke, and ahead there were screams, more screams, but the drums had stopped.

Another growing crescendo of the noise that was like no other noise on earth, like a great waterfall that hissed and seethed and roared, and the flames drove sparks and smoke backwards and Sharpe saw the glows going far into the smoke fog, some rising, and the red glows did not stop as they struck men, but went on out of sight and he called the cease fire.

The order was repeated by officers and sergeants. 'Cease fire! Cease fire!'

Silence. No, not silence. A seeming silence because the death was not sounding now, just the dying. Moans, cries, sobbing, calls for help, curses for a life ended, and in the wash of that pain Sharpe felt the anger of fighting ebb from him. 'Captain Brooker?'

'Sir?'

'Two ranks on the rubble. You may attend to your wounded.'

'Sir.' Brooker's face seemed appalled. He had not wanted to fight here, he had thought Sir Augustus Farthingdale a man of prudence and sense, and he could not believe that they had fought and won.

Sharpe's voice was irritable. 'There's more to come, Captain! Get on with it!'

'Sir!'

More to come. But the smoke cleared slowly, lifted by the breeze that carried it over the British dead and wounded, and as the smoke went Sharpe saw the fruits of his work. The scorch marks that fanned out from the shallow earthwork, and then the blood. It hardly looked like bodies after battle, it looked as if a giant hand had squeezed the enemy to death, had scattered fragments of flesh and blood on the winter grass beneath the lowering clouds, and then he saw distinct bodies, broken and burned, and the wounded stirred in the carnage like creatures heaving up from a pall of blood.

The Rocket Troop had burned hands and faces, scorched marks on their uniforms, but they grinned as they stood up in their trench, grinned because they had lived, and they beat soil from their greatcoats and trousers and then turned to look at their enemy.

Sharpe looked too, looked where the rockets had pierced and twisted through the ranks. Flames showed where the sticks burned, one giving fire to a wounded Frenchman's uniform and the man could not struggle free and his ammunition pouch exploded, gouting more smoke on the grass, and the dead seemed to stretch halfway back to the village, and Sharpe had not seen a field after battle like it. It sounded like a field after battle, the noise, the small noise usually, of men who are dying.

'Captain Gilliland?'

'Sir?'

'I thank you for your efforts. Tell your men so.'

'Yes, sir.' Gilliland's voice was subdued, like Sharpe's. The Rifle officer still stared at the field. He could see two horsemen halfway to the village, horsemen who stared as he stared, while beyond them the French infantry was slowly ordered into ranks before the village. Sharpe shook his head. Fifteen cannons firing canister would have caused more destruction, but there was something about the scorch marks, the burned dead, the spread of the wounded and corpses that was unlike anything he had seen. 'I suppose one day all battlefields will look like this.'

'Sir?'

'Nothing, Captain Gilliland. Nothing.' He shook the mood off him, turned, and saw the Bugler still had his rifle on one skinny shoulder. Sharpe took the rifle from him, dragging the sling free of the left arm, tears stinging his eyes because the boy had a musket ball buried in his brain. It would have been quick, but the boy would never be a Rifleman.

The first flake of snow fell as Sharpe walked away. It fell soft as love, seemed to hesitate, then settled on the bugler's forehead. It melted, turning red, and disappeared.

CHAPTER 24

The second truce in a day, a truce that would last till four o'clock. This time the General had ridden forward with Dubreton so he could see this Sharpe for himself, and he had agreed to the four hour truce because he knew there would be no passage of the pass this day. He needed time to draw up new orders to get round the delay imposed on him by the tall, scarred, grim looking Rifleman. He needed time to collect the wounded from in front of the Castle, to take them from that place of roasted flesh and scorched grass.

So many wounded, so many dead. Sharpe had tried to count from the gatehouse turret, but the bodies were too dense on the valley floor, and he wrote on a piece of paper merely that they had destroyed more than a Battalion of the enemy. Most were wounded, overcrowding the French surgeons' rooms, carried back by the light ambulances or on slow stretchers through the falling snow.

North-east of the village, caught in a tangle of thorns, some Lancers found a rocket that had exhausted itself and which had not exploded. They took it back to Adrados, but not before one of them saw riders on the hillcrests, saw a stab of musket flame, and when they handed over the weapon to Major Ducos they gave him news of a fresh enemy in the hills. Partisans.

Ducos bent low over the rocket in the inn, peering at its construction, prising the metal tube away from the head so he could see where the fuse had somehow worked itself free. He straightened up, his eyes losing their focus, and wondered how much of the stick had been burned away. It should be possible, he thought, to cram more powder into the cylinder, put a new stick onto it, and test fire the weapon. He began taking measurements of the rocket head, jotting the figures on paper in his cramped handwriting, while above him the wounded screamed as doctors peeled charred cloth from burned skin.

In the Castle courtyard the Fusiliers boiled water, then poured the water into their musket barrels to clear the fouled deposits of powder. They filled their ammunition pouches, watched the snow settle, and hoped the French had had enough.

In the Castle dungeons Obadiah Hakeswill rubbed his wrists where the ropes had been, grinned at the other prisoners, and promised them escape. In the dim light, far from the straw torches that lit the steps where the guards were, he pulled himself along the back wall, through the ordure and the cold puddles, till he was in the darkest corner. There he stood up, his nakedness pale against the dark stones, and his head twitched as he pulled at a stone high on the wall. He moved slowly, quietly, not wanting to attract attention. He had remembered the one thing that everyone else seemed to have forgotten.

On the watchtower hill Frederickson wrote on a piece of the sketching paper, then gave it to the French officer. 'My father's address, though God knows if I'll be living near him.'

Pierre had a formal calling card, on the back of which he put his own address. 'After the war, perhaps?'

'You think it will end?'

Pierre shrugged. 'Aren't we all tired of it?'

Frederickson was not, but it seemed hardly polite to say so. 'After the war, then?' He looked at the captured German Lancer whose spear had been decorated with a dirty white cloth. The Lancer was not happy, hating to carry the makeshift flag, and Frederickson switched to German. 'If you don't carry it your own people will shoot you.' He looked back to Pierre, changed back into the French language. 'You'll observe all the usual nonsense? Wait to be exchanged, no fighting against us until then?'

'I will observe all the usual nonsense.' Pierre smiled.

'And no telling what you've seen up here?'

'Of course not. Though I can't speak for him.' Pierre glanced at the Lancer.

'He hasn't seen the rockets in the tower. He can't tell anything.' Frederickson grinned cheerfully through the lie, knowing that Sergeant Rossner had described in graphic detail the non-existent rockets stacked on the hilltop to the young Lancer. 'I'm sorry to see you go, Pierre.'

'It's good of you to let me. Good luck! Come and see us after the war!'

Frederickson watched them go. He looked at one of his Sergeants. 'A thoroughly nice man, that.'

'So it seems, sir.'

'Sensible, too. Much prefers Salamanca's old Cathedral to the new.'

'Really, sir?' The Sergeant had not noticed one Cathedral in Salamanca, let alone two.

Frederickson turned to see Lieutenant Wise coming up through the thorns. 'Well done, Lieutenant! Any casualties?'

'Corporal Baker lost a finger, sir.'

'Left or right hand?'

'Left, sir.'

'Well, he can still fire a rifle. Splendid! And when we run out of ammunition we can throw snowballs!' He grinned at the Sergeant. 'Come the four corners of the world in arms, Sergeant, and we will shock them.'

'A chance would be a fine thing, sir.'

'It will come, Sergeant, it will come!'

To the north of the village, well away from the Rifle sharpshooters on the watchtower hill, two batteries of French guns unlimbered. The horses were taken away, the ready ammunition piled by the guns, and the snow settled on the bulbous roundshot piles and on the serge bags of powder. The artillerymen were strong and confident. The infantry had failed, and now the General was sensibly calling in the artillery. Not just the artillery, the French artillery, Napoleon's own weapon. Every gunner in France was proud that the Emperor was an artilleryman. A Sergeant swept the snow off the wreathed 'N' on a gun's breech and squinted along the barrel at the Convent. Soon, my lovely, he thought, soon. He patted the gun as though the brass, iron and timber monster were a favoured child.

Sharpe crossed to the Convent during the truce, his boots leaving fresh prints on the snow, and he stopped at the gates to look at the foreshortened barrels of the guns, guns that looked straight at him. He went inside, past the hornbeam which was decorated anew with a delicate tracery of snow, and it seemed impossible that only yesterday morning he had watched the German Riflemen decorate the bare branches.

He spoke to the officers, surprising them with his words, and he made them repeat his orders and then walk him through their positions so he knew they had understood. The Fusilier officers seemed relieved by his words. 'We will not defend the Convent, gentlemen.'

'Something up your sleeve, sir?' Harry Price grinned.

'No, Harry.'

Sharpe went downstairs and found Harper. 'Patrick?'

'Sir?' The big grin.

'All well?'

'Aye. So what's happening?' Sharpe told him and the broad Irish face nodded. 'The lads will be glad to be back with you, so they will, sir.'

'I'll be glad to have them back. Tell them.'

'They know that. How's my friend Private Hakeswill?'

'Rotting in the dungeon.'

'I heard so.' Harper grinned. 'That's good.'

'Did you spike the gun?'

'Aye, they'll not fire that in a hurry.' Harper had driven a nail into the touchhole, then filed the cut nail smooth with the breech. The whole touch-hole would have to be drilled out, then replaced with an iron wedge block, in which a new touch-hole was bored, that was inserted from the inside of the barrel and shaped so that each subsequent firing of the gun would drive it further home. Harper scratched his temple. 'You reckon it will be tonight, sir?'

'Dusk?'

'Aye.'

'Good luck.'

'The Irish don't need luck, sir.'

'Just the English off their backs, yes?' Sharpe laughed.

Harper grinned. 'You see how promotion brings sense to you, sir?'

Sharpe walked back across the valley, the snow falling thicker now, only a few tussocks of grass visible above the clean whiteness. He thought it would be the Convent that the French would attack, though it was possible that the siting of the guns was an attempt to mislead him, but he did not think so. The French wanted the Convent so they could put their big guns behind the protection of its wall and hammer at the Castle's northern ramparts. Then they would try for the watchtower so their guns could plunge fire into the courtyard, and most of all he feared the howitzers that would lob their shells high in the clouds before they fell among the defenders. Tomorrow.

The snow crunched under his boots, settled on his face, touched the old ramparts with a white shading which was curiously beautiful. The snow had covered the dark stains on the grass. He wondered how long they could hold this position. The weather could only delay any relief, and now they were down to just four hundred rockets. Gilliland had not been able to bring more because of the necessity of bringing the Fusiliers' supplies, but somehow Sharpe did not think the rockets would be used much more in the Gateway of God. He had one idea for them, an idea of desperation, but they had served their purpose, as had the quick-fuses which he had taken from Gilliland for another purpose. The fuses were for firing batches of rockets, and Gilliland had been unhappy at losing them, but their time would come.

Upstairs in the Castle the Fusilier surgeon sawed at a leg. He had pushed back the flap of skin that would fold over the stump, sliced through the muscle, tying off the blood vessels, and he worked fast with his short saw. Orderlies held the Fusilier down on the table, the man was trying to hold back his scream, gagging down on the folded leather pad that had already subdued the pain of fifteen other men, and the surgeon grunted as the bone splintered and powdered beneath the saw's teeth. 'Almost there, son. Good lad! Good lad!'

In the trench where the rockets had been fired Cross's German Riflemen buried their two dead. They had deepened the trench, put the bodies in, and then covered them with rocks that would prevent the scavengers' paws from scrabbling up the dead meat. They had piled the earth on top, watched as Cross said sad, inadequate words, and then, as the snow mottled the mounded grave, they had sung the new song which the Germans of this war had taken to their hearts. *'Ich hatt' einen Kameraden, Einen bess'ren findst du nicht . . .'* Their voices reached Sharpe in the Castle keep. 'I had a comrade once, you couldn't find a better.'

Captain Brooker stood opposite Sharpe. The Fusilier Captain was shaved, his uniform brushed, and he made Sharpe feel dirty and tattered. 'What's the bill, Captain?'

'Fifteen dead, sir. Thirty-eight badly wounded.'

'I'm sorry.' Sharpe took the paper from him, tucked it into his pouch. 'Ammunition?'

'Plenty, sir.'

'Rations?'

'Two days, sir.'

'Let's hope it won't be that long.' Sharpe rubbed his face. 'So we're down to a hundred and eighty Fusiliers in the Castle?'

'A hundred and eighty-two, sir. With officers, of course, there's more.'

'Yes.' Sharpe grinned, trying to break through Brooker's reserve. 'And we're holding off a whole army.'

'Yes, sir.' Brooker sounded gloomy.

'Don't worry, Captain. You'll get ninety Fusiliers from the Convent tonight.'

'You think so, sir?'

Sharpe almost snapped that he would not have said it if he did not think so, but he bit back the reproof. He needed Brooker's co-operation, not his enmity. 'And there's still nearly a hundred and fifty on the watchtower hill.'

'Yes, sir.' Brooker's face was lugubrious, like a Methodist preacher who revelled in hell-fire predictions.

'You checked the prisoners?'

Brooker had not, but he was frightened of Sharpe. 'Yes, sir.'

'Good. I don't need those bastards up my backside. Put fresh men on as guards tonight.'

'Do we feed them, sir?'

'No. Let the bastards starve. Do you have the time, Captain?'

Brooker pulled a heavy turnip watch from his pocket. 'A quarter to four, sir.'

Sharpe walked to a great hole in the wall where stones had fallen from an arrow slit. The snow was slanting down over the valley. It was dark outside, the sky almost black, the clouds bringing a premature dusk. Below him he saw Captain Cross by a new grave, a smaller grave, and he saw a Rifleman who had once been a bugler put the dead boy's instruments to his lips. First he played the Buglers' call, short and simple, the notes clear in the darkening valley. Then, a long call, requested by Sharpe for the dead lad, the call that was for setting the watch. It ended in long, slow notes, played sweetly. *Ich hatt' einen Kameraden.*

There was a scrape of feet at the door, a cough for attention, and Sharpe turned to see a Rifleman. 'Yes?'

'Compliments of Captain Frederickson, sir.' He held out a piece of paper.

'Thank you.' Sharpe unfolded it. 'Partisans to north, east and south. Password tonight? Do I get a fight or not?' This time it was signed 'Captain William Frederickson, 5th Batt', 60th, retired.' Sharpe smiled, borrowed a pencil from Brooker, and rested the paper on the broken ledge of the arrow slit. 'Password tonight; patience. Countersign; virtue. Expect your fight at dawn. During night no patrols of mine will go east of stream. Good hunting. Richard Sharpe.' He gave it to the Rifleman, watched him go, then gave the password to Brooker. 'And you'd better warn the sentries about Partisans. Some may want to come in in the night.'

'Yes, sir.'

And cheer up, you bastard, Sharpe wanted to add. 'Carry on, Captain Brooker.'

The minutes passed. Artillerymen brushed snow from the touch-holes of guns that would soon be too hot for the snow that lay an inch deep on the brass barrels, each barrel more than seven feet long between the five foot high wheels. Each gun caisson had dropped forty-eight roundshot, the trail boxes on the guns themselves contained another nine each, and the gunners would be happy to fire all those shots to bring the eastern face of the Convent crashing to the ground to let in the Battalion of attacking infantry. This Battalion had been at the rear of the Column, virtually untouched by the rockets, and they would attack in the very last light. Then the guns would move in under the cover of darkness, embrasures would be hacked in the south wall, and these twelve-pounder monsters would take on the Castle itself. Let the gunners show how it ought to be done.

By five minutes to four the valley seemed deserted. The

Fusiliers were behind stone walls, the Riflemen on the hill were in the shallow scoops they had fashioned beneath the thorns, the French were masked by the village.

Sharpe climbed the gatehouse turret, stamped his feet on the cold snow, talked with the Riflemen whose post this was. 'Must be nearly time.'

Serge bags were thrust down barrels, then the roundshot that was strapped to the wooden shoe which would burn off in flight. Spikes were thrust into touch-holes to pierce the powder bags, then the priming tube thrust home, the slant of the touch-hole making the quills slant forward so that they would be expelled in that direction. The Colonel looked at his watch. Two minutes to four. 'A pox on those bastards. Fire!'

Eight guns slammed back, eight trails gouging the clean snow, and the crews were instantly to work, straightening the guns with handspikes and ropes, other men sponging out the hissing barrel, others ready with the next charge.

The first shots bounced a hundred yards short of the convent, rose, and slammed into the wall. As the barrels grew hotter that first bounce would creep towards the Convent till there was no bounce at all. 'Fire!'

The guns were hidden from the gatehouse, but the long muzzle flames spread red flashes on the snow and Sharpe watched each volley bloom rose-red on the whiteness. They were good. The shots came faster, the rhythm creeping up to the swinging team-work of well trained artillerymen where each man knew his job, and each man took pride in doing it well, and the rose-red flashed, the balls smashed at the Convent, and the wall, which had not been built for defence, cracked and crumbled.

'Fire!'

The smoke drifted towards the convent, drifted slowly with the falling snow, and now the flakes hissed as they hit the hot barrels, and again the guns bucked back, wheels bouncing, and again the teams dragged them round, rammed them, primed them, fired them, and the gates of the Convent had already gone.

'Fire!'

And each volley seemed to tinge the drifting cloud with red so that the sky was grey-black, the valley white, and the northern edge a place of redness. 'Fire!'

The noise echoed from the hills, jarred snow from the eaves of the village houses, tinkled the glasses in the inn's kitchen.

'Fire!'

A length of wall collapsed, dust looking like smoke, and the next roundshot smashed through an interior wall, breaking plaster and old stone, and the guns smashed back again, their crews hot and sweating despite the cold, and the gunner Colonel grinned in pleasure for his men.

'Fire!'

The upper cloister was open to the valley now, the closed Convent torn apart by the close range gunnery, and the first acrid smoke of the early volleys was drifting between broken pillars and fallen carvings.

'Fire!'

The hornbeam was struck on the trunk, it seemed to fly in the air, roots tearing up tiles and snow, and the buttons and ribbons that had decorated it were thrown to the ground with the falling tree.

'Fire!'

The cat that had walked so delicately on the Christmas morning tiles now hissed, claws outstretched, in the cellar. The fur on its back was upright. The building seemed to shake around it.

'Fire!'

A Rifleman on the gatehouse pointed. 'Sir?'

The French Battalion were moving along the northern fringe of the valley, their blue coats dark in the gloom where the smoke rolled over the snow.

'Fire!'

The last volley, crashing down a carved archway, bringing tiles slipping in an avalanche of clay and snow from the roof, and the Voltigeurs cheered, ran clumsily on the snow, and the first muskets fired at the Convent.

'Now.' Sharpe said. 'Now!'

'Sir?'

'Nothing.' It was nearly dark, so much so that his eyes played tricks in the gloom.

The Convent's defenders, sheltered in the inner cloister, ran as they had been ordered to run. Up the stairs, up the ramp of the cloister furthest from the guns, and then to their places. One volley, muskets and rifles pricking the dusk, and then they jumped. Some went down rubble into the upper cloister, clambered over the wreckage of the wall, and sprinted towards the Castle. Others jumped from the roof, falling clumsily on the snow covered slope, and they too ran for the safety of the ramparts. Sharpe looked up the valley. There was no cavalry, there was no need to send out the three Companies of Fusiliers to cover the retreat.

The French saw them go, cheered, fired a hasty farewell volley and then the Battalion scrambled over the wreckage made by the guns, and French cheers sounded in the valley for they had their first victory.

'Limber up!' The Colonel wanted the guns moved swiftly to the Convent. The howitzers, which had not fired, were already hitched to their horses.

The Battalion spread through the Convent, finding the barrels of liquor that Sharpe had left them, barrels he hoped would make them drunk and helpless. The officers saw them too, levelled pistols, and blew the strakes from the bottom so the liquor flowed into the snow. 'Move! Move! Move!' A passage had to be cleared for the guns.

The Convent's defenders came in through the archway of the Castle. One man limped, his ankle sprained by the fall, another cursed because a French musket bullet was lodged in his buttocks. Laughter greeted his pained announcement.

Sharpe leaned over the turret into the courtyard. 'Call the roll!'

The Fusiliers reported first. 'All present!'

Cross's Riflemen. 'Present!'

'Lieutenant Price?'

The Lieutenant's face was white as he looked up. 'Harps is missing, sir!' There was disbelief in his voice. Around him the men of Sharpe's Company stared up at the turret and on their faces was a hope that Sharpe could bring off a miracle.

Lieutenant Price's voice was anguished. 'Did you hear me, sir?'

'I heard you. Block the gate.'

There was a gasp from below. 'Sir?'

'I said block the gate!' Anger in Sharpe's voice.

He turned and the snow drifted gentle in the dusk, drifted past the ramparts to settle on the graves, drifted down the long pass where help must come, settled on the shattered east wall of the Convent.

Harper had said that the Irish do not need luck. Sharpe flinched as musket shots sounded deep within the Convent from which only Sergeant Patrick Harper had not escaped.

Lieutenant Price was on the turret, panting from his swift climb up the winding stair. 'He was with us, sir! I didn't see anything happen to him!'

'Don't worry, Harry.'

'We can go back in the night, sir!' Price was eager.

'I said don't worry, Harry.' Sharpe stared northwards into the smoking twilight.

Ich hatt' einen Kameraden, Einen bess'ren findst du nicht.

CHAPTER 25

In war, as in love, few campaigns go exactly as planned, and the French General remade his plans before the fire at the inn. 'The object is still the same, gentlemen, to draw the British north. If we cannot make Vila Nova, then we can still make Barca de Alva. It will have the same effect.' He turned to the gunner Colonel. 'How long before your guns are in place?'

'Midnight, sir.' The guns had to be manhandled into the Convent, embrasures made in the southern wall, but the work was going fast. They had feared that the British might send Riflemen to harry the progress, but none had come.

'Good. Sunrise, someone?'

'Twenty-one minutes past seven.' Ducos was always exact about these things.

'These long nights! Still, we knew of them when we started.' The General sipped muddy coffee, looked back to the gunner. 'Howitzers, Louis. I don't want a man to be able to move in that courtyard tomorrow.'

The Colonel grinned. 'Sir. I can put two more in there.'

'Do it.' The General smiled at Dubreton. '*Merci*, Alexandre.' He took the offered cigar, rolled it between finger and thumb, and accepted a light. 'When can we open fire?'

The gunner shrugged. 'When you want, sir.'

'Seven? And we put two more batteries on the southern edge of the village to fire straight across the breach, yes?' The Colonel nodded. The General smiled. 'Canister, Louis. That will stop their damned rockets. I don't want a man living if they leave the shelter of the walls.'

'They won't, sir.'

'But your gunners will be in range of those damned Riflemen on the hill.' The General spoke slowly, thinking aloud. 'I think we must keep them busy. Do you believe this report they have rockets?' He had turned to Dubreton.

'No, sir. I can't see how they could fire them through the thorns.'

'Nor me. So. We'll send a Battalion up the hill, eh? They can keep the Riflemen busy.'

'Just one, sir?'

The fire crackled in the hearth, sparks spitting onto the boots that dried before the flames, and the plans were meticulously made. A battalion, reinforced by Voltigeurs, would assault the watchtower while two twelve-pounders, instead of going into the Convent, would soak the thorns with canister to kill the hidden Greenjackets. The howitzers in the Convent would make the Castle courtyard into a place of shell-born death, while guns south of the village would rake the rubble and earthworks so no rockets could be carried to their launchers. And the infantry would attack again in mid-morning, an infantry that would be protected by the guns, that would take their bayonets to a shattered, demoralized garrison. Then the French could march on to the bridge at Barca de Alva, to victory. The General raised a glass of brandy. 'To victory in the Emperor's name.'

They murmured the toast, drank it, and only Dubreton muttered a doubt. 'They gave the Convent up pretty easily.'

'They had few men there, Alexandre.'

'True.'

'And my guns had softened them.' The Colonel of Artillery smiled.

'True.'

The General raised his glass again. 'And tomorrow we win.'

'True.'

The breeze drifted the snow into piles inside the Castle

courtyard. The flakes hissed in the fire, melted on the backs of the Rocket Troop horses who were huddled inside the keep's courtyard, settled wet and cold on the greatcoats of the men who stared into the night and feared a screaming attack from the darkness. Rags were wrapped round the locks of muskets and rifles, rags to stop the wetness reaching the powder in the pans. Fires had been lit in the Convent and the flames showed where French soldiers struggled at the old gateway, heaving and hammering stones into a crude ramp up which the guns could be pushed. Occasionally a rifle shot cracked in the valley and its bullet would chip stone by the French or throw a man down, cursing and wounded, but then the French protected the place with an empty ammunition caisson, and the Riflemen saved their ammunition. Other Riflemen, from Frederickson's Company, patrolled into the valley. Their orders were to keep the French awake, to fire at lights, shadows, to wear on the night-time nerves of the enemy, while on the hill the Fusiliers cursed and swore and wondered what kind of maniac would order to them to search by night for rabbit holes. Rabbit holes!

Men slept uneasily, their uniforms half dried by the fires, their muskets always within reach. Some woke in the darkness, wondering for an instant where they were, and when they remembered the chill fear would come back. They were in a bad place.

Major Richard Sharpe seemed distracted. He was polite, attentive to every detail, secretive about tomorrow's plans. He stayed on the gatehouse turret till midnight, till the snow stopped falling, and then he had joined his Company for a thin meal of boiled dried beef. Daniel Hagman had assured Sharpe that Harper would survive, but there had been little conviction in the old poacher's voice and Sharpe had just smiled at him. 'I know, Dan. I know.' There had been little conviction in Sharpe's voice as well.

Sharpe walked every rampart, spoke to every sentry, and the tiredness was like a pain in every part of his body. He wanted to be warm, he wanted to sleep, he wished that Harper's huge and genial presence was in the Castle, but he knew, too, that he would have little sleep this night. An hour or two, perhaps, huddled in some cold corner. The room that Farthingdale had made his own, the room with the fireplace, had been given to the wounded, and no man in the valley had a worse night than them.

The wind was cold. The snow seemed almost luminous on the valley floor, a white sheet that would betray an enemy movement. The sentries fought to stay awake on the ramparts, listened for their Sergeants' footsteps, wondered what the dawn would bring from the east.

To the south there was a glow in the sky, a red suffusion that marked where Partisans were spending the dark hours. Somewhere, just once, a wolf gave a sobbing howl that was ghostlike in the high, dark night.

Sharpe's final visit to the sentries was to the men who guarded the hole hacked in the southern side of the keep. He looked at the snow-covered thorns of the hill and knew that, should tomorrow they be overwhelmed, that was the escape route. Many would never take it, but would lie dying in the Castle, and he remembered the winter four years before when he had led the single Company of Riflemen, in weather worse than this, on a retreat that had been as desperate as tomorrow's might be. Most of those men were dead now, killed by disease or by the enemy, and Harper had been one of the men who had struggled south in the Galician snows. Harper.

He went to the steps which led straight and broad down to the dungeons. Lightly wounded Fusiliers guarded the prisoners and they did so in a stench that was vile, a stench that rose from the crammed, foul bodies in the dark. The guards were nervous. There was no door to the dungeons, just the stairway, and they had made a barricade, chest high, at the bottom of the steps and lit it with flaming straw torches that showed the slick wetness of the nearest patch of floor. Each guard had three muskets, loaded and cocked, and the thought was that no prisoner would have time to clamber the barricade before a bullet would throw him back. The guards were pleased to see Sharpe. He sat with them on the steps. 'How are they?'

'Bleeding cold, sir.'

'That'll keep them quiet.'

'Gives me the creeps, sir. You know that big bastard?'

'Hakeswill?'

'He got free.'

Sharpe looked into the darkness beyond the torches. He could see the half-naked bodies piled together for warmth, he could see some eyes glittering at him from the heap, but he could not see Hakeswill. 'Where is he?'

'He stays at the back, sir.'

'Given you no trouble?'

'No.' The man spat a stream of tobacco juice over the unbalustraded edge of the stairs. 'We told them if they came within ten feet of the barricade, we'd fire.' He patted the butt of his musket, one captured from Pot-au-Feu's men.

'Good.' He looked at the half-dozen men. 'When are you relieved?'

'Morning, sir.' Their self-elected spokesman said.

'What do you have to drink?'

They grinned, held up canteens. 'Rum, sir.'

He walked down the steps and pushed at the barricade. It seemed firm enough, a mixture of stones and old timber, and he stared into the darkness and understood why this damp place would scare a man. It was called a dungeon, though in truth it was more like a huge, branching cellar, arched low with massive stones, but doubtless it had been a place where men had died through the ages. Like the men Hakeswill had killed here, like the Muslim prisoners who would have defended their faith by refusing to convert despite the Christian knives, racks, burning irons, and chains. He wondered if anyone had ever been happy in this place, had ever laughed.

309

This was a tomb for happiness, a place where no sunlight had reached for centuries, and he turned back to the stairs, glad to be leaving this place.

'Sharpy! Little Dick Sharpy!' The voice was behind him now, a voice Sharpe knew too well. He ignored Hakeswill, began climbing the steps, but the cackle came, mocking and knowing. 'Running away, are we, Sharpy?'

Despite himself, Sharpe turned. The figure shuffled into the torchlight, face twitching, body wrapped with a shirt taken off another prisoner. Hakeswill stopped, pointed at Sharpe, and gave his cackling laugh. 'You think you've won, don't you, Sharpy?' The blue eyes were unnaturally bright in the flames of the torch, while the grey hair and yellow skin looked sallow, as if Hakeswill's whole body, except his eyes, were a leprous growth.

Sharpe turned again, spoke loud to the sentries. 'If he comes within fifteen feet of the barricade, shoot him.'

'Shoot him!' The scream was from Hakeswill. 'Shoot him! You poxed son of a poxed whore, Sharpe! You bastard! Get others to do your dirty work for you?' Sharpe turned, halfway up the stairs, and saw Hakeswill smile at the guards. 'You think you can shoot me, lads? Try, go on! Try now! Here I am!' He spread his naked arms wide, grinning, the head on its long neck twitching at them. 'You can't kill me! You can shoot me, but you can't kill me! I'll come for you, lads, I'll come and squeeze your hearts out in the dark.' The hands came together. 'You can't kill me, lads. Plenty's tried, including that poxed bastard who calls himself a Major, but no one's killed me. Never will. Never!'

The guards were awed by the force of Hakeswill, by the passionate conviction in the harsh voice, by the hatred.

Sharpe looked at him, hating him. 'Obadiah? I'll send your soul to hell within a fortnight.'

The blue eyes were unblinking, the twitching gone, and Hakeswill's right hand came slowly up to point at Sharpe. 'Richard bloody Sharpe. I curse you. I curse you by wind and by water, by fog and by fire, and I bury your name on the stone.' It seemed as if his head would twitch, but Hakeswill exerted all his will, and the twitch was nothing more than a mouth-clenched judder, a judder followed by a great scream of rage. 'I bury your name on the stone!' He turned back to the shadows.

Sharpe watched him go, then turned himself and, after a word with the guards, climbed to the very top of the Castle's keep. He climbed the turning stairs until he was in the cold, clean air that blew from the hills, and he breathed deep as though he could cleanse his soul of all the bad deeds. He feared a curse. He wished he had carried his rifle, for on the butt of the gun he had carved away a small sliver so that a patch of bare wood was not covered with varnish, and he could have pressed a finger on the wood to fight the curse. He feared a curse. It was a weapon of evil, and a weapon that always brought evil upon the person who made the curse, but Hakeswill had no future but evil and so could deliver the words.

A man could fight bullets and bayonets, even rockets if he understood the weapon, but no man understood the invisible enemies. Sharpe wished he knew how to propitiate Fate, the soldiers' Goddess, but She was a capricious deity, without loyalty.

It came to him that if he could see just one star, just one, then the curse would be lifted, and he turned on the ramparts and he searched the dark sky, but there was nothing in the heavens but cloud and heaviness. He searched desperately, looking for a star, but there was no star. Then a voice called to him from the courtyard, wanting him, and he went down the twisting stair to wait for morning.

CHAPTER 26

There were ghosts in the Gateway of God, so said the people of Adrados, and so the soldiers believed even though they had not been told. The buildings were too old, the place too remote, the imaginations too receptive. The wind sounded on shattered stone, rustled long-spiked thorn, sighed on the edge of the pass.

Four French soldiers were sentries by the gun in the cellars of the Convent. They stared at the Castle and their view was obscured by the gusts of wind that picked up bellying sails of snow and snatched them over the edge of the pass so that, for moments at a time, the air between Convent and Castle was beautiful with glittering white folds in the darkness.

And behind them, behind the spiked gun, were the piled skulls, the stuff of ghosts, and the soldiers shivered and watched the British sentries on the ramparts who were outlined by the fires in the Castle courtyard, and then another gust of wind would snatch the white ghost-like snow into waving plumes that went westward to settle again in the pass.

Sledge-hammers sounded above them, the crashes muffled by the intervening stones. The gunners would have their embrasures in the southern wall.

One of the Frenchmen smoked a short pipe, his back comfortable against the skulls, though the others had seen him lean there and had sketched the sign of the cross on their greatcoats.

'Steam.' One of them said.

'What?'

'I've been thinking about it. Steam, that's what they were. Steam.'

They had been talking of the strange weapon that had torn into the column. One of the men spat into the darkness. 'Steam.' He was scornful.

'Have you ever seen a steam engine?' Asked the first man. 'No.'

'I saw one in Rouen. Bloody great noise! Just like this morning! Fire, smoke, noise. Has to be steam!'

A new conscript who had hardly spoken all night plucked up courage to say something. 'My father says the future is with steam.'

The first man looked at him, dubious of this unmoustached support. He decided it was welcome. 'There you are then! I tell you! I saw one in a mill. A bloody great room with bloody great beams going up and down, and smoke everywhere! Like hell it was, like hell!' He shook his head, intimating that he had seen things that they had not seen, horrors of which they could have no comprehension, though in truth his glimpse had been brief at best, and incomprehensible as well. 'Your father's right, son. Steam! It'll be everywhere.'

Another man laughed. 'You'll have a steam musket, Jean.'

'And why not?' The first man had been carried away by his vision of the future. 'Steam infantry. I tell you! It'll happen! You saw what happened this morning.'

'I could do with a steam whore right now.'

There was a crash outside, a cheer, and a section of the wall fell into the snow. The man with the pipe blew smoke that was snatched into the pass. 'They should block this hole up.'

'They should march us back to bloody Salamanca.'

There were footsteps in the cellar behind and Jean peered between the skulls. 'Officer.'

They swore quietly, pulled their uniforms straight, and adopted poses that suggested an unceasing watch on the snow outside. The Lieutenant stopped at the gun. 'Anything?'

313

'No, sir. All quiet. Reckon they're tucked up in bed.'

The officer fingered the filed nail in the touch-hole. 'It'll soon be over, lads.'

'That's what they told them, sir.' The man with the pipe jerked its stem at the skulls of the nuns.

The Lieutenant looked at the skulls. 'Bit eerie, aren't they?'

'We don't mind, sir.'

'Well, it'll soon be over. We've got four howitzers upstairs. There'll be four other guns as well. They're just putting them into place. Another hour and we'll open fire.'

'Then what, sir?' Jean asked.

'Then nothing!' He grinned at them. 'We guard the guns and watch the attack.'

'Really!'

'Truly.'

The soldiers grinned. Someone else would be doing the fighting and the dying. The Lieutenant peered through the great hole and watched the snow smoke off the crest of the pass. 'It'll soon be over.'

The hour passed slowly. Overhead the gunners prepared the tools of their trade, their rippers and wormheads, rammers and swabbers, buckets and portfires, spikes and fuses. The howitzers, obscenely squat guns, pointed into the air and the gunners fussed about them. The range was short and the officers were debating how much powder to put into each barrel and the gunners waited with their long-handled scoops to feed the skyward muzzles that would lob the six inch shells over the valley. The hornbeam had long been taken away as fuel for the fires that burned in the lower courtyard.

To the east there was the faintest lightening of a strip of sky over the horizon, a false dawn that was seen by few except the Riflemen on the watchtower hill, and for the four sentries alone again in the room of skulls and bones the night was as dark as ever. It seemed to them that the dawn would never come, that they were trapped eternally in this cold place, this dark place, where the skulls of the dead reached to the ceiling, and they .shivered, watched the night above the snow, and hoped for dawn. One of them looked suddenly alarmed. 'What was that?'

'What?'

'A noise! In here. Listen!'

They listened. The conscript shook his head. 'A rat?'

'Shut your bloody face!'

Jean, his enthusiasm of an hour before gone, leaned back against the gunwheel. 'Rats. Must be thousands of bloody rats. Anyway, I don't know how you can hear a bloody thing with all that thumping upstairs. What are they doing up there? Mardi Gras?'

The gunners were spiking the trails of the twelve-pounders to face the same spot on the Castle wall.

The gunner Colonel had ridden to the Convent and now he strode into the other cloister, his hands rubbing together, and grinned at his men. 'All ready?'

'Yes, sir.'

'How much powder in the howitzers?'

'Half pound, sir.'

'Too much. Still! It'll warm the barrels. Christ! It's cold.' He walked into the chapel, open now to the south, and saw two of his twelve pounders that had been dragged through the widened door and now pointed through gaping holes at the Castle. 'Those Riflemen worrying you?'

'No, sir.'

'Let's hope the bastards are low on bullets.' He walked across the wreckage of the chapel and found a curious lump of granite that stuck through the floor. The top of it was polished smooth and he wondered why it was there. Typical of the bloody Spanish not to clear the site properly before they built the Convent, though why anyone would want to build a Convent in this benighted spot was beyond him. No wonder the nuns had left. He went back to the door. 'Well done, lads! You did a good job moving them in here!' They had too.

In the cloister he looked east and saw the first faint flush of the real dawn to the east. Snow was two inches deep on the shattered remains of the Convent's wall. 'All right! Let's try the howitzers! You'll fire over, you'll see!'

A Captain shouted at a Lieutenant on the roof to watch the fall of shot, and then he yelled the order to fire and four linstocks touched four fuses, and the howitzers seemed to try and bury themselves into the snow-trampled tiles, and the noise shook snow from the tiles and the smoke was thick and choking and the Lieutenant on the roof shouted into the courtyard. 'Two hundred over!'

'Told you so!'

Morning in the Gateway of God. The cough of howitzers, the sudden almost imperceptible streak of burning fuses hurtling into the air, falling, and the shells bounced on the hillside to the south of the keep, rolled, then exploded in dirty smoke. The snow was streaked black, thorns cracked as the fragments hurtled outwards.

Then the twelve-pounders fired, hammering the loose plaster of the chapel, loosening flakes of gold paint that fluttered into the dust on the floor, and the solid shot smashed at the Castle wall, chipped great shards from it, and Sharpe, on the turret, shouted to the ramparts below. 'Don't fire till my order!'

Over fifty Riflemen lined the northern ramparts, Riflemen who had been put there by Sharpe and then forbidden to fire at the ragged embrasures which had just blossomed flame and smoke into the morning darkness. The Fusiliers guarded into the dawn, facing the rising sun, but the Riflemen had been summoned by Sharpe. 'Wait!'

The firing of the guns was a signal. It shook the sleep from men throughout the valley, warned them that death was striding again into the Gateway, but most of all it was a signal to one man. He stretched massive muscles, wondering if the cold had made him useless, and he prayed for one more deafening volley from the guns above him. His right hand curled about the lock of the seven-barrelled gun.

Sharpe and Harper had told no one of this plan, no one, for a single prisoner taken in the night could have blurted the truth. Harper had made a lair in the bones, a lair that was lined with blankets and supported by a table, the legs of which had been sawed short so there was just room for the huge Irishman to lie flat. When Price had bellowed the order to run Harper had echoed the shout, had pushed men on, and then stepped aside into a shadow to watch his comrades scramble out of the Convent. No one had missed him, they were all too intent on escaping the French whose shouts were audible beyond the wrecked wall, and Harper had turned back to the ossuary. He had wriggled backwards beneath the wooden shelter, drawn blankets about him, piled skulls in front of his face, and waited.

Waited through the cold, through the utter darkness, with the closeness of the dead about him, and he had clutched his crucifix and sometimes he had slept. Sometimes he listened to the voices just feet away from him and tried to reckon how many men he would have to kill.

His cave was at one side of the room, at the back of the bone-pile, and he had ensured that the weight of the skeletons above him was not too heavy. He fingered the flint of the seven-barrelled gun, wondering why the guns did not fire again, and then they did and sent their recoil shuddering through the stones of the Convent.

The four sentries heard the bones rattle as the guns fired. They looked across the valley to see where the shells would fall.

Harper groaned as his back took the weight of table and dead, the groan rising to a war bellow as he rose, and the young conscript was the first to see that the dead were moving! Skulls fell, grinning faces shifted in the pile, and the bones were lifting in the darkness. The other sentries turned as the bones cascaded outwards and a dark figure, teeth bared as the skulls' teeth were bared, came at them from the place of the dead.

Harper's bellow was drowned by the crash of the seven-barrelled gun, the muzzle flaming livid in the ossuary's gloom, the smoke white as the skulls' domes, and the sentries did not even have time to turn their muskets onto the sudden apparition. Two died instantly, both with bullets in their heads, a third was flung backwards, hit in the chest, and only the conscript was untouched.

Harper staggered with the recoil of the gun, almost tripped on a skull that crunched beneath his boot-heel, and the conscript gibbered in fear.

'No trouble, lad,' the Irish voice growled. 'Stay still.'

The heavy gun was reversed, the brass butt came forward once, and the conscript slumped into unconscious silence. Harper glanced once at the other three, but none would trouble him, and then he turned to the corridor leading into the Convent's interior.

Silence. No shouts of alarm, no footsteps, but he did not want to be disturbed so, with a muttered apology to the dead, he put his shoulder against one of the great piles of bones and heaved. They swayed, but were remarkably anchored together, and he wondered if the cold had sapped his strength and heaved again. He felt them shift, scraping and cracking, and he grunted as he put all his strength against the bones which suddenly collapsed into the corridor. He ploughed into the destruction, feet crunching on dry bones, and hauled at the still standing parts of the ossuary. He reached up and his fingers hooked into dead eye-sockets, grated on yellowed teeth, and more of the pile clattered down. He went on pulling until the blockage was higher than his own height and until the first voice at the far end shouted a nervous question into the darkness.

He ignored it. He went back to the sentries and found, by the wounded man, a fallen pipe, its tobacco still alight, and

Harper picked it up, sucked on it until the bowl was glowing fierce, and then he turned back towards his lair.

He heaved the table from where it had fallen, raked bones aside with his foot, and on the wall, hanging like a bundle of white cords, were the fuses. They led to powder barrels stacked beneath the floors of the Convent's eastern end, powder barrels that Harper had himself put in place during three long cold hours of crawling in utter darkness. He had stacked rocks about the barrels and then led the fuses to the ossuary.

More voices shouted at him, voices that were stilled by an officer who then shouted himself. Harper did not understand what was being said, but he answered anyway. '*Oui*'

There was a second's silence. '*Qui vive?*'

'Eh?' He touched the glowing pipe bowl to the fuses and the fire seemed to leap up them, spitting sparks and smoking, and he stayed only a second or two until he was sure that the fire had taken and the Convent was doomed. One minute. Less.

He backed out over the bones, stooped for his seven-barrelled gun and slung it on his shoulder, and he could hear the French pulling at the bones at the far end of the blocked corridor. The wounded sentry looked mutely at him, but there was nothing Harper could do for the man. He would die anyway. 'I'm sorry, mate.' He leaned down, picked up the man's fallen musket and aimed it at the ceiling halfway above the bones. 'Here's one from Ireland!'

The ball ricocheted from the ceiling, slammed downwards to smash a skull at the French Lieutenant's feet.

'All right, son. Let's go.' Harper scooped the conscript in his arms, glanced once at the blackened, burned fuse dangling from the dark space that led beneath the Convent floors, and jumped through the gap into the snow-covered pass.

'Number one section, fire!' Sharpe shouted.

A dozen Rifles, warned to ignore the crude embrasure from which Harper stumbled and slipped, fired at the Convent's parapet.

Harper cursed, struggled on the snow, and threw the

conscript aside when he judged that the boy would avoid the effects of the explosion. He put his head down and sprinted at the white slope, imagining the French infantry behind him, and the first musket ball sprayed snow at his feet.

'Fire!' Sharpe shouted, and the remaining Rifles spat flame over the Castle ramparts and the bullets cracked on stone or whirred in the air about the heads of the French.

'*Tirez!*' Cold Frenchmen fumbled with locks, picked at the rags that some had not taken from their guns, and the giant Rifleman was running further and the smoke of the first muskets was obscuring the target. '*Tirez!*' More smoke and flames decorated the Convent's cornice and the bullets jerked at the shallow snow at the lip of the pass.

'Run!' Sharpe yelled. He thought for one awful moment that Harper was hit for the big man fell, rolled down the slope, but then the Irishman was up, legs pumping, and the Riflemen on the Castle wall were reloaded and they slid the barrels across the stone and gave him covering fire.

The rumble was hardly audible at first, like the first hints of far-away thunder on a summer's night.

The old builders would not have chosen the edge of the pass as a place to build the Convent, but the Virgin Mary had chosen it herself and so the builders had to negotiate the difficulties she had bequeathed them. The granite boulder had to be the centre-piece of the chapel, the Holy Footfall would have its proper, holy place, and so the old masons had built a platform of stone about the tip of the rock and supported the platform on solid arches which, to the west, made rooms for cells, a hall, and the Convent kitchens. To the east, though, there was not space for rooms and so the ground sloped up towards the stone platform and it was in that space, dark and cold, that the barrels of powder took the fire.

Eight caches of barrels, barrels taken from the stack which the Spanish had delivered to Adrados instead of Ciudad Rodrigo, waited in the darkness. Much of their force went sideways, but enough lifted the bed of stone so that, to an astonished gunner, it seemed as if the howitzers were being lifted up from the surface of the cloister, and then the tiles ripped apart, smoke and flame surged upwards, and the noise rose to drown the valley in sound. Flame lanced upwards, flame that for a second seemed like a spike of the sun itself, and then the powder for the howitzers caught the fire and a flame sheet spread sideways as the chapel floor heaved up. The serge bags for the twelve pounder guns added their power and to the watchers in the valley it seemed as if the whole south east corner of the ancient building was melting in fire and smoke.

Harper panted, stopped, and turned to watch his handi-work. He brushed snow from his uniform.

Lieutenant Harry Price was on the gatehouse turret. 'You knew!' He was accusing. 'Then why didn't you say?'

Sharpe grinned. 'Suppose one of you had been captured and held in the Convent overnight. Could you have kept silent?'

Price shrugged. 'But you might have told us when we got back.'

'I thought the surprise might cheer you up.'

'Jesus.' Price sounded disgusted. 'I was worried!'

'I'm sorry, Harry.'

The Convent was boiling smoke now, flames licking where they found fuel, and men stumbled, blackened and burned, from the wreckage. Most of the building still stood, but the wheels of all but two of the guns were broken, the ammunition was gone, and the Convent was no longer a threat to the Castle.

Patrick Harper was in the courtyard, grinning, demand-ing breakfast for a big man, while the Fusiliers and Riflemen cheered because their day had begun with another victory.

In the Convent daylight filtered through the smoke and dust, past broken stone and burning beams, and the light touched a polished piece of granite that had not seen daylight in eight hundred years.

Sunday, the 27th of December, 1812, had begun.

CHAPTER 27

The French still had guns and now the gunners were fired by anger and the south of the village was wreathed in ragged smoke while the canister rattled like metal rain on the Castle walls. There were howitzers firing too, and even though they could no longer fire from the flank and thus keep firing until the infantry were at the very brink of the courtyard, they could lob their shells from the protection of the village and make the Castle a place of seething iron.

One hour, two, and the guns still fired, and the canister killed sentries and the cobbles were scorched by the exploding shells where the snow had turned to black slush.

There was no truce this time. The gunner Colonel was dead, crushed by a falling howitzer barrel, and it was still dangerous to go into the Convent's upper part because of the howitzer shells that still exploded and added fresh smoke to the funeral pyre of more than a hundred men. The French General swore his revenge, and ordered the guns to start it. The gunners fought for their dead Colonel.

Two guns doused the watchtower hill in canister, the musket balls flaying through the thorns, jerking snow from the branches, snapping twigs and spines down onto the Riflemen who crouched in their pits. Rabbits know where to dig, and a rabbit hole was a rifle pit that was well started, and Frederickson urged the gunners on. 'Fire, you bastards! We're ready for you!' He was too. He expected them to come from the east or the north and his strength was ready for them, strength that would push the attack towards the cleared space on the northern slope of the hill down which he

planned to roll his barrels of powder, fuses protected from
the snow with sewn leather sheaths, and with the barrels
would go the four inch round shells left for the Spanish gun.
'Come on, you bastards!' His men grinned, listening to
Sweet William's battle cry. He had kept most of the Fusiliers
on the reverse slope of the hill, away from the artillery fire,
and he would only use them if the French turned his line of
hidden Riflemen.

Most of the guns worked on the Castle. They broke open
the stable roof, started fire in its rafters and in Gilliland's
empty carts that blazed high and melted the slush for yards
around. The French dislodged the single gun on the Castle's
eastern wall, lifting it in an explosion and sliding it in a
tumble of stone, snow, brass and timber down to the rubble.
One shell penetrated the inner courtyard, bouncing off the
walls of the keep, and its blast killed six horses outright and
the Fusiliers forced their way through the screaming, panicked beasts, sliding on a mixture of blood and slush and horse
urine to finish off the wounded beasts. And still the guns
fired.

The Castle filled with the smoke of the explosions, shook
with the crash of shot, and the twelve-pounders mixed
roundshot with the canister and some of the balls hit ancient,
loosened stone and a Rifleman screamed because a slab fell
on his legs.

On the snow in front of the eastern wall the howitzer shells
that fell short made star-shaped patterns in the snow, stars
black and violent, craters of heat in the whiteness, and one
shell landed on the gatehouse turret where a Rifleman, old in
war, ran to it with the butt of his rifle raised. The fuse smoked
crazily as the shell span, the Rifleman paused a second, then
struck one glancing blow on the iron ball. The fuse was
jerked out clean as a blade, and the shell was harmless. The
man grinned at his frightened companions. 'Always come
out if you hit 'em right.'

The Colours had gone, taken back to the Fusiliers who

crouched behind a low barricade that guarded the entrance to the keep. They would fight with their own standards on this last fight and they wondered how long they must endure the blast of the explosions outside, the screaming of the horses behind, the noise of the guns that filled the valley more dreadfully than any file of French drummers.

Sharpe crouched beside Captain Gilliland high in the keep. He had to shout over the noise of the cannonade. 'You know what to do?'

'Yes, sir.' Gilliland was unhappy. The rest of his rockets would be used in a manner he did not like. 'How long, sir?'

'I don't know! An hour? Maybe two?'

Men wanted the French to come, wanted this storm of metal to end, wanted to have this fight done.

Frederickson yelled at the French to attack, called them yellow bastards, women to a man, afraid of a little hill with a few straggly thorns, and still the infantry did not come. One Rifleman screamed in pain because a canister ball was in his shoulder and Frederickson bawled at him to be silent.

The gunners slaved at their machines, served them, hauled at them, fed them with revenge for their dead Colonel.

High on the eastern side of the keep Sharpe watched the village. Once he flinched as a high canister shot struck shards of razor sharp stone from the hole he peered through. Somewhere a man screamed, the scream cut short, and the noise rolled about the valley and the smoke of the guns was drifted high over the pass and still the metal came at the walls and the shells cracked apart in the yard.

'Sir?' Harper pointed.

The French were coming.

Not in a column, not in one of France's proud columns, but uncoiling like snakes from the village, four men in a file, and three Battalions were marching down the road, marching fast, and still the guns thundered, and still Sharpe's men died in ones and twos, and still the shells battered at the defenders.

Fifteen hundred men, bayonets fixed, staying in the centre of the valley well away from the flight of the guns.

Sharpe watched them. He had held this place for a day now and he had desperately hoped for two. It would not be. He had one card left to play, just one, and when that was played it would all be over. He would retreat south through the hills, hoping the French cavalry had better targets to chase than his depleted force, and he would leave his wounded to the mercy of the French. He had made the garrison pile their coats and packs at the southern exit from the keep, the exit Pot-au-Feu's men had used and which was now guarded by twenty Fusiliers to stop the faint-hearted leaving early. He grinned at Harper. 'It was a good fight, Patrick.'

'It's not over yet, sir.'

Sharpe knew different. The curse was on him like a lead weight, and he supposed the curse would bring defeat, would let the French through the pass, and he wondered if he would have time to go to the dungeon before the panic of the scramble southwards and kill the yellow-faced misshapen man. That would lift the curse.

In the dungeon Hakeswill listened. He could read a battle by its sound and he knew the moment was not yet. He had hoped it would be in the night, but a Fusilier Lieutenant had sat with the sentries through much of the darkness, and Hakeswill had done nothing. Soon, he promised himself, soon.

Sharpe turned to the man who had replaced the bugler. 'Ready?'

'Yes, sir.'

'In a minute. Wait.'

The French were close, the Battalions turning towards the Castle, coming over the place where yesterday the rockets had shredded the ranks, but today there was no weapon that fired at them.

The guns stopped. It seemed like silence in the valley.

The left hand Battalion of the French broke into a run, curving further left, heading south-east, and they ran towards the watchtower hill because they would attack from the one direction where Dubreton had rightly guessed there were few defences.

The other two Battalions raised a cheer, lowered their bayonets, and ran at the rubble of the eastern wall. No muskets fired from the defenders, no rifles, and the gun that would have flanked them lay on its side, shattered, useless on the stones. The two men who would have fired it sprawled lifeless on the cobbles.

A Rifleman on the keep's ramparts shouted for Sharpe, shouted loud, but the message never reached him. The French were in the courtyard.

CHAPTER 28

The news had come from Salamanca, where so much news came from because the Rev. Dr Patrick Curtis had been Professor of Astronomy and Natural History at the University of Salamanca. Strictly speaking Don Patricio Cortes, as the Spanish called him, was still Professor, and still Rector of the Irish College, but he had been in temporary residence in Lisbon ever since the French had discovered that the seventy-two year old Irish priest was interested in things other than God, the stars, and the natural history of Spain. Don Patricio Cortes was also Britain's chief spy in Europe.

The news reached Dr Curtis in Lisbon two evenings before Christmas. He was hearing confessions in a small church, helping out the local priest, and one of the penitents had nothing to confess and gave news through the grille instead. Hurriedly Dr Curtis left his booth, smiling apologetically at the parishioners, and after hastily crossing himself he undid the papers that had been sent to him across the border. The messenger, a trader in horses who sold to the French so he could travel unimpeded, shrugged 'I'm sorry it's late, Father. I couldn't find you.'

'You did well, my son. Come with me.'

But time was desperately short. Curtis went to Wellington's quarters and there he fetched Major Hogan from dinner, and the small Irish Major, who was also in charge of what Wellington liked to call his 'intelligence', rewarded the messenger with gold and then hurried the captured French despatch to the General.

'God damn.' The General's cold eyes looked at Hogan. 'Any doubt?'

'None, sir. It's the Emperor's code.'

'God damn.' Wellington gave the smallest apologetic shrug towards the elderly priest, then blasphemed again. 'God damn.'

There was time to send word to Ciudad Rodrigo and Almeida, to roust Nairn out of Frenada and have the Light Division moving, but that was not what worried the Peer. He was worried by the French diversionary attack that would come from the hills and descend on the valley of the Douro. God damn! This spring Wellington planned a campaign the like of which had never been seen in the Peninsula. Instead of attacking along the great roads of invasion, the roads that led eastward from Ciudad Rodrigo and from Badajoz, he was taking troops where the French thought they could not go. He would lead them north-east from the hills of Northern Portugal, lead them on a great circuit to cut the French supply road and force battle on a perplexed and outflanked enemy. To do it he would need pontoons, the great clumsy boats that carried roadways across rivers, because his invasion route was crossed by rivers. And the pontoons were being built at the River Douro and the French force was planning to descend on that area, an area that would normally be of small importance except this winter. God damn and damn again.

'Apologies, Curtis.'

'Don't mention it, my Lord.'

Messengers went north that night, messengers who changed horses every dozen miles or so, messengers who rode to warn the British that the French were coming, and Wellington followed them himself, going first to Ciudad Rodrigo because he feared to lose that great gateway into Spain. With any luck, he thought, Nairn could hold the French at Barca de Alva.

Major General Nairn looked once at the order, thought for

a moment, then disobeyed. The Peer had forgotten, or else had not connected the name Adrados with the Gateway of God, that the British already had a force that could block the French. A pitifully small force, a single Battalion with a raggle-taggle collection of Riflemen and Rockets, but if it could hold the pass just twelve hours then Nairn could reinforce it. His cold magically disappeared.

And now he was late. The snow had held him up and he feared he was too late. He had met Teresa coming from the pass and he had listened to her message, charmed her, and then taken her along with his troops who struggled against the snow. Next came Sir Augustus Farthingdale, icy and angry, who insisted that .there were complaints, serious complaints, that he wished to make against Major Richard Sharpe, but Nairn politely declined to listen, then rudely insisted, and finally ordered Sir Augustus and Lady Farthingdale on their way. On the evening of December 26th the wind brought more snow and the grumble of guns.

They marched before dawn and Nairn heard a mighty explosion in the hills, and the light showed a great pall of smoke that blew towards him, yet still the guns sounded. March to the guns, always to the guns, and he sent his best troops ahead with orders to climb fast and Teresa went with a Spanish Battalion of light troops that could climb the hills beside the pass and come down on the French flank. She would guide them, and they struggled through the cold, the snow, listening always to the guns that told them the battle still lived, that their help was needed, and then the guns stopped.

A seeming silence in the hills. The guns rested.

The French were in the courtyard. They were cheering, running, swarming over the stones of the eastern wall and there was no enemy.

The French officers had their swords drawn. They looked at ramparts and turrets for targets for their men, but the Castle seemed empty and silent, and then a shout from a

Frenchman and they could see the Fusiliers crammed in the archway behind their low barricade of stone. 'Charge!'

'Fire!' The Fusilier volley drove an avenue of musket fire into the courtyard.

'Fire!' The second rank pushed past the first.

'Fire!' The third was at the front, two more behind it, while the ranks that had fired reloaded and came up behind.

'Fire!' The archway was safe.

'Doors!' French officers led their men to the doorways into the gatehouse and north-western turret, but the doors had been blocked solid with stone, as had the steps to the northern ramparts, and still the French infantry piled into the courtyard and believed they had victory.

'Now!' Sharpe snarled at the bugler. 'Now!'

Dubreton had foreseen this. He had known that the courtyard would be a deathtrap, a cul de sac, unless the men could fight their way into the keep.

French officers shouted at their men. 'Fire! Fire at the archway!'

And then the bugle sounded. The notes climbed the full octave once, twice, three times. 'Open fire'.

The sticks had been taken from the remaining rockets much to Gilliland's disgust and now the Rocket Troop put fire to the fuses, waited to see the fire catch, and then tossed the stickless cylinders out of arrow-slits, through gaps in the stones, over ramparts, and down to the courtyard crammed with French.

The cylinders tumbled, smoke intricate behind them, and then they coughed and roared into life and without the sticks they could not fly but hurled themselves in aimless frantic patterns in the yard.

'Come on! Throw!'

More came, more rockets, shells beginning to explode in their heads, and still more came, their tails flaying the French with fire, the rockets whipping erratically about the

330

stones, breaking ankles, lodging in bodies, exploding, burning, and Sharpe yelled at the men to throw more. Some snaked their way to the stables where they added to the fire and pumped smoke at the disorganized French, while most carved gaps in the crowded ranks and exploded their iron fragments in circles of death, while the solid-tipped rockets hurled their weight against feet and legs and wounded bodies and the French shouted in alarm, in confusion, and still more came.

'Downstairs!' Sharpe led Harper and the bugler down to where the Fusiliers waited for this moment. Two hundred of them waited with their Colours and Sharpe pushed the bugler forward. 'Sound the cease-fire!' He looked at the Fusiliers, those who were not guarding the archway. 'Fix bayonets!'

The bugle was sounding its message to the Rocket Troop again and again, but Sharpe did not hear it. He heard only the scraping and clicking as the seventeen-inch blades were slotted onto muskets and he drew his own sword, the metal bright in the archway's gloom, and he waited until he was sure no more rockets were being thrown. 'We go to the rubble! No further!' He would clear the yard, kill the enemy, for in this hour of defeat he could still claw and maim this French force and hope to weaken it so that it could not perform whatever duty it had been sent to do.

'Charge!'

This was the way to end it! Sword in hand and charging, and even though the battle was lost he could still make these French regret the day they had come to the Gateway of God. He could put fear in them for their next battle, he would make them remember this place with sourness. 'Get them!' The sword twisted in his hand as it glanced off bone, but the man was down, and then he heard the bellow of the seven-barrelled gun, and Sharpe had a glimpse of the Fusiliers, teeth bared over white crossbelts on red uniforms, blades reaching ahead, and the yard was full of smoke and stinking

331

rocket carcasses and the French were running from the line of men who had erupted into the gloom and Sharpe saw an officer trying to rally them and he lunged at the man, felt the Frenchman's sword scrape the length of his blade, and then he was onto the man, beating down with the blade, and he could see the rubble ahead. 'On!'

He tugged the sword free, looked for another enemy, but the French had gone back, the courtyard was his, and he screamed at Brooker to line the Fusiliers on the rubble. He saw the two Colours, ragged and blackened, proud over the line and he stood in front of them, sword red in his hand, and there was a mad impulse to charge on into the valley as if his two hundred Fusiliers could sweep the French clear out of the hills.

That was the last card, the last surprise, the final twisting of the French tail. There was nothing left now but muskets, rifles, and bayonets. He would have to retreat before the next attack, and a small part of him said it would be sensible to go now, go while the French were not pressing behind, while he could still extricate Frederickson from the hill, but Sharpe would not retreat until he could see the enemy's face. He would not.

He could hear firing to his left and he wondered if the French were attacking through the gate. 'Watch the gate, Mr Brooker!'

'Sir!'

Where were the bastards? Why did they not come? This was the moment of their victory, the moment when Sharpe could not fight them, and then he wondered whether the guns would start again and the canister would spray the Fusiliers red and ragged off the stones, but still he stared into the smoke of the rockets and wondered why the enemy did not come.

The smoke drifted slowly, cleared thin, and he saw why the guns did not fire.

The Battalion that had attacked the watchtower hill was

in full retreat, streaming across the valley. Sharpe grinned. Sweet William had blooded them.

Sweet William was mad with anger. 'You bastards! You bastards!' He shook his fist at men in sky-blue uniforms, men who had swept from behind the Castle and charged with bayonets at the Battalion which had been coming for Frederickson. 'You bastards!' The Spaniards had cheated him of a fight.

'Sir!' Harper was pointing left. 'Sir!' His voice was triumphant.

Riflemen. Scores of Riflemen! Greenjackets! How the hell had they got here, Sharpe wondered? And he felt the weight of defeat lift from him and he stared, almost unbelieving, at the French running from the Convent, at the skirmish line that was on his flank, and then he looked right and saw the Spanish uniforms on the hill. They had won!

'Fusiliers! Forward!'

And Hakeswill struck.

CHAPTER 29

Only a fraction of the gold that Sharpe and Dubreton had fetched so laboriously to the Gateway of God had been found. Handfuls had been taken off the prisoners, lost forever into the pouches of French and British soldiers, but the bulk of it still lay in the Castle. It was hidden for gold was a useful thing to hide, a cache that could be retrieved at leisure when the enemy had gone, and Hakeswill had hidden it well. It was in the dungeon, behind the gore-splashed wall where he had tortured and murdered the men and women who had displeased him. Now he needed the gold.

He did not take all of it. Enough to last him a few weeks and enough to get him out of the Castle, and when he judged by the sound of the battle that the Castle keep was short of defenders, he acted.

He threw one coin. It clinked heavily, rolled down two steps, and shuddered to a halt. A sentry, nervous because of the battle sounds, stared disbelieving at the gold.

Another coin came from the darkness, caught the light of the straw torch, and bounced on the stone of the bottom step.

The sentry grinned, went down to the cellar floor, and a comrade, jealous of his luck, called out a sour warning to be careful, but then a shower of gold glittered in the light, fell in rich harvest on the stairs, and the sentries whooped for their luck and shouted at each other for someone else to watch the prisoners while they scooped the coins into their pouches.

More gold came. Gold that was more than a Fusilier could earn in five years service, gold flickering from the darkness, gold that rang heavy on the stones and Hakeswill watched

334

the sentries go down on hands and knees to make themselves rich. 'Now!'

One sentry managed to scramble back, to pull a trigger and send a deserter backwards over the barricade with a bullet in his brain, but then he too was caught by the half naked men, men who stank in his nostrils, who beat him with fists and then stamped the life from him with the butt of his own musket.

'Stop!' Hakeswill crouched halfway up the steps, next to the bloody body of the one man who had fought back. 'Wait, lads, wait.'

He carried his bag of gold in his hand, crept up the stairs, and saw the passageway beyond the door empty. Packs and greatcoats were piled in the passage and, better still, muskets piled against a wall. The muskets had been put there by Sharpe for the final desperate defence of the Castle, muskets captured from Pot-au-Feu's men and now returned to them.

Hakeswill moved fast. He went left and peered into the inner courtyard and swore silently when he saw the picquet that guarded the southern exit. He went the other way, plucking a greatcoat as he went, and he saw that the courtyard was oddly empty except of French dead and strange, smoking cylinders that lay on the cobbles. He went back to the cellar steps. 'Coats up here, lads, and muskets. Get one each, then follow me.' He would go through the courtyard, across the wall, then break right into the thorns. He prepared himself, steeled himself for the rush, planned the route he would take south. He grinned at his fellow deserters, waited for a twitching of his head to stop. 'They can't kill me, lads. Nor you, while you're with me.'

He looked at the daylight in the Castle yard, at the smoking cylinders, at the dead, and he thought only of life. Of his new chance for life. He cackled to himself, and pushed lank hair from his eyes. Obadiah Hakeswill could not be killed. 'Come on!'

They ran, naked feet slipping on the slick cobbles, but

desperation forcing them on. They faced nothing but a firing squad if they were marched westward, and it was better to run into the savage southern hills in this winter than to face the line of muskets in some Portuguese field. They scrambled over the rubble, some hauling themselves by gripping the fallen Spanish gun, and then Hakeswill was in the open, turning right, and a Spanish soldier saw him, was scared of the huge, yellow-faced man who seemed naked beneath his unbuttoned coat, and the Spaniard jerked his unloaded musket into his shoulder.

The movement saved his life. Hakeswill saw only the threat of the bullet, saw the sky-blue uniforms in the thorns behind the man, and he broke left again, into the open valley and led his ragged, dirty band into the clear, clean air of Adrados' fields. 'Run!'

They were like rats that had run from a fire only to find themselves ringed by fire. To the left were Fusiliers and Riflemen, to the right the Spaniards who still came through the thorns, and ahead were the French. Already the Spanish were cutting off the deserters, shouting at them to surrender, and even though the Spaniards did not know this was an enemy, they knew that this filthy, villainous crew were not friends.

Hakeswill ran into the open valley, his breath harsh in his ears, his feet numbed by the snow, and he glanced left and saw he had far outrun the Fusiliers, and he thought he saw Sharpe, but that was no concern for this moment, and then he saw the Riflemen beyond Sharpe and he feared their weapons so he cut right, sprinting in desperation, the gold in his greatcoat pocket, the musket heavy in his hand. The French! There was nowhere else to go, nowhere! He would offer his services to the French, desert properly, and though it was not much of a choice it was better than being cut down like a dog in this snowfield. He ran for the nearest Battalion of French infantry, a Battalion that retreated towards the village, and then he heard the hooves behind him.

The hooves had been muffled by the snow and he realized, desperately, that the horseman was close. He turned, toothless mouth aghast with the horror, and he saw the lifted weapon that threatened to crush his skull with a heavy brass hilt and he fumbled with his musket, brought it round as he fell away from the downward stroke, and pulled the trigger.

He laughed maniacally. Death, his master, had not deserted him, and this he had prayed for too! Not this way, perhaps, but he laughed as he saw the bullet lift the rider from the horse, a bullet that went through the lower throat, travelling upwards, and death was as swift as death can be. The body was lifted upwards, the horse swerved away, and the body fell, spread-eagled, thumping onto the snow and the rifle, unloaded, that had threatened his life with its brass-bound butt, fell into the coldness.

Hakeswill paused. It was a moment of sweet victory, a moment to be remembered in the days to come, and he gibbered his victory call at the low clouds and his half-naked body jigged with the joy of it! He had lived! Death was still favouring him! And then he turned and ran for the French ranks. 'Don't shoot! Don't shoot!'

Hakeswill would live yet! He staggered into the French Battalion, gasping with pained lungs, and he grinned as his head twitched. He had escaped.

CHAPTER 30

Sharpe had watched Hakeswill break into the open field, had sworn, but then a voice had hailed him from behind and he turned to see Major General Nairn beaming at him from a horse. 'Sharpe! My dear Sharpe!'

'Sir!'

Nairn groaned as he slid from the horse. 'Major Sharpe! You've had a full-scale war while my back is turned!'

'Looks that way, sir.' Sharpe grinned.

'You disturb my Christmas, force me to drag weary bones up into the snows of winter!' He smiled a huge smile. 'I thought you'd all be gone by now!'

'It crossed my mind, sir.'

'Sir Augustus said you'd be dead.'

'He did?'

Nairn laughed at Sharpe's tone. 'I sent him packing with his lady wife. She's a rare looker, Sharpe!'

'Yes, sir.'

'Mind you, your lady wife told me she was too fat! Told me something else, too, which I'm sure can't be true. Something to do with the fact that the lady's not a lady at all! Can you believe that, Sharpe?'

'I wouldn't know, sir.'

Nairn grinned, but said nothing. He was looking at the French back at the village, and he glanced left and right where his first troops had secured the wreckage of the Convent and now reinforced the watchtower hill. Nairn stamped his feet on the ground. 'I think our froggie friends will call that a day! Don't you?' He clapped his hands in delight. 'They won't attack again, and in a couple of hours I'll be in a position to attack them.' He looked at Sharpe. 'Well done, Major! Well done!'

'Thank you, sir.' Sharpe was not looking at Nairn. He was looking up the valley at a loose horse, at a dark figure on the snow, and his voice was far away, distracted.

'Sharpe?'

'Sir?' But Sharpe was already walking away, and the walk broke into a run, and he still stared at the figure on the snow.

The hair was black against the pure whiteness, long and black. He had seen it like that on a white pillow when she had teasingly raised her head and splayed her hair in a great tempting fan. The blood at her throat was like a broken necklace of rubies, half spilt onto the snow, and her eyes stared unseeing at the clouds.

He knelt beside her, wordless, and he felt the thickness in his throat, the sting of tears in his eyes, and he put his arms about the slim body, raised her, and her head fell backwards so that the big ruby in the hollow of her neck leaked a slow trickle towards her chin. He put a hand under her head, feeling where the cold snow was on her hair, and he pressed her cheek against his and he wept for Teresa was dead.

Her hands were in the snow, cold hands frozen by the ride, yet there was still warmth in her. Warmth that would fade. He held her to him as though he could force life back into the body and he sobbed into the black hair. She had loved him with a pure, simple love that forgave, understood, and she had loved him.

He had no picture of her. She would be a memory that would fade as her warmth would fade, but would fade over the years, and he would forget the passion that gave life to this face. She had seethed with life. She had been restless and forceful, a killer of the border hills, yet she had a childlike faith in love. She had given herself to him and never doubted the wisdom of the gift as he had sometimes doubted it. She had kept the faith, and she was dead.

He cried, not caring who watched, and he rocked her in his arms and held her tight because he had not held her enough when she lived. They had met through war, war had held them apart, and now war had done this. It should have been himself who died, he thought, not this, and his grief was formless, incoherent, a pain that was betrayed love and filled the universe.

'Sharpe?' Nairn touched his shoulder, but Sharpe did not hear, did not see, he only rocked the body in his arms. His left arm was entwined in her hair, gripping it because he did not want to lose her, he did not want to be alone, and she was the mother of his child, his motherless child, and Nairn heard the moan, half howl, that came from Sharpe's throat. Nairn saw the face of the body and straightened up. 'Oh God.'

Patrick Harper crouched opposite Sharpe. 'There'll be a priest with the Spanish, sir.' He had to repeat it, and then Sharpe looked up, eyes strange to Harper.

'What?'

'A priest, sir. She must be shriven.'

Sharpe appeared not to understand. He was holding Teresa as though Harper would take her away, but then he frowned. 'After death?'

Harper was not embarrassed by the tears. 'Aye, sir. It can be done.' He put out a hand and, with extraordinary gentleness, closed the eyelids. 'We must send her to heaven, sir. She'd be best laying down, so she would.' He spoke as if to a child and Sharpe obeyed.

He knelt by the body till the priest came and he was in the confused world of the grief and he babbled promises at her and inside was the insane hope that the eyes would open and she would smile at him, tease him as she used to tease him, but there was no movement in her. Teresa was dead.

Her cloak was open at the waist and he pulled it over her and felt the lump tucked into the sash she wore. He pulled out the cloth bundle, unwrapped it, and he looked at the Rifleman which was his daughter's present and he did not

340

think it worthy of her so he broke it, tore it, scattered the small shreds on the snow.

He stood unseeing as the priest knelt by the body, as the Latin words whirled over the snow like meaningless, dead things. The wafer was put to dead lips, the sign of the cross made, and Sharpe stared at the face that was so calm and still and utterly without life.

'Sharpe?' Nairn touched his elbow. Pointed eastwards.

Dubreton was riding slowly towards them and behind the French Colonel was Sergeant Bigeard, walking, and in Bigeard's grip once more was Hakeswill. Hakeswill clutched the greatcoat about his nakedness and jerked helplessly against the big Frenchman's hold.

Dubreton saluted Nairn, spoke softly with him, and then turned to Sharpe who had stepped protectively towards Teresa's body. 'Major Sharpe?'

'Sir?'

'He did it. We saw it. I give him to you.' He spoke very simply.

'He did it?'

'Yes.'

Sharpe looked at the twitching, yellow-faced man who cringed in fear because Bigeard was holding him towards Sharpe. Sharpe felt the uselessness of the hatred he had for Hakeswill when measured against the pain of this loss. His sword was lying a few feet away, dropped there when he had run to the body, but there was no desire to pick it up, to bury it in this lumpen man whose curse had killed the mother of Sharpe's child. Sharpe wanted this place of her death to be peaceful. 'Sergeant Harper?'

'Sir?'

'Take the prisoner. He's to live for a firing squad.'

'Sir.'

The wind stirred the snow in powdery ripples that banked against Teresa's boots. Sharpe hated this place.

Dubreton spoke again. 'Major?'

'Sir?'

'It's all over now.'

'Over, sir?'

Dubreton shrugged. 'We're going. You won, Major. You won.'

Sharpe looked uncomprehending at the French Colonel. 'Won, sir?'

'You won.'

Won so that a child's present could be strewn in the snow. Won so that he could feel this pain that was bigger than anything he had ever felt.

By the village Major Ducos watched through his telescope as Sharpe lifted the body from the snow and walked with it towards the Castle. He watched the big Sergeant pick the sword out of the snow and then Ducos snapped the glass shut. He had sworn his revenge on Sharpe, on the Rifleman who had thwarted this winter victory, but revenge, Ducos believed with the Spanish proverb, was a dish best eaten cold. He would wait.

Snow drifted over the broken doll in the Gateway of God.

Christmas was finished.

EPILOGUE

Sharpe was in the room where it had all started last year. Last year. That seemed strange, but 1813 was already ten days old, Teresa's death two weeks in the past, the spring would come and with it would come a new campaign.

The fire burned in the same hearth by which Sharpe had learned with such joy of his promotion. There was no joy now.

Wellington looked at Hogan as if for help, but the Major shrugged. The General put levity into his voice. 'I'll have to keep those damned rockets, Sharpe. You saw to that.'

Sharpe looked up from the fire. 'Yes, my Lord.' He supposed he had seen to that. After their success at Adrados they could hardly be sent back to England. 'I'm sorry, my Lord.'

'We'll fit them in somewhere.' Wellington paused. 'As we'll fit you in somewhere, Major.' He gave one of his rare smiles. 'You took a lot on yourself, Sharpe. A whole Battalion under your command!'

Sharpe nodded. 'Sir Augustus complained I took too much on myself, my Lord.'

Wellington grunted. 'Good thing you did. What was the matter with the man? Lily-livered?' His voice was suddenly harsh.

Sharpe shrugged, then decided the truth was better than politeness. 'Yes, sir.'

'How did it feel to fight a Battalion? Good?'

'At times, sir.'

'Like being a General, eh? Perhaps you'll find that out, Sharpe.'

'I doubt it, sir.'

Wellington's piercing blue eyes watched him. The General stood in muddied boots in front of the fire, the skirts of his riding coat lifted by clasped hands. 'The glory gets tarnished, yes?'

'Yes, sir.'

'Some people never learn that. They think I enjoy this, but its a job, Sharpe, that's all, a job. Like being a street-sweeper or a slaughterman. Someone has to do it or the filth will overwhelm us.' He seemed embarrassed to have said so much.

'Yes, my Lcrd.'

Wellington waved a hand towards the door. 'I'll send for you, Major Sharpe. We must find you employment. A Major who fights my battles must be given employment!'

Sharpe moved to the door, Hogan with him, shepherding him protectively, but the General stopped them. 'Sharpe?'

'My Lord?'

This time Wellington really did seem embarrassed. He glanced at the armchair, then back to Sharpe. 'Would it seem amiss, Sharpe, if I say that all things pass?'

'No, my Lord. Thank you.'

Major Michael Hogan, as old a friend as almost any in the army, walked with Sharpe through Frenada's streets. 'You're sure of this, Richard?'

'Yes, I'm sure.'

They walked in silence for a minute and Hogan hated the heaviness in his friend, the seemingly inconsolable and private grief that festered inside. 'I'll meet you afterwards.'

'Afterwards?'

'Afterwards.' Hogan spoke decisively. This evening he planned to make Sharpe drunk. He planned to force the grief out into the open and he would do it as the Irish knew how to do it, with a wake. It was overdue, but he and Harper had

344

agreed to it, had forced agreement on Sharpe, and the Rifle Captain, Frederickson, would come too. Hogan had liked Frederickson instantly, had been amused at the man's complaint that no one would fight him, and had been pleased to see Frederickson's modest disclaimer when he had read the words of Sharpe's report. A wake, a decent, drunken, laughing wake. Hogan had ordered Harry Price to attend and he would force Sharpe to drink, to talk, to remember Teresa, and in the morning the grief would already be turning into healthy regret. 'Afterwards, Richard.' Hogan stepped across a deep rut in a cross-roads. 'You heard that Sir Augustus has requested home leave?'

'I heard.'

'And "Lady Farthingdale" is back in Lisbon?'

'Yes. I heard.' Josefina had written Sharpe a bitter letter, a letter that complained he had broken his word by revealing his knowledge to Sir Augustus, a letter that reeked of her lost future fortune. It had ended by saying a friendship was over and Sharpe had torn the letter into shreds and put the shreds on the fire, and then remembered how Teresa had seen him flirting with Josefina and he had cried because of the hurt he might have given to his wife. His wife.

She was buried in Casatejada, in the stone crypt in the tiny chapel where her family was buried. Antonia would grow up speaking Spanish, knowing neither mother nor father, and Sharpe would ride to see her soon, to look at his daughter who would grow up not knowing him.

Sometimes he woke in the night and he was happy for a moment until he remembered Teresa was dead. Then the happiness went.

Sometimes he saw long black hair on a slim woman in the street and his heart leaped inside, joy welled up uncontrollable, and then the shroud of knowledge would sink again. She was dead.

The South Essex had marched north to Frenada and they were drawn up in a hollow square, one side left open, and in the open side was a hornbeam tree. Not a sapling like the one the Germans had decorated for Christmas, but a full grown tree and in front of the tree was an open grave and beside the grave was an empty box.

When the corpse was put in the box they would make the whole Battalion march past and the order would be given. 'Eyes left!' Every man must look on the punishment for desertion.

The provosts brought him, and the firing squad watched as he was tied to the hornbeam, but Sharpe did not watch. It was late afternoon and he stared at the snow which was on the hilltops around Frenada and he waited until a provost officer reported to him. 'We're ready, sir.'

It was a cloudless sky, a winter's day of sharp clarity, a day when a deserter would die.

He did not want to die. He had cheated death before and he pulled at the bonds, his head twitching, and the spittle frothed at his lips as he swore and jerked, snatched at the ropes and threw himself from side to side so that the fourteen muskets of the firing party went from side to side.

'Fire!'

Fourteen muskets slammed into fourteen shoulders and Hakeswill was twitched against the trunk, blood spattering the shirt he wore, yet still he lived. He slumped down, a cough rasping in his throat, and then he was cackling in triumph, the madness on him because he knew he had cheated death again, and he jerked, twisted, and the blood spotted his trousers, the earth, and the blue eyes in the yellow face came up to watch the Rifle officer walk slowly towards him. 'You can't kill me! You can't kill me! You can't kill me!'

It was supposed to be done with a pistol, but Sharpe pulled back the flint of his Rifle and he knew that the curse would be gone when the flint snapped forward. Hakeswill was hanging in the ropes, the face turned up, the voice screaming and spitting blood and spittle.

The Rifle barrel came slowly up.

346

'You can't kill me!' And this time the voice collapsed into sobs, sobs that were child-like because Obadiah knew that he was lying. 'You can't kill me.'

The bullet killed him. It twitched his head for the very last time, killing him instantly, killing the man who could not be killed. Sharpe had dreamed of this moment for nigh on twenty years, but there was none of the pleasure he had expected.

Behind him, unseen, the evening star was showing pale against a winter sky. A small wind stirred the hornbeam twigs.

Two bodies marked this winter. The one whose hair had been spread on the snows of the Gateway of God, and now this one. Obadiah Hakeswill, being lifted into his coffin, dead. Sharpe's enemy.

HISTORICAL NOTE

The idea that a private 'army' of deserters, drawn from every nationality fought in the Peninsular War, may stretch credulity too far. Not as far, perhaps, as the idea of a 'Rocket Troop'. Yet both existed.

Pot-au-Feu lived, a renegade French Sergeant who promoted himself to Marshal, and who survived by terrorising a wide patch of Spanish countryside. His followers included French, British, Spanish and Portuguese soldiers, and his crimes included kidnapping, rape, and murder. I fear I have made him into a man pleasanter than he really was. The French General de Marbot tells how the French destroyed him and then handed the allied deserters over to Wellington's forces. Sharpe, I fear, has taken credit for a French success.

In another distortion of history I have brought the Rocket Troop to Spain a few months early. Wellington first saw a demonstration of Sir William Congreve's Rocket System in 1810 when a Naval detachment brought some weapons ashore in Portugal. Wellington was unimpressed. By 1813, however, a Rocket Troop had joined his army and it enjoyed the enthusiastic patronage of the Prince Regent. In its workings I have stayed close to the Instruction Book written by Sir William Congreve himself (even down to the detachable lance-heads, surely a triumph of inventor's hope over judgment). It was an extraordinary system that had, at its most ambitious, a 'Light-Ball' rocket that delivered a parachute flare for night fighting. And this in 1813! The Rocket Corps itself came into formal existence on January 1st, 1814, though it had already been deployed in the Peninsula and, indeed, Congreve's system had been sold in 1808 to the Austrian army where it was known as the *Feuerwerkscorps*. Wellington continued to mistrust it, though he used it at the crossing of the Adour, while in Northern Europe, it had its most successful day at the Battle of Leipzig where foreign observers were much impressed. A rocket battery was present at Waterloo and in some pictures of that engagement the rocket trails can be seen over the battlefield.

Though it was never a great success, the Rocket Corps has enshrined itself in history thanks to one of the enemies against whom it was so ineffectively employed (the problem was simply accuracy, which is why Sharpe chose to wait until they could hardly avoid hitting the enemy). Rockets were deployed in the war of 1812 against the United States, used by the British in their siege of Fort McHenry. A song was written about that siege and then put to the music of a drinking song used by the Anacreon Club in London. Those words and that tune now comprise, of course, the American National Anthem. It is strange to think that whenever 'The Star-Spangled Banner' is sung, before every baseball and football game, Britain's erstwhile enemies recall Sir William Congreve's invention in the line 'the rockets' red glare'. Thus did Britain's secret weapon find lasting fame!

Sir Augustus Farthingdale plagiarized his book mainly from Major Chamberlin's book, and now I must confess to a plagiarism. Sharpe's Christmas meal, and the hare stew that Pot-au-Feu ate in the Convent, all came from Elizabeth David's magnificent *French Provincial Cooking*, a book that has given me more pleasure than most. If any reader would like to recreate Sharpe's Christmas meal (a rewarding experience!) then I refer to them to Mrs David's magnificent work. *Potage de marron Dauphinois* (Chestnut soup), *Perdreau Roti au Four* (Roast Partridge), and the *Cassoulet de Toulouse à la Menagère*, to which I added roast potatoes for Sharpe's sake, and changed the recipe to fit the foods which might have been available in winter Spain. The hare stew exalts in the name *Le Civet de Lievre de Diane de Chateaumorand*. Strictly speaking it is not a stew, but I will not attempt the impossible and try to rival Elizabeth David as a cookery writer. My thanks to her.

Beyond the army of deserters and the rocket system, all else in *Sharpe's Enemy* is fiction. There is no Gateway of God, nor was any battle fought over the Christmas of 1812. The 60th existed, the Royal American Rifles, but all other Regiments are fictitious. I wanted to write one story that reflected the last winter when the British would be pinned back again in Portugal. Despite Napoleon's crushing defeat in Russia it must still have seemed to many soldiers that the war could last forever, yet within months Wellington's strategy changed the whole Peninsular War and never again were the British to retreat. Sharpe and Harper will march again.